P9-DVO-591

CALGARY PUBLIC LIBRARY

JAN   2015

NNEWTS

BOOK ONE
Escape from the Lizzarks

Doug TenNapel
with color by Katherine Garner

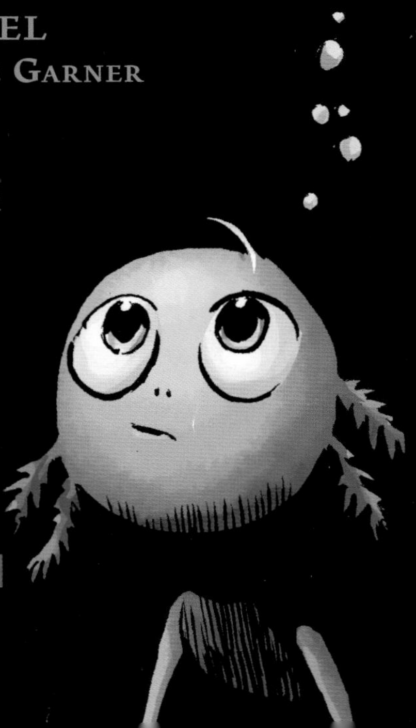

graphix
An Imprint of
SCHOLASTIC

Copyright © 2015 by Doug TenNapel

All rights reserved. Published by Graphix, a division of Scholastic Inc.,
Publishers since 1920. SCHOLASTIC, GRAPHIX, and associated logos are trademarks
and/or registered trademarks of Scholastic Inc.

No part of this publication may be reproduced, stored in a retrieval system,
or transmitted in any form or by any means, electronic, mechanical, photocopying,
recording, or otherwise, without written permission of the publisher. For information
regarding permission, write to Scholastic Inc., Attention: Permissions
Department, 557 Broadway, New York, NY 10012.

Library of Congress Control Number: 2014939372

ISBN 978-0-545-67647-2 (Hardcover)
ISBN 978-0-545-67646-5 (Paperback)
12 11 10 9 8 7 6 5 4 3 2 1   15 16 17 18 19
Printed in China   38

First edition, January 2015
Edited by Adam Rau
Book design by Phil Falco
Creative director: David Saylor

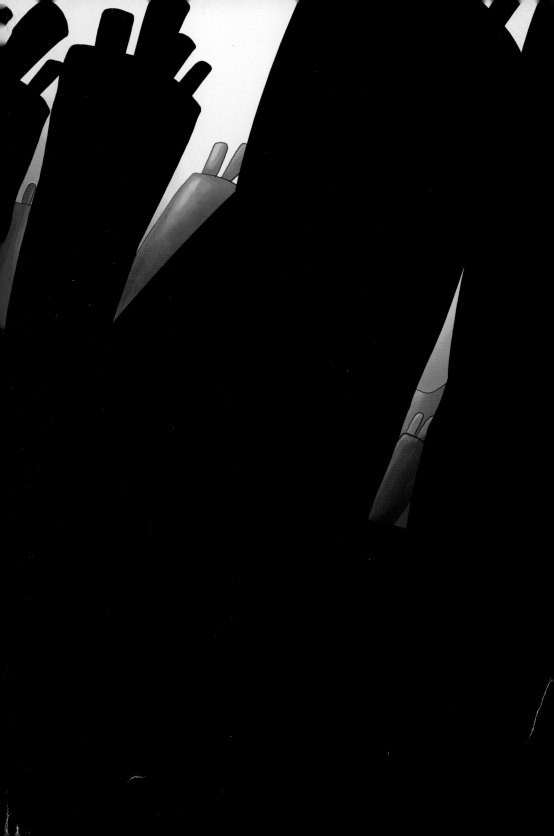

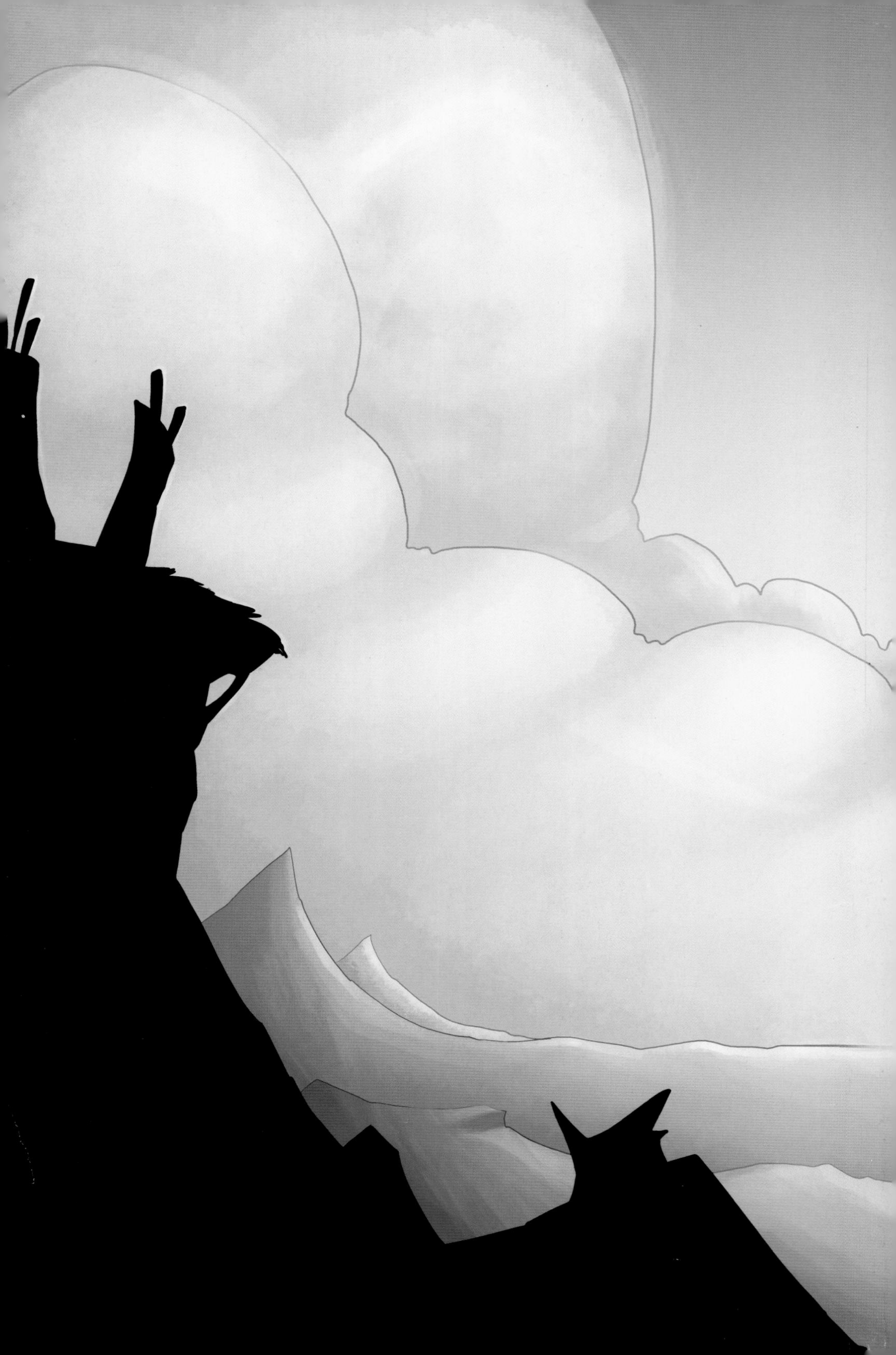

For Mr. Watanabe

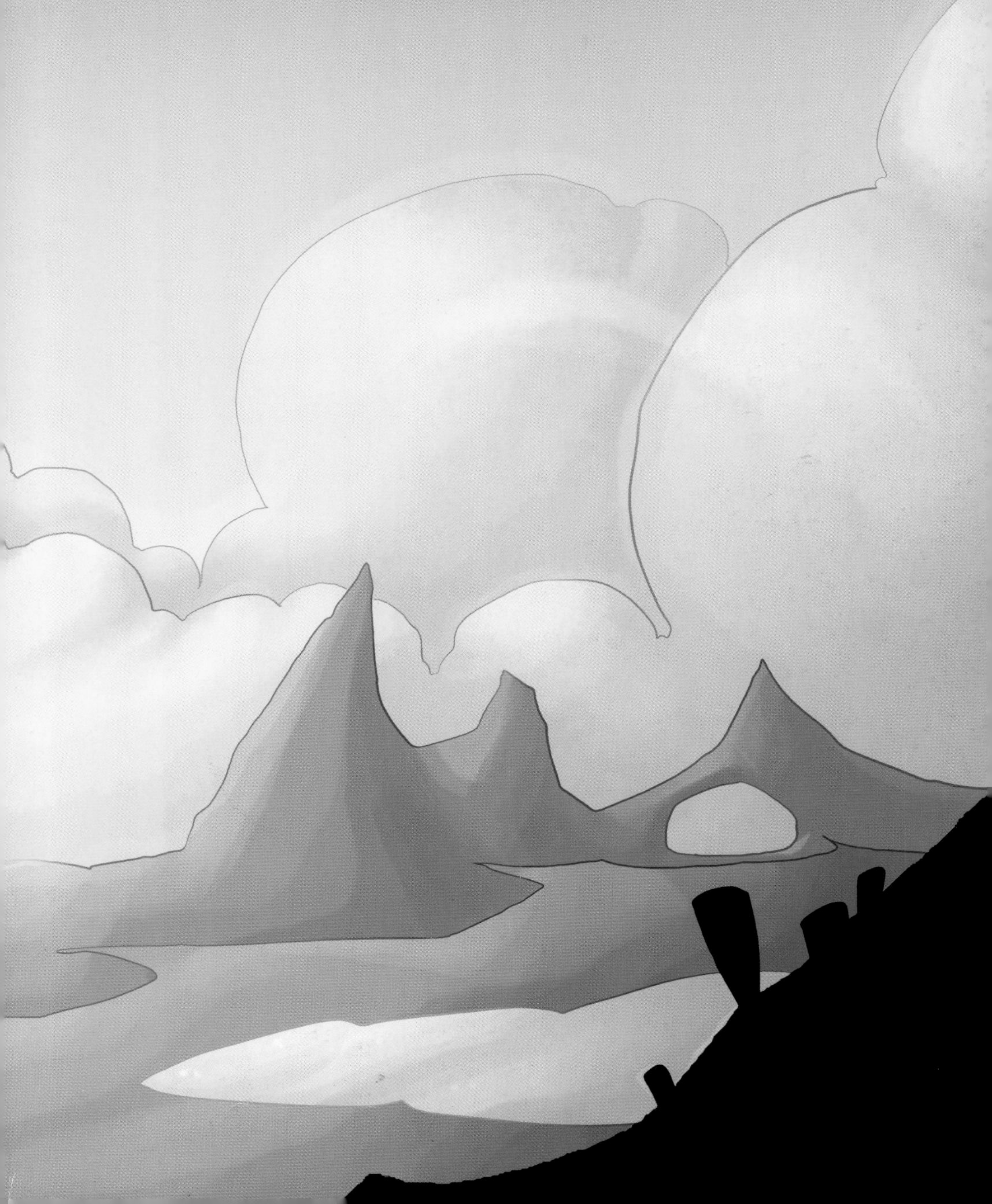

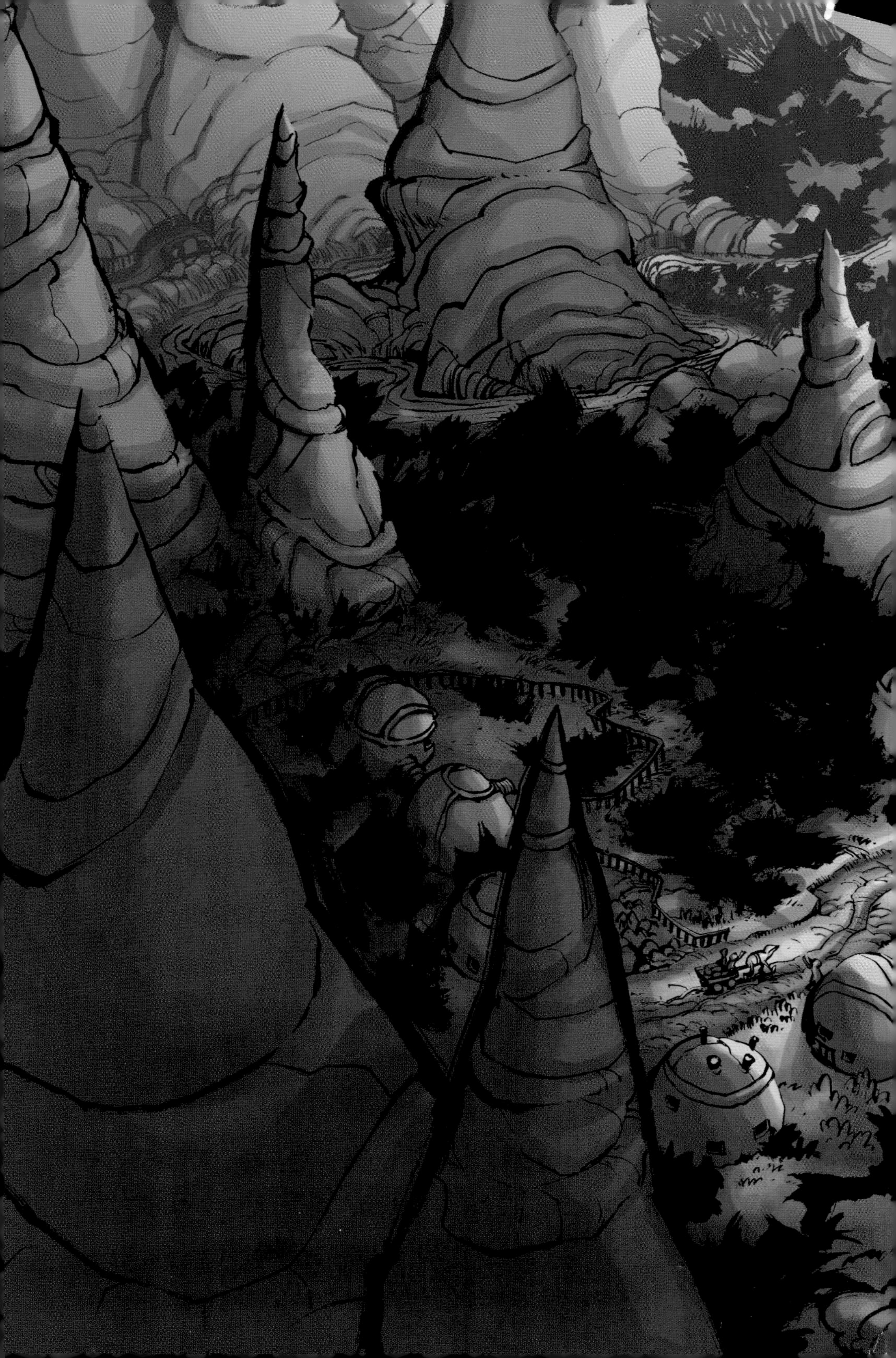

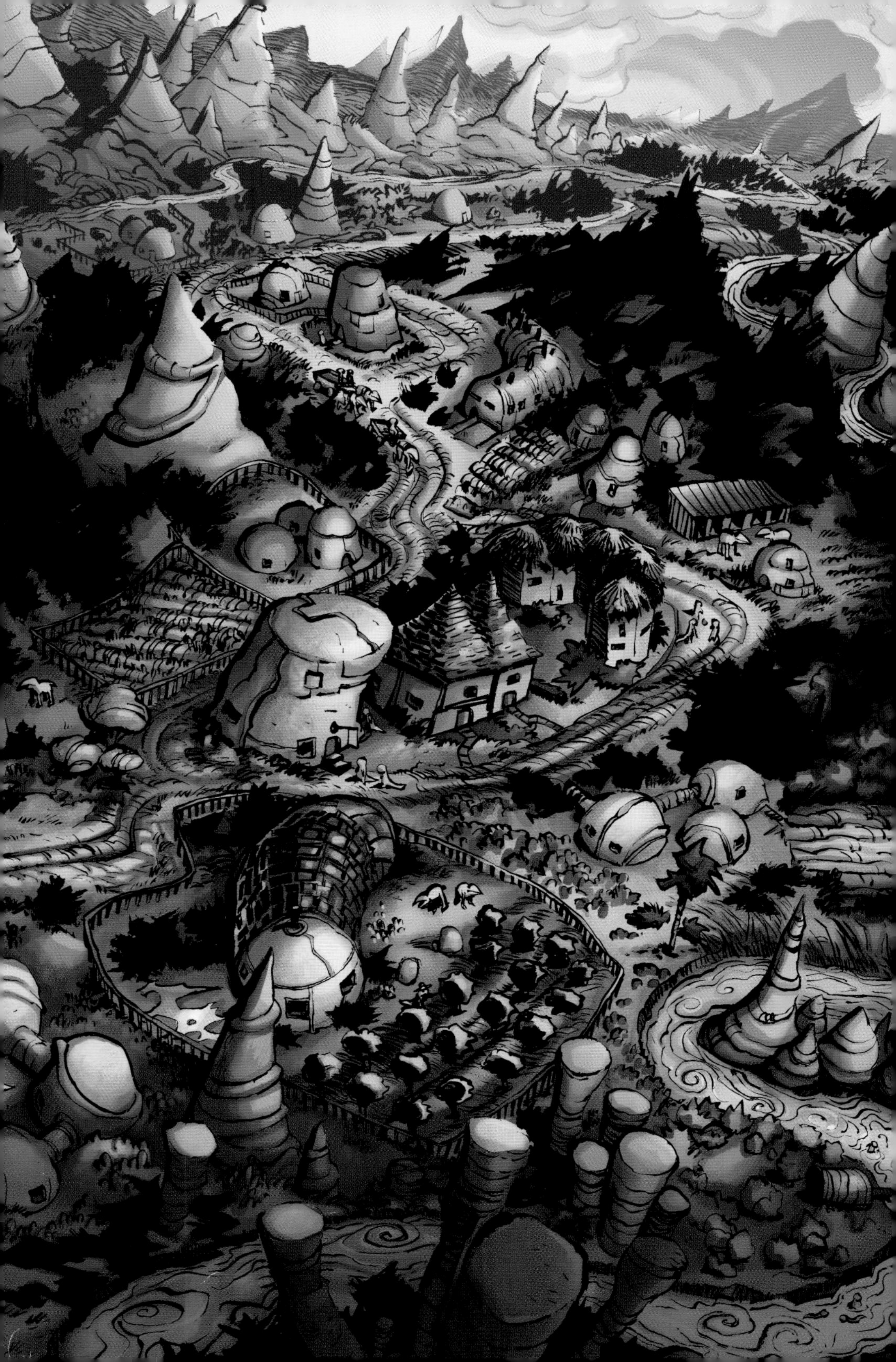

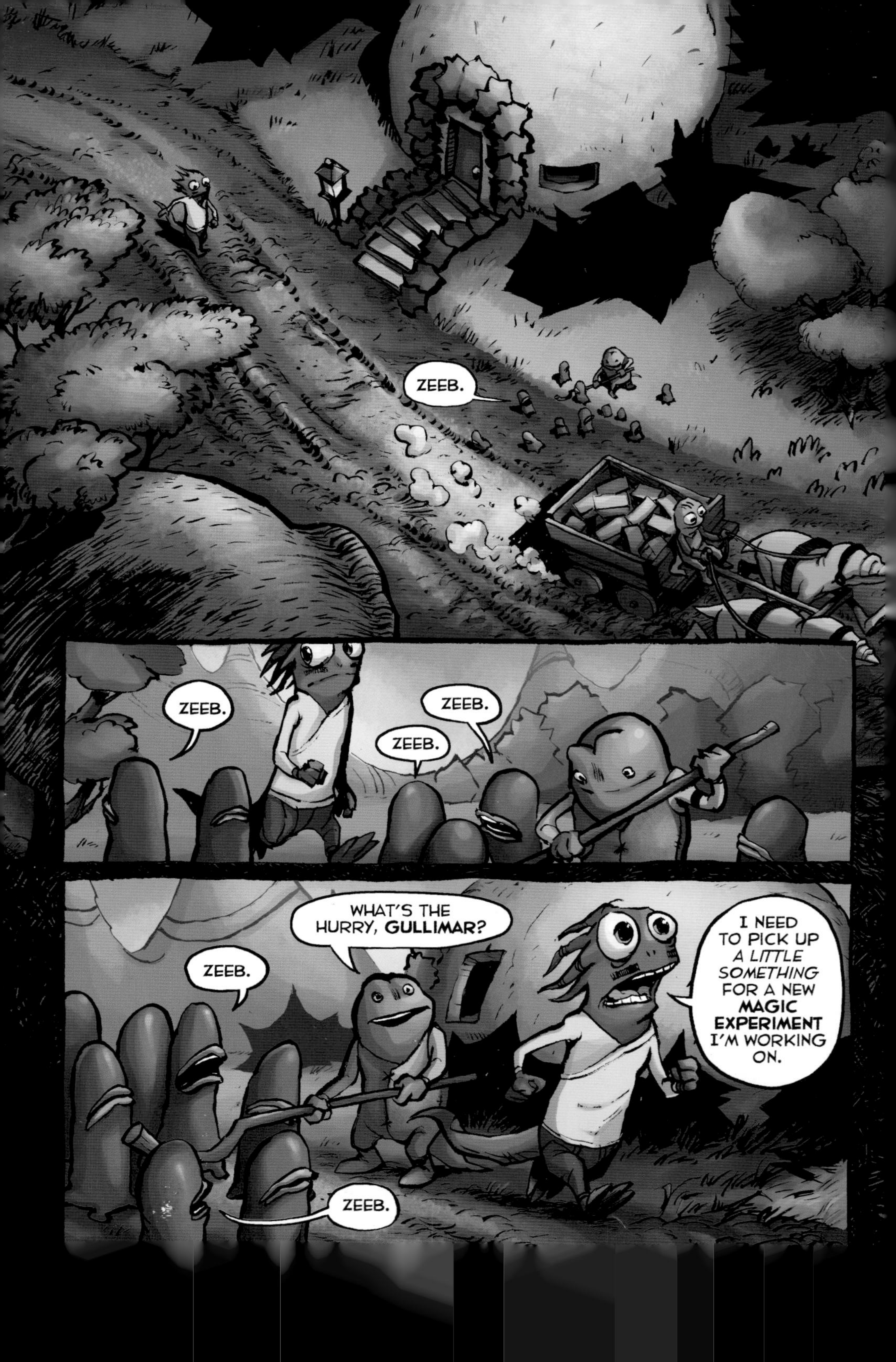
ZEEB.
ZEEB.
ZEEB.
ZEEB.
WHAT'S THE HURRY, **GULLIMAR?**
ZEEB.
I NEED TO PICK UP *A LITTLE SOMETHING* FOR A NEW **MAGIC EXPERIMENT** I'M WORKING ON.
ZEEB.

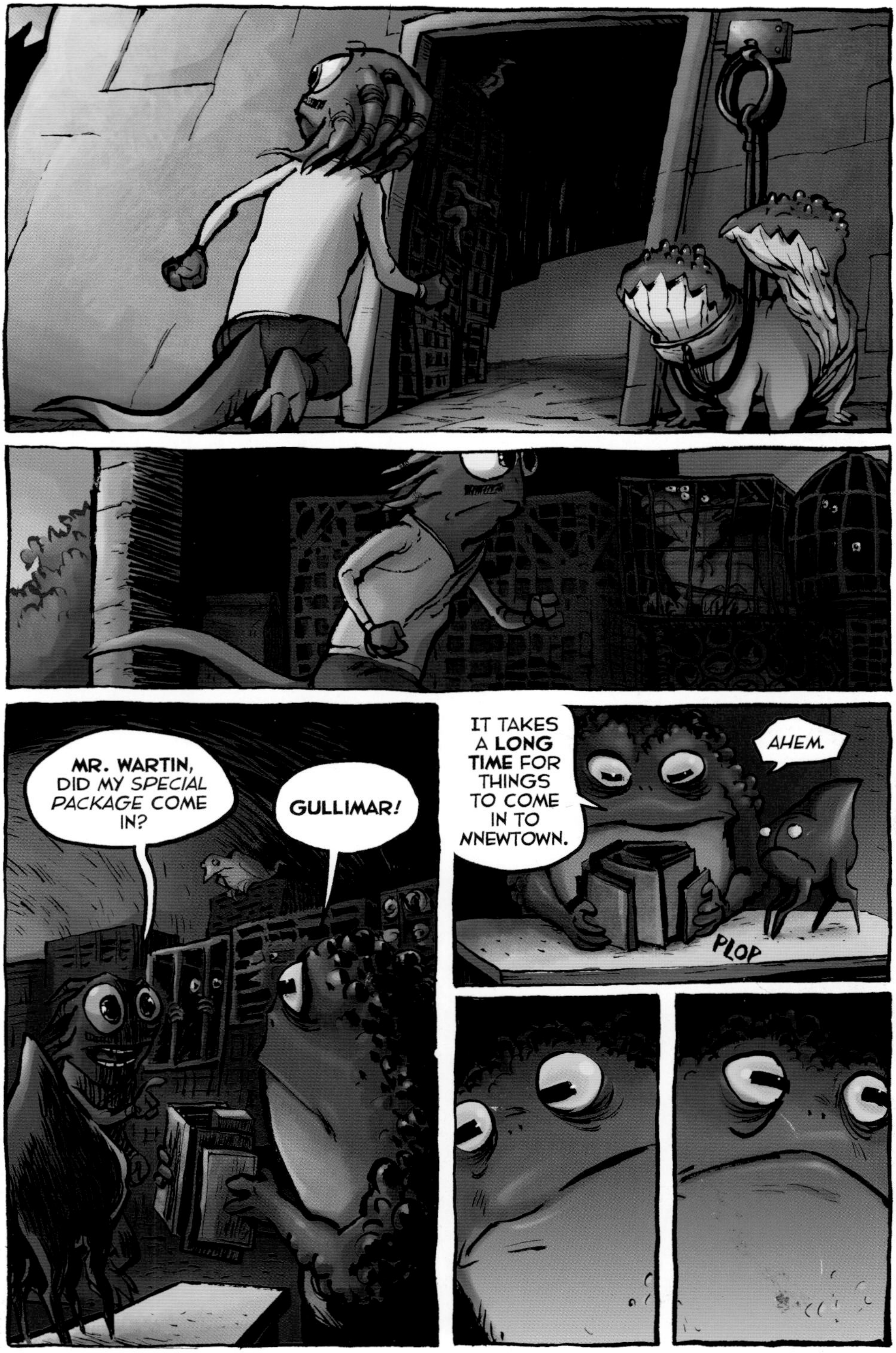
MR. WARTIN, DID MY SPECIAL PACKAGE COME IN?
GULLIMAR!
IT TAKES A LONG TIME FOR THINGS TO COME IN TO NNEWTOWN.
AHEM.
PLOP

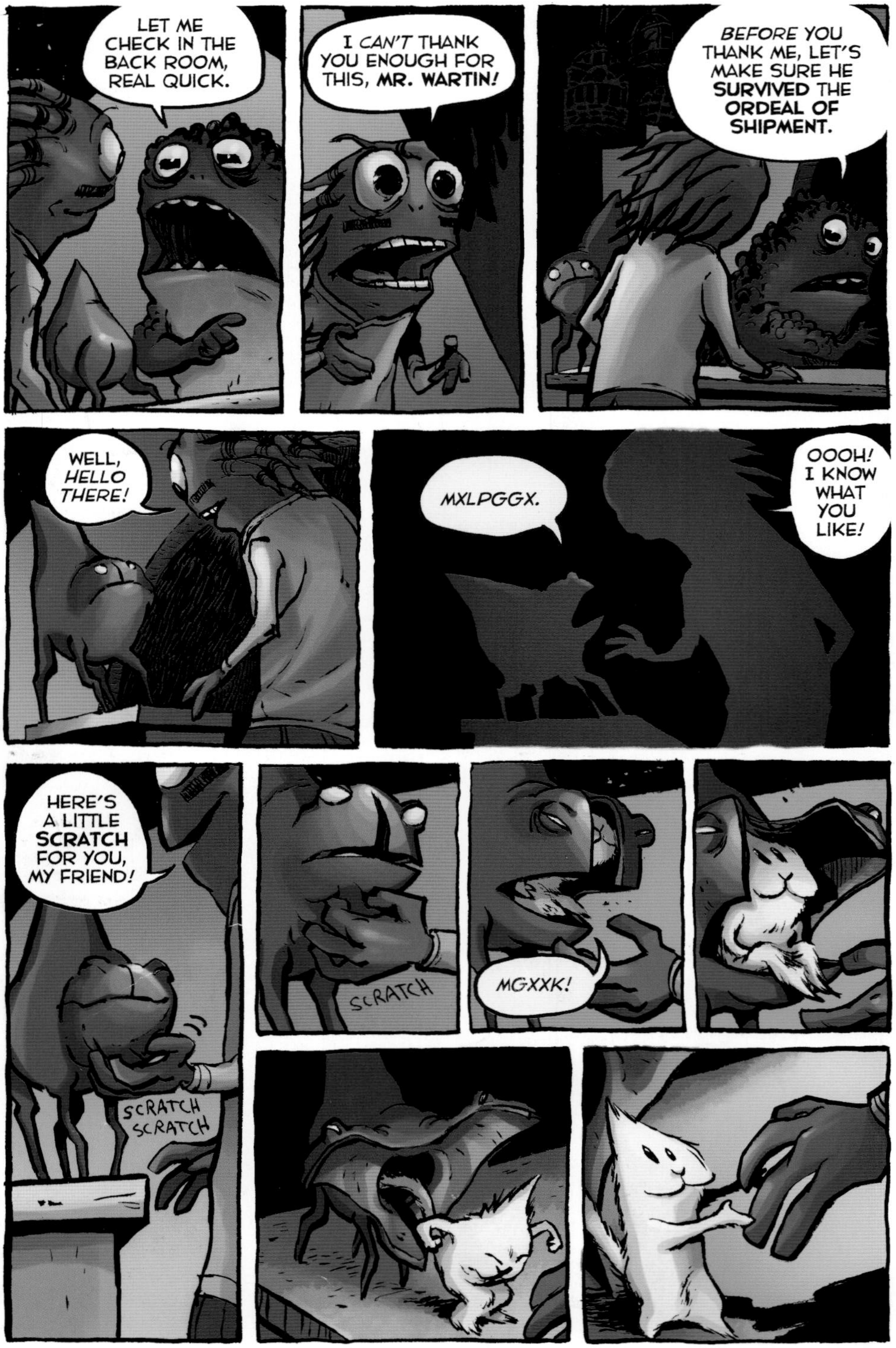
LET ME CHECK IN THE BACK ROOM, REAL QUICK.
I CAN'T THANK YOU ENOUGH FOR THIS, MR. WARTIN!
BEFORE YOU THANK ME, LET'S MAKE SURE HE SURVIVED THE ORDEAL OF SHIPMENT.
WELL, HELLO THERE!
MXLPGGX.
OOOH! I KNOW WHAT YOU LIKE!
HERE'S A LITTLE SCRATCH FOR YOU, MY FRIEND!
SCRATCH SCRATCH
SCRATCH
MGXXK!

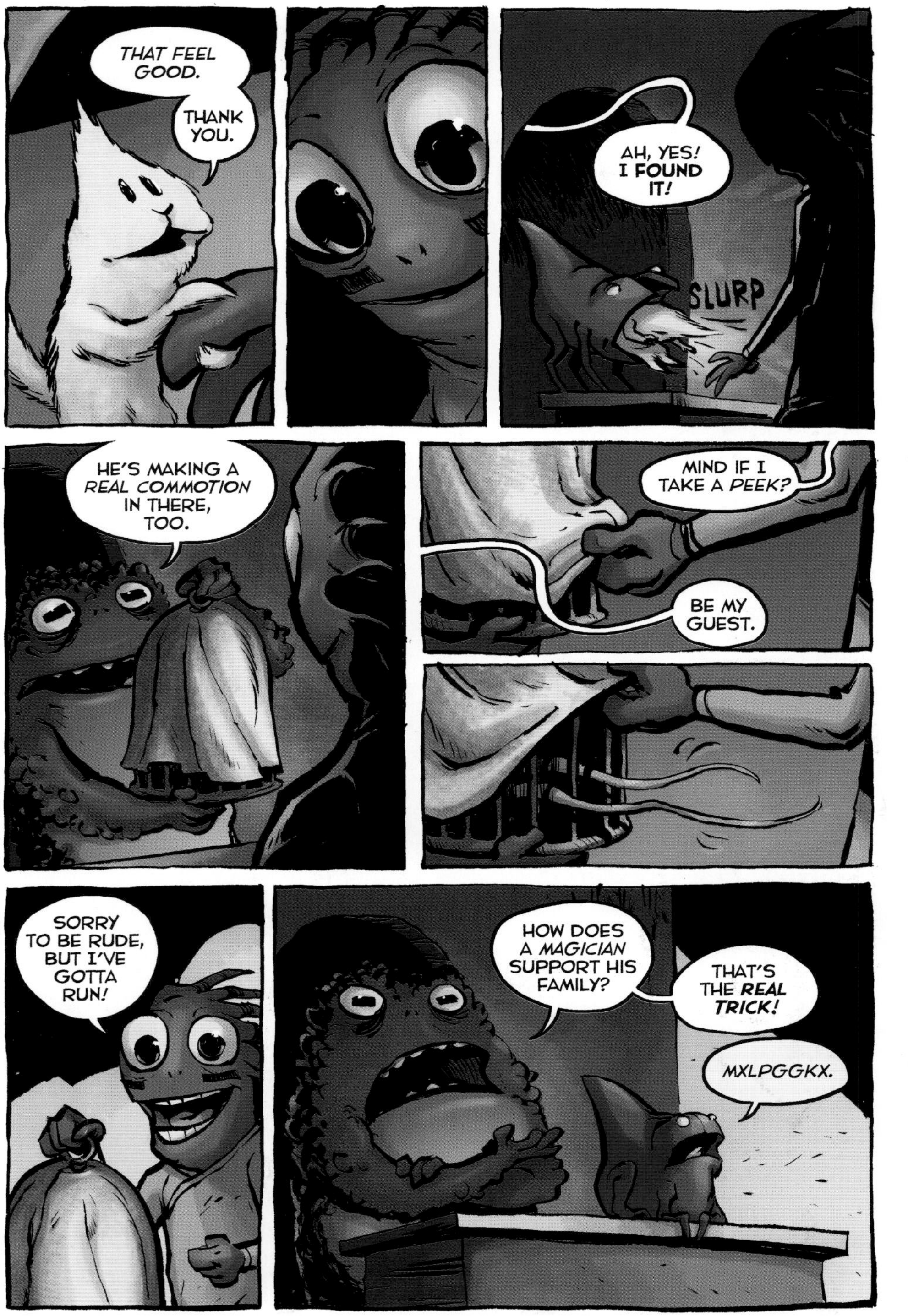
THAT FEEL GOOD.
THANK YOU.
AH, YES! I FOUND IT!
SLURP
HE'S MAKING A REAL COMMOTION IN THERE, TOO.
MIND IF I TAKE A PEEK?
BE MY GUEST.
SORRY TO BE RUDE, BUT I'VE GOTTA RUN!
HOW DOES A MAGICIAN SUPPORT HIS FAMILY?
THAT'S THE REAL TRICK!
MXLPGGKX.

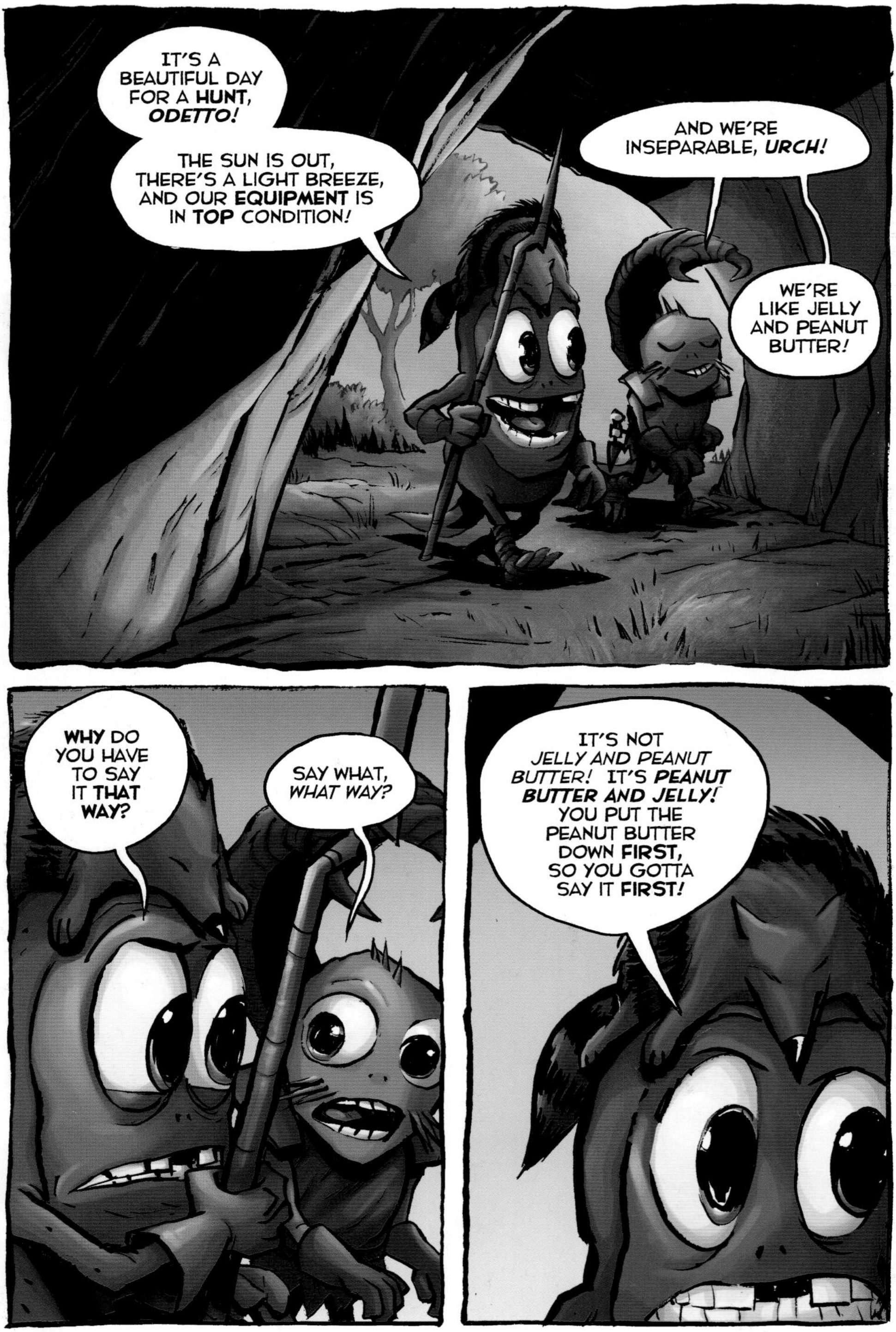
IT'S A BEAUTIFUL DAY FOR A **HUNT**, ***ODETTO!***
THE SUN IS OUT, THERE'S A LIGHT BREEZE, AND OUR **EQUIPMENT** IS IN **TOP** CONDITION!
AND WE'RE INSEPARABLE, ***URCH!***
WE'RE LIKE JELLY AND PEANUT BUTTER!
WHY DO YOU HAVE TO SAY IT **THAT WAY?**
SAY WHAT, *WHAT WAY?*
IT'S NOT *JELLY AND PEANUT BUTTER!* IT'S ***PEANUT BUTTER AND JELLY!*** YOU PUT THE PEANUT BUTTER DOWN **FIRST,** SO YOU GOTTA SAY IT **FIRST!**

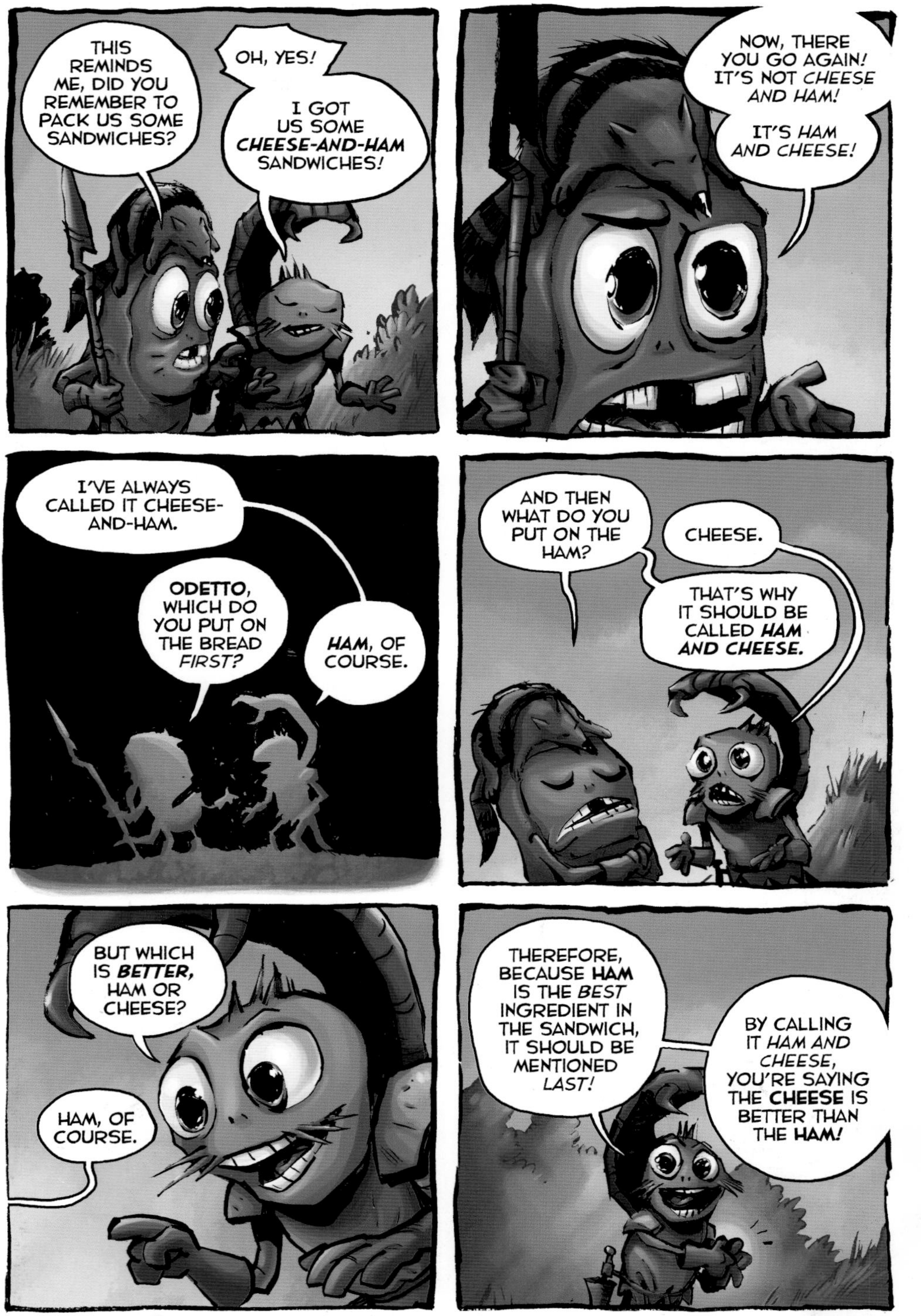
THIS REMINDS ME, DID YOU REMEMBER TO PACK US SOME SANDWICHES?
OH, YES!
I GOT US SOME **CHEESE-AND-HAM** SANDWICHES!
NOW, THERE YOU GO AGAIN! IT'S NOT *CHEESE AND HAM!*
IT'S *HAM AND CHEESE!*
I'VE ALWAYS CALLED IT CHEESE-AND-HAM.
ODETTO, WHICH DO YOU PUT ON THE BREAD *FIRST?*
HAM, OF COURSE.
AND THEN WHAT DO YOU PUT ON THE HAM?
CHEESE.
THAT'S WHY IT SHOULD BE CALLED **HAM AND CHEESE.**
BUT WHICH IS ***BETTER***, HAM OR CHEESE?
HAM, OF COURSE.
THEREFORE, BECAUSE **HAM** IS THE *BEST* INGREDIENT IN THE SANDWICH, IT SHOULD BE MENTIONED *LAST!*
BY CALLING IT *HAM AND CHEESE*, YOU'RE SAYING THE **CHEESE** IS BETTER THAN THE **HAM!**

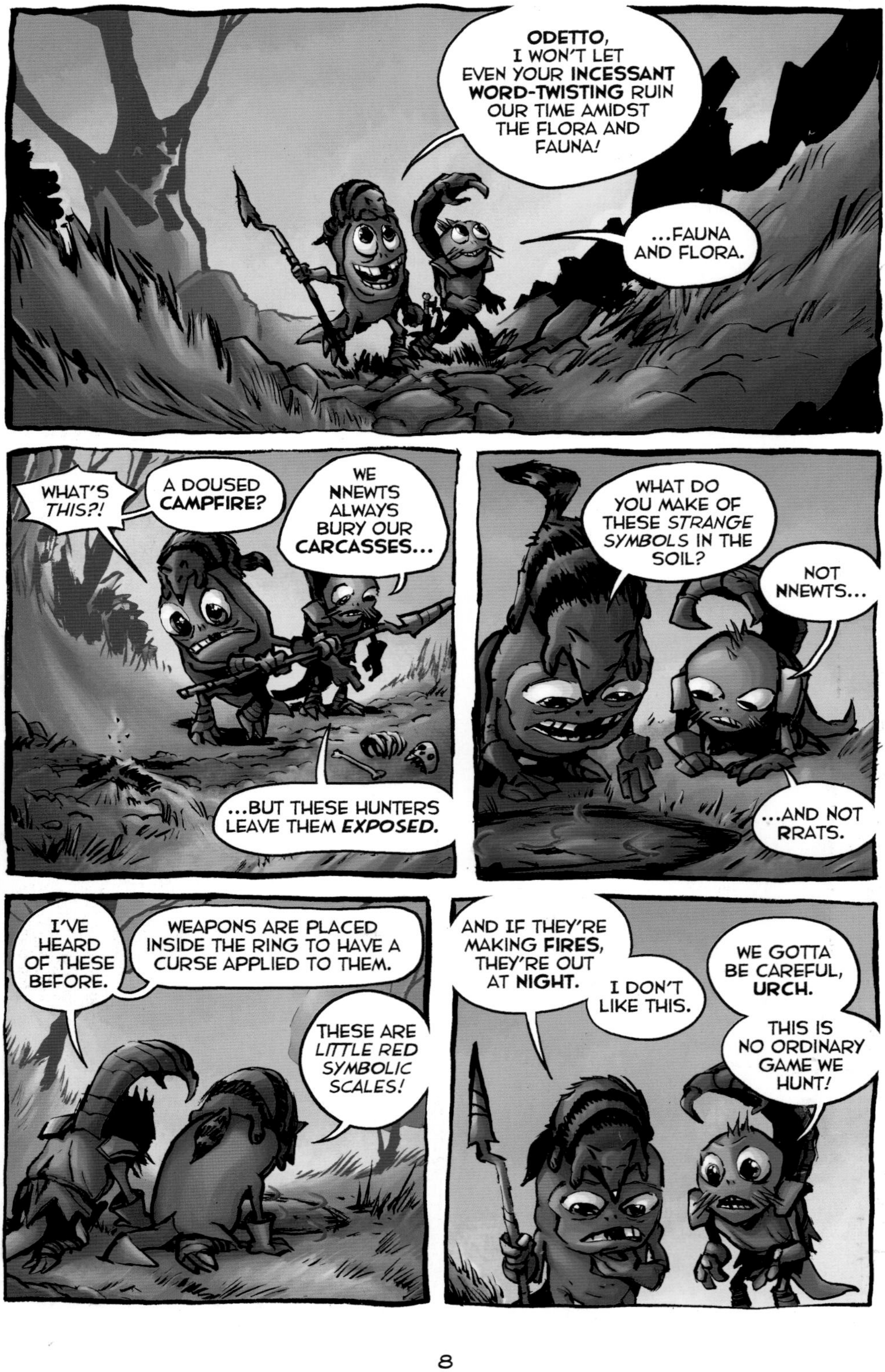
ODETTO, I WON'T LET EVEN YOUR INCESSANT WORD-TWISTING RUIN OUR TIME AMIDST THE FLORA AND FAUNA!
...FAUNA AND FLORA.
WHAT'S THIS?!
A DOUSED CAMPFIRE?
WE NNEWTS ALWAYS BURY OUR CARCASSES...
...BUT THESE HUNTERS LEAVE THEM EXPOSED.
WHAT DO YOU MAKE OF THESE STRANGE SYMBOLS IN THE SOIL?
NOT NNEWTS...
...AND NOT RRATS.
I'VE HEARD OF THESE BEFORE.
WEAPONS ARE PLACED INSIDE THE RING TO HAVE A CURSE APPLIED TO THEM.
THESE ARE LITTLE RED SYMBOLIC SCALES!
AND IF THEY'RE MAKING FIRES, THEY'RE OUT AT NIGHT.
I DON'T LIKE THIS.
WE GOTTA BE CAREFUL, URCH.
THIS IS NO ORDINARY GAME WE HUNT!

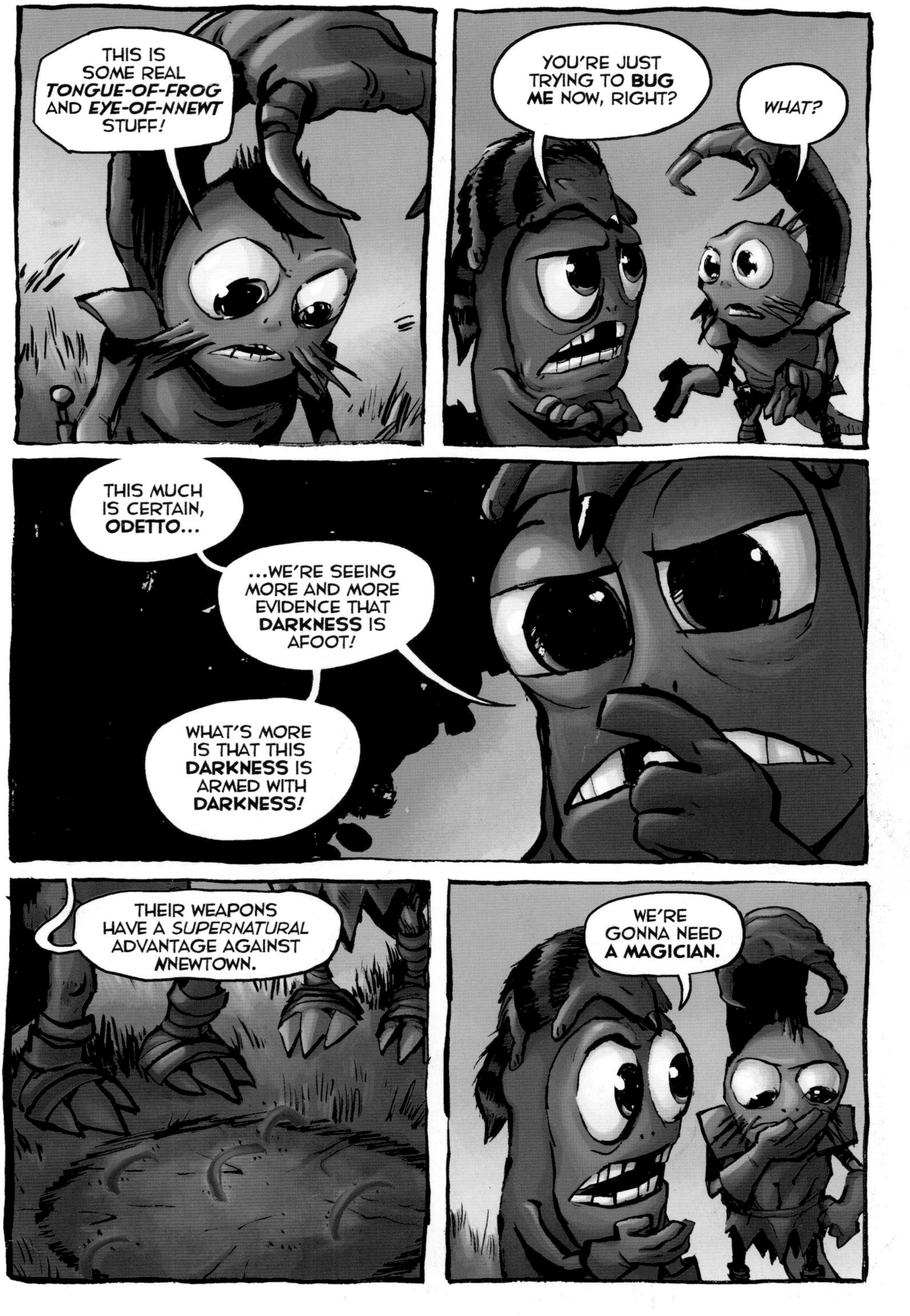
THIS IS SOME REAL TONGUE-OF-FROG AND EYE-OF-NNEWT STUFF!
YOU'RE JUST TRYING TO BUG ME NOW, RIGHT?
WHAT?
THIS MUCH IS CERTAIN, ODETTO...
...WE'RE SEEING MORE AND MORE EVIDENCE THAT DARKNESS IS AFOOT!
WHAT'S MORE IS THAT THIS DARKNESS IS ARMED WITH DARKNESS!
THEIR WEAPONS HAVE A SUPERNATURAL ADVANTAGE AGAINST NNEWTOWN.
WE'RE GONNA NEED A MAGICIAN.

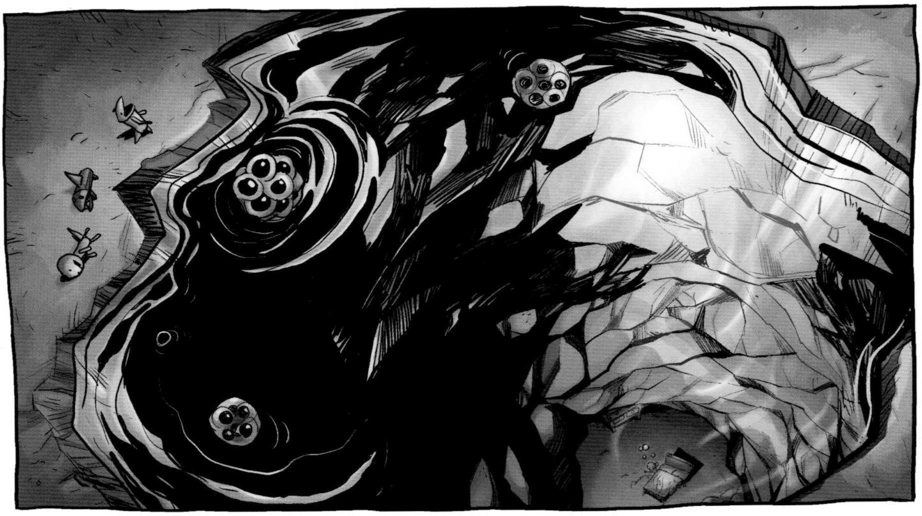

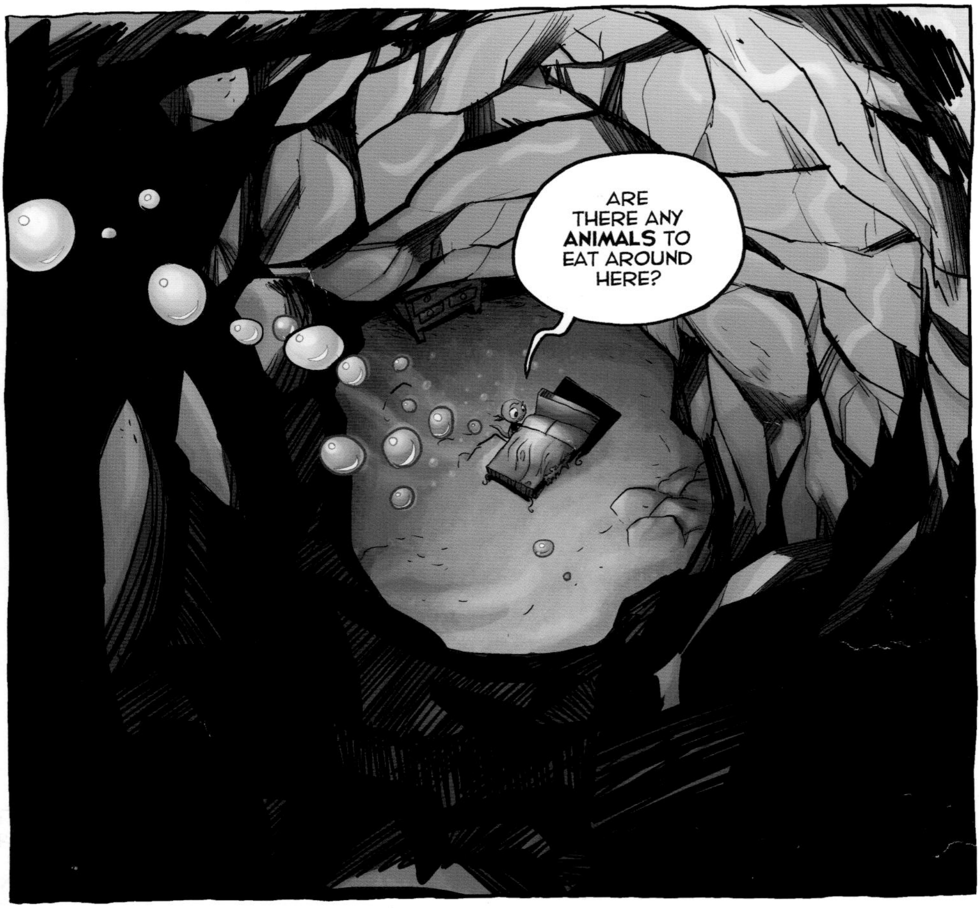
ARE THERE ANY ANIMALS TO EAT AROUND HERE?

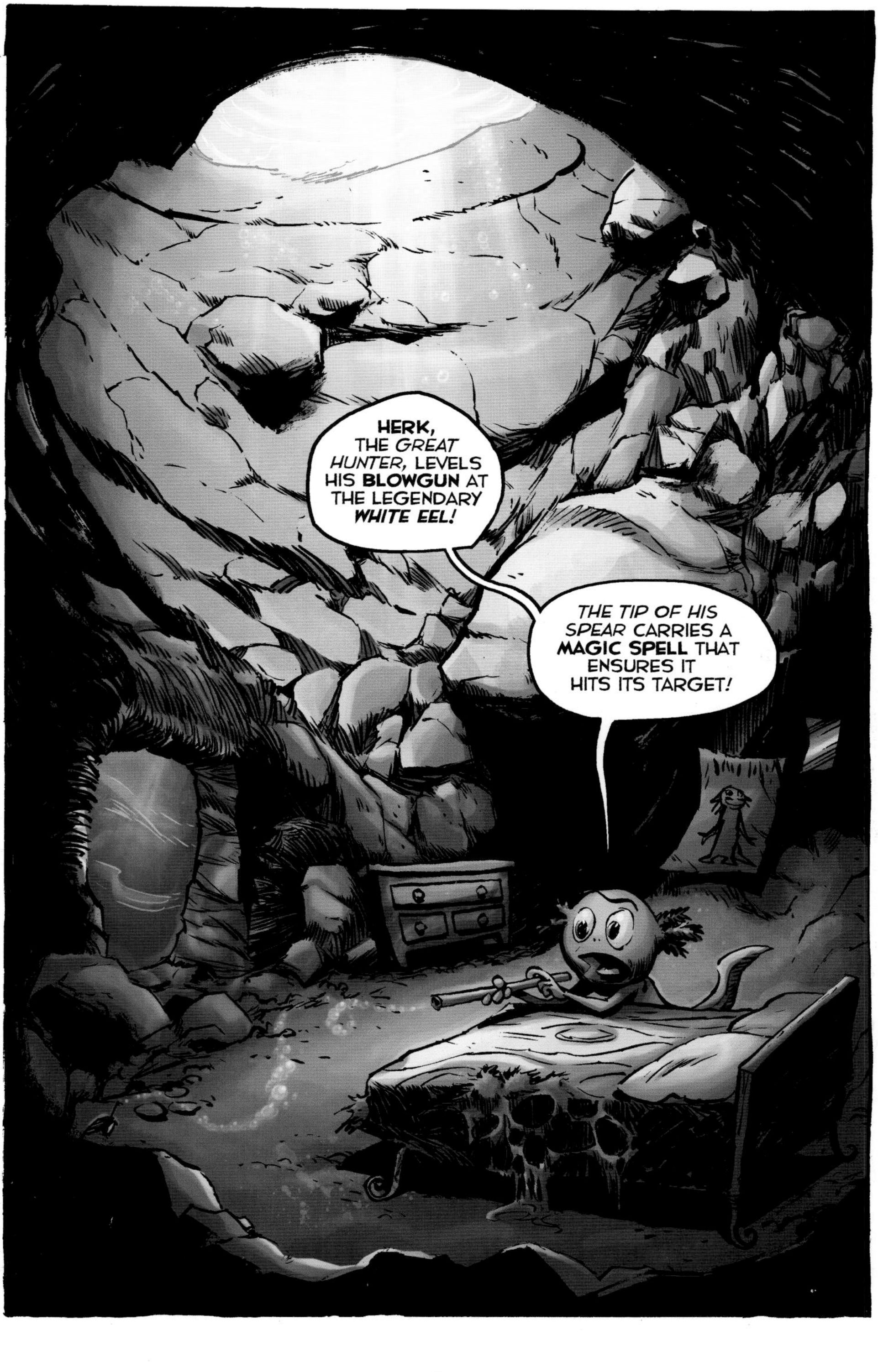
HERK, THE GREAT HUNTER, LEVELS HIS BLOWGUN AT THE LEGENDARY WHITE EEL!
THE TIP OF HIS SPEAR CARRIES A MAGIC SPELL THAT ENSURES IT HITS ITS TARGET!

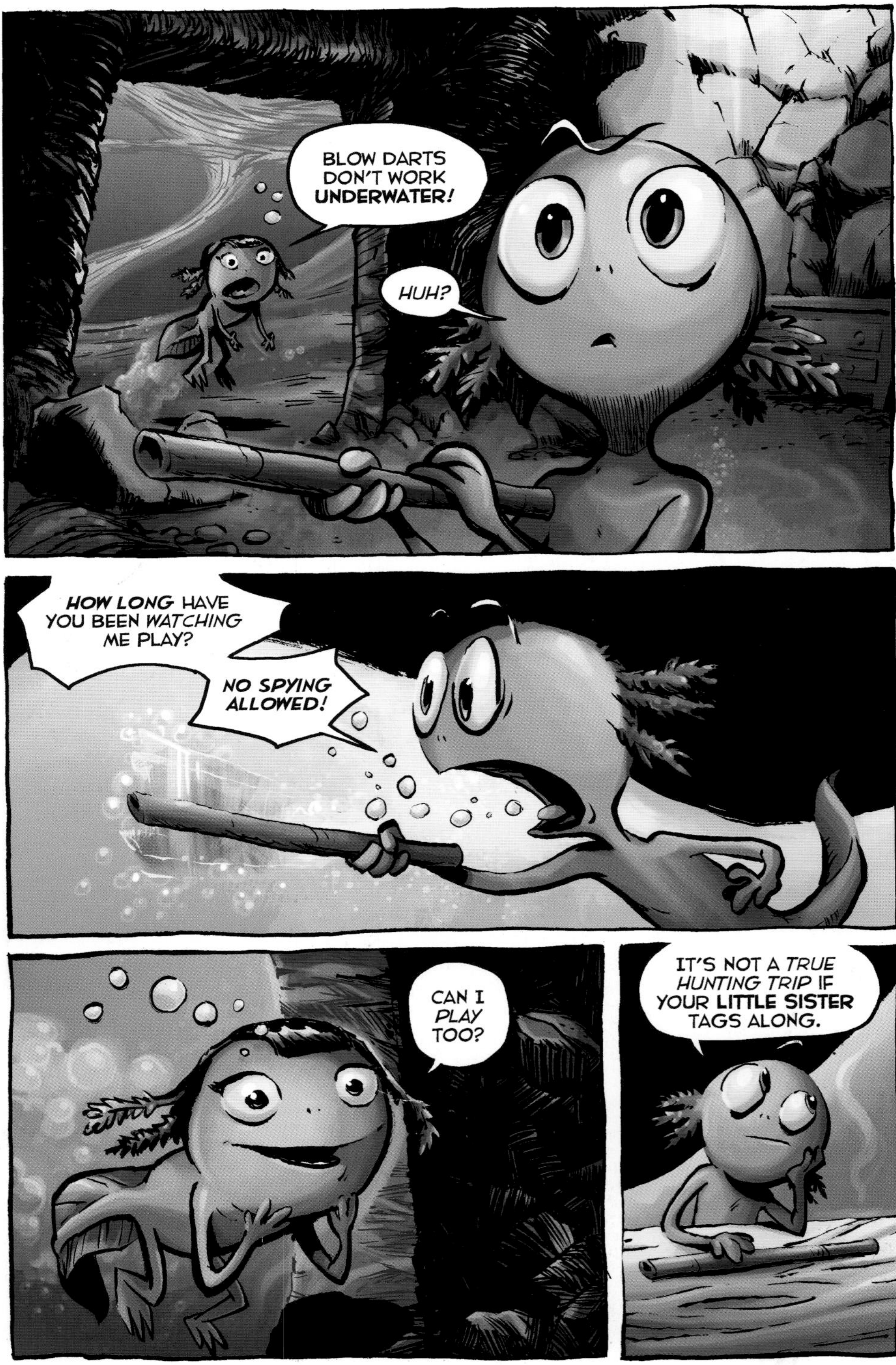
BLOW DARTS DON'T WORK **UNDERWATER!**
HUH?
HOW LONG HAVE YOU BEEN *WATCHING* ME PLAY?
NO SPYING ALLOWED!
CAN I *PLAY* TOO?
IT'S NOT A *TRUE HUNTING TRIP* IF YOUR **LITTLE SISTER** TAGS ALONG.

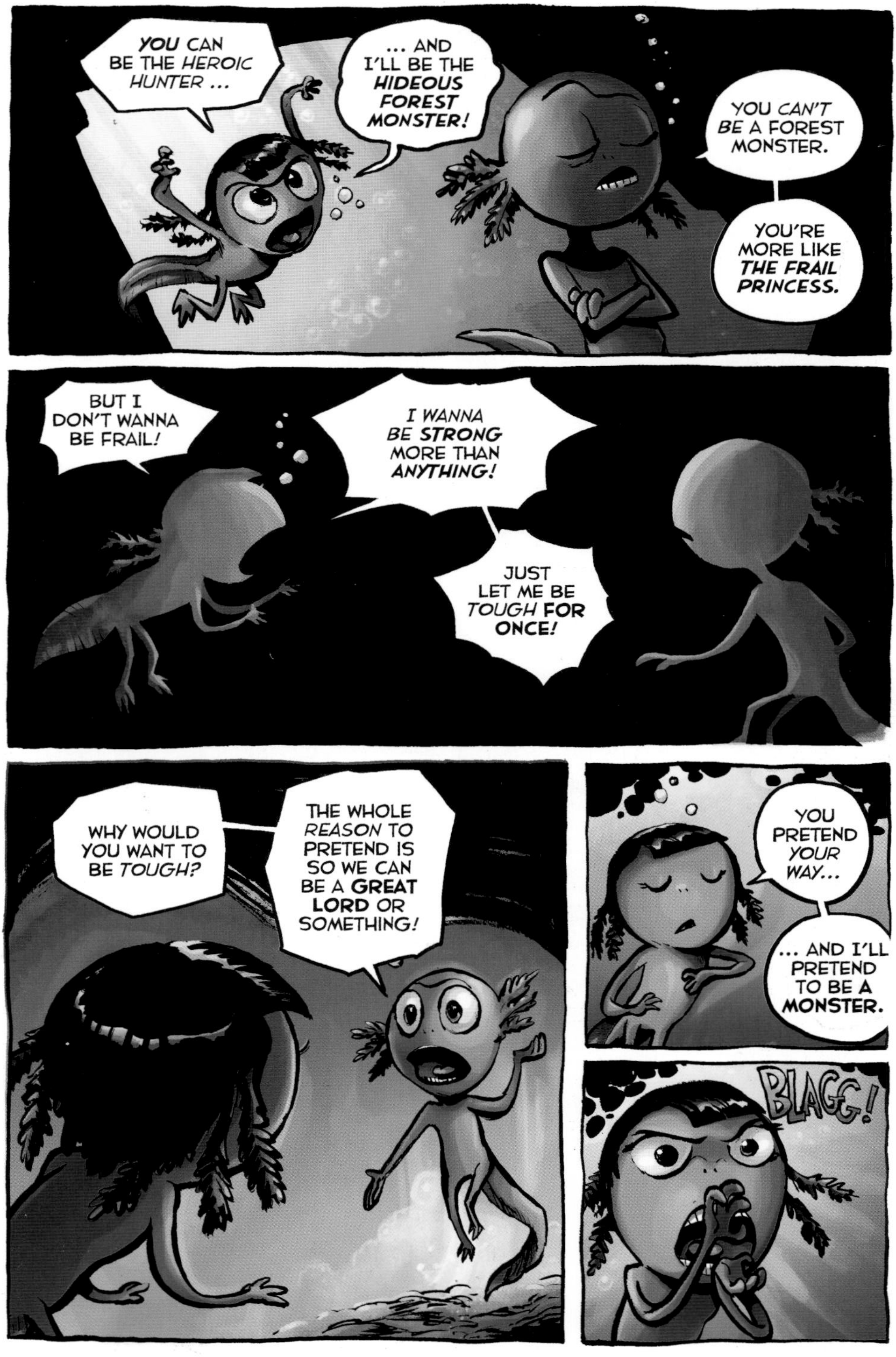

YOU CAN BE THE HEROIC HUNTER ...
... AND I'LL BE THE HIDEOUS FOREST MONSTER!
YOU CAN'T BE A FOREST MONSTER.
YOU'RE MORE LIKE THE FRAIL PRINCESS.
BUT I DON'T WANNA BE FRAIL!
I WANNA BE STRONG MORE THAN ANYTHING!
JUST LET ME BE TOUGH FOR ONCE!
WHY WOULD YOU WANT TO BE TOUGH?
THE WHOLE REASON TO PRETEND IS SO WE CAN BE A GREAT LORD OR SOMETHING!
YOU PRETEND YOUR WAY...
... AND I'LL PRETEND TO BE A MONSTER.
BLAGG!

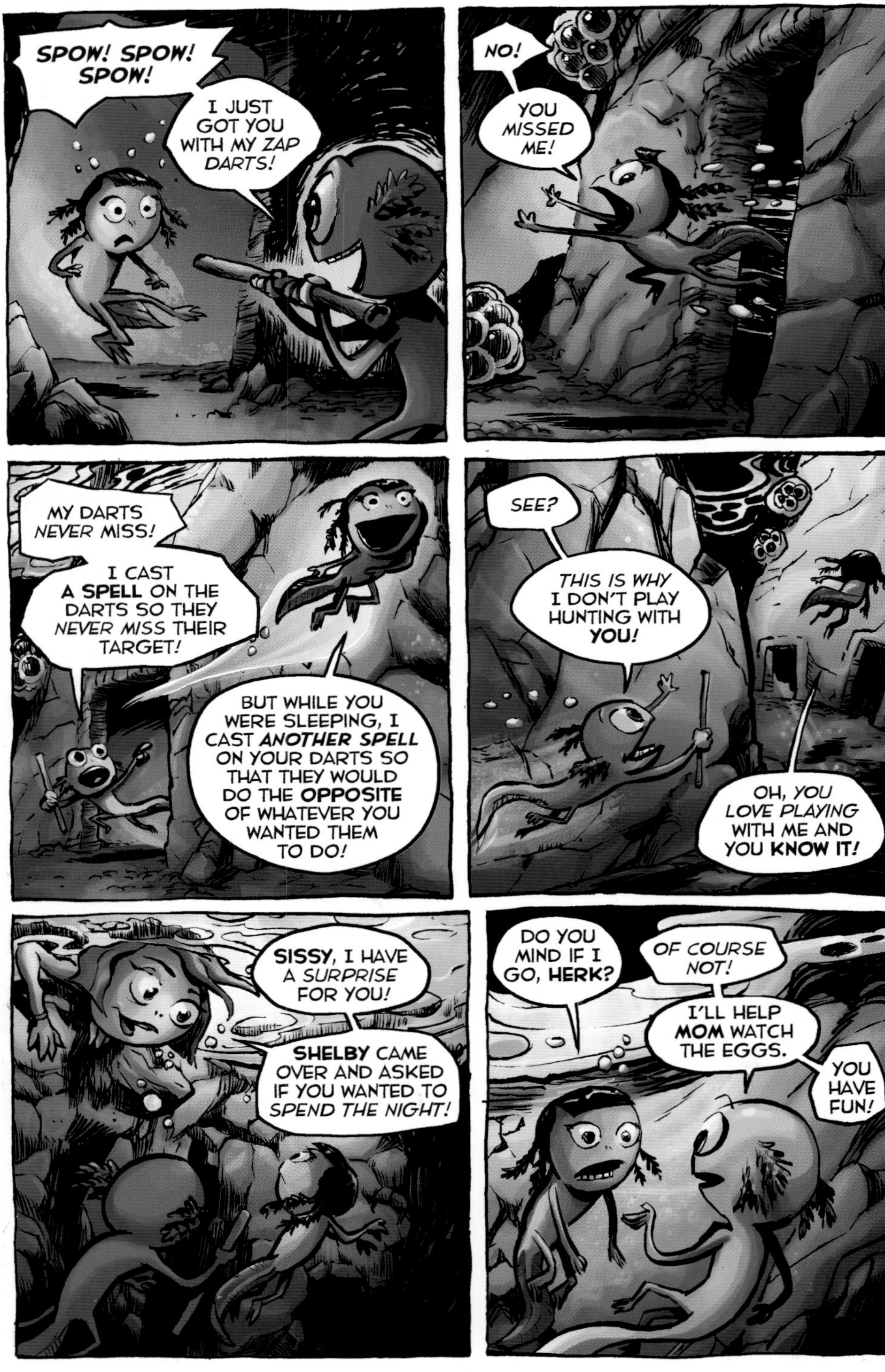
SPOW! SPOW! SPOW!
I JUST GOT YOU WITH MY ZAP DARTS!
NO!
YOU MISSED ME!
MY DARTS NEVER MISS!
I CAST A SPELL ON THE DARTS SO THEY NEVER MISS THEIR TARGET!
BUT WHILE YOU WERE SLEEPING, I CAST ANOTHER SPELL ON YOUR DARTS SO THAT THEY WOULD DO THE OPPOSITE OF WHATEVER YOU WANTED THEM TO DO!
SEE?
THIS IS WHY I DON'T PLAY HUNTING WITH YOU!
OH, YOU LOVE PLAYING WITH ME AND YOU KNOW IT!
SISSY, I HAVE A SURPRISE FOR YOU!
SHELBY CAME OVER AND ASKED IF YOU WANTED TO SPEND THE NIGHT!
DO YOU MIND IF I GO, HERK?
OF COURSE NOT!
I'LL HELP MOM WATCH THE EGGS.
YOU HAVE FUN!

LITTLE LEGS...

...BIG HEART!

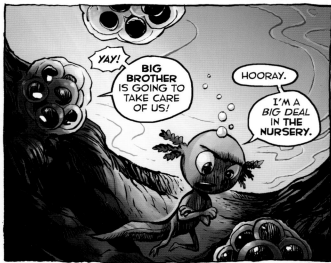

YAY!

BIG BROTHER IS GOING TO TAKE CARE OF US!

HOORAY.

I'M A BIG DEAL IN THE NURSERY.

YOU WON'T BE A BURDEN TO HER MOTHER, RIGHT?

GIVE HER A HAND WITH SOME CHORES JUST LIKE YOU WERE WORKING FOR ME.

OH, MOM!

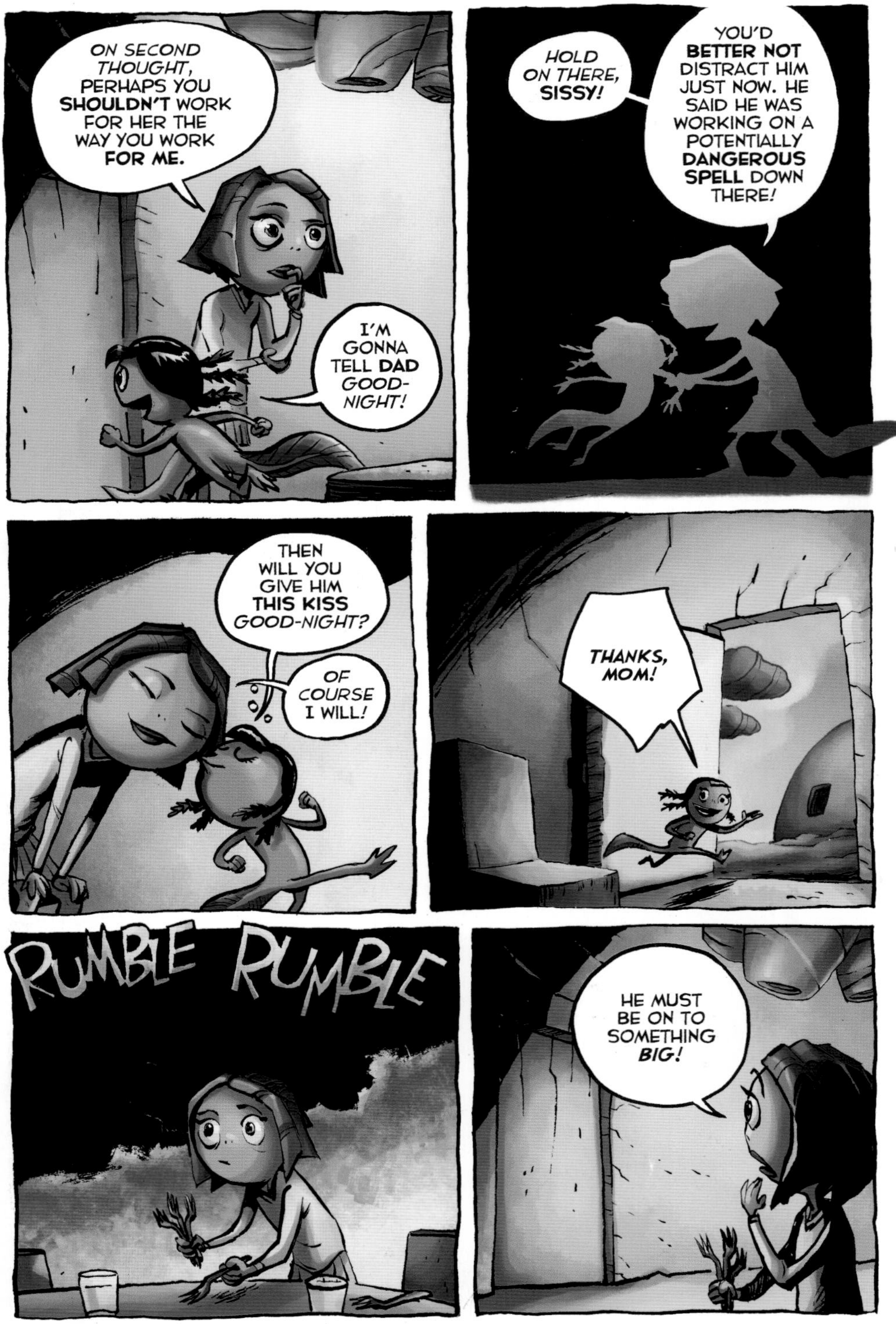
ON SECOND THOUGHT, PERHAPS YOU SHOULDN'T WORK FOR HER THE WAY YOU WORK FOR ME.
I'M GONNA TELL DAD GOOD-NIGHT!
HOLD ON THERE, SISSY!
YOU'D BETTER NOT DISTRACT HIM JUST NOW. HE SAID HE WAS WORKING ON A POTENTIALLY DANGEROUS SPELL DOWN THERE!
THEN WILL YOU GIVE HIM THIS KISS GOOD-NIGHT?
OF COURSE I WILL!
THANKS, MOM!
RUMBLE RUMBLE
HE MUST BE ON TO SOMETHING BIG!

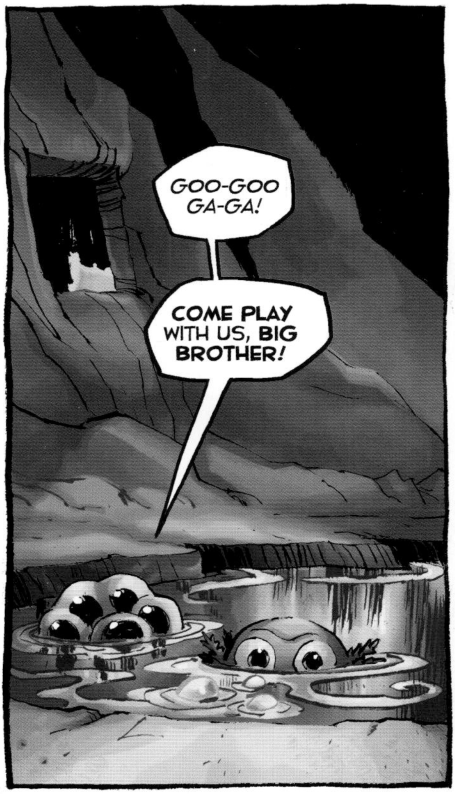
GOO-GOO GA-GA!
COME PLAY WITH US, **BIG BROTHER!**

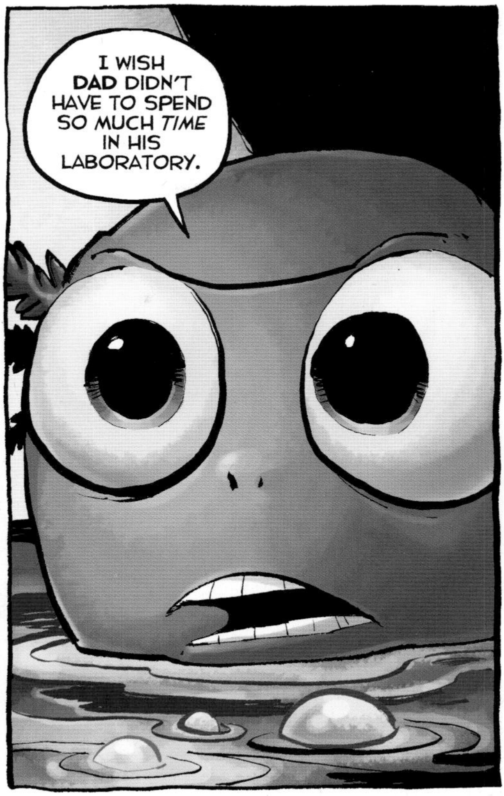
I WISH **DAD** DIDN'T HAVE TO SPEND SO MUCH *TIME* IN HIS LABORATORY.

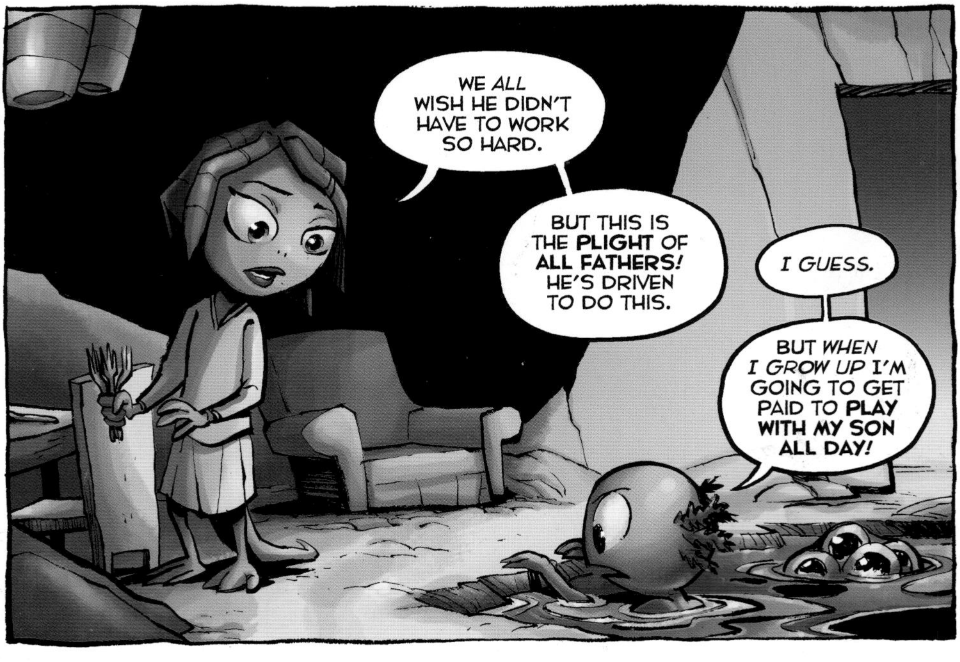
WE *ALL* WISH HE DIDN'T HAVE TO WORK SO HARD.
BUT THIS IS THE **PLIGHT** OF **ALL FATHERS!** HE'S DRIVEN TO DO THIS.
I GUESS.
BUT *WHEN I GROW UP* I'M GOING TO GET PAID TO **PLAY WITH MY SON ALL DAY!**

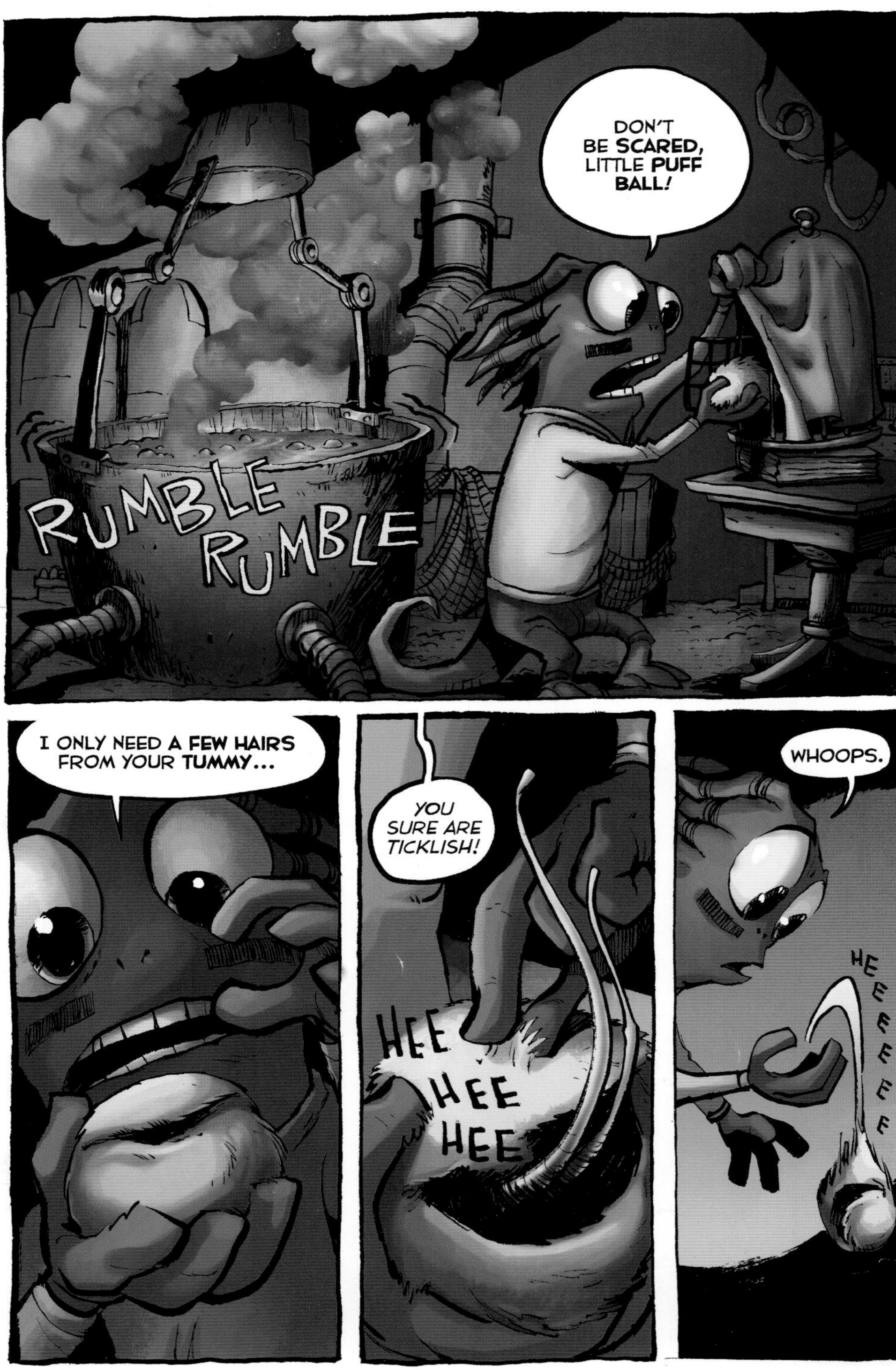
DON'T BE **SCARED**, LITTLE **PUFF BALL**!
RUMBLE RUMBLE
I ONLY NEED A **FEW HAIRS** FROM YOUR **TUMMY**...
YOU SURE ARE TICKLISH!
HEE HEE HEE
WHOOPS.
HEEEEEEE

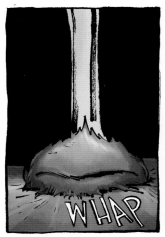

WHAP

GET BACK HERE!

IF I LOSE YOU, I DON'T THINK I'LL EVER BE ABLE TO AFFORD ANOTHER!

NOT UP THERE! IT'S FULL OF PEST TRAPS!

NO! NOT THAT WAY!

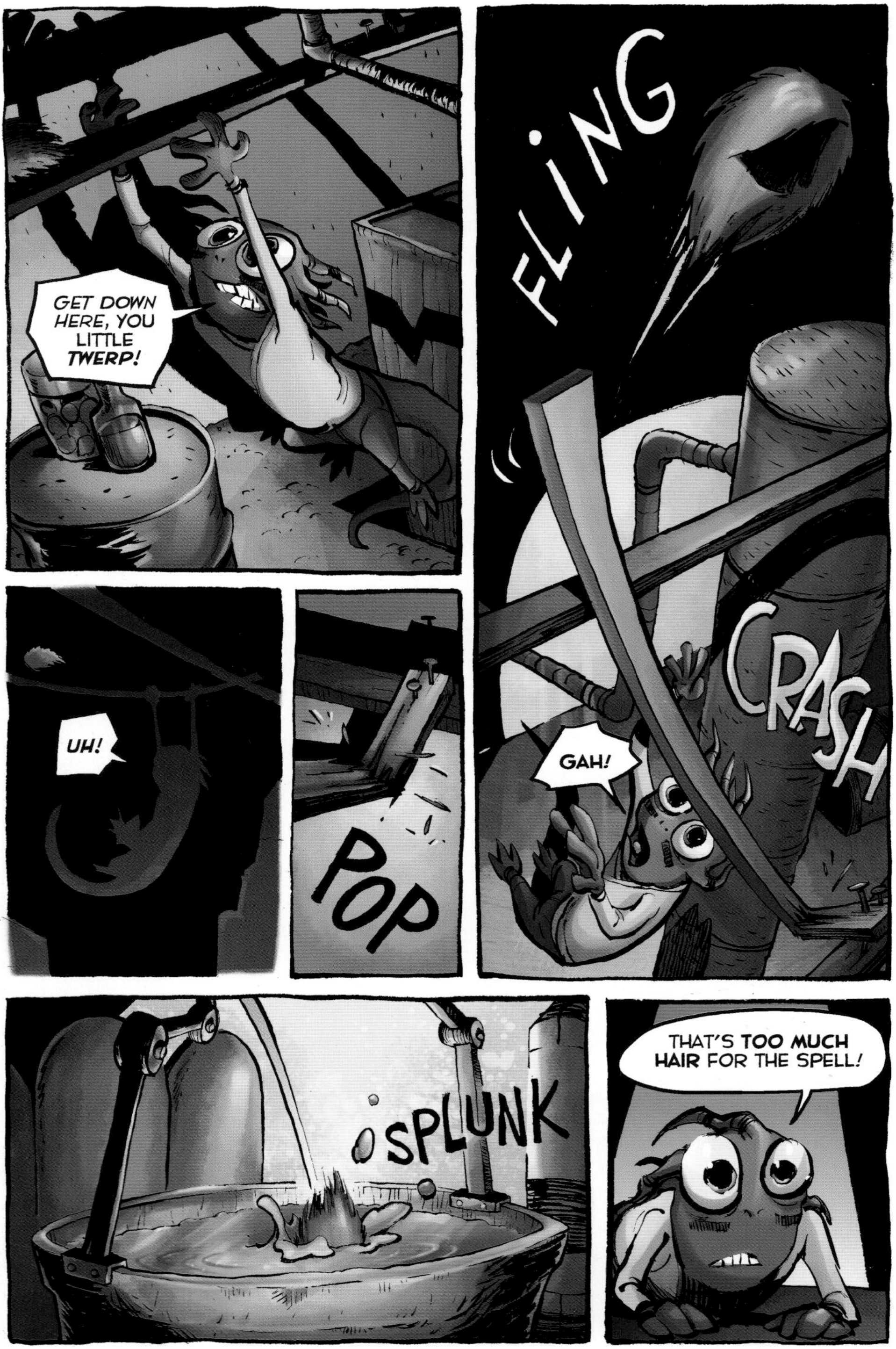
GET DOWN HERE, YOU LITTLE TWERP!
FLING
UH!
POP
CRASH
GAH!
SPLUNK
THAT'S TOO MUCH HAIR FOR THE SPELL!

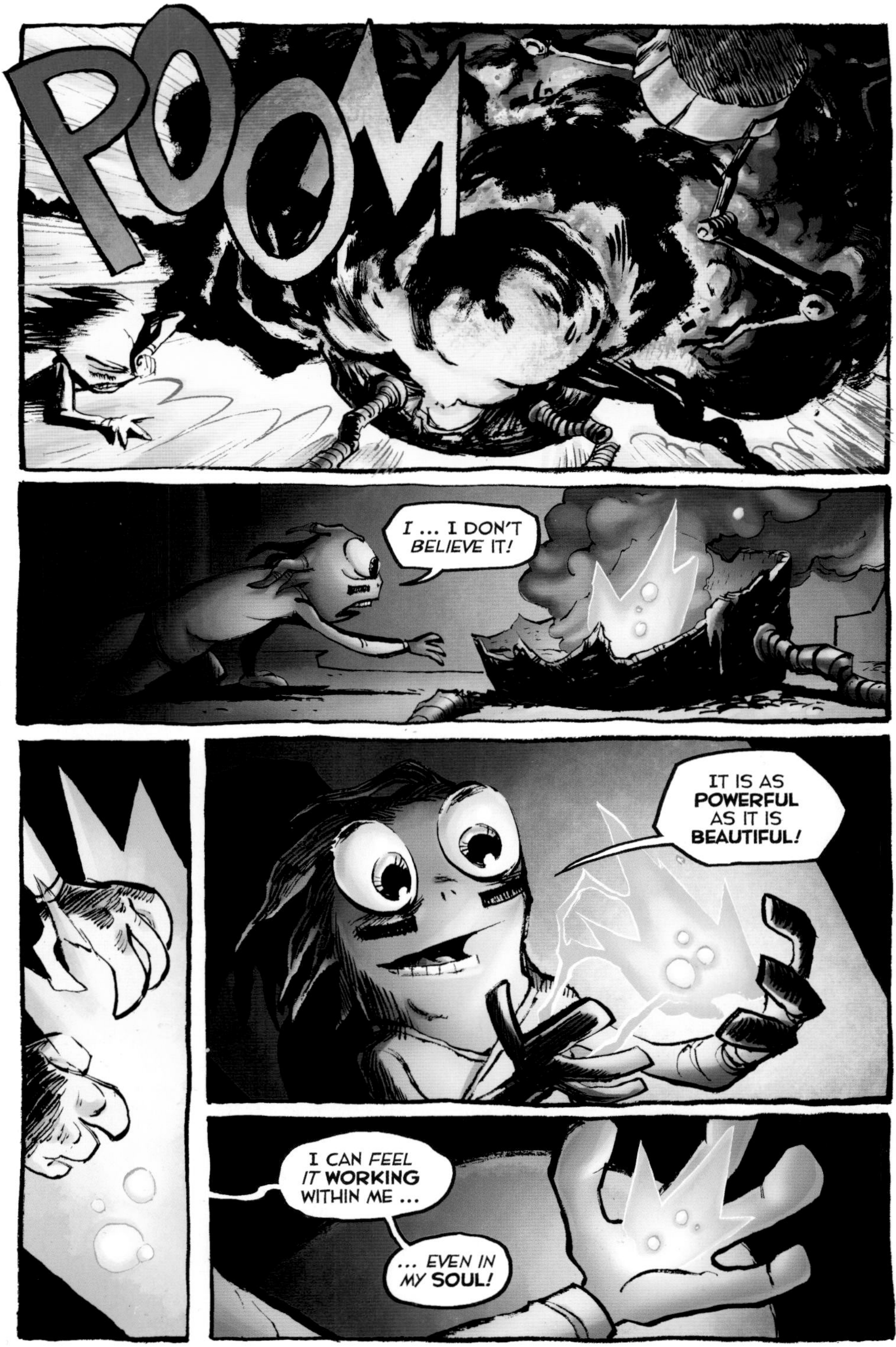
POOM
I ... I DON'T *BELIEVE* IT!
IT IS AS **POWERFUL** AS IT IS **BEAUTIFUL!**
I CAN *FEEL IT* **WORKING** WITHIN ME ...
... *EVEN IN MY* **SOUL!**

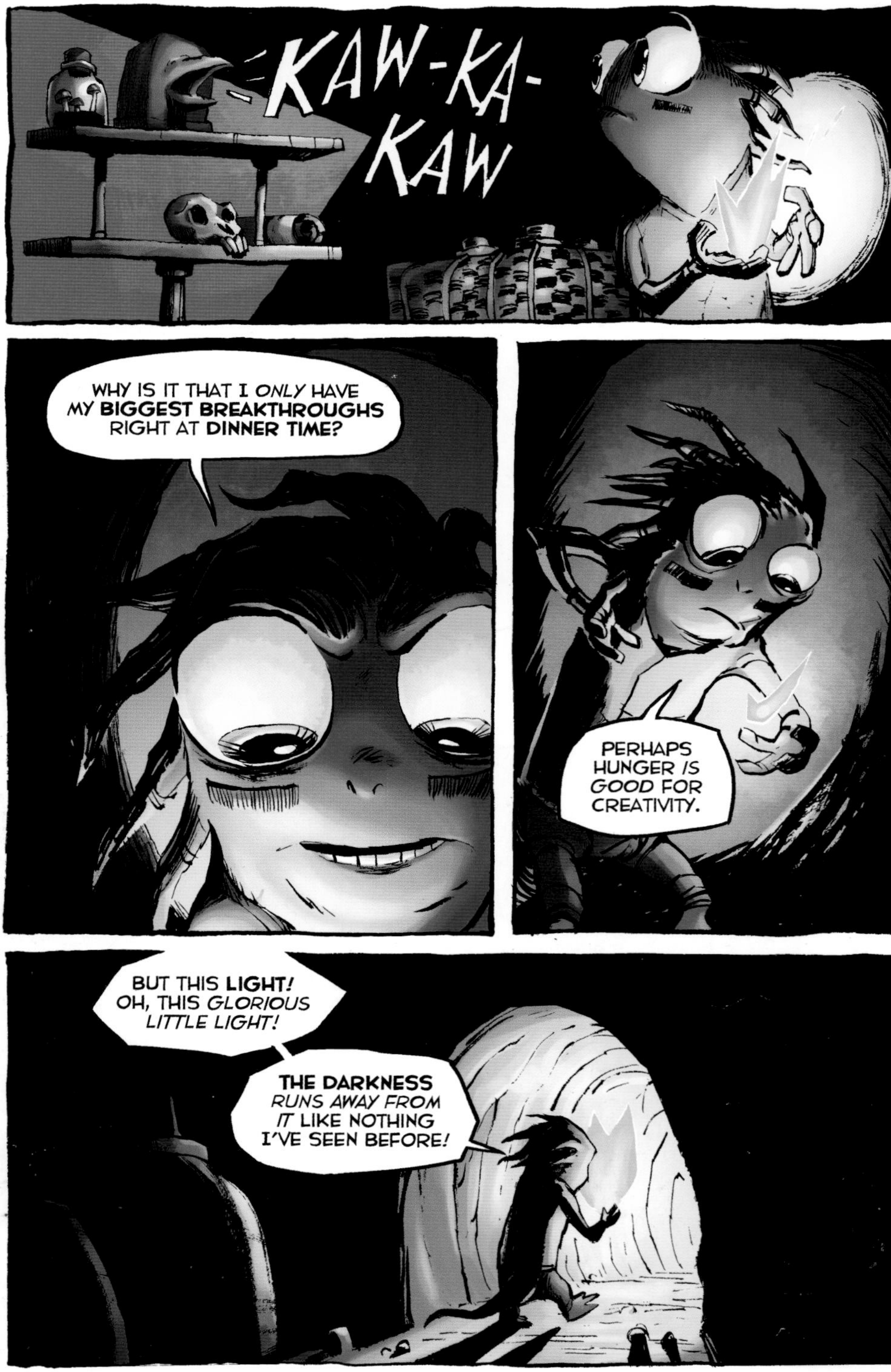
KAW-KA-KAW
WHY IS IT THAT I *ONLY* HAVE MY **BIGGEST BREAKTHROUGHS** RIGHT AT **DINNER TIME?**
PERHAPS HUNGER *IS* *GOOD* FOR CREATIVITY.
BUT THIS **LIGHT!** OH, THIS *GLORIOUS* *LITTLE LIGHT!*
THE DARKNESS *RUNS AWAY FROM* *IT* LIKE NOTHING I'VE SEEN BEFORE!

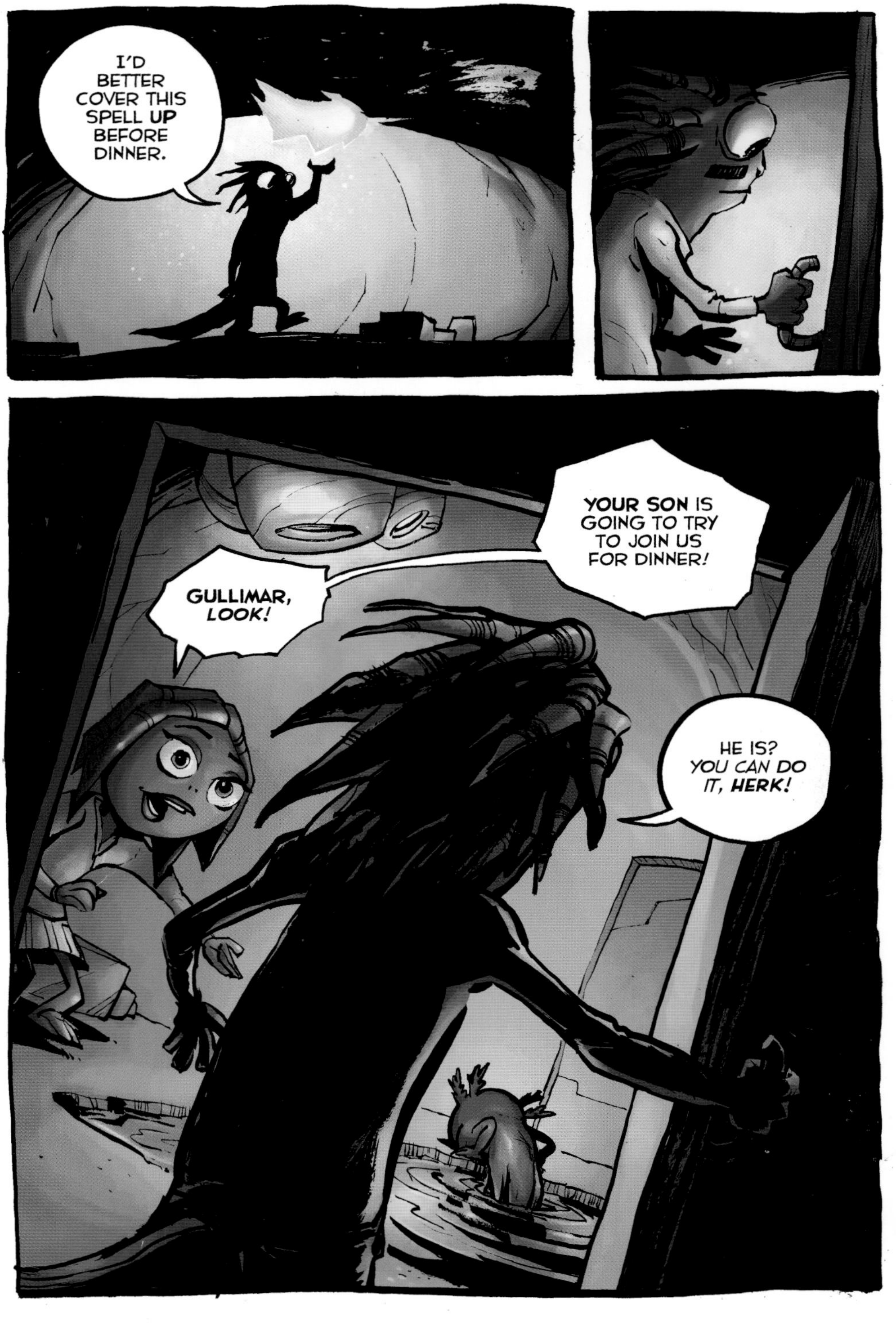
I'D BETTER COVER THIS SPELL UP BEFORE DINNER.
GULLIMAR, LOOK!
YOUR SON IS GOING TO TRY TO JOIN US FOR DINNER!
HE IS? YOU CAN DO IT, HERK!

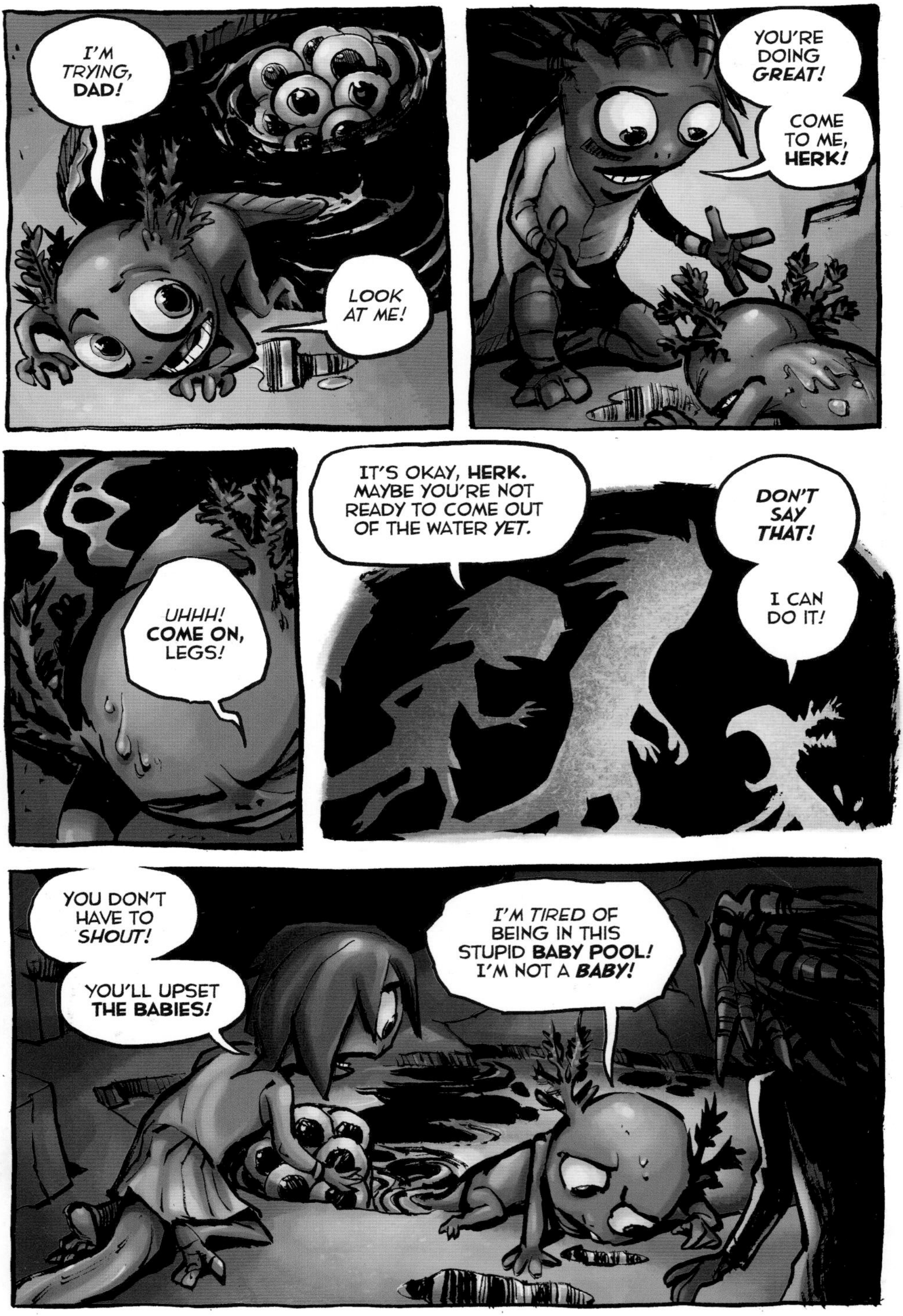
I'M *TRYING*, **DAD!**
LOOK AT ME!
YOU'RE DOING ***GREAT!***
COME TO ME, **HERK!**
UHHH! **COME ON,** *LEGS!*
IT'S OKAY, **HERK.** MAYBE YOU'RE NOT READY TO COME OUT OF THE WATER *YET.*
DON'T SAY THAT!
I CAN DO IT!
YOU DON'T HAVE TO ***SHOUT!***
YOU'LL UPSET **THE BABIES!**
I'M TIRED OF BEING IN THIS STUPID **BABY POOL!** I'M NOT A ***BABY!***

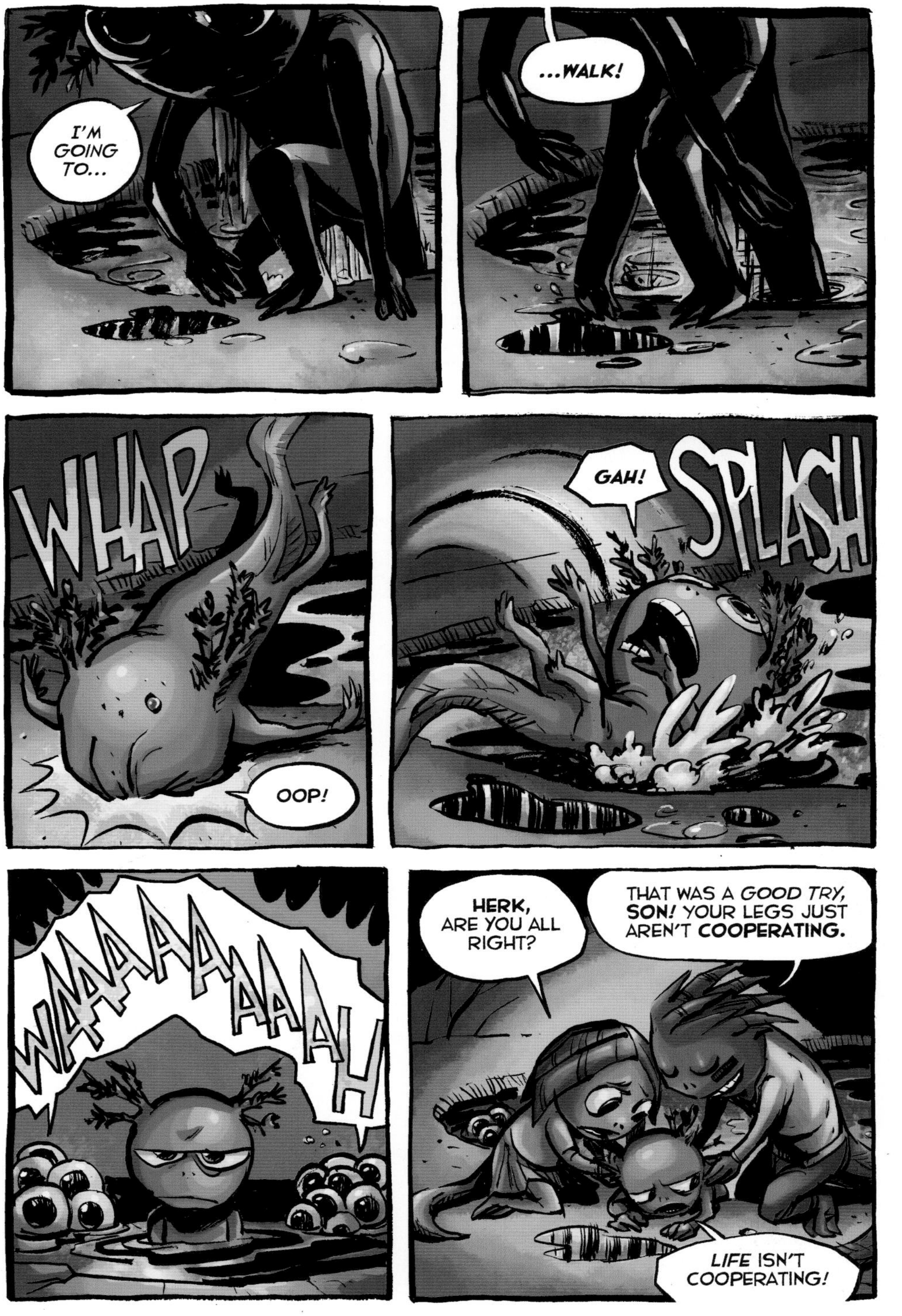
I'M GOING TO...
...WALK!
WHAP
OOP!
GAH!
SPLASH
WAAAAAAAAAAH
HERK, ARE YOU ALL RIGHT?
THAT WAS A *GOOD TRY*, **SON!** YOUR LEGS JUST AREN'T **COOPERATING.**
LIFE ISN'T COOPERATING!

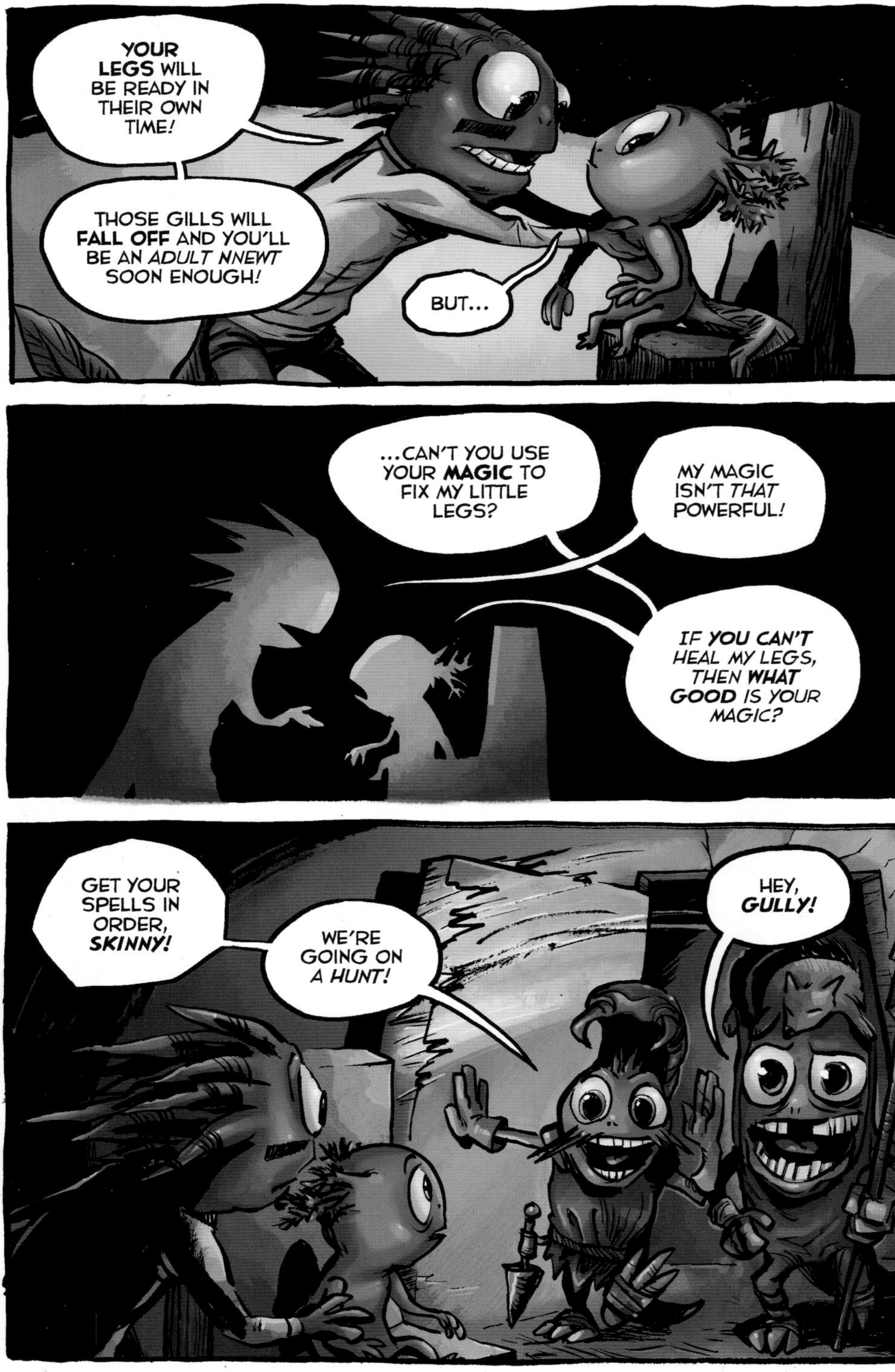
YOUR LEGS WILL BE READY IN THEIR OWN TIME!
THOSE GILLS WILL FALL OFF AND YOU'LL BE AN ADULT NNEWT SOON ENOUGH!
BUT...
...CAN'T YOU USE YOUR MAGIC TO FIX MY LITTLE LEGS?
MY MAGIC ISN'T THAT POWERFUL!
IF YOU CAN'T HEAL MY LEGS, THEN WHAT GOOD IS YOUR MAGIC?
GET YOUR SPELLS IN ORDER, SKINNY!
WE'RE GOING ON A HUNT!
HEY, GULLY!

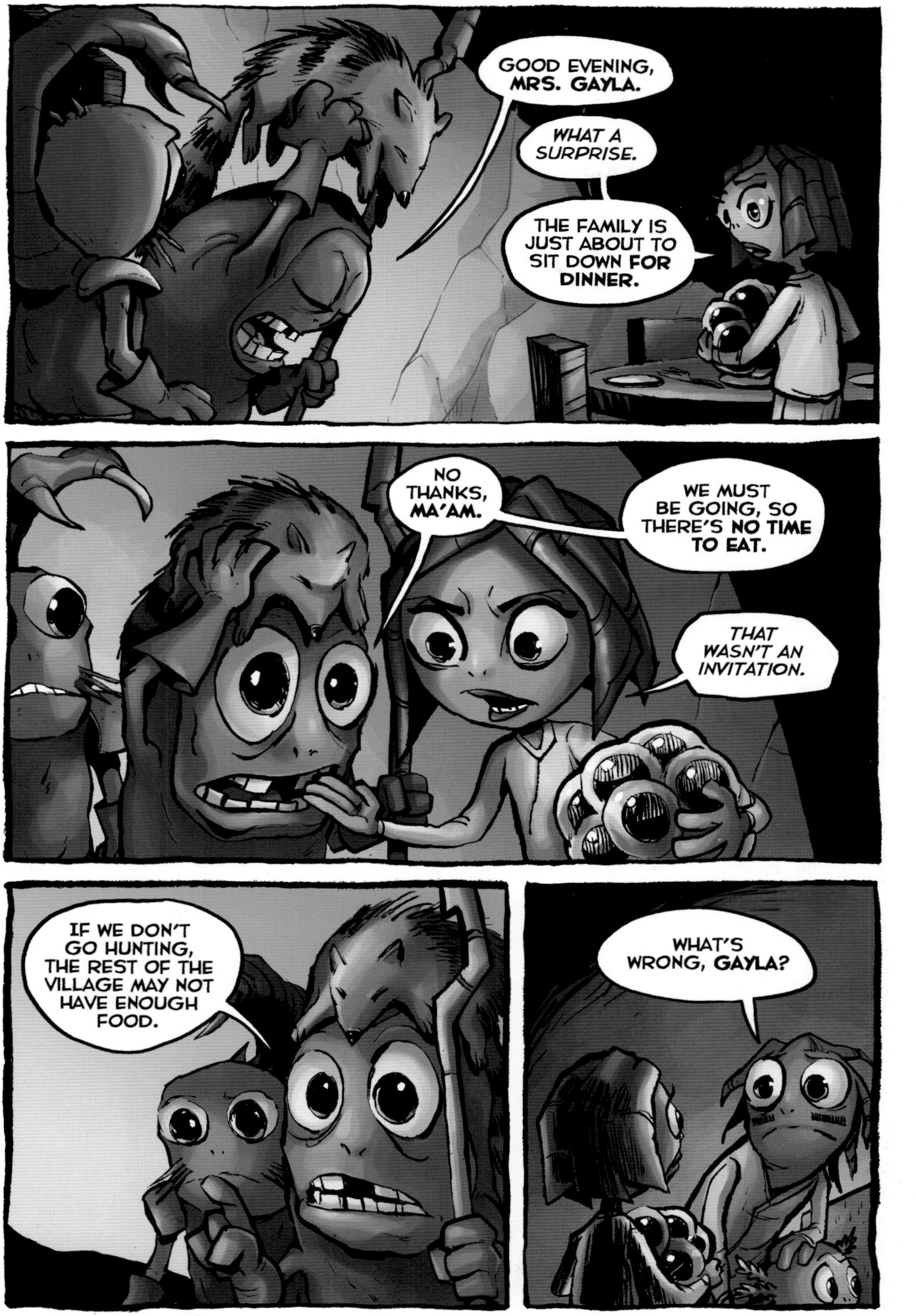
GOOD EVENING, MRS. GAYLA.
WHAT A SURPRISE.
THE FAMILY IS JUST ABOUT TO SIT DOWN FOR DINNER.
NO THANKS, MA'AM.
WE MUST BE GOING, SO THERE'S NO TIME TO EAT.
THAT WASN'T AN INVITATION.
IF WE DON'T GO HUNTING, THE REST OF THE VILLAGE MAY NOT HAVE ENOUGH FOOD.
WHAT'S WRONG, GAYLA?

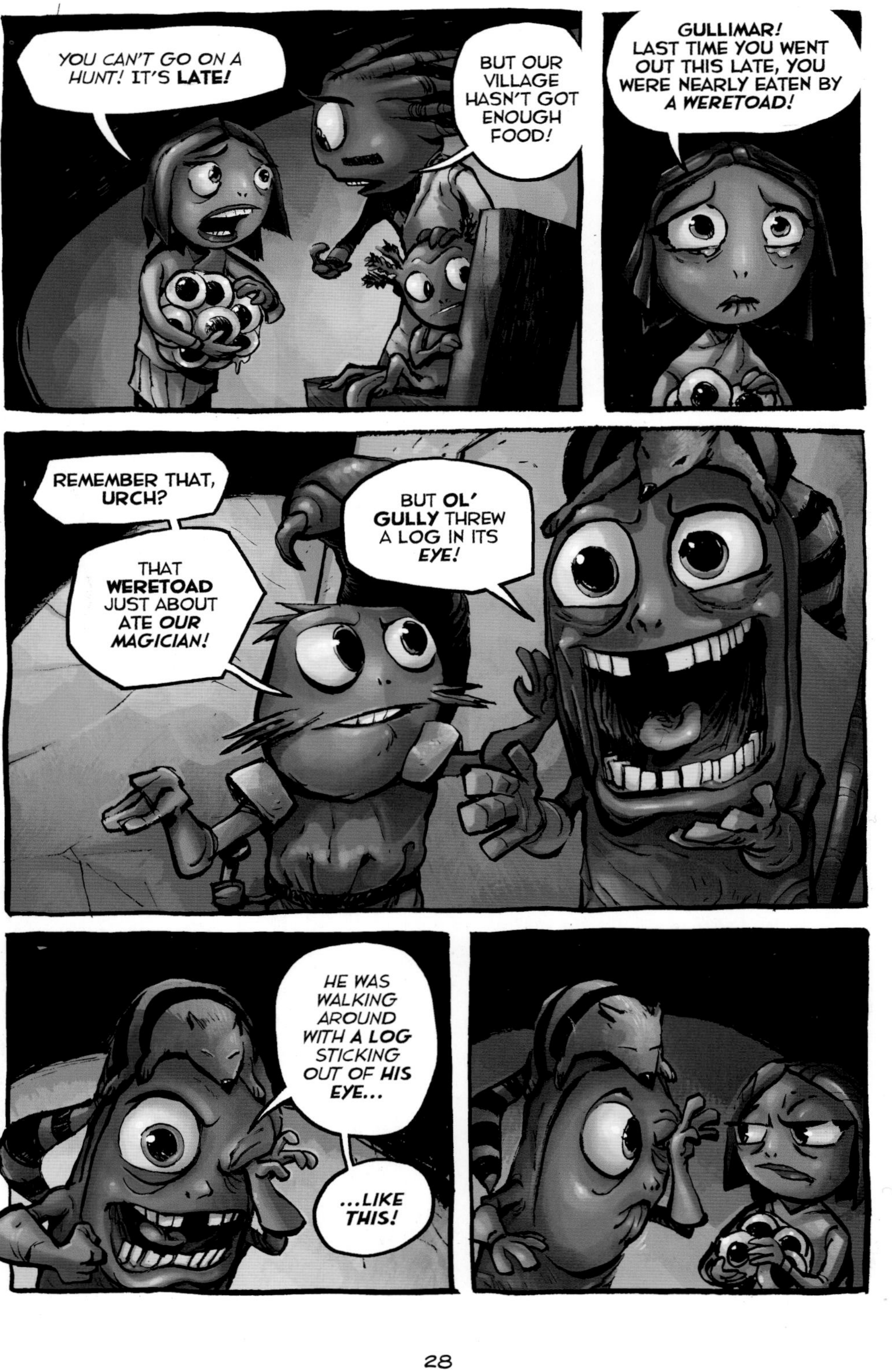
YOU CAN'T GO ON A HUNT! IT'S **LATE!**
BUT OUR VILLAGE HASN'T GOT ENOUGH FOOD!
GULLIMAR! LAST TIME YOU WENT OUT THIS LATE, YOU WERE NEARLY EATEN BY ***A WERETOAD!***
REMEMBER THAT, **URCH?**
THAT **WERETOAD** JUST ABOUT ATE ***OUR MAGICIAN!***
BUT **OL' GULLY** THREW A LOG IN ITS ***EYE!***
HE WAS WALKING AROUND WITH **A LOG** STICKING OUT OF **HIS EYE...**
...LIKE THIS!

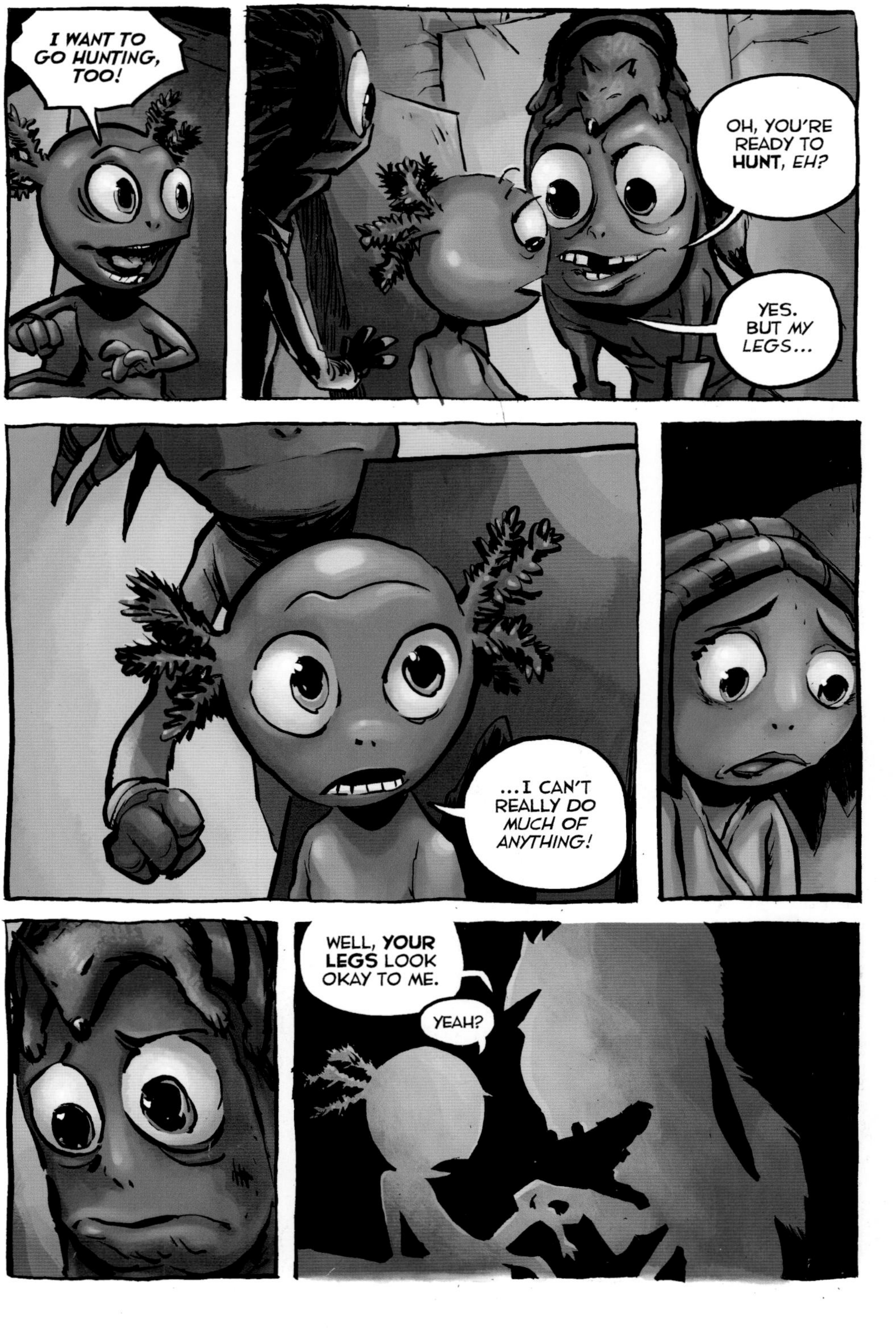
I WANT TO GO HUNTING, TOO!
OH, YOU'RE READY TO HUNT, EH?
YES. BUT MY LEGS...
...I CAN'T REALLY DO MUCH OF ANYTHING!
WELL, YOUR LEGS LOOK OKAY TO ME.
YEAH?

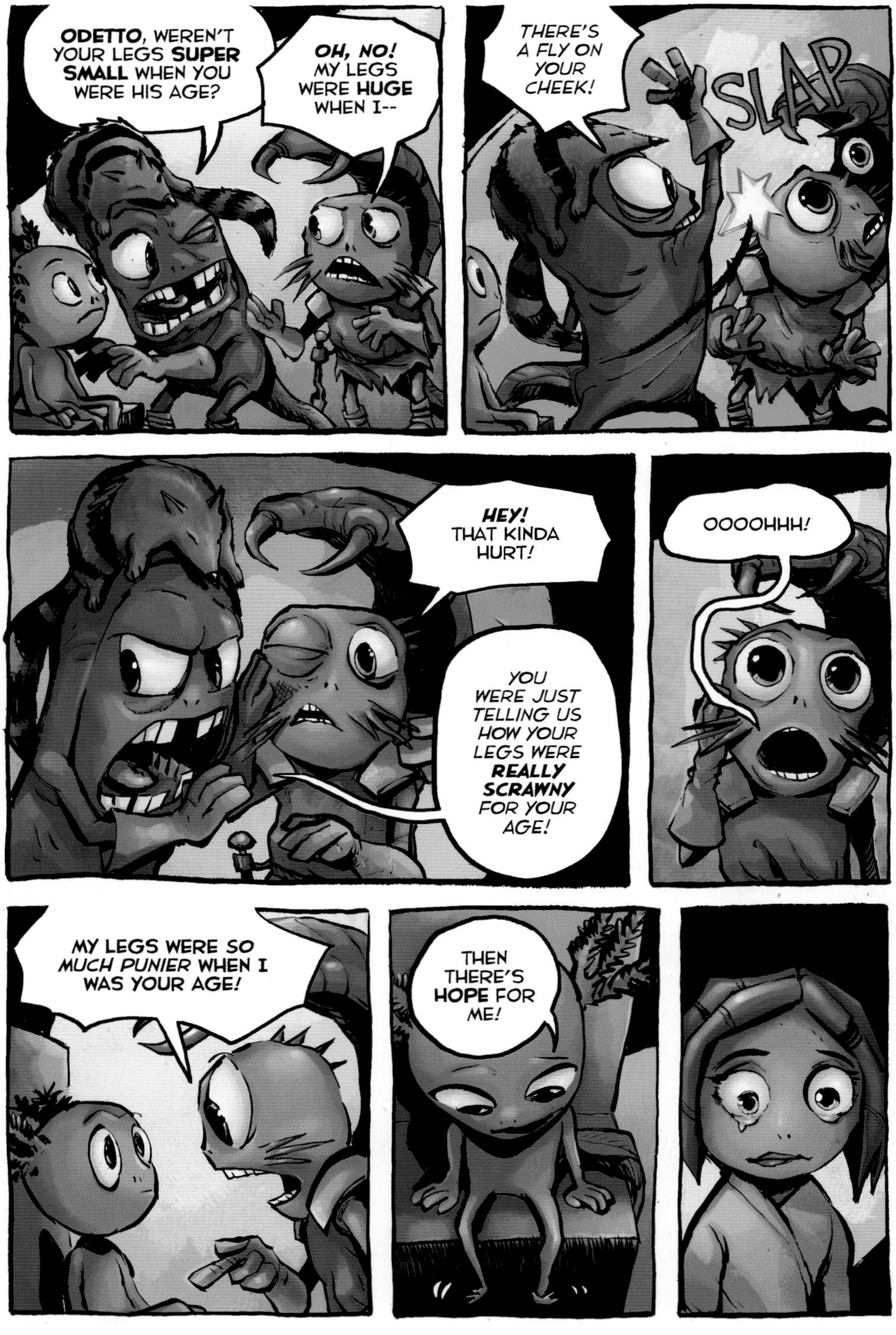
ODETTO, WEREN'T YOUR LEGS SUPER SMALL WHEN YOU WERE HIS AGE?
OH, NO! MY LEGS WERE HUGE WHEN I--
THERE'S A FLY ON YOUR CHEEK!
SLAP
HEY! THAT KINDA HURT!
YOU WERE JUST TELLING US HOW YOUR LEGS WERE REALLY SCRAWNY FOR YOUR AGE!
OOOOHHH!
MY LEGS WERE SO MUCH PUNIER WHEN I WAS YOUR AGE!
THEN THERE'S HOPE FOR ME!

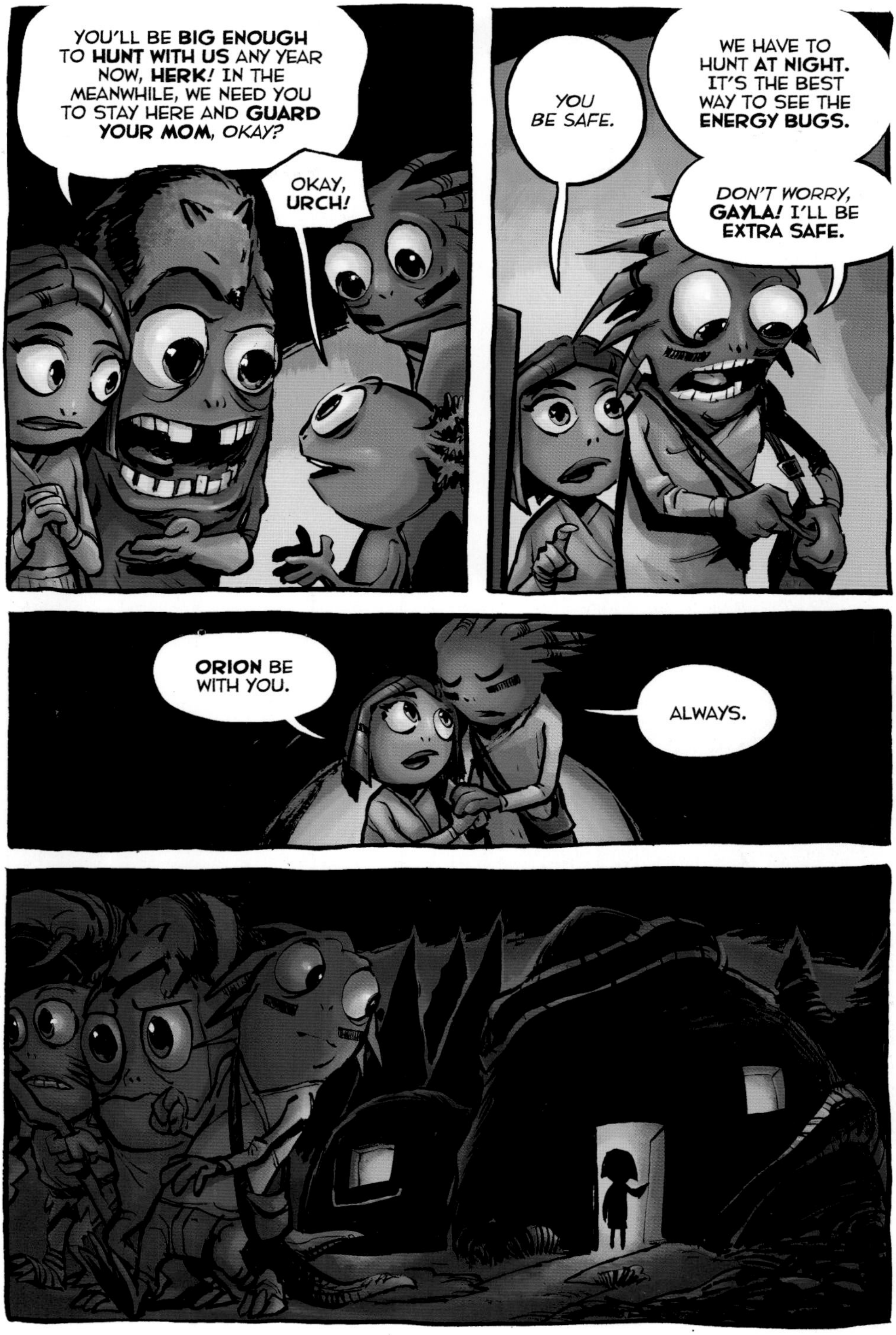
YOU'LL BE **BIG ENOUGH** TO **HUNT WITH US** ANY YEAR NOW, **HERK!** IN THE MEANWHILE, WE NEED YOU TO STAY HERE AND **GUARD YOUR MOM**, *OKAY?*
OKAY, **URCH!**
YOU BE SAFE.
WE HAVE TO HUNT **AT NIGHT.** IT'S THE BEST WAY TO SEE THE **ENERGY BUGS.**
DON'T WORRY, **GAYLA!** I'LL BE **EXTRA SAFE.**
ORION BE WITH YOU.
ALWAYS.

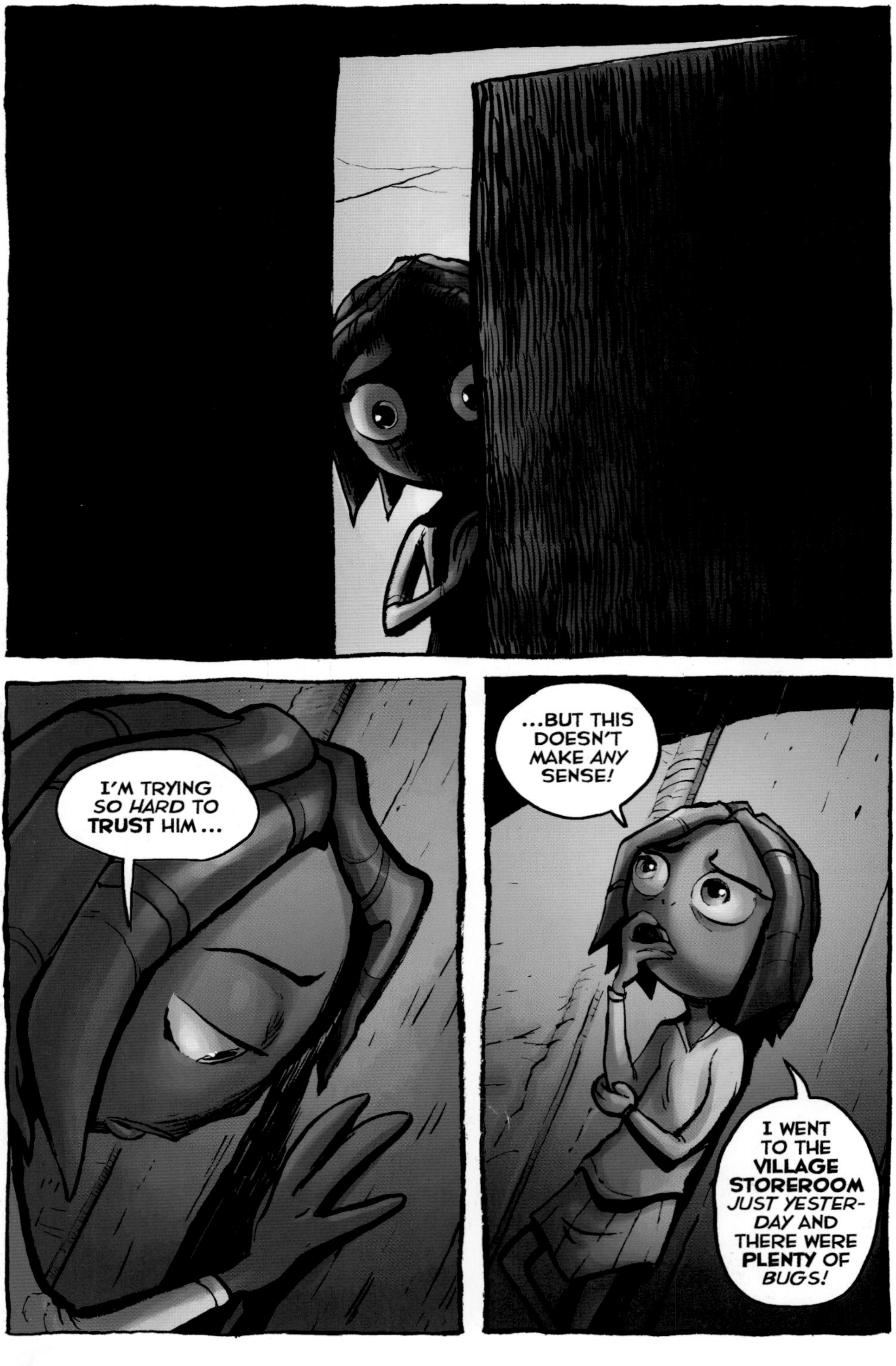
I'M TRYING SO HARD TO TRUST HIM...
...BUT THIS DOESN'T MAKE ANY SENSE!
I WENT TO THE VILLAGE STOREROOM JUST YESTER-DAY AND THERE WERE PLENTY OF BUGS!

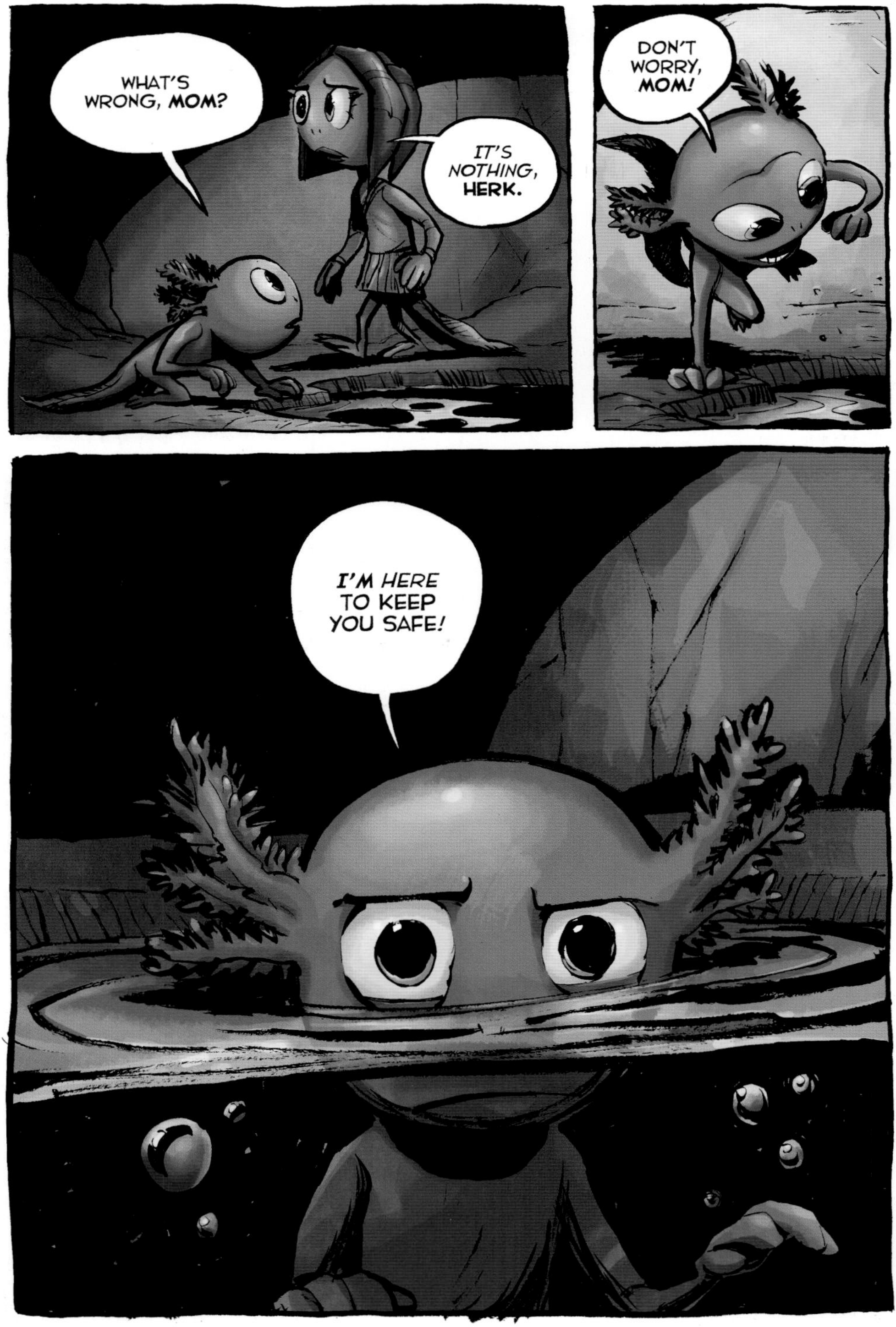
WHAT'S WRONG, MOM?
IT'S NOTHING, HERK.
DON'T WORRY, MOM!
I'M HERE TO KEEP YOU SAFE!

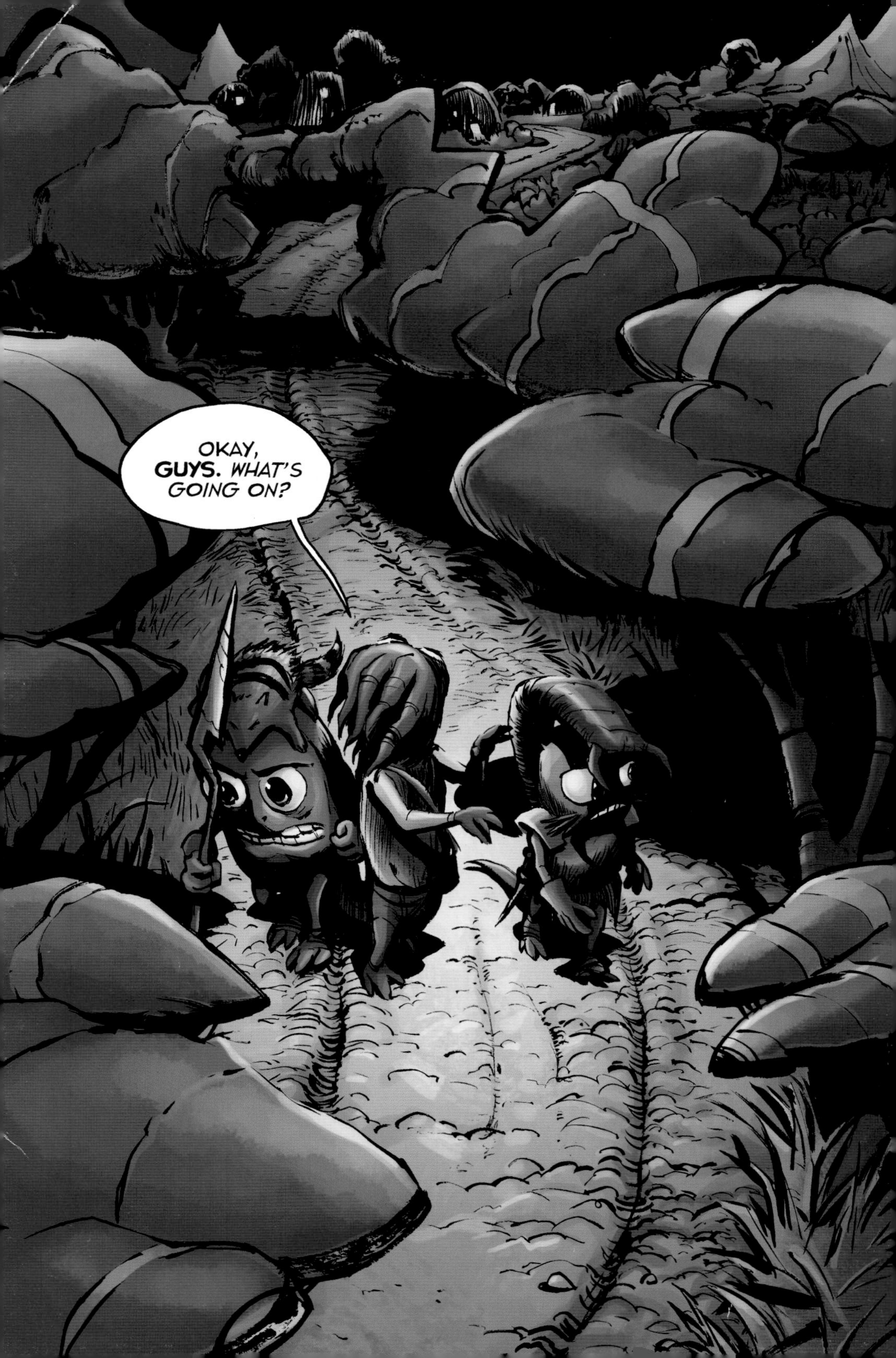
OKAY, GUYS. WHAT'S GOING ON?

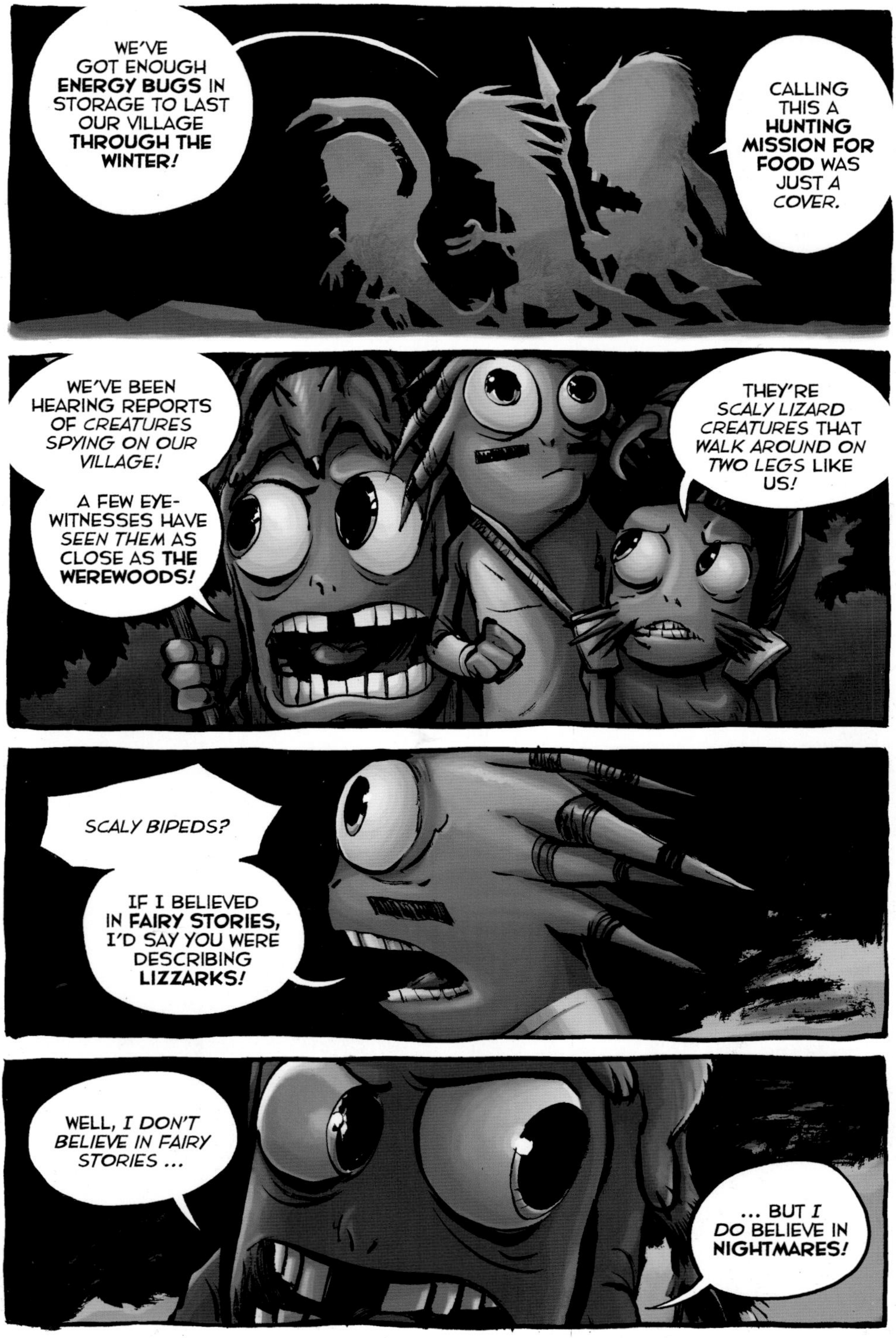
WE'VE GOT ENOUGH ENERGY BUGS IN STORAGE TO LAST OUR VILLAGE THROUGH THE WINTER!
CALLING THIS A HUNTING MISSION FOR FOOD WAS JUST A COVER.
WE'VE BEEN HEARING REPORTS OF CREATURES SPYING ON OUR VILLAGE!
A FEW EYE-WITNESSES HAVE SEEN THEM AS CLOSE AS THE WEREWOODS!
THEY'RE SCALY LIZARD CREATURES THAT WALK AROUND ON TWO LEGS LIKE US!
SCALY BIPEDS?
IF I BELIEVED IN FAIRY STORIES, I'D SAY YOU WERE DESCRIBING LIZZARKS!
WELL, I DON'T BELIEVE IN FAIRY STORIES ...
... BUT I DO BELIEVE IN NIGHTMARES!

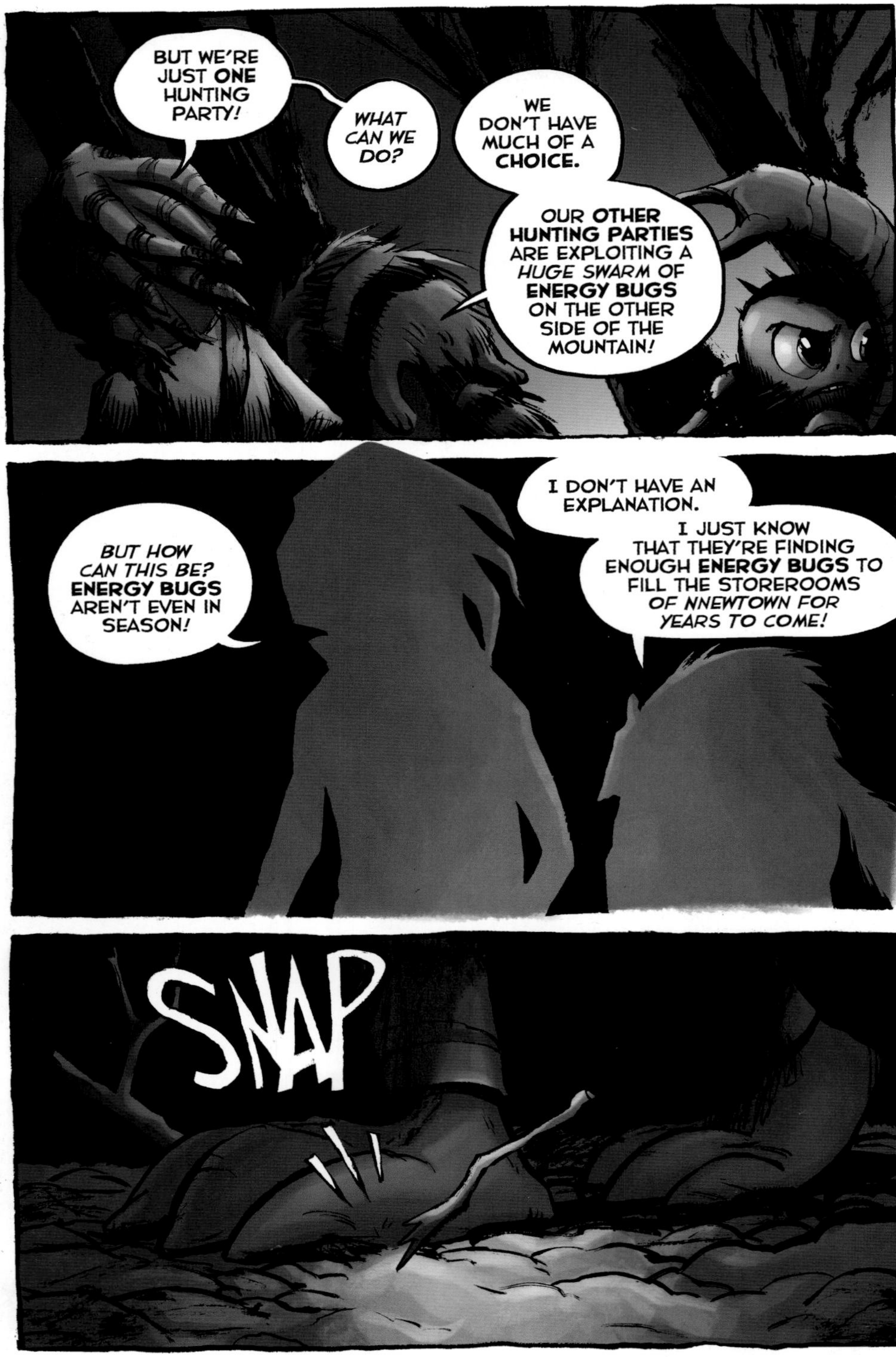
BUT WE'RE JUST **ONE** HUNTING PARTY!
WHAT CAN WE DO?
WE DON'T HAVE MUCH OF A **CHOICE.**
OUR **OTHER HUNTING PARTIES** ARE EXPLOITING A *HUGE SWARM* OF **ENERGY BUGS** ON THE OTHER SIDE OF THE MOUNTAIN!
BUT HOW CAN THIS BE? **ENERGY BUGS** AREN'T EVEN IN SEASON!
I DON'T HAVE AN EXPLANATION.
I JUST KNOW THAT THEY'RE FINDING ENOUGH **ENERGY BUGS** TO FILL THE STOREROOMS *OF NNEWTOWN FOR YEARS TO COME!*
SNAP

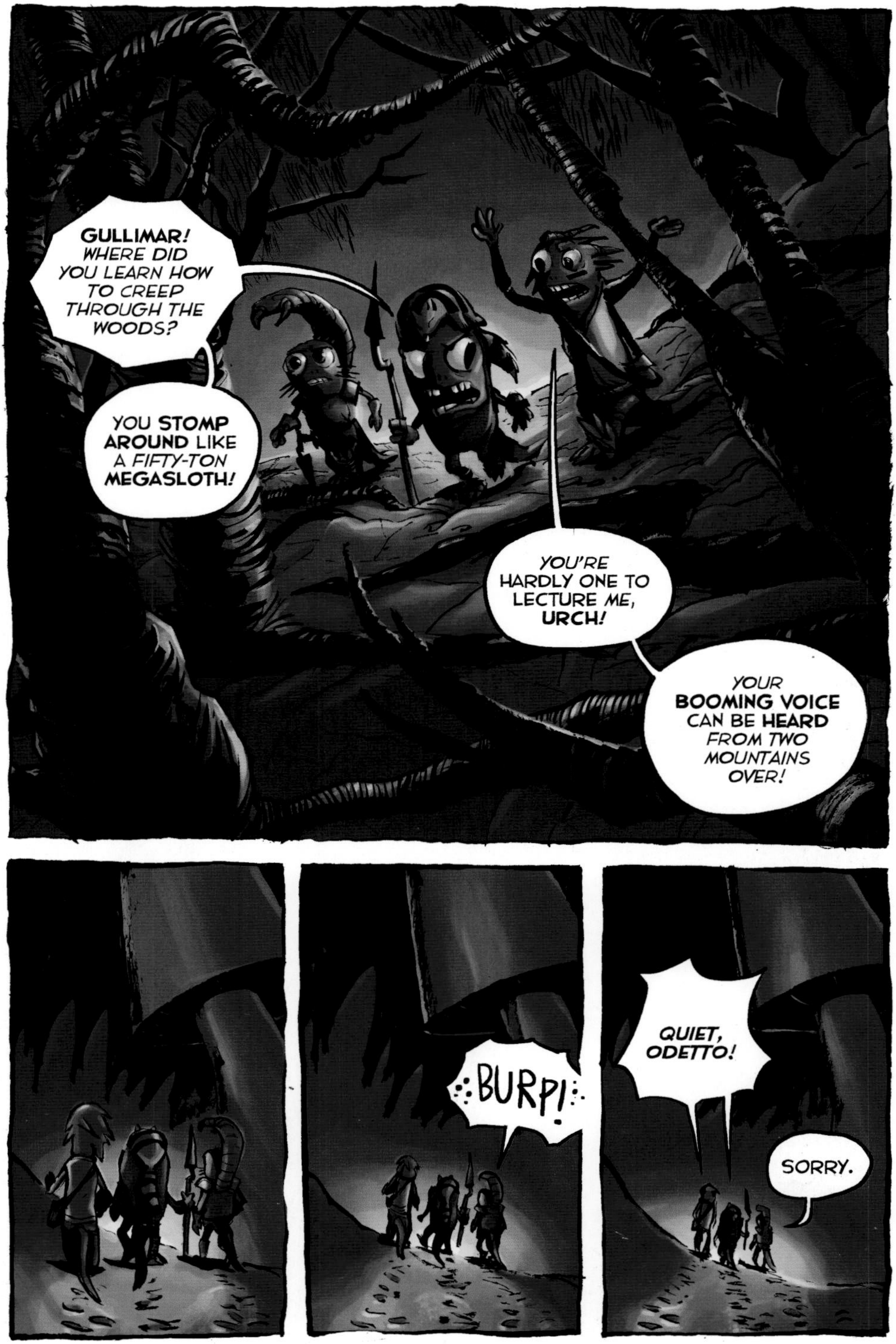

GULLIMAR! WHERE DID YOU LEARN HOW TO CREEP THROUGH THE WOODS?
YOU STOMP AROUND LIKE A FIFTY-TON MEGASLOTH!
YOU'RE HARDLY ONE TO LECTURE ME, URCH!
YOUR BOOMING VOICE CAN BE HEARD FROM TWO MOUNTAINS OVER!
BURP!
QUIET, ODETTO!
SORRY.

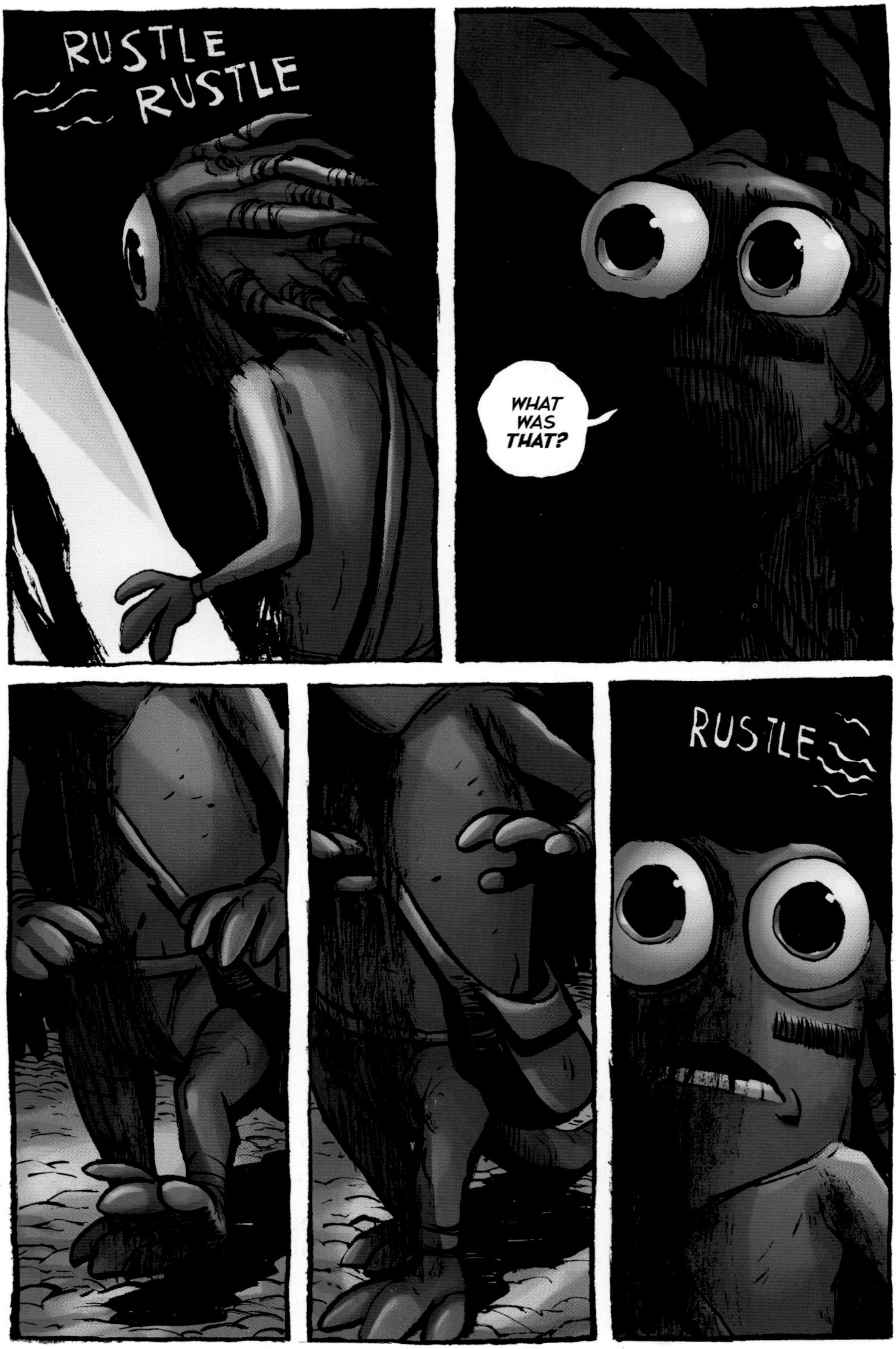
RUSTLE
RUSTLE
WHAT WAS THAT?
RUSTLE

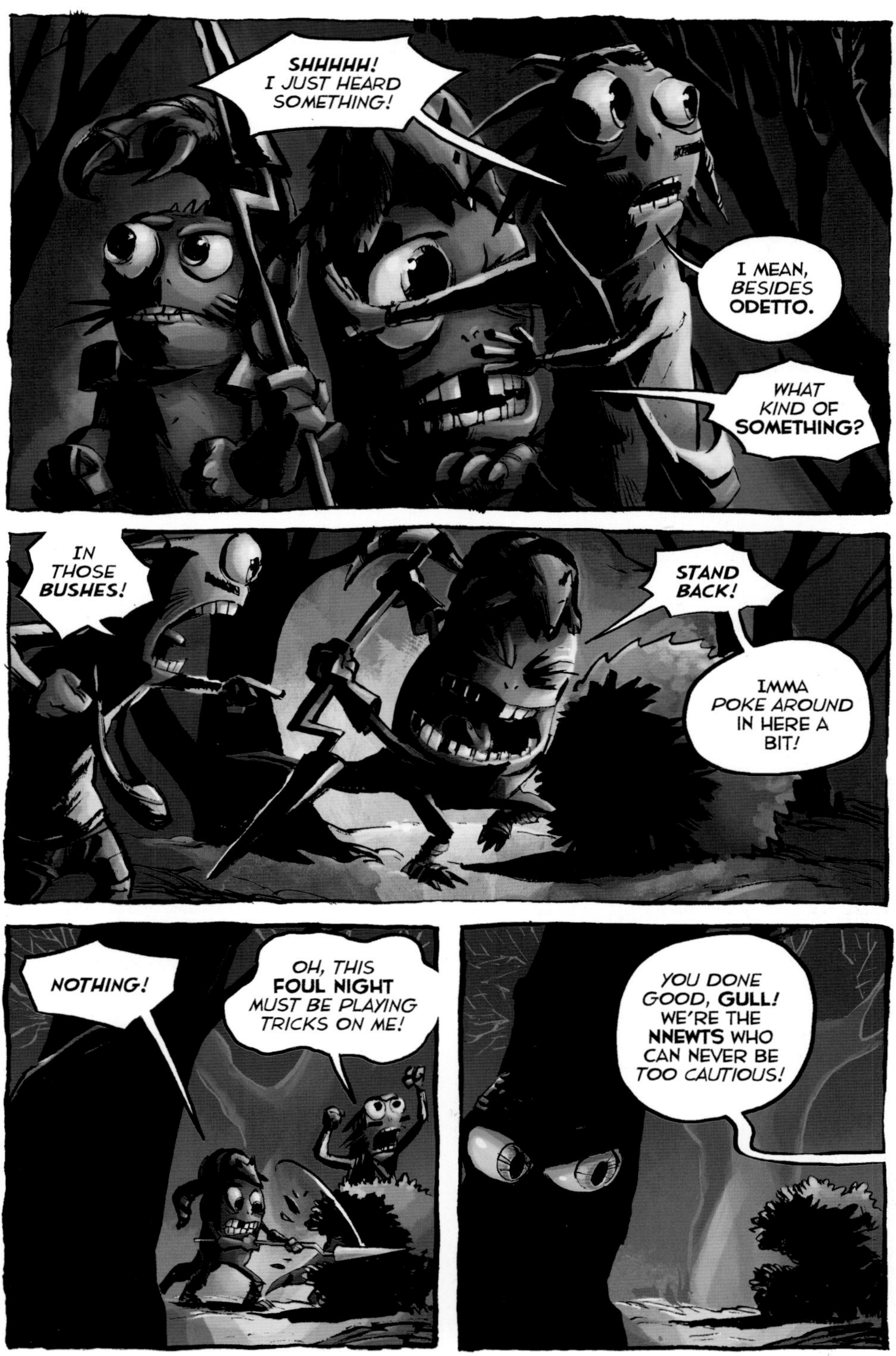
SHHHHH! I JUST HEARD SOMETHING!
I MEAN, BESIDES ODETTO.
WHAT KIND OF SOMETHING?
IN THOSE BUSHES!
STAND BACK!
IMMA POKE AROUND IN HERE A BIT!
NOTHING!
OH, THIS FOUL NIGHT MUST BE PLAYING TRICKS ON ME!
YOU DONE GOOD, GULL! WE'RE THE NNEWTS WHO CAN NEVER BE TOO CAUTIOUS!

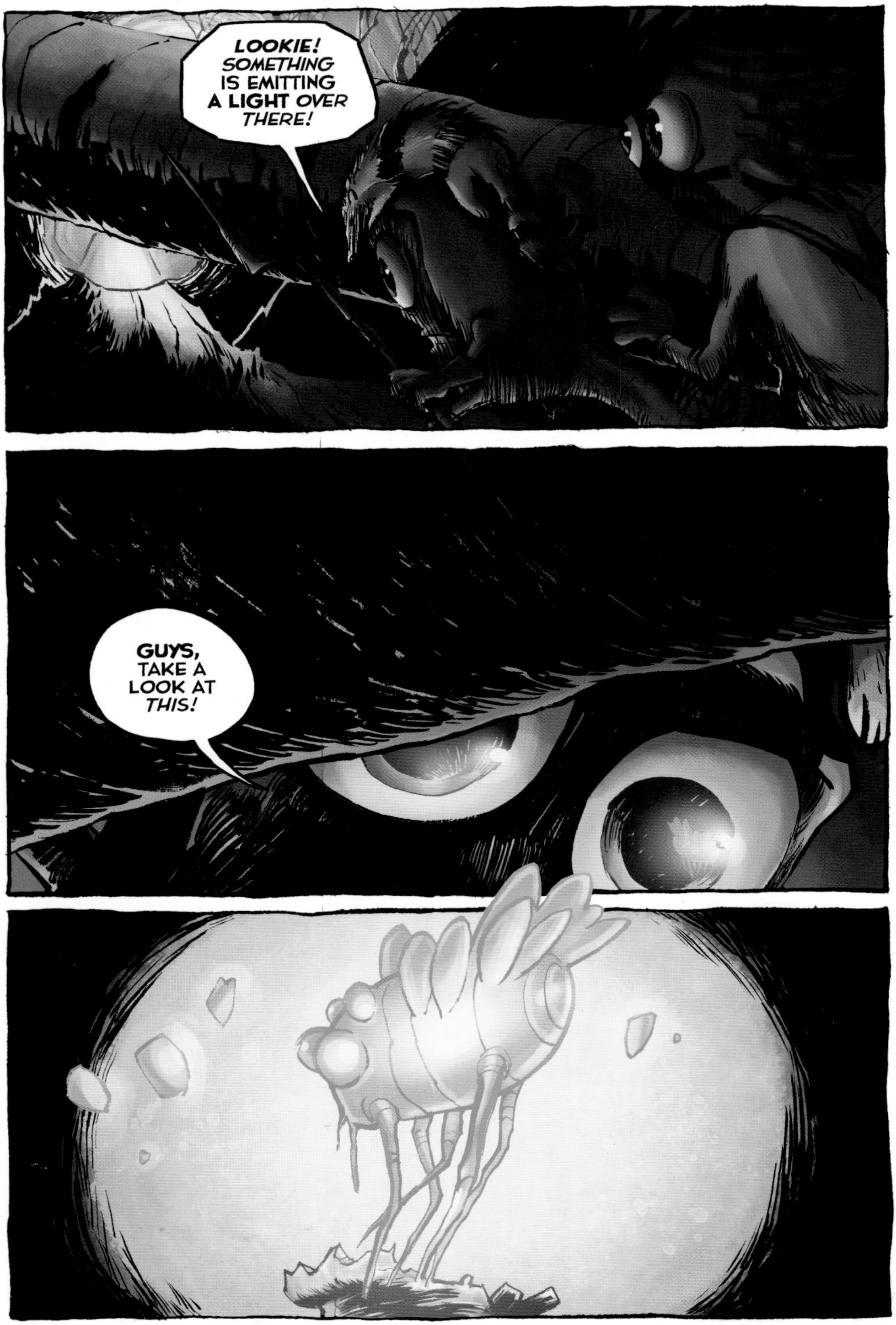
LOOKIE! SOMETHING IS EMITTING A LIGHT OVER THERE!
GUYS, TAKE A LOOK AT THIS!

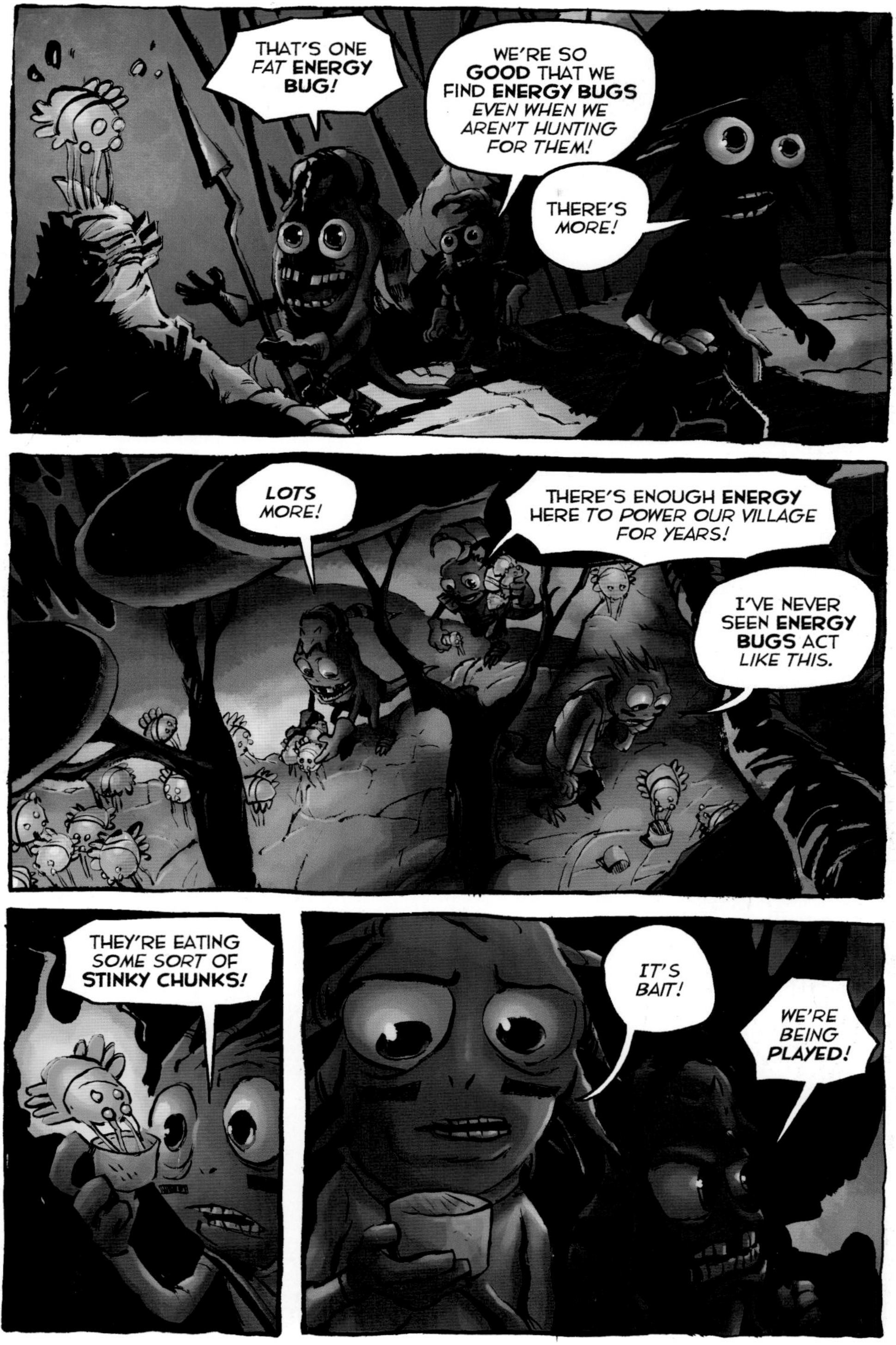
THAT'S ONE FAT ENERGY BUG!
WE'RE SO GOOD THAT WE FIND ENERGY BUGS EVEN WHEN WE AREN'T HUNTING FOR THEM!
THERE'S MORE!
LOTS MORE!
THERE'S ENOUGH ENERGY HERE TO POWER OUR VILLAGE FOR YEARS!
I'VE NEVER SEEN ENERGY BUGS ACT LIKE THIS.
THEY'RE EATING SOME SORT OF STINKY CHUNKS!
IT'S BAIT!
WE'RE BEING PLAYED!

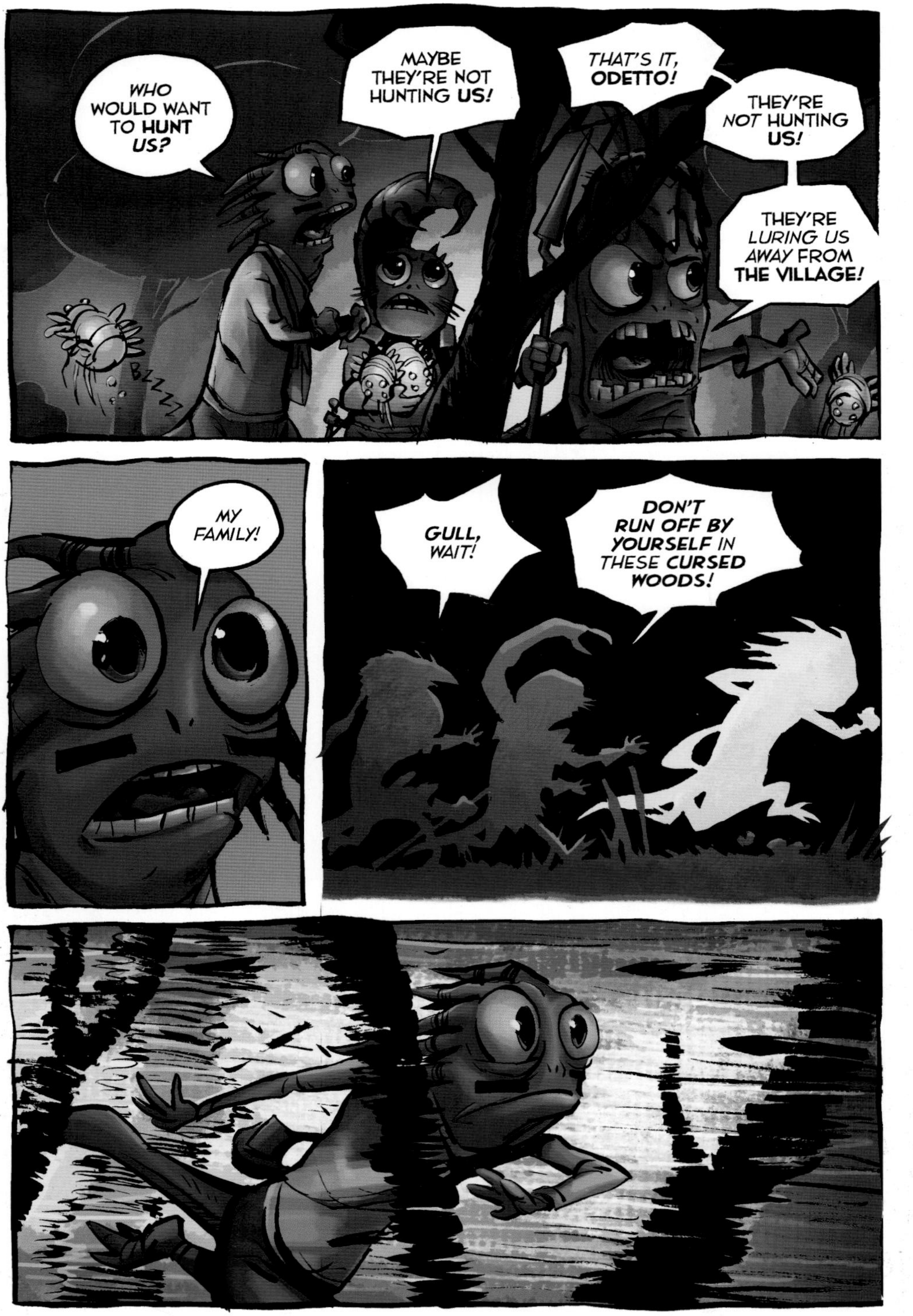
WHO WOULD WANT TO HUNT US?
MAYBE THEY'RE NOT HUNTING US!
THAT'S IT, ODETTO!
THEY'RE NOT HUNTING US!
THEY'RE LURING US AWAY FROM THE VILLAGE!
BZZZZ
MY FAMILY!
GULL, WAIT!
DON'T RUN OFF BY YOURSELF IN THESE CURSED WOODS!

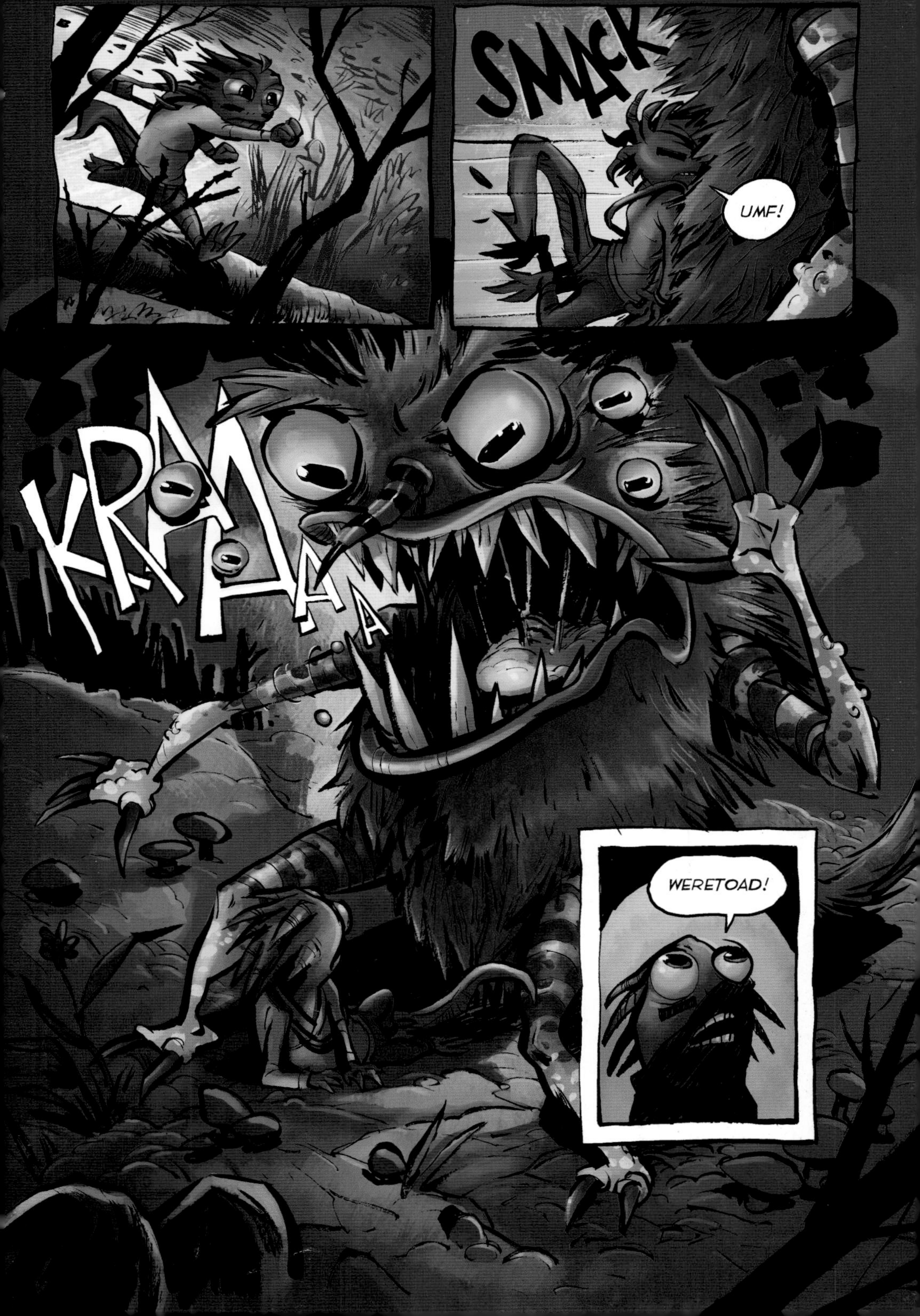

SMACK
UMF!
KRAAAAA
WERETOAD!

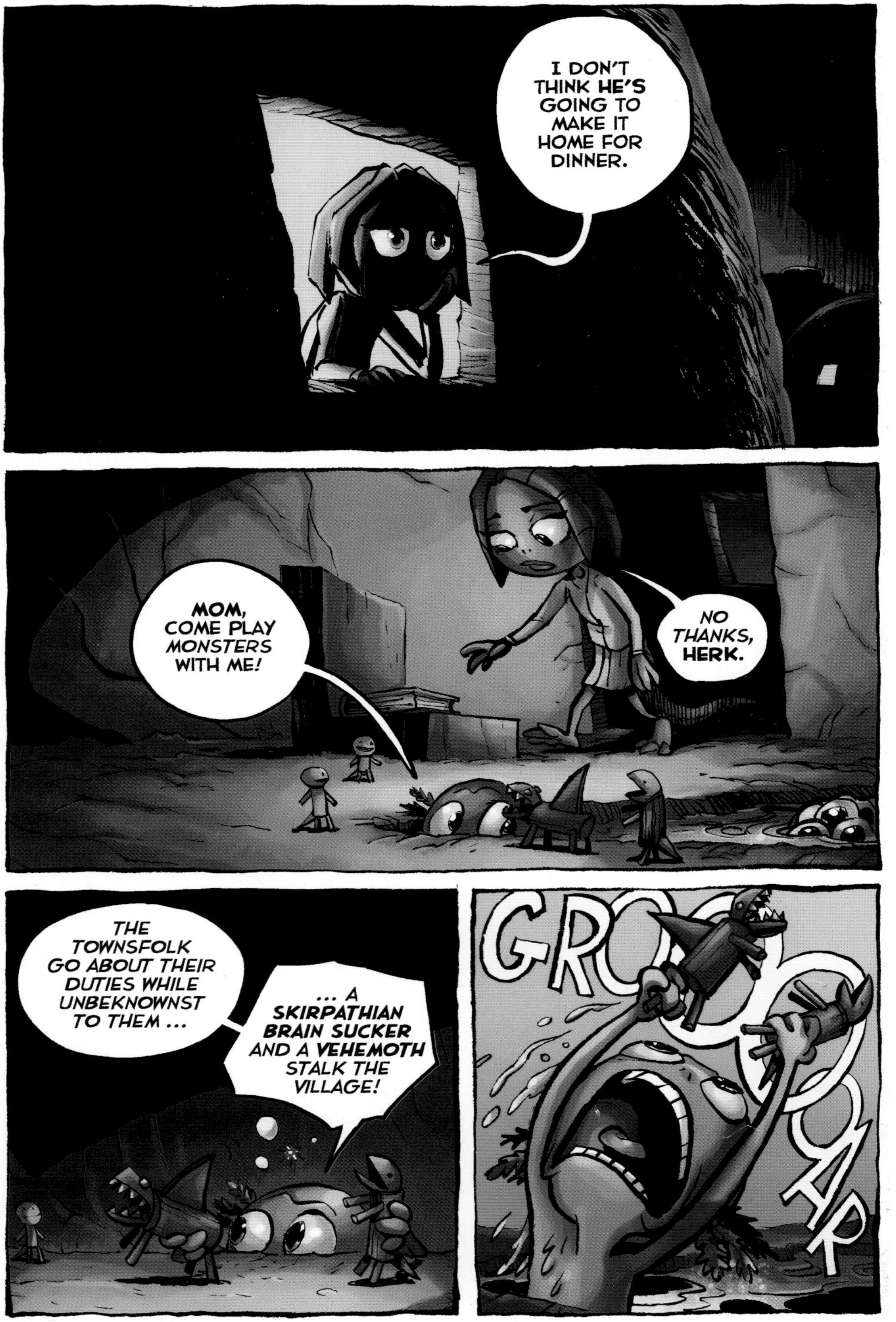
I DON'T THINK HE'S GOING TO MAKE IT HOME FOR DINNER.
MOM, COME PLAY MONSTERS WITH ME!
NO THANKS, HERK.
THE TOWNSFOLK GO ABOUT THEIR DUTIES WHILE UNBEKNOWNST TO THEM ...
... A SKIRPATHIAN BRAIN SUCKER AND A VEHEMOTH STALK THE VILLAGE!
GROOOOOAR

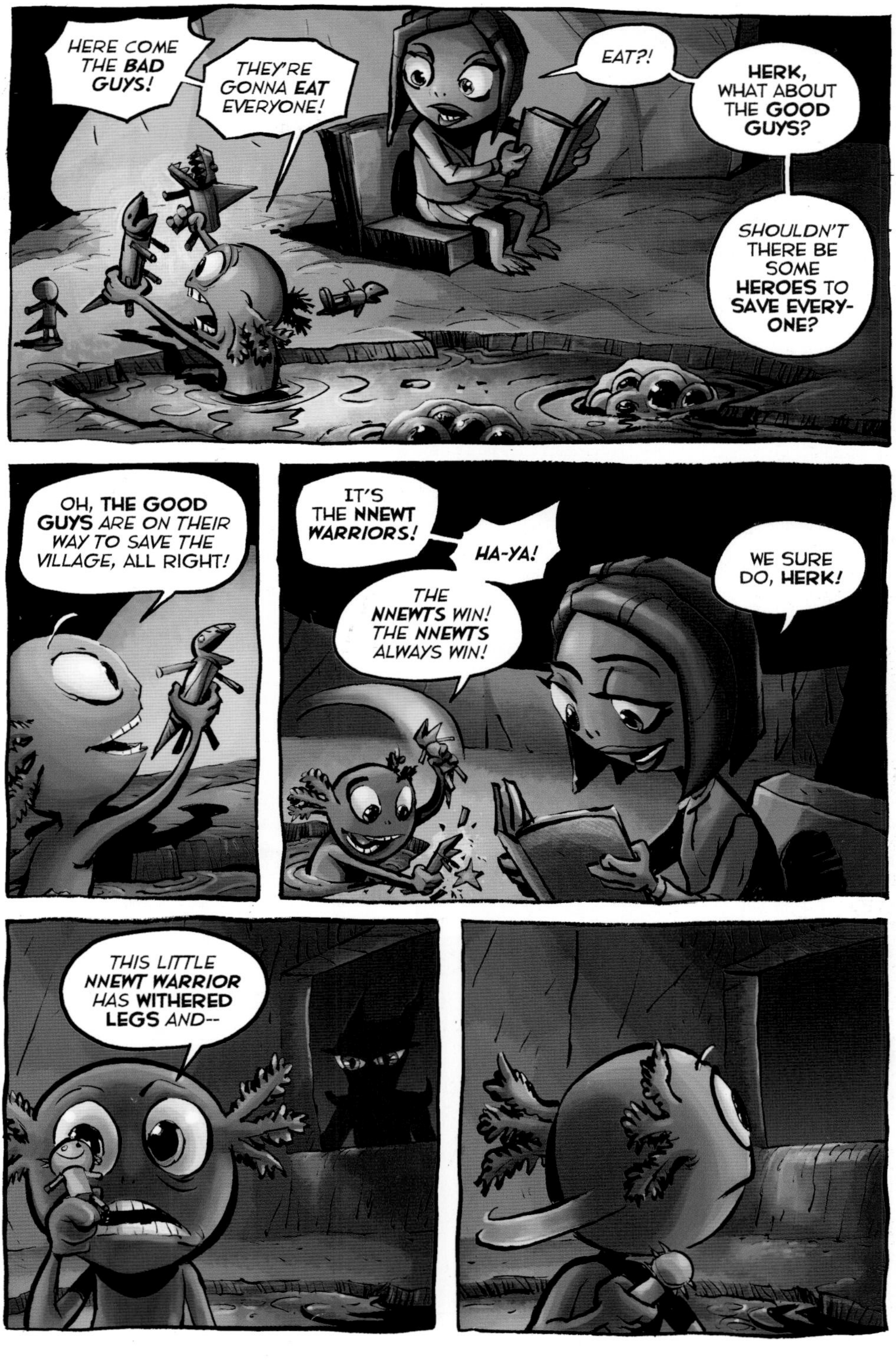
HERE COME THE BAD GUYS!
THEY'RE GONNA EAT EVERYONE!
EAT?!
HERK, WHAT ABOUT THE GOOD GUYS?
SHOULDN'T THERE BE SOME HEROES TO SAVE EVERY-ONE?
OH, THE GOOD GUYS ARE ON THEIR WAY TO SAVE THE VILLAGE, ALL RIGHT!
IT'S THE NNEWT WARRIORS!
HA-YA!
THE NNEWTS WIN! THE NNEWTS ALWAYS WIN!
WE SURE DO, HERK!
THIS LITTLE NNEWT WARRIOR HAS WITHERED LEGS AND--

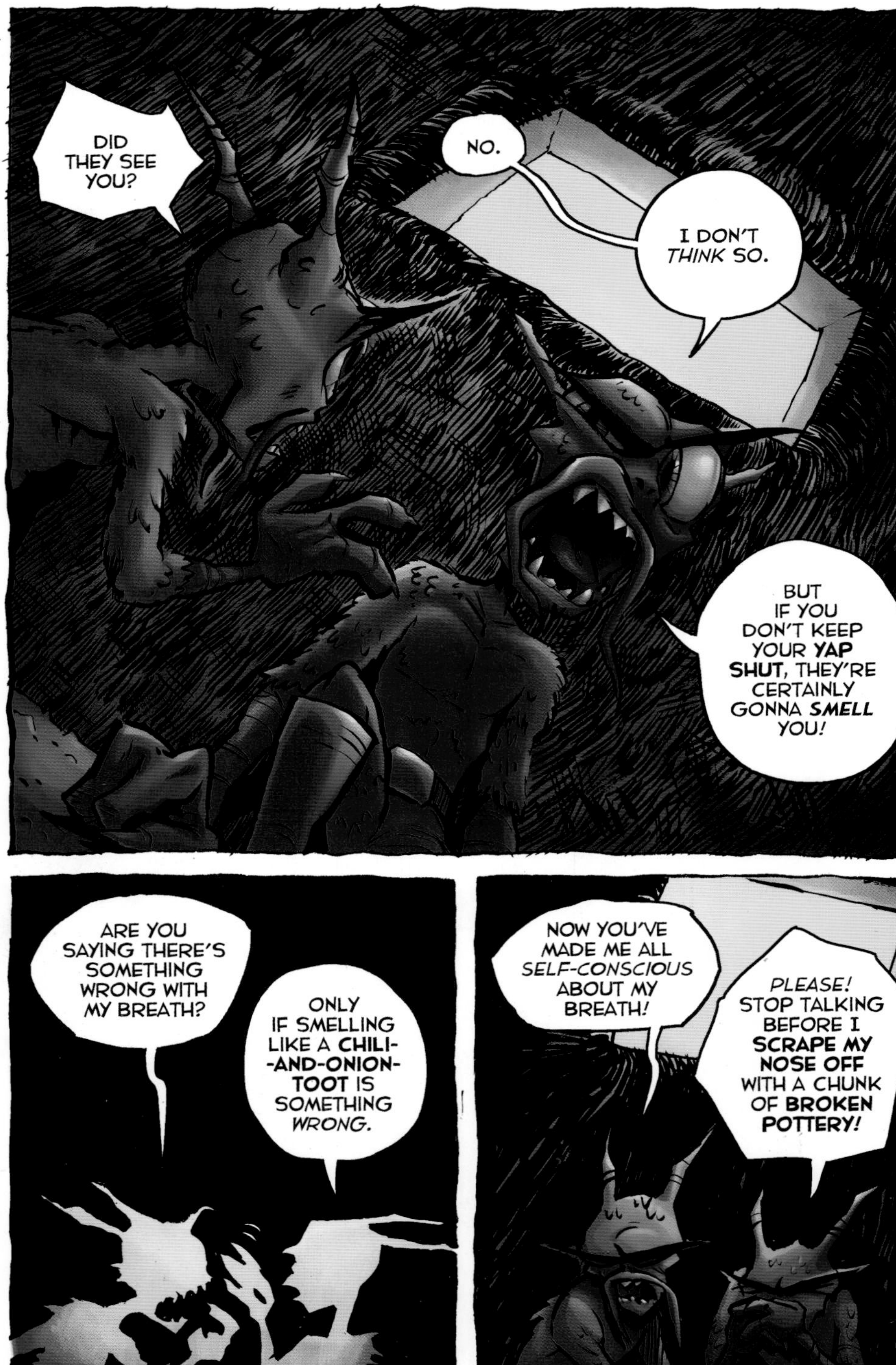
DID THEY SEE YOU?
NO.
I DON'T *THINK* SO.
BUT IF YOU DON'T KEEP YOUR **YAP SHUT**, THEY'RE CERTAINLY GONNA **SMELL** YOU!
ARE YOU SAYING THERE'S SOMETHING WRONG WITH MY BREATH?
ONLY IF SMELLING LIKE A **CHILI-AND-ONION-TOOT** IS SOMETHING *WRONG*.
NOW YOU'VE MADE ME ALL *SELF-CONSCIOUS* ABOUT MY BREATH!
PLEASE! STOP TALKING BEFORE I **SCRAPE MY NOSE OFF** WITH A CHUNK OF **BROKEN POTTERY!**

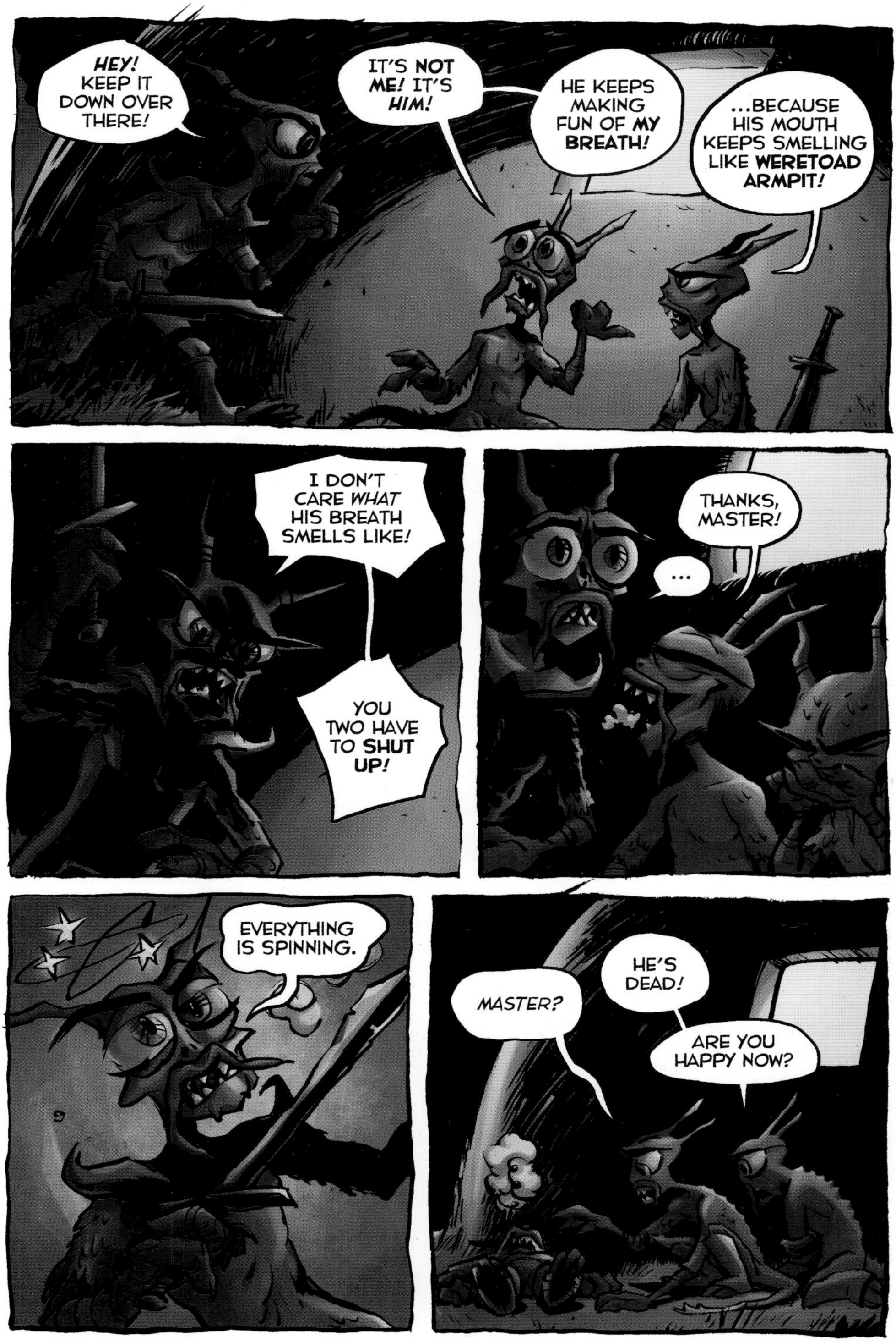
HEY! KEEP IT DOWN OVER THERE!
IT'S **NOT ME!** IT'S ***HIM!***
HE KEEPS MAKING FUN OF **MY BREATH!**
...BECAUSE HIS MOUTH KEEPS SMELLING LIKE **WERETOAD ARMPIT!**
I DON'T CARE *WHAT* HIS BREATH SMELLS LIKE!
YOU TWO HAVE TO **SHUT UP!**
THANKS, MASTER!
...
EVERYTHING IS SPINNING.
MASTER?
HE'S DEAD!
ARE YOU HAPPY NOW?

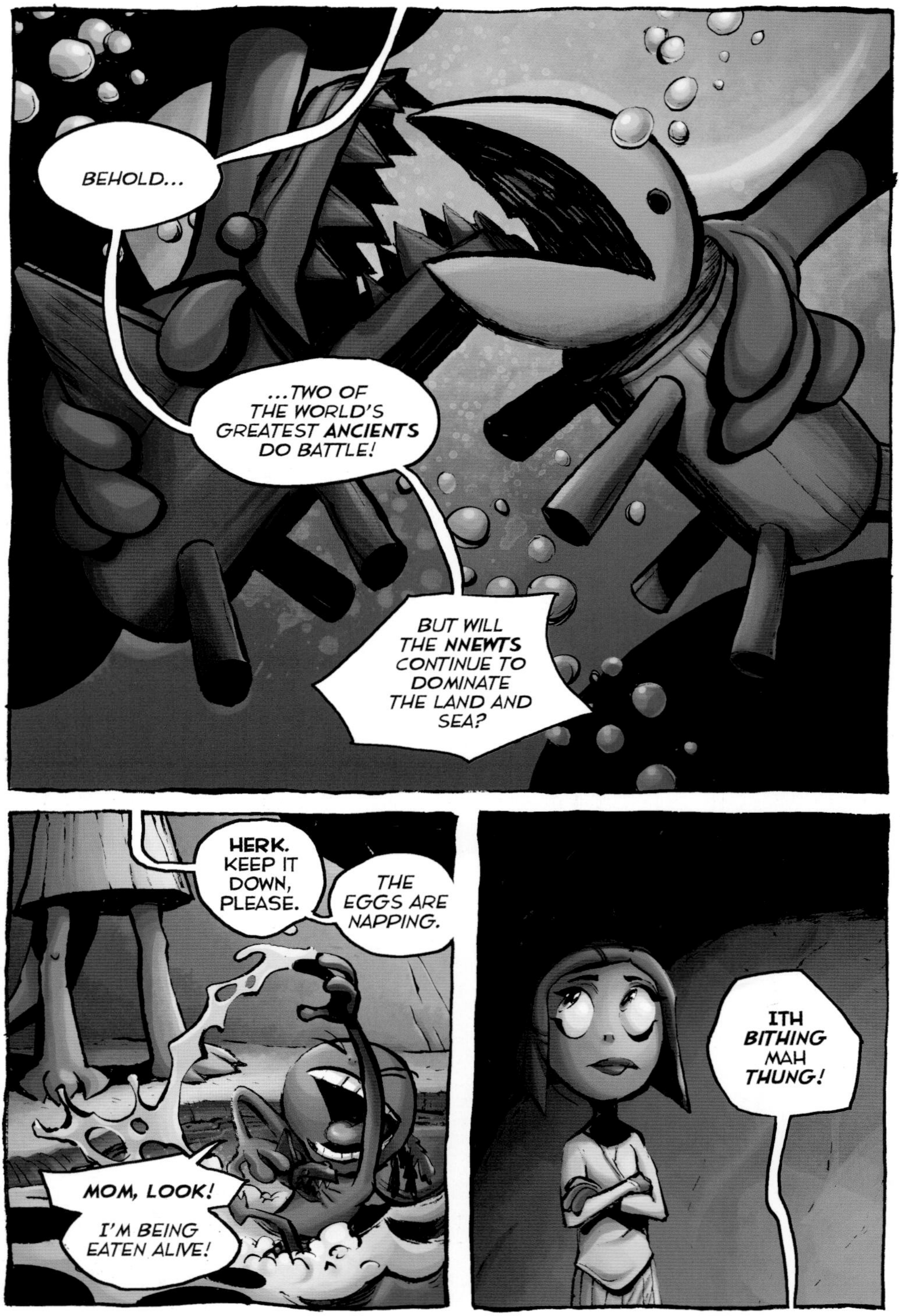
BEHOLD...
...TWO OF THE WORLD'S GREATEST ANCIENTS DO BATTLE!
BUT WILL THE NNEWTS CONTINUE TO DOMINATE THE LAND AND SEA?
HERK. KEEP IT DOWN, PLEASE.
THE EGGS ARE NAPPING.
MOM, LOOK!
I'M BEING EATEN ALIVE!
ITH BITHING MAH THUNG!

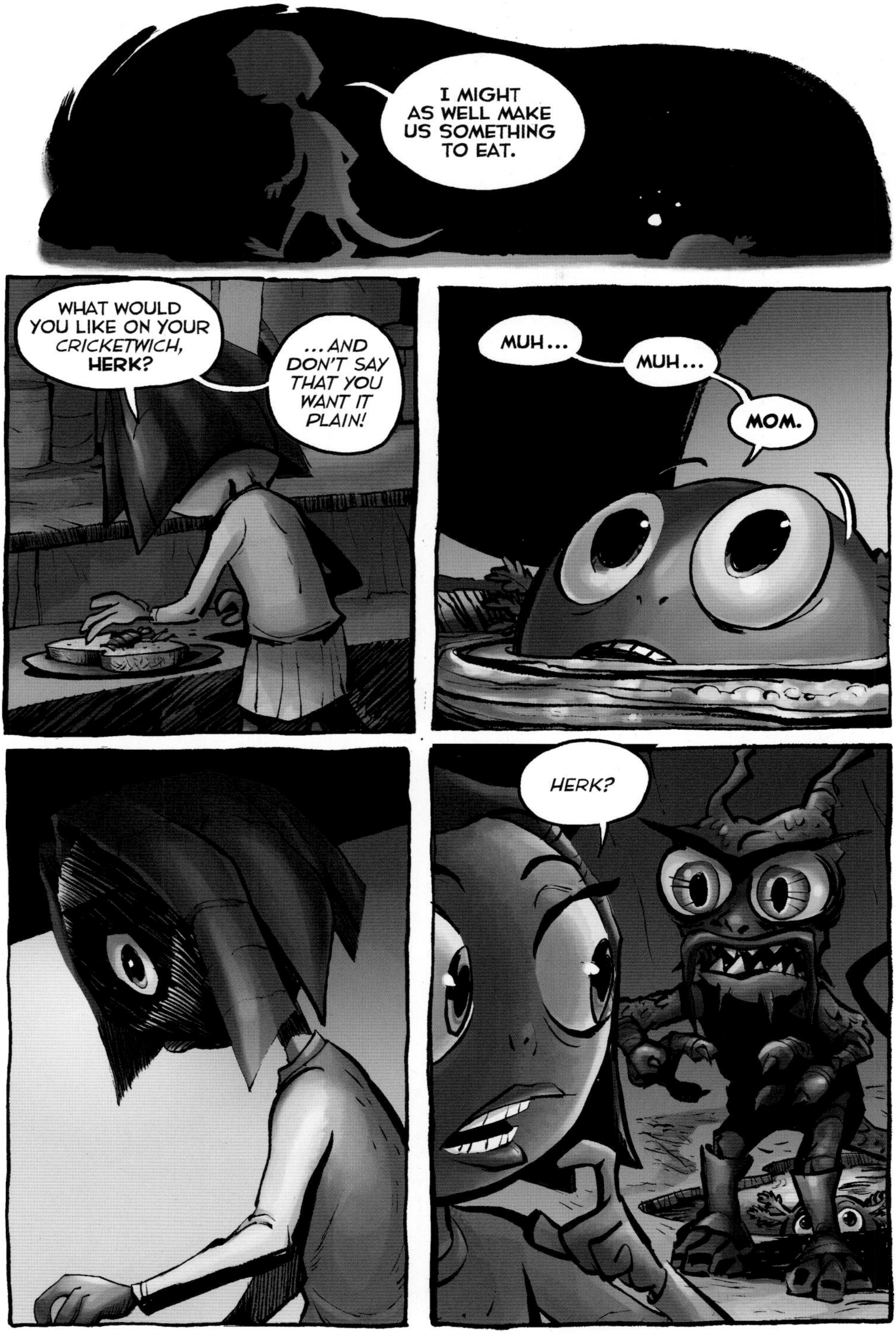
I MIGHT AS WELL MAKE US SOMETHING TO EAT.
WHAT WOULD YOU LIKE ON YOUR *CRICKETWICH*, **HERK?**
...AND DON'T SAY THAT YOU WANT IT PLAIN!
MUH...
MUH...
MOM.
HERK?

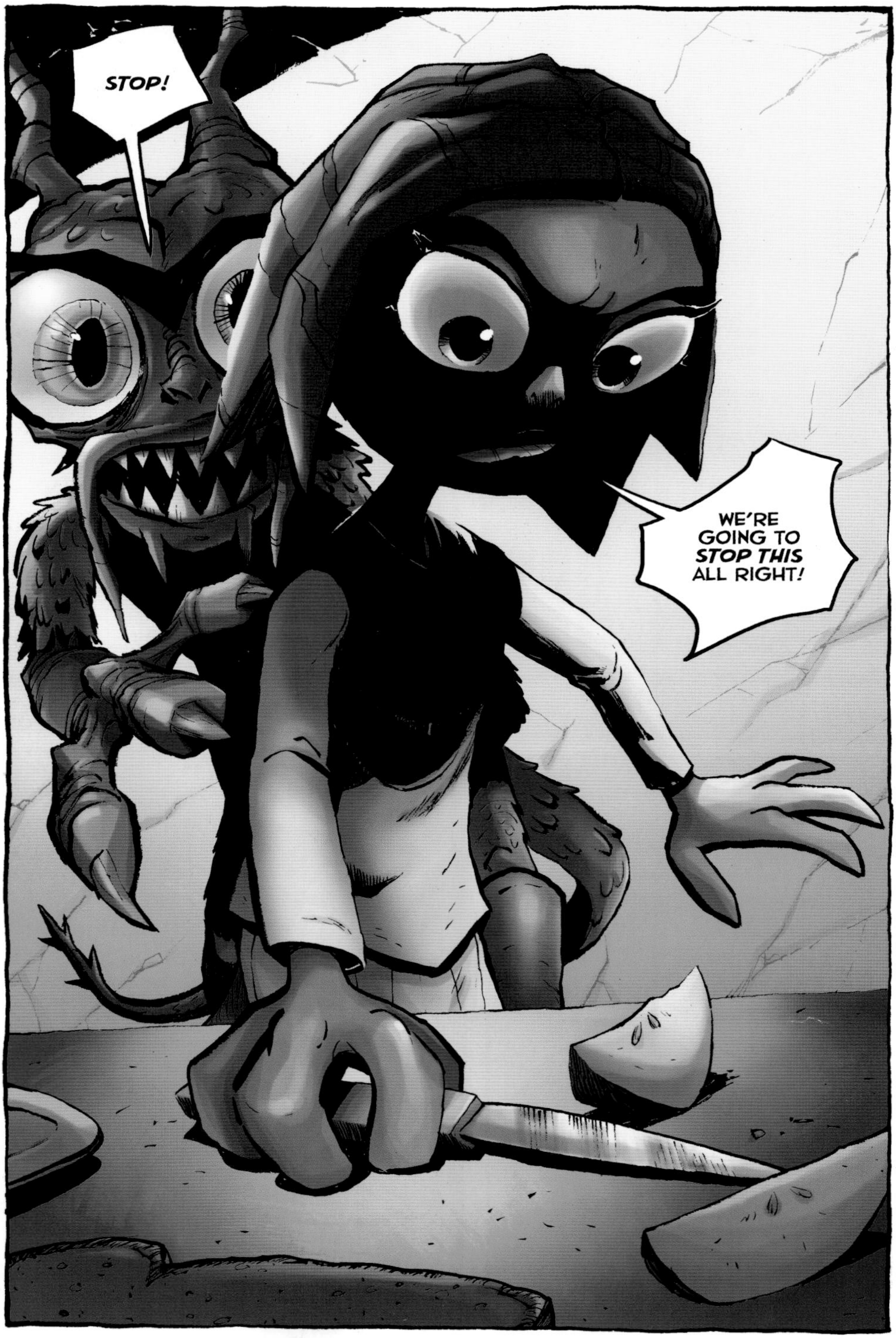
STOP!
WE'RE GOING TO *STOP THIS* ALL RIGHT!

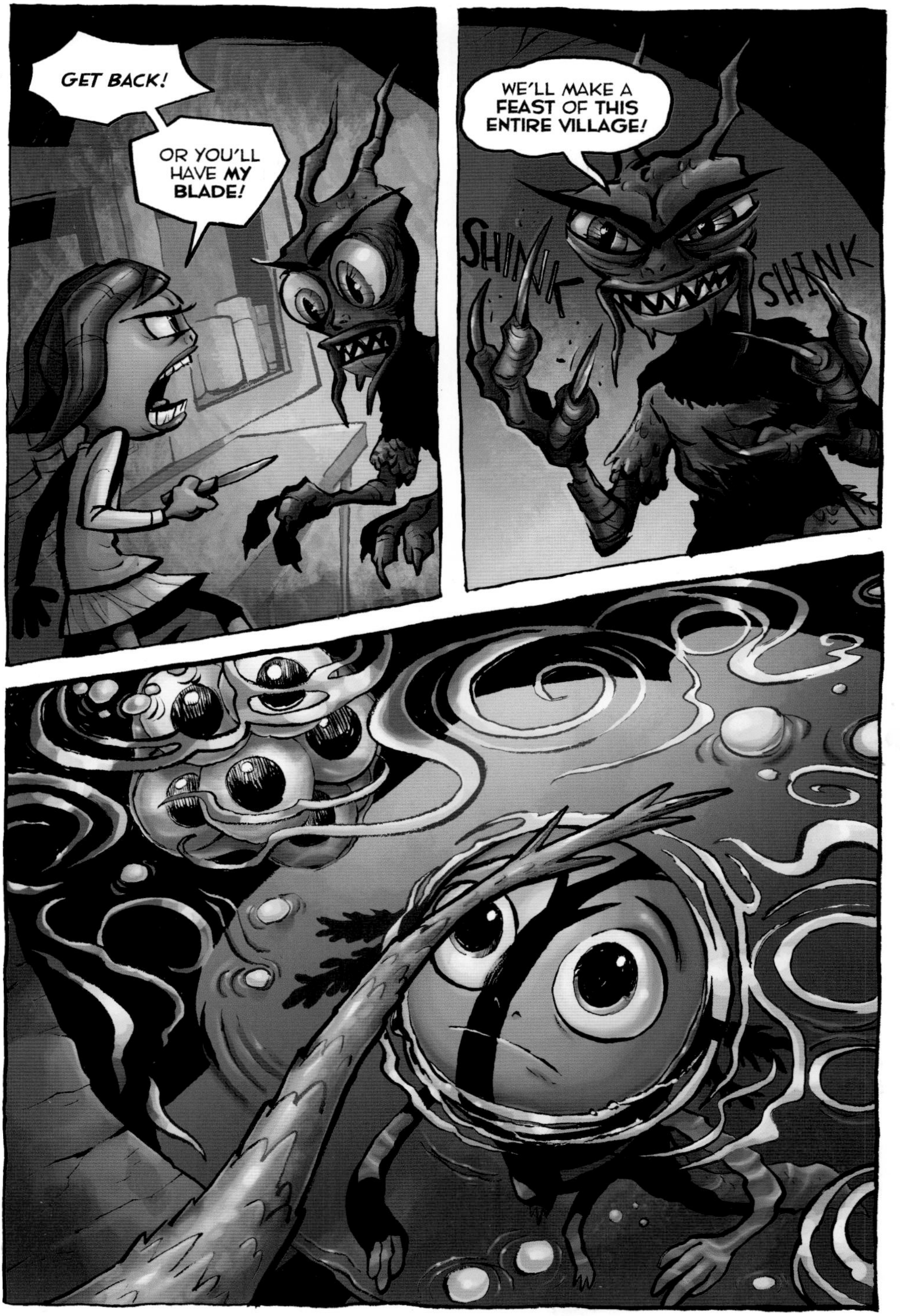
GET BACK!
OR YOU'LL HAVE MY BLADE!
WE'LL MAKE A FEAST OF THIS ENTIRE VILLAGE!
SHINK
SHINK

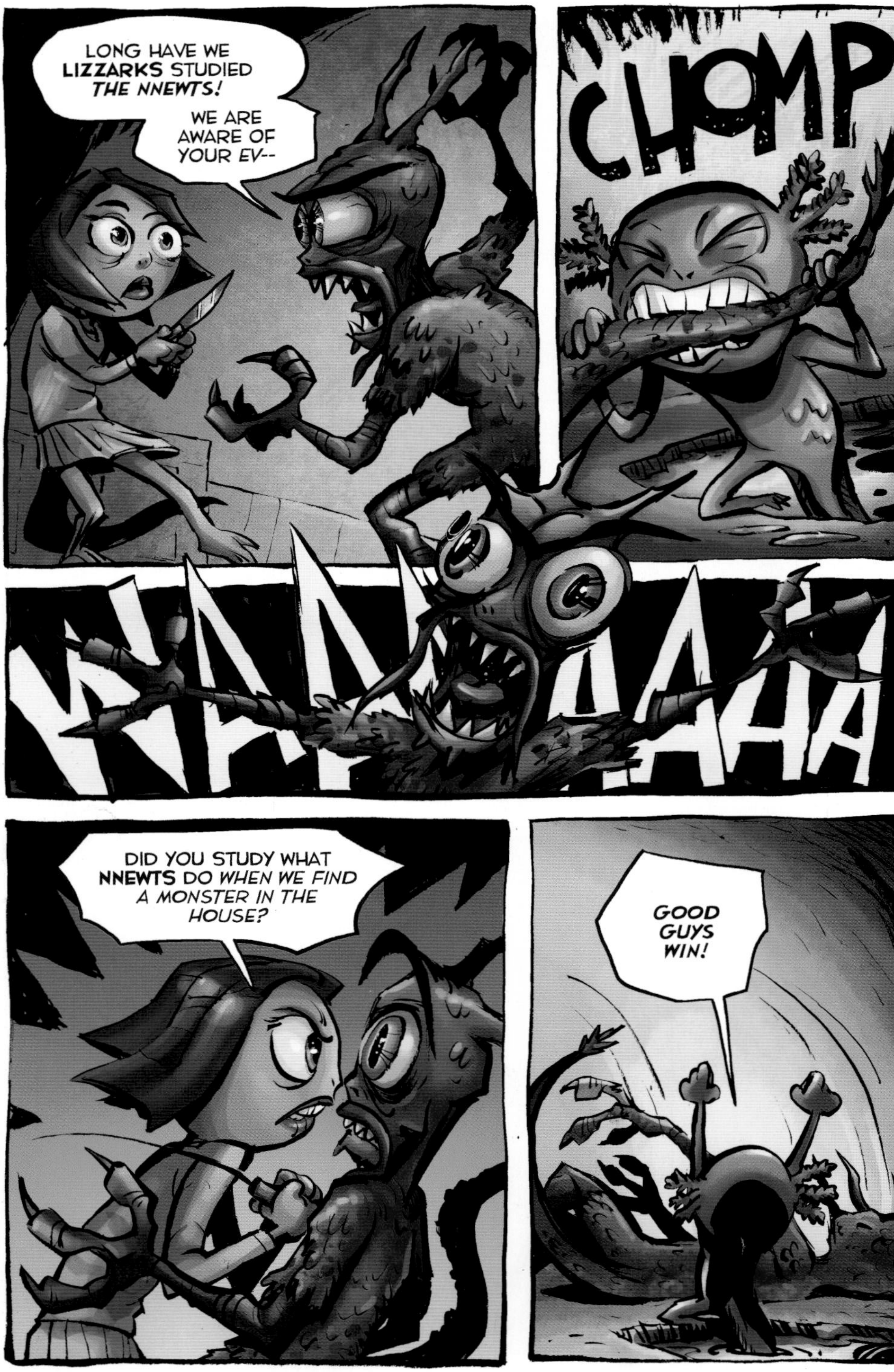
LONG HAVE WE LIZZARKS STUDIED THE NNEWTS!
WE ARE AWARE OF YOUR EV--
CHOMP
WAAAAAAHA
DID YOU STUDY WHAT NNEWTS DO WHEN WE FIND A MONSTER IN THE HOUSE?
GOOD GUYS WIN!

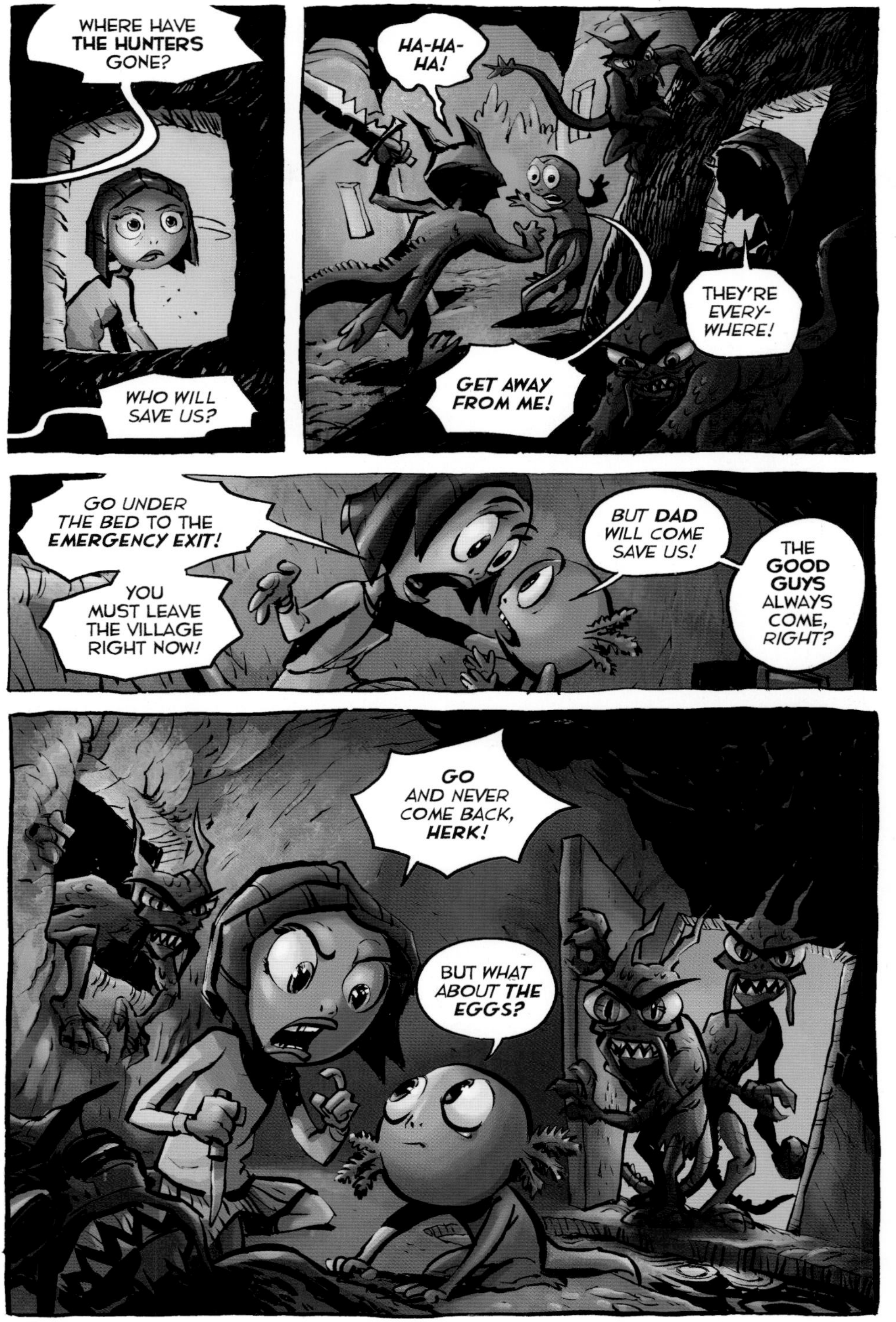
WHERE HAVE THE HUNTERS GONE?
WHO WILL SAVE US?
HA-HA-HA!
THEY'RE EVERY-WHERE!
GET AWAY FROM ME!
GO UNDER THE BED TO THE EMERGENCY EXIT!
YOU MUST LEAVE THE VILLAGE RIGHT NOW!
BUT DAD WILL COME SAVE US!
THE GOOD GUYS ALWAYS COME, RIGHT?
GO AND NEVER COME BACK, HERK!
BUT WHAT ABOUT THE EGGS?

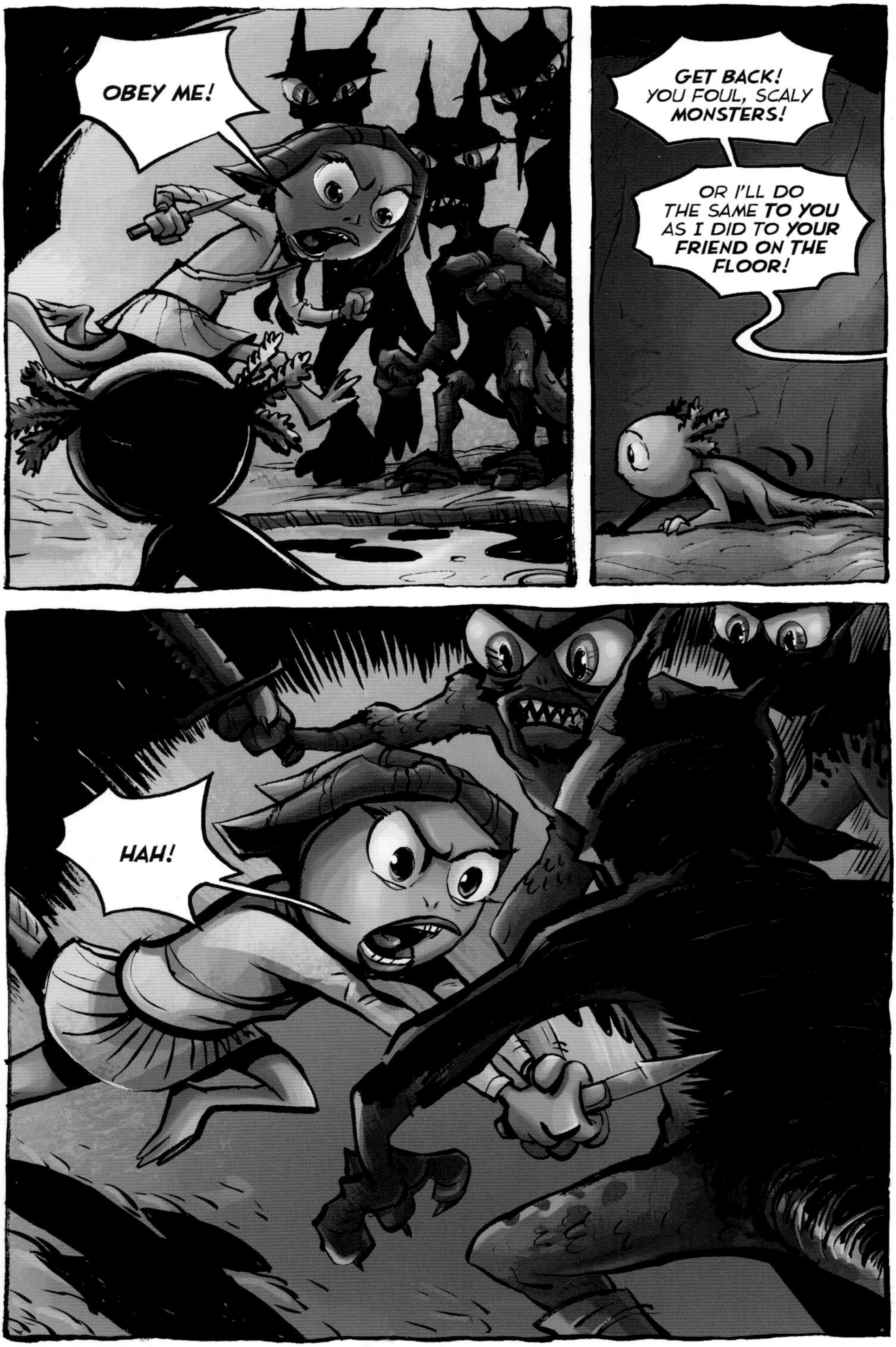
OBEY ME!
GET BACK! YOU FOUL, SCALY MONSTERS!
OR I'LL DO THE SAME TO YOU AS I DID TO YOUR FRIEND ON THE FLOOR!
HAH!

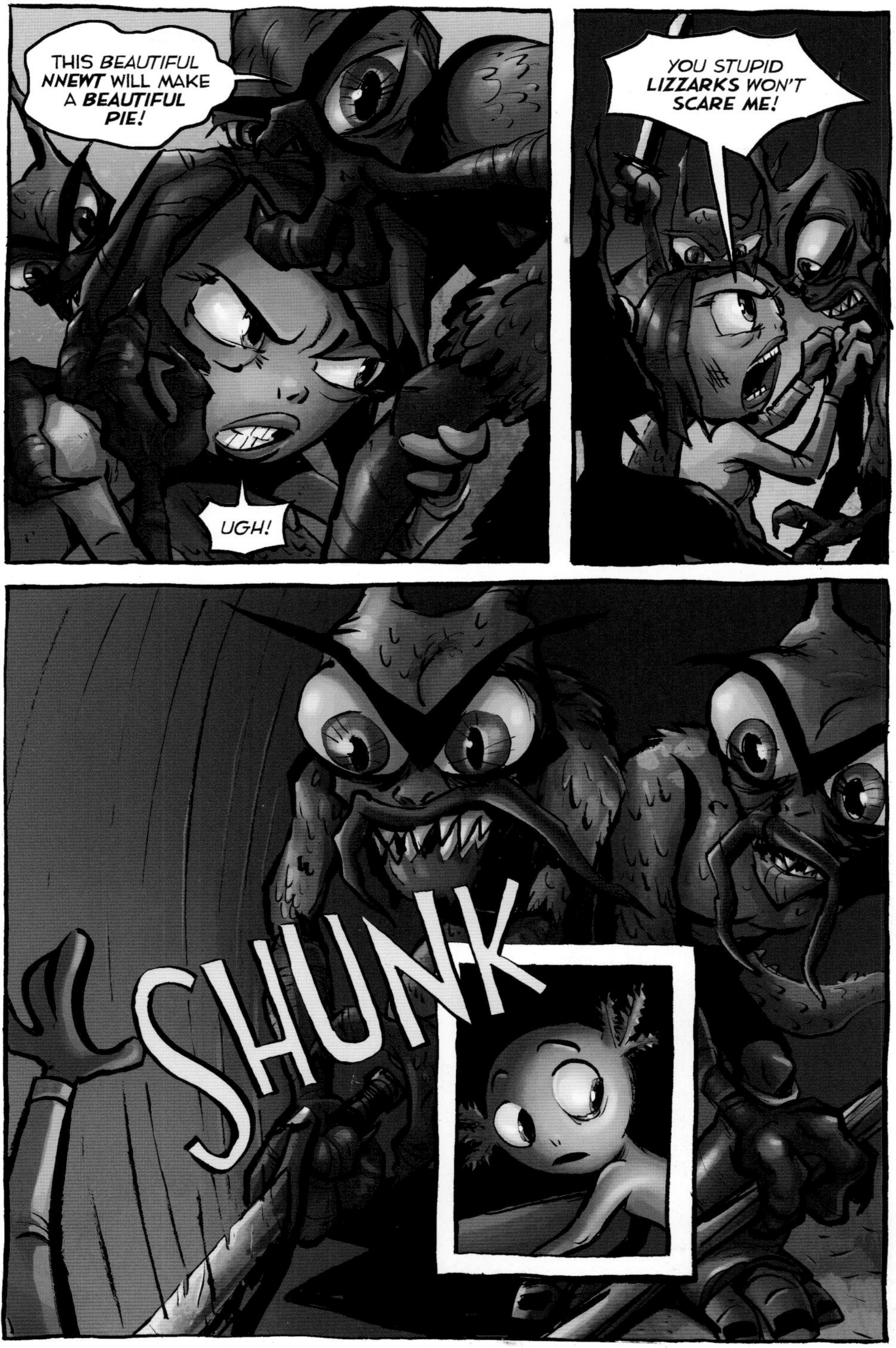
THIS *BEAUTIFUL* **NNEWT** WILL MAKE A **BEAUTIFUL PIE!**
UGH!
YOU STUPID **LIZZARKS** *WON'T* **SCARE ME!**
SHUNK

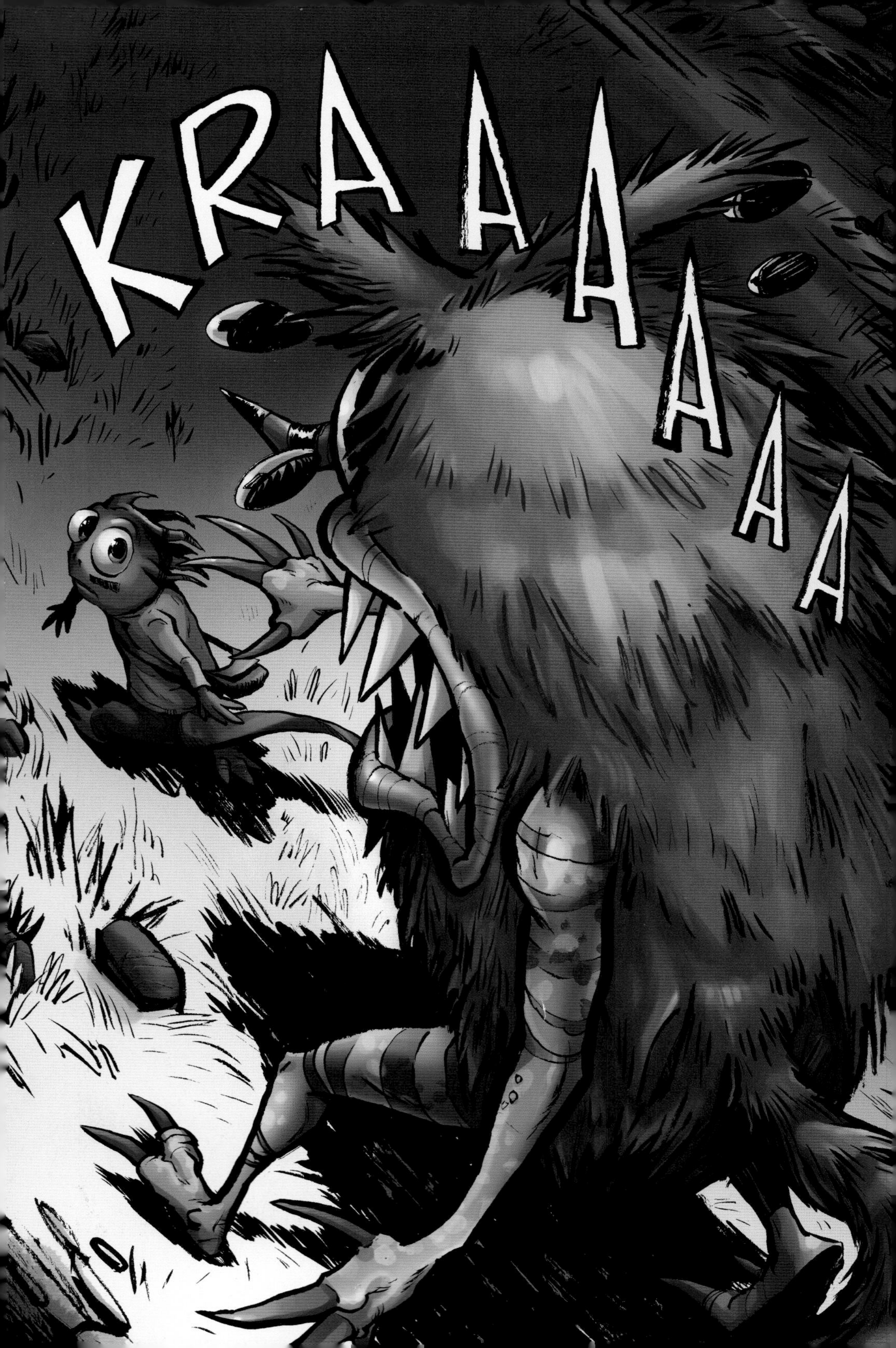
KRAAAAAAAA

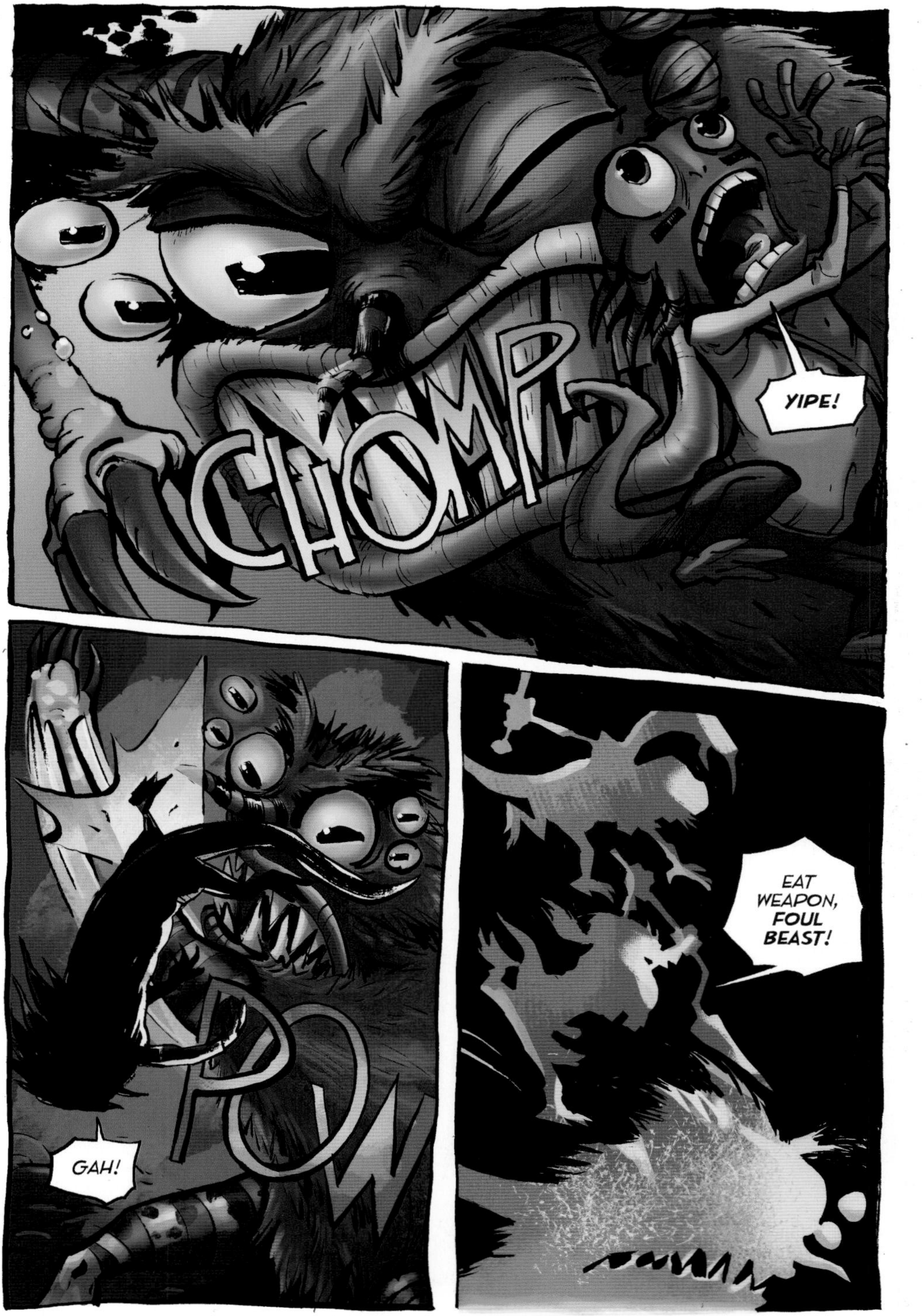
CHOMP
YIPE!
POW
GAH!
EAT WEAPON, FOUL BEAST!

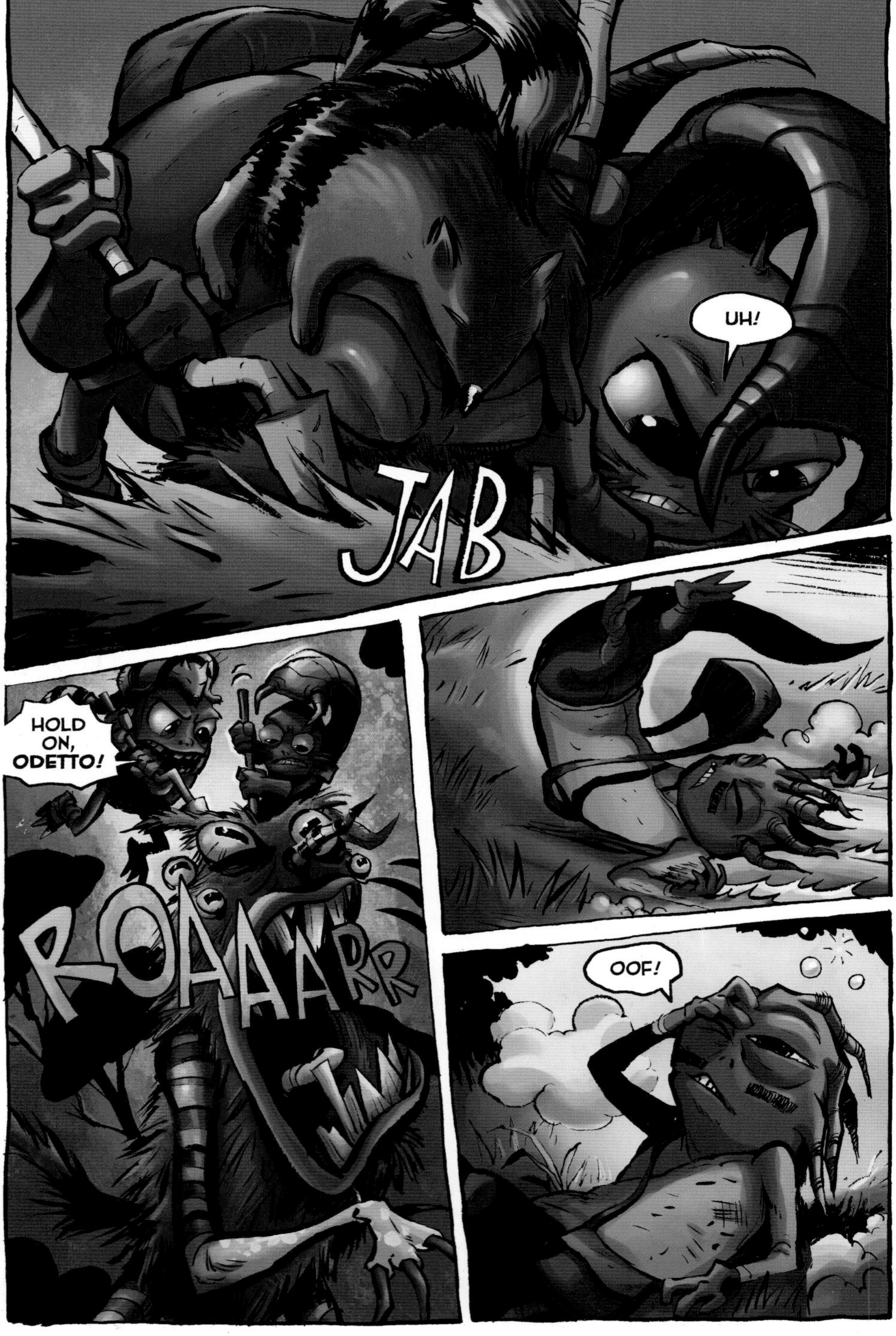
UH!
JAB
HOLD ON, ODETTO!
ROAAAARR
OOF!

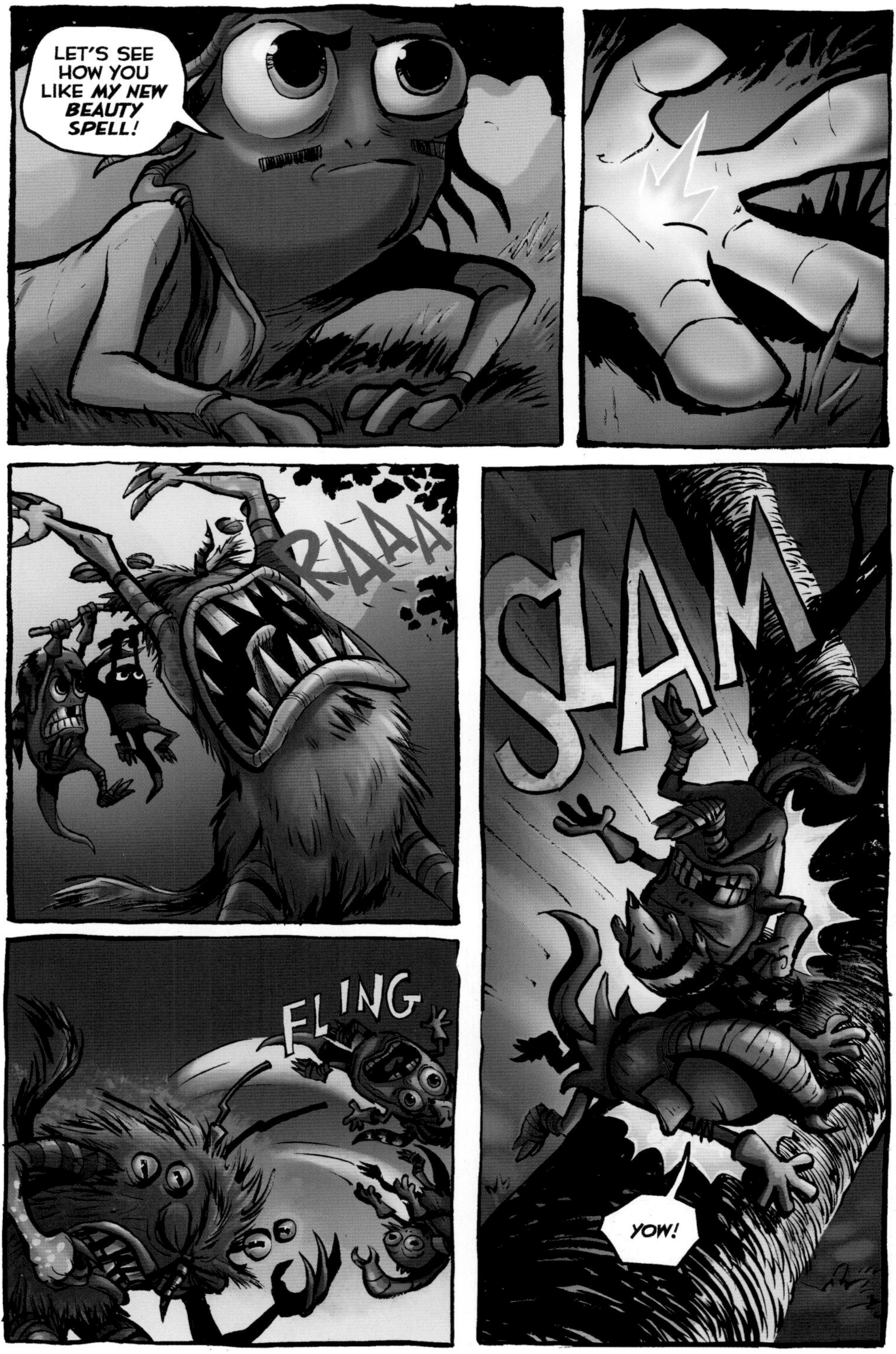
LET'S SEE HOW YOU LIKE *MY NEW BEAUTY SPELL!*
RAAA
SLAM
FLING
YOW!

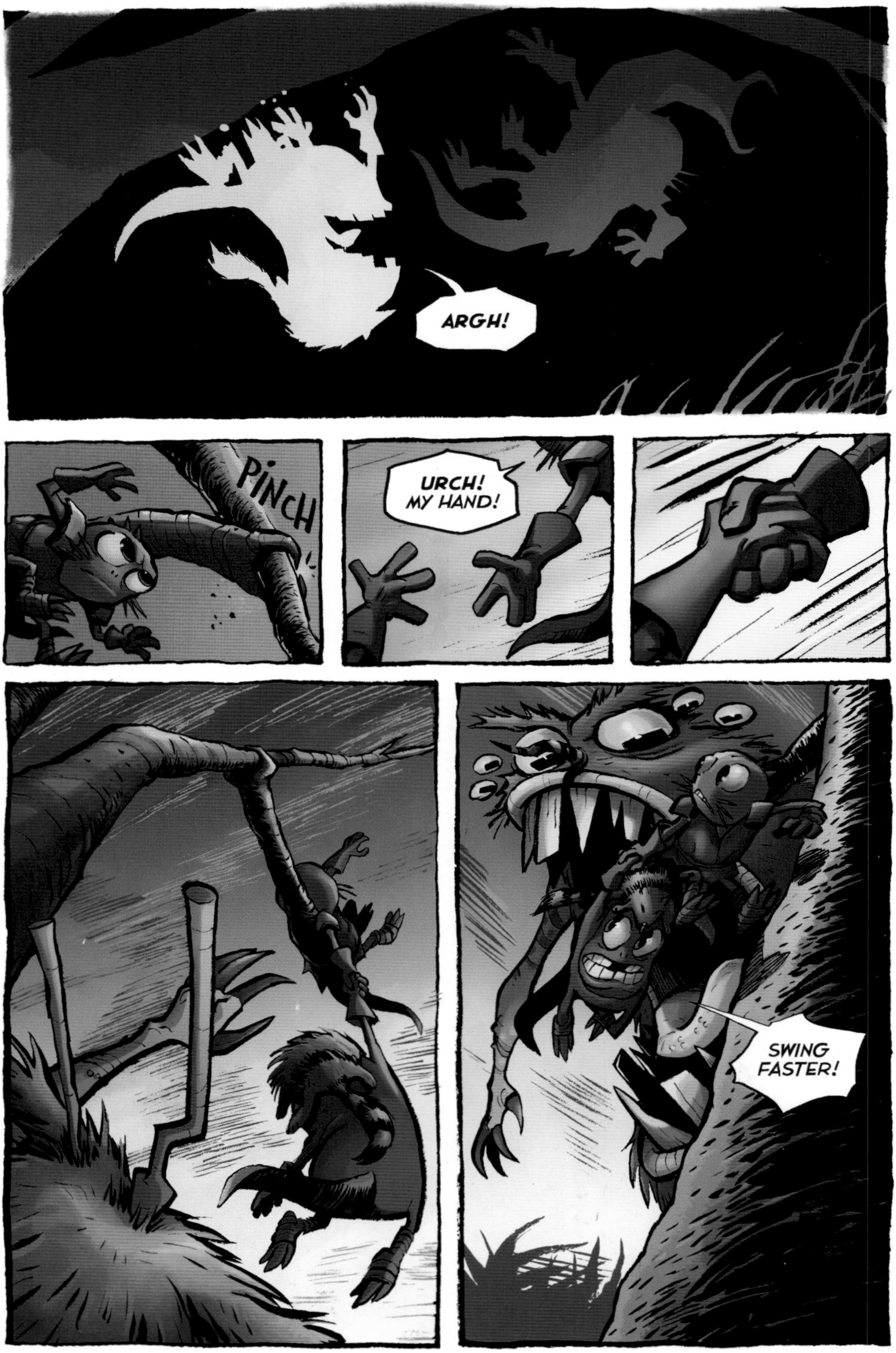
ARGH!
PINCH
URCH! MY HAND!
SWING FASTER!

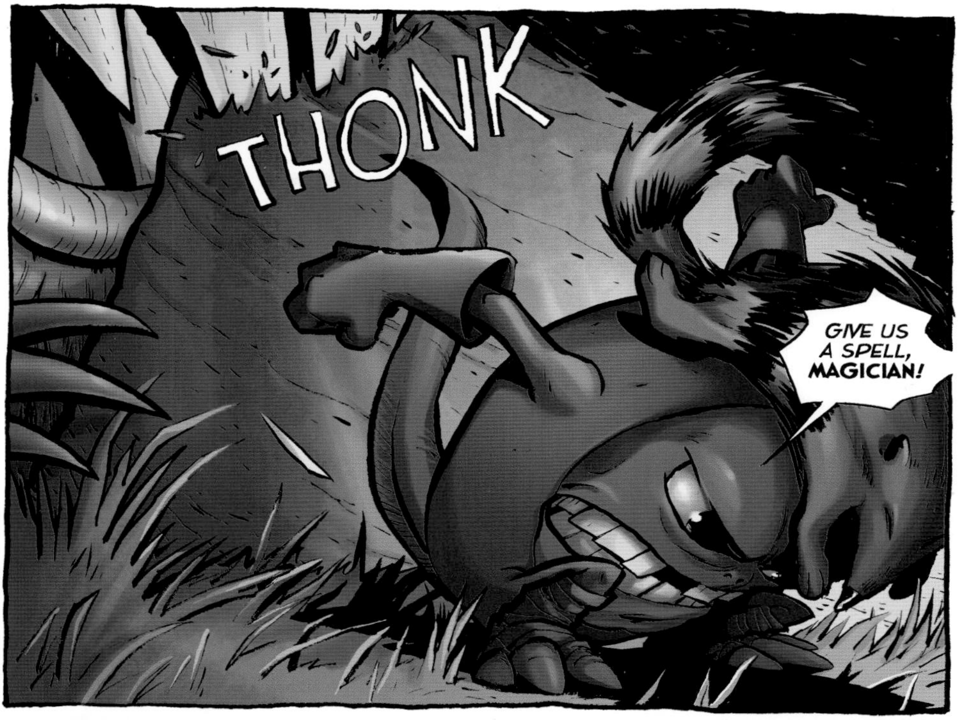
THONK
GIVE US A SPELL, **MAGICIAN!**

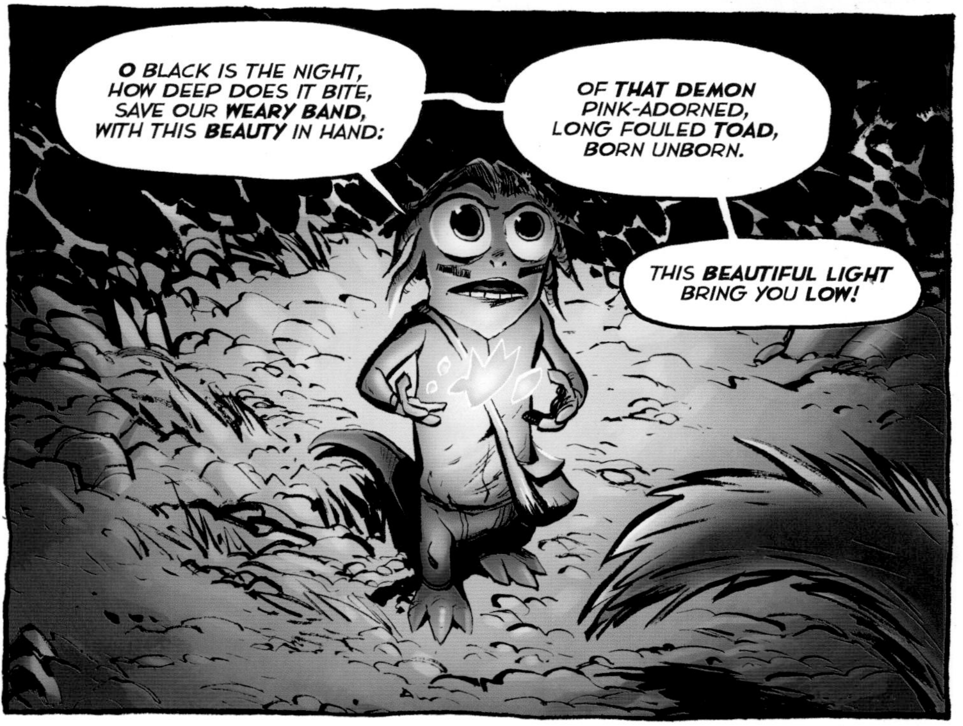
O BLACK IS THE NIGHT, HOW **DEEP** DOES IT BITE, SAVE OUR **WEARY BAND**, WITH THIS **BEAUTY** IN HAND:
OF **THAT DEMON** PINK-ADORNED, LONG FOULED **TOAD**, BORN UNBORN.
THIS **BEAUTIFUL LIGHT** BRING YOU **LOW!**

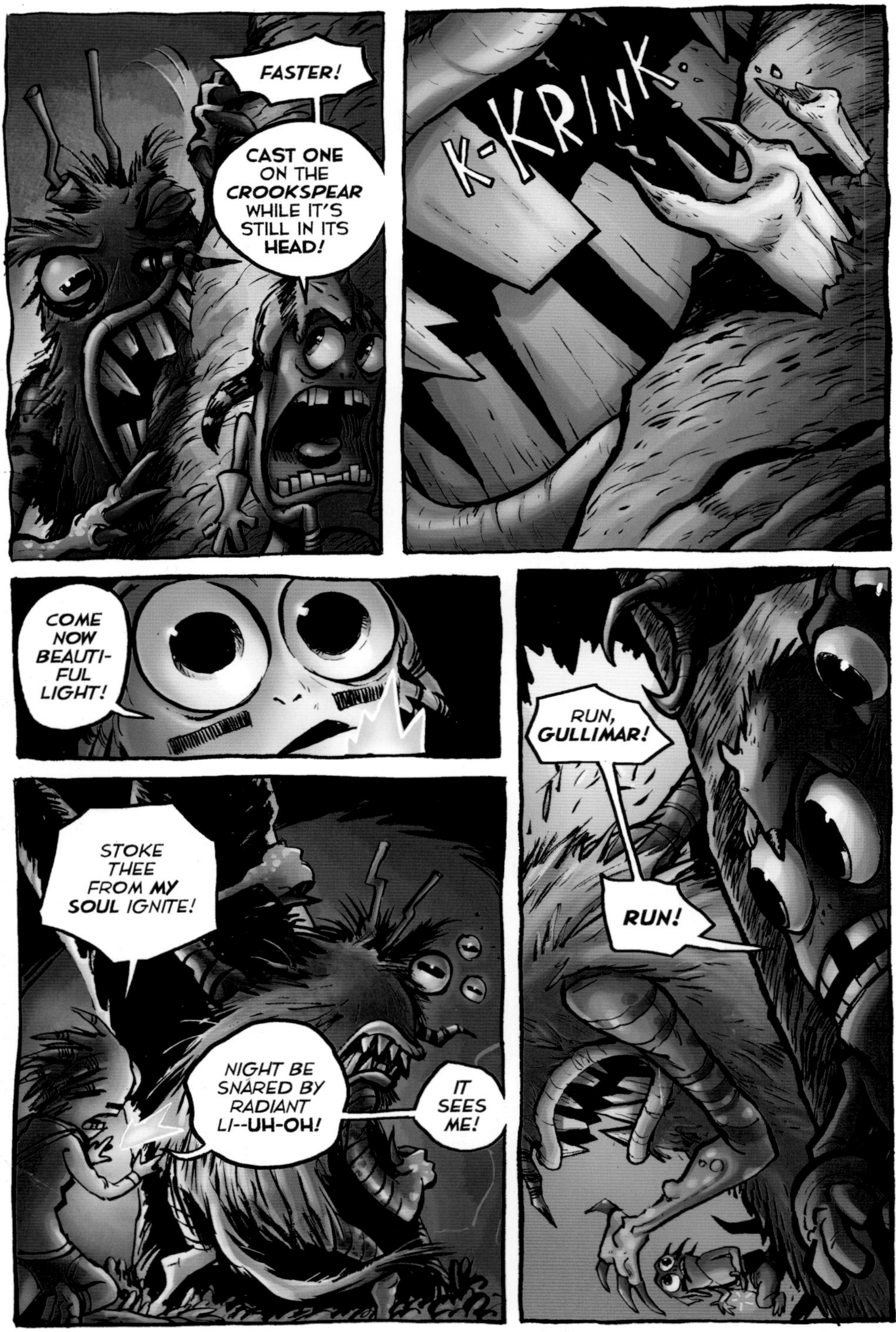
FASTER!
CAST ONE ON THE CROOKSPEAR WHILE IT'S STILL IN ITS HEAD!
K-KRINK
COME NOW BEAUTIFUL LIGHT!
STOKE THEE FROM MY SOUL IGNITE!
NIGHT BE SNARED BY RADIANT LI--UH-OH!
IT SEES ME!
RUN, GULLIMAR!
RUN!

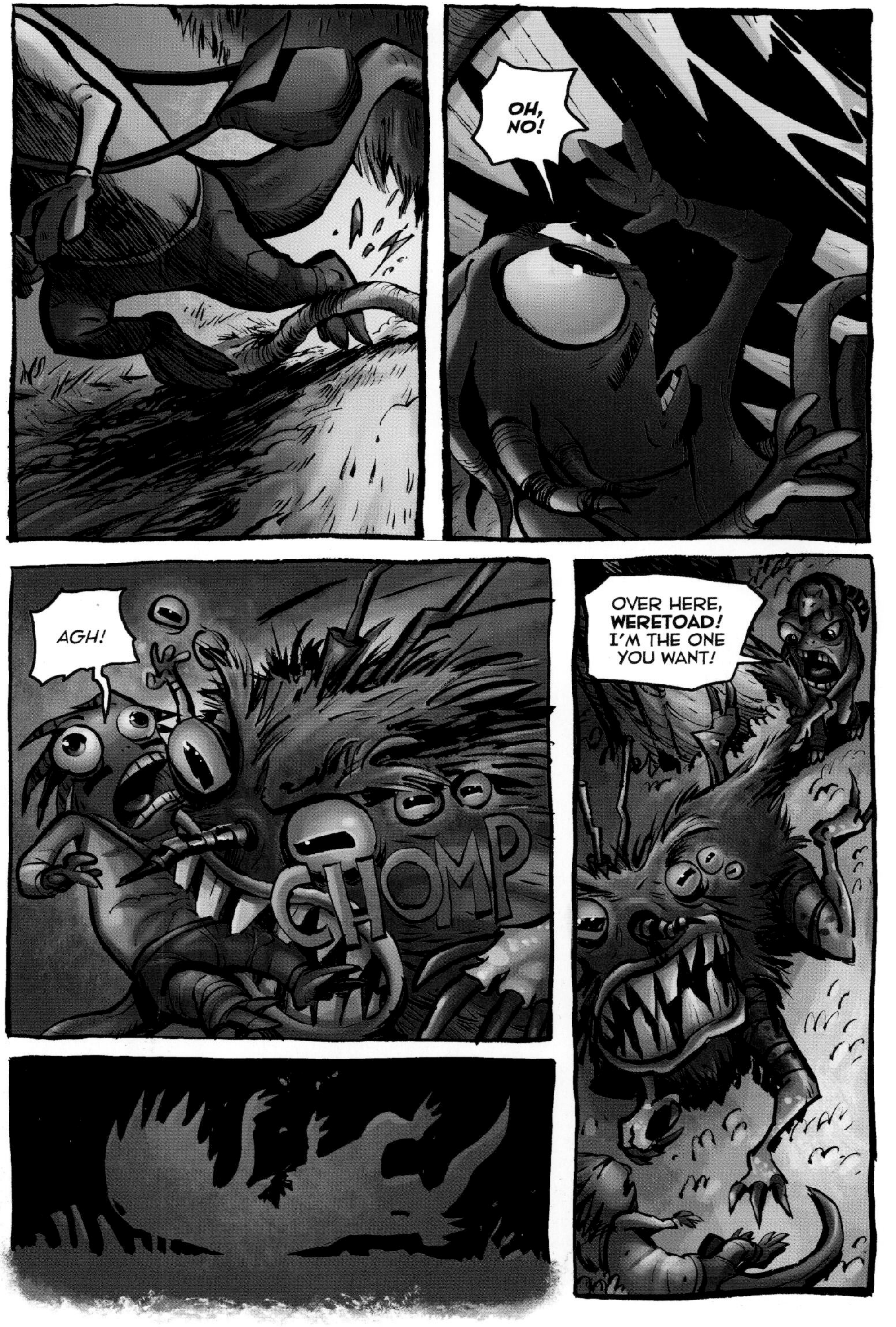
OH, NO!
AGH!
CHOMP
OVER HERE, WERETOAD! I'M THE ONE YOU WANT!

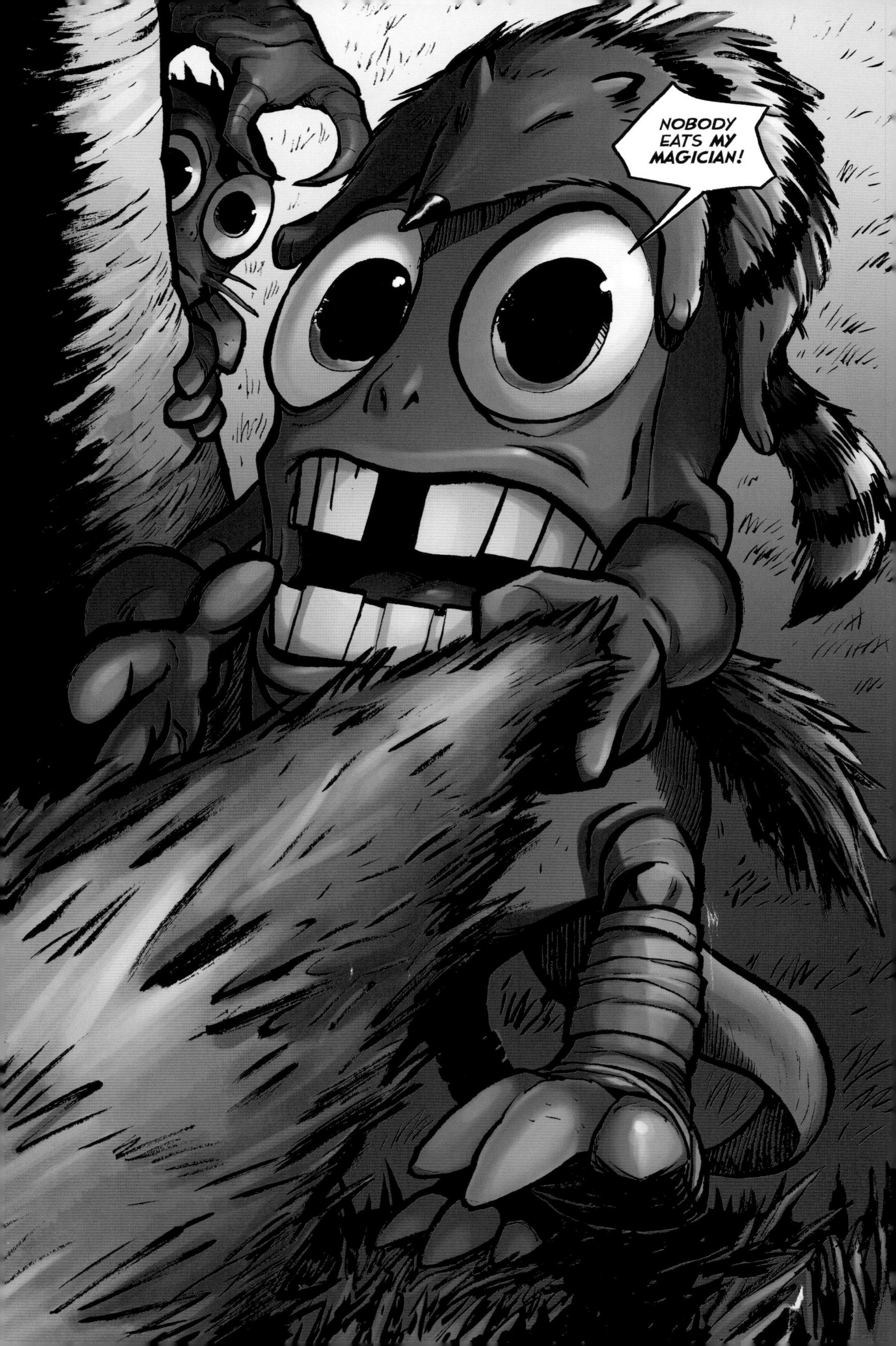
NOBODY EATS MY MAGICIAN!

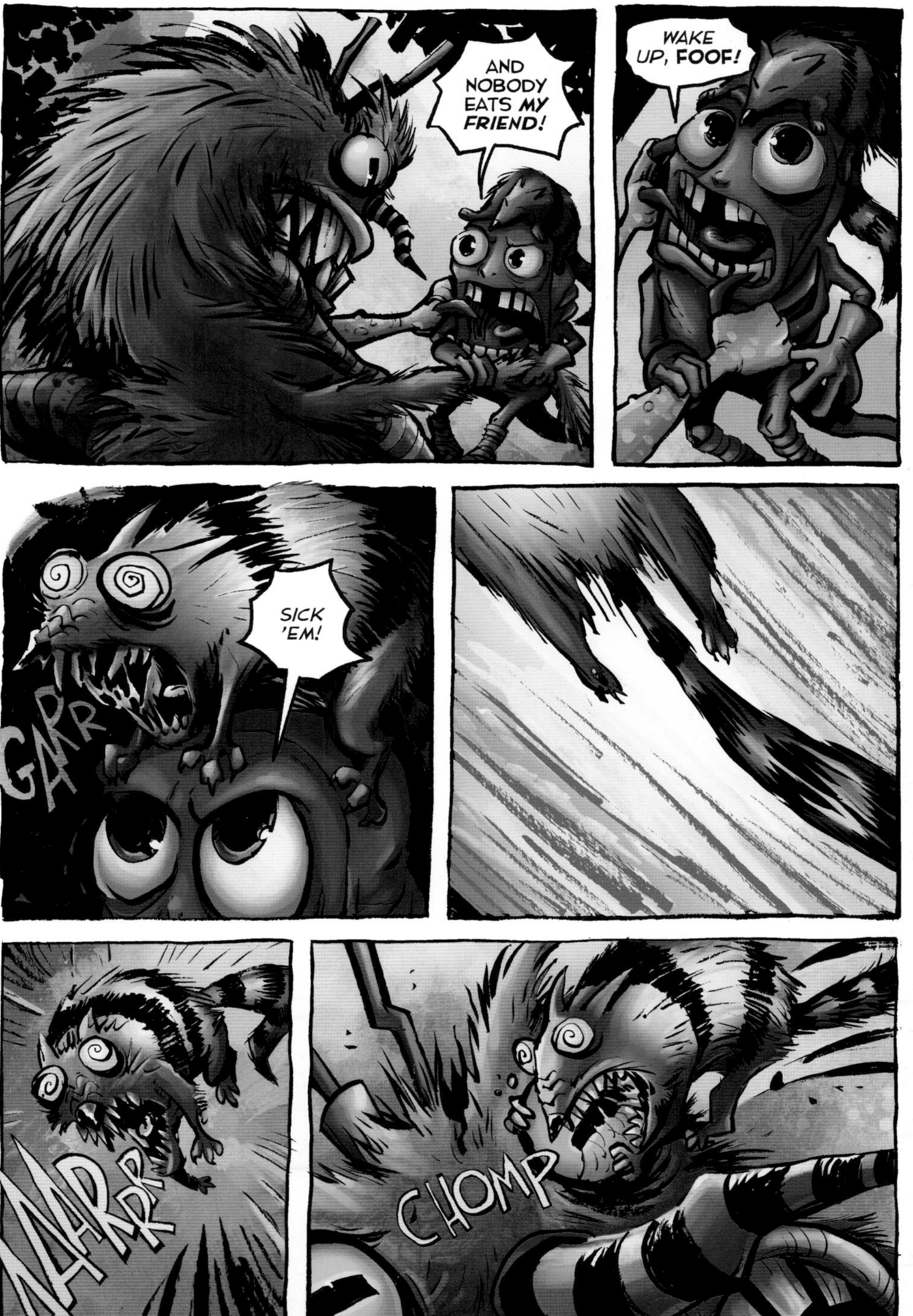
AND NOBODY EATS MY FRIEND!
WAKE UP, FOOF!
SICK 'EM!
GARR
AAARRR
CHOMP

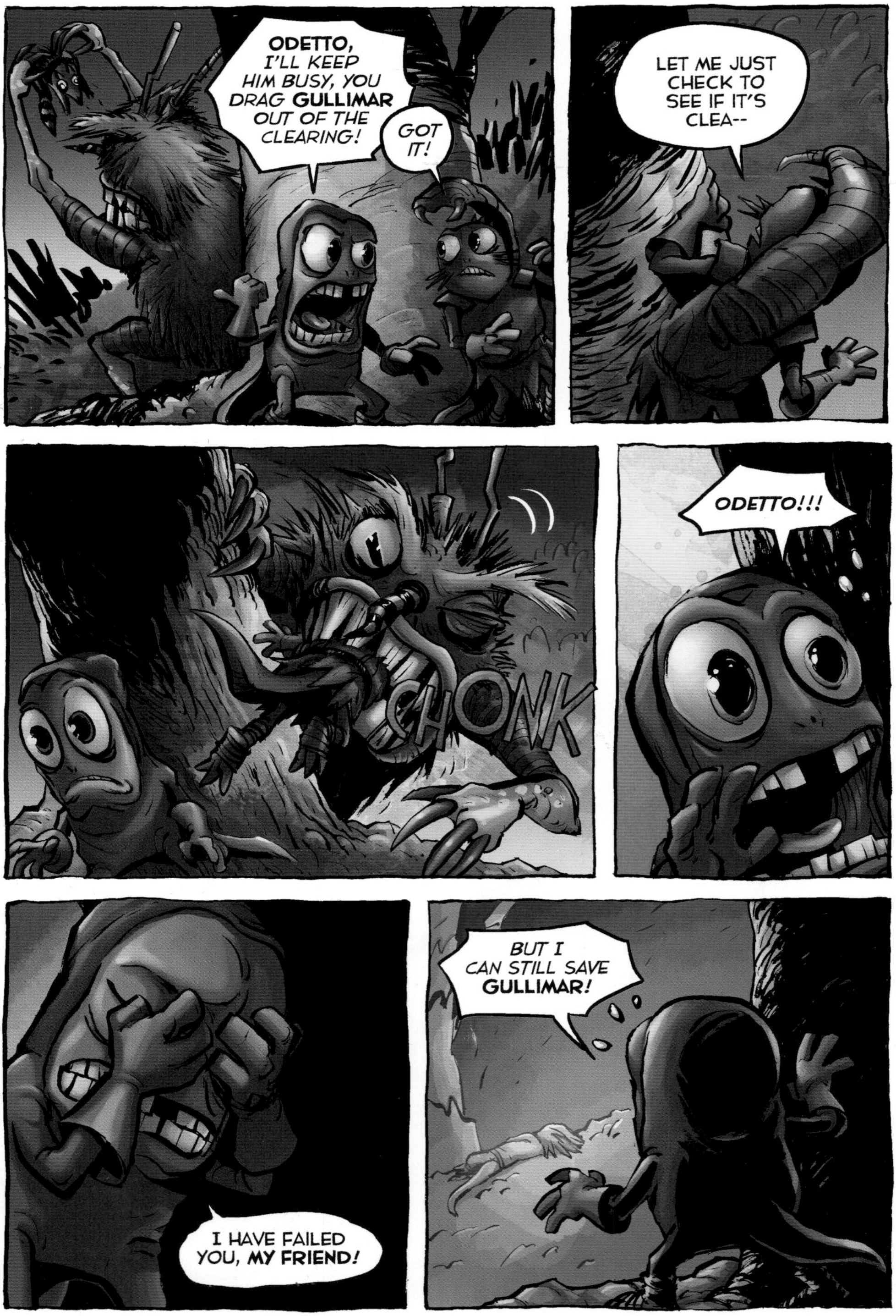
ODETTO, I'LL KEEP HIM BUSY, YOU DRAG GULLIMAR OUT OF THE CLEARING!
GOT IT!
LET ME JUST CHECK TO SEE IF IT'S CLEA--
CHONK
ODETTO!!!
I HAVE FAILED YOU, MY FRIEND!
BUT I CAN STILL SAVE GULLIMAR!

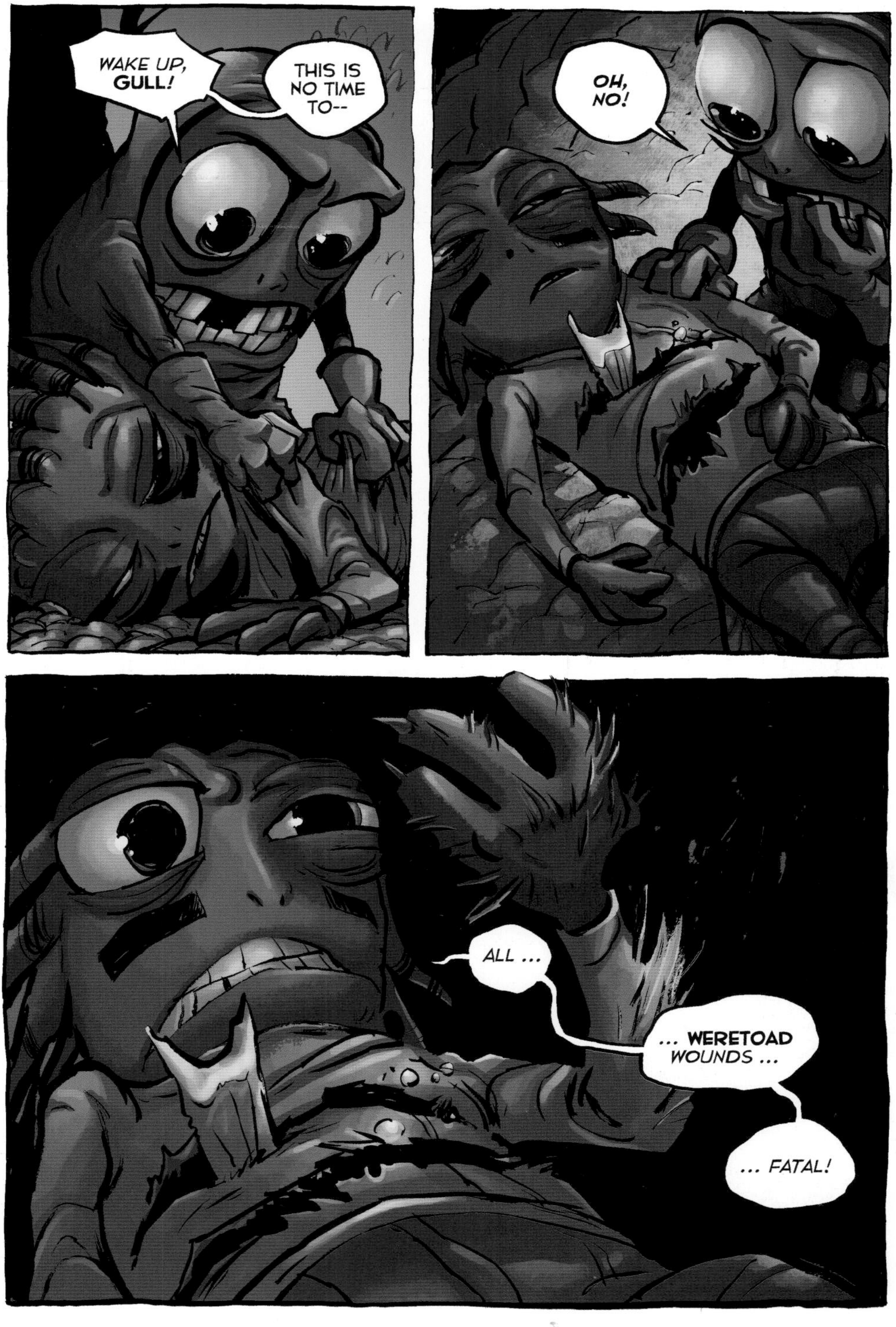
WAKE UP, GULL!
THIS IS NO TIME TO--
OH, NO!
ALL ...
... WERETOAD WOUNDS ...
... FATAL!

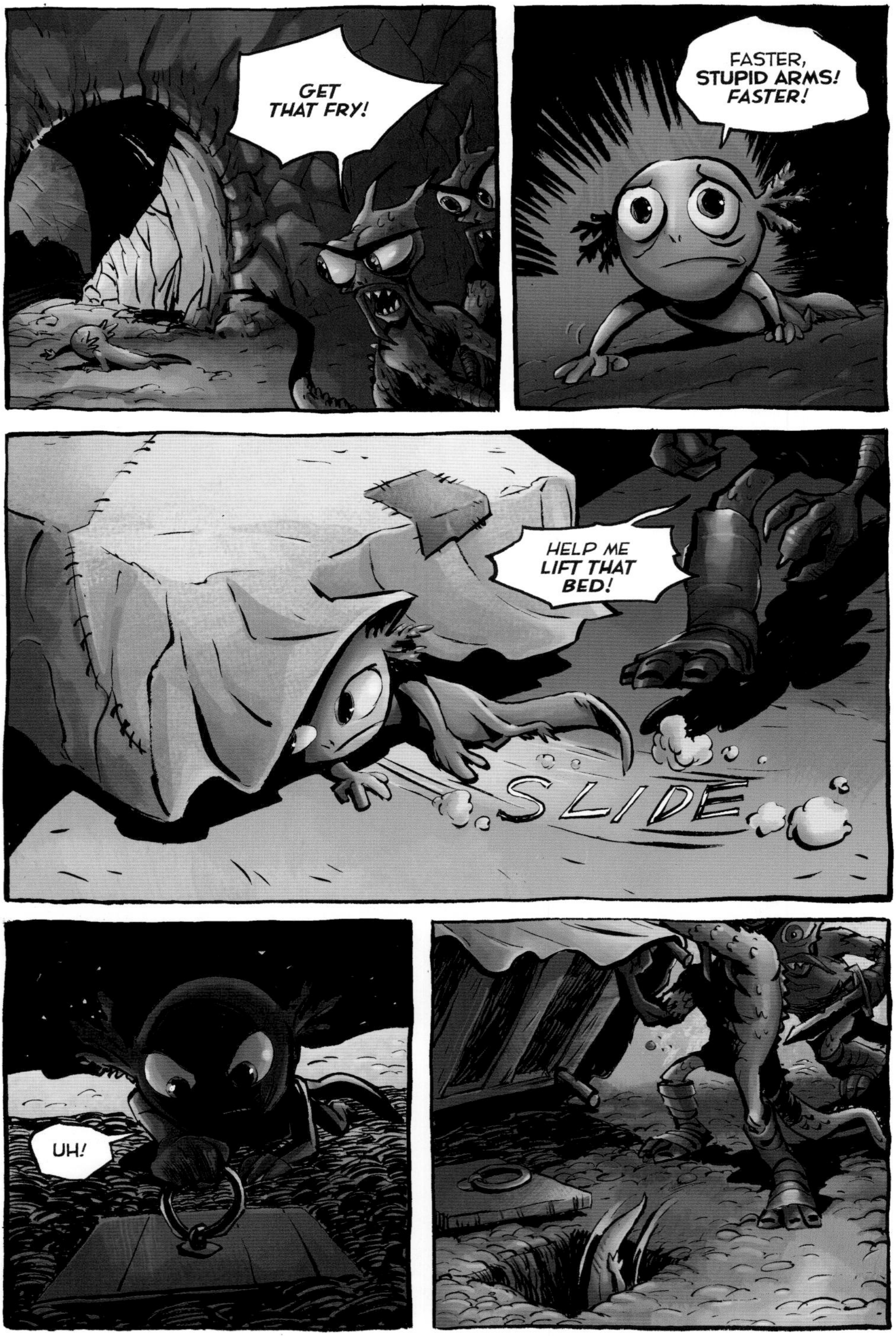
GET THAT FRY!
FASTER, STUPID ARMS! FASTER!
HELP ME LIFT THAT BED!
SLIDE
UH!

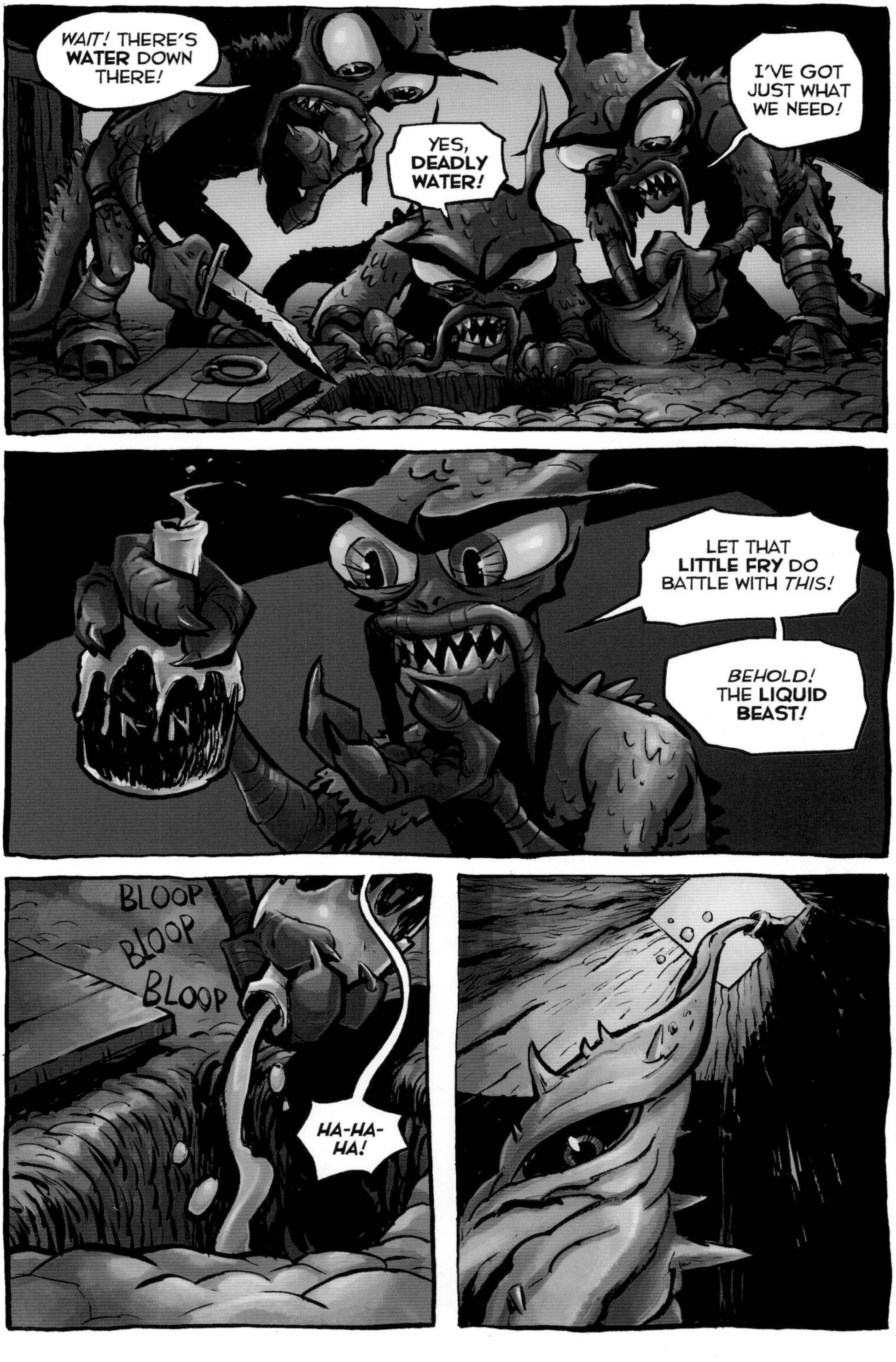
WAIT! THERE'S WATER DOWN THERE!
YES, DEADLY WATER!
I'VE GOT JUST WHAT WE NEED!
LET THAT LITTLE FRY DO BATTLE WITH THIS!
BEHOLD! THE LIQUID BEAST!
BLOOP BLOOP BLOOP
HA-HA-HA!

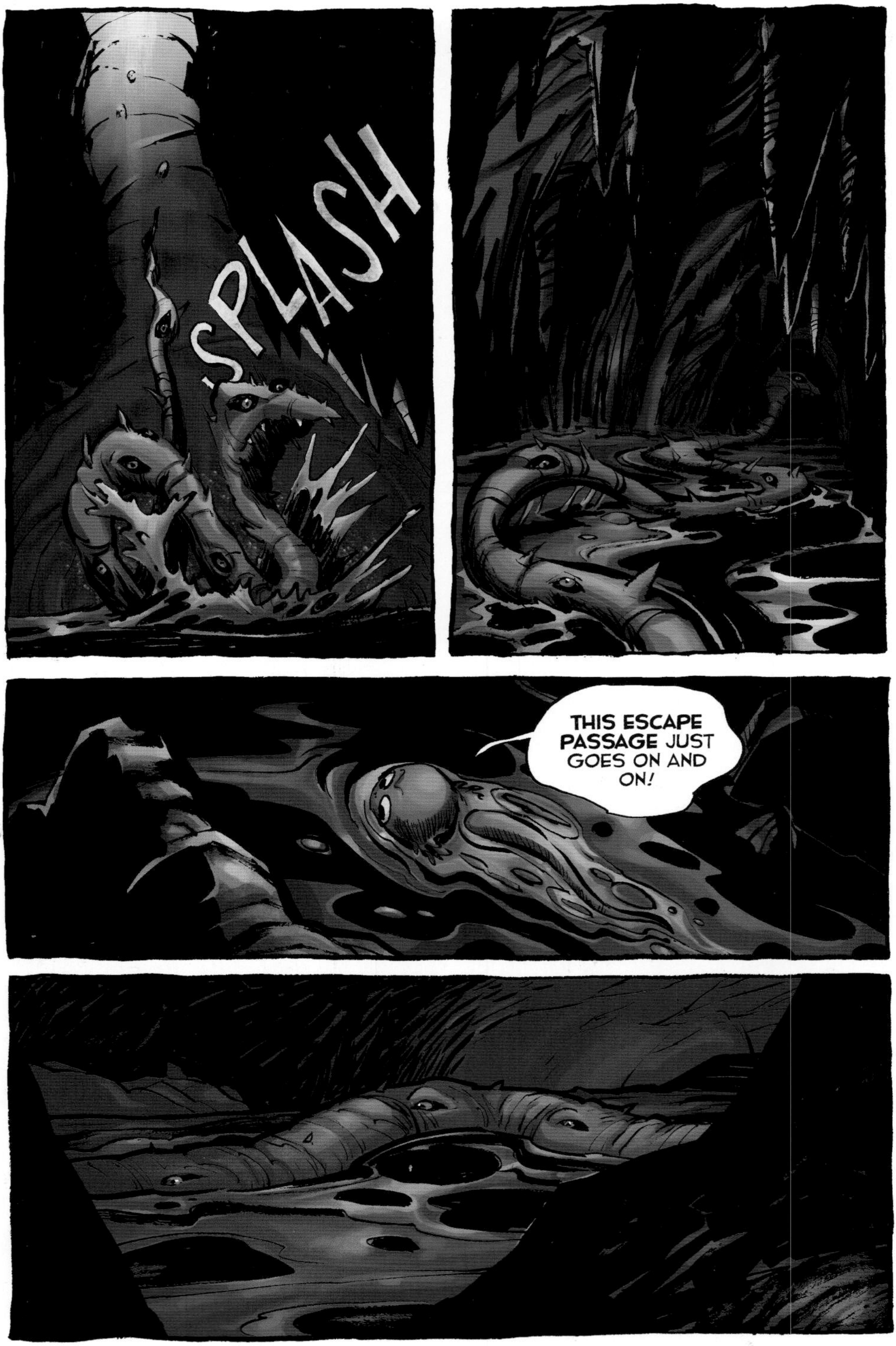
SPLASH
THIS ESCAPE PASSAGE JUST GOES ON AND ON!

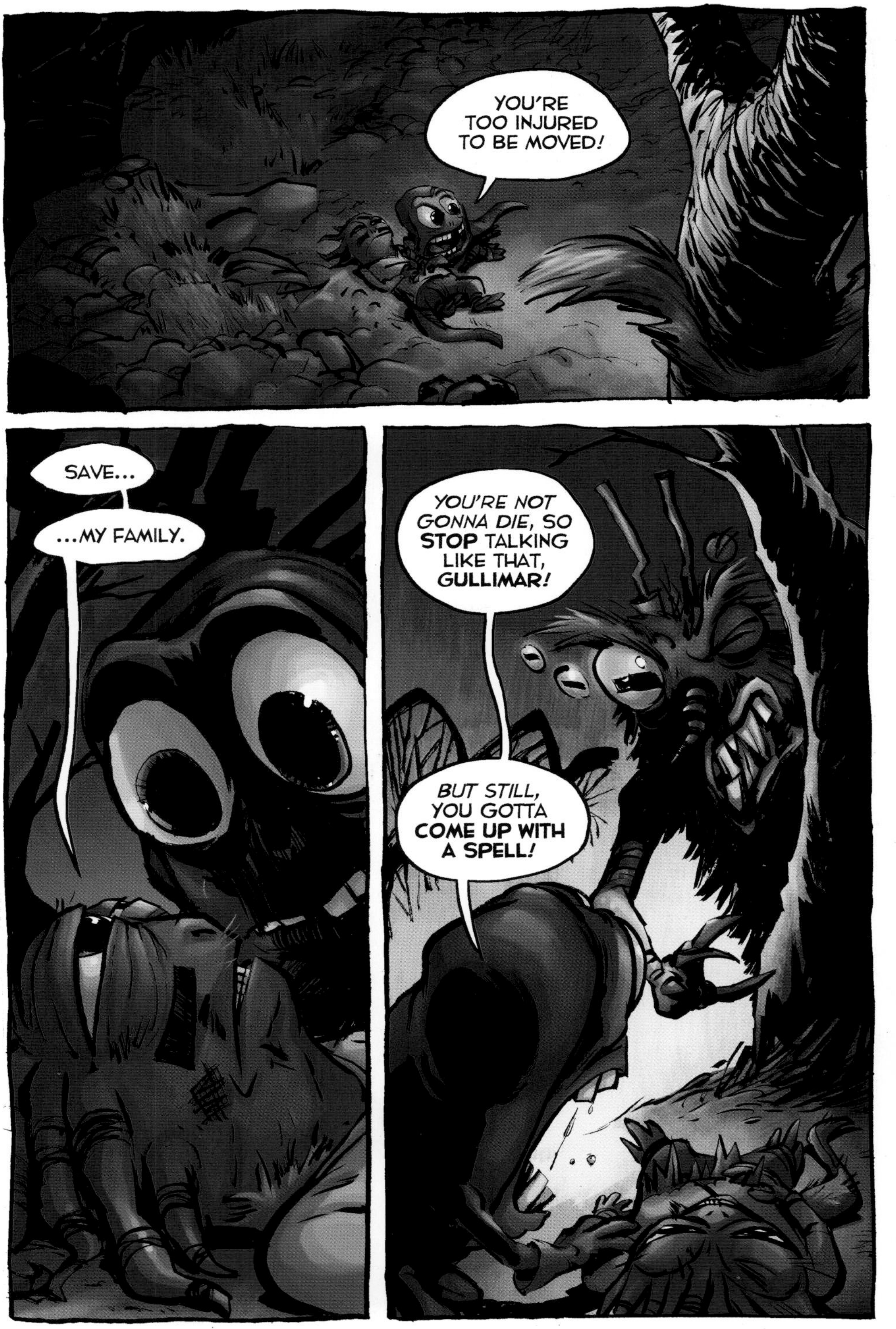
YOU'RE TOO INJURED TO BE MOVED!
SAVE...
...MY FAMILY.
YOU'RE NOT GONNA DIE, SO **STOP** TALKING LIKE THAT, **GULLIMAR!**
BUT STILL, YOU GOTTA **COME UP WITH A SPELL!**

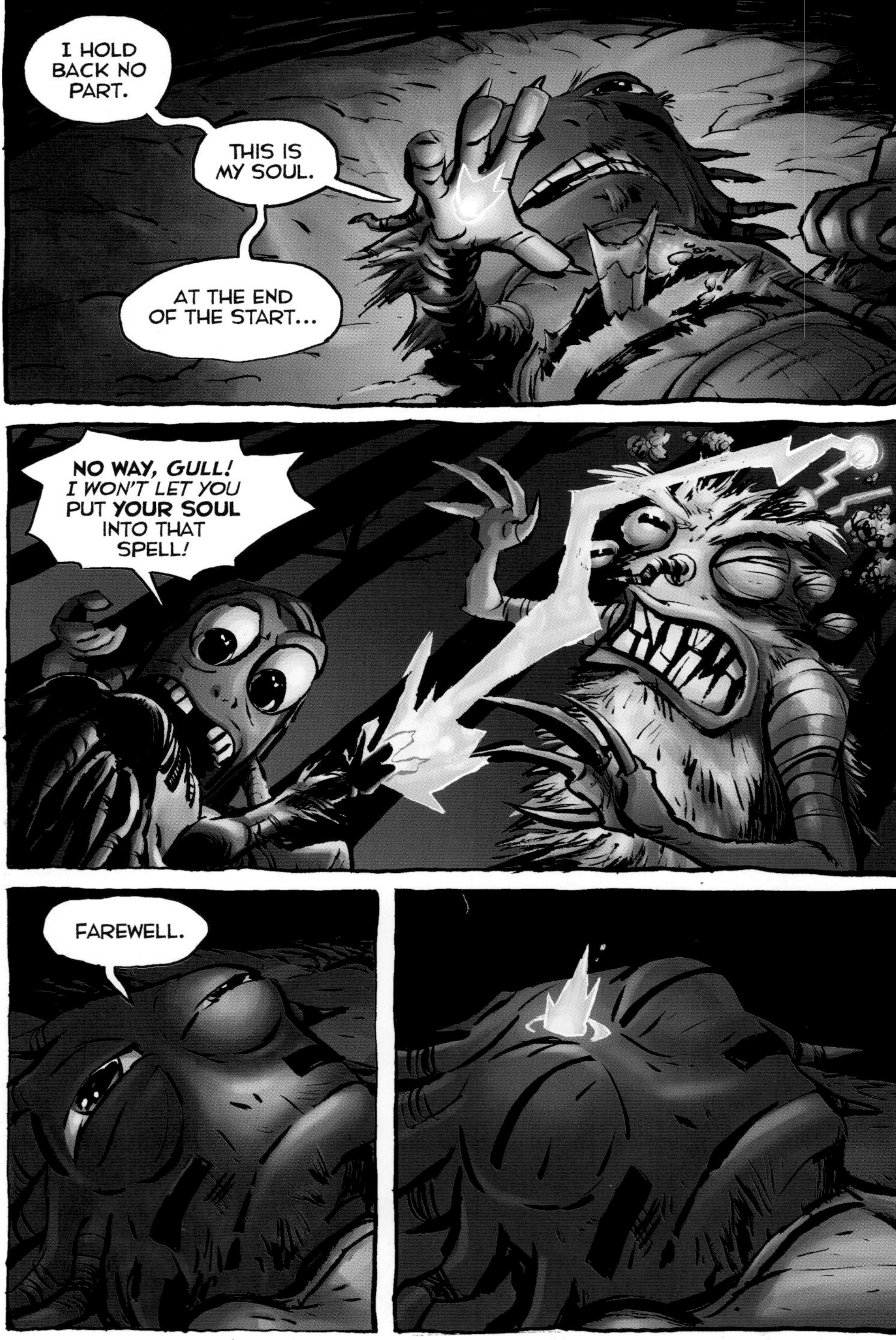
I HOLD BACK NO PART.
THIS IS MY SOUL.
AT THE END OF THE START...
NO WAY, GULL! I WON'T LET YOU PUT YOUR SOUL INTO THAT SPELL!
FAREWELL.

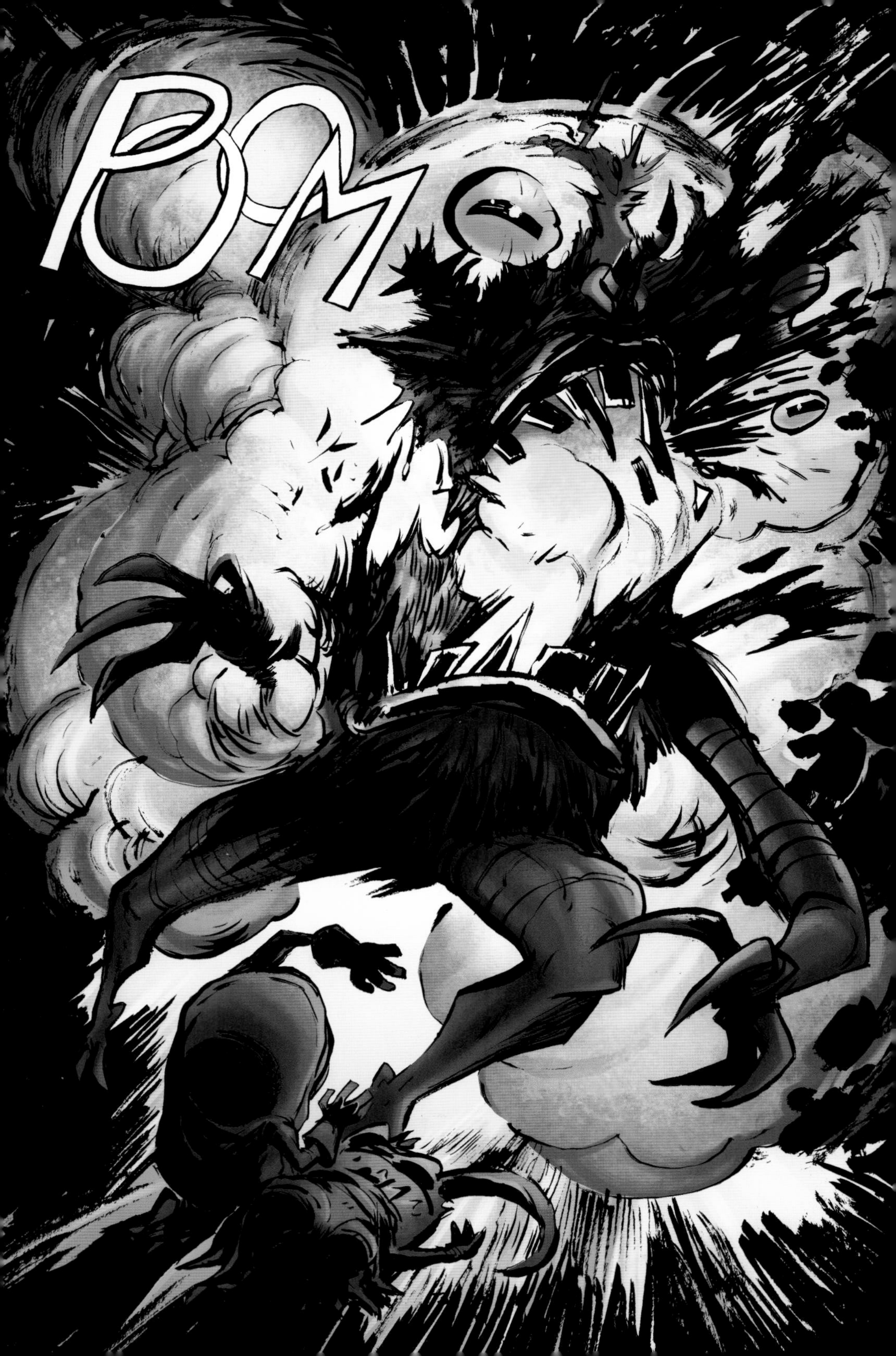
POM

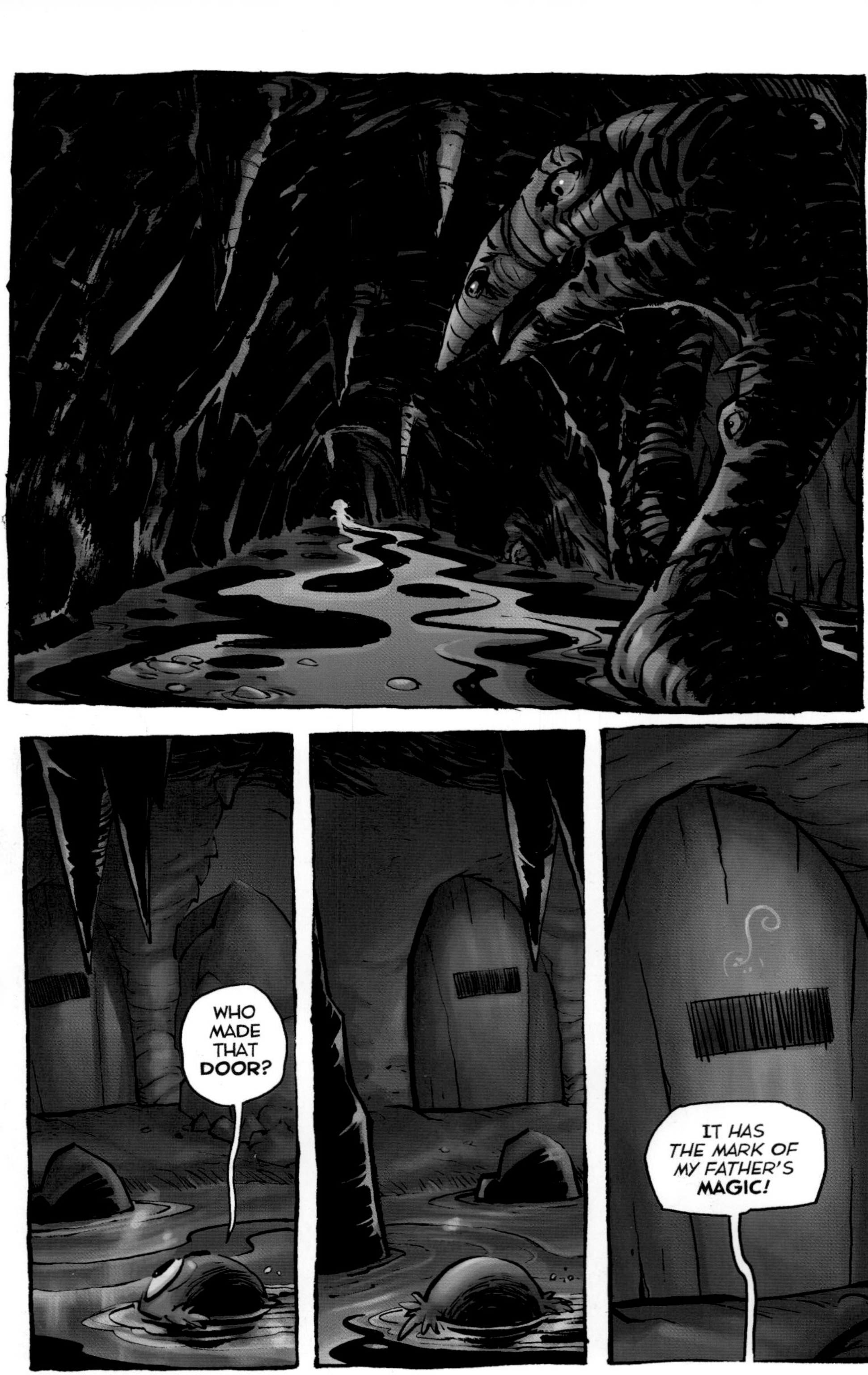
WHO MADE THAT DOOR?
IT HAS THE MARK OF MY FATHER'S MAGIC!

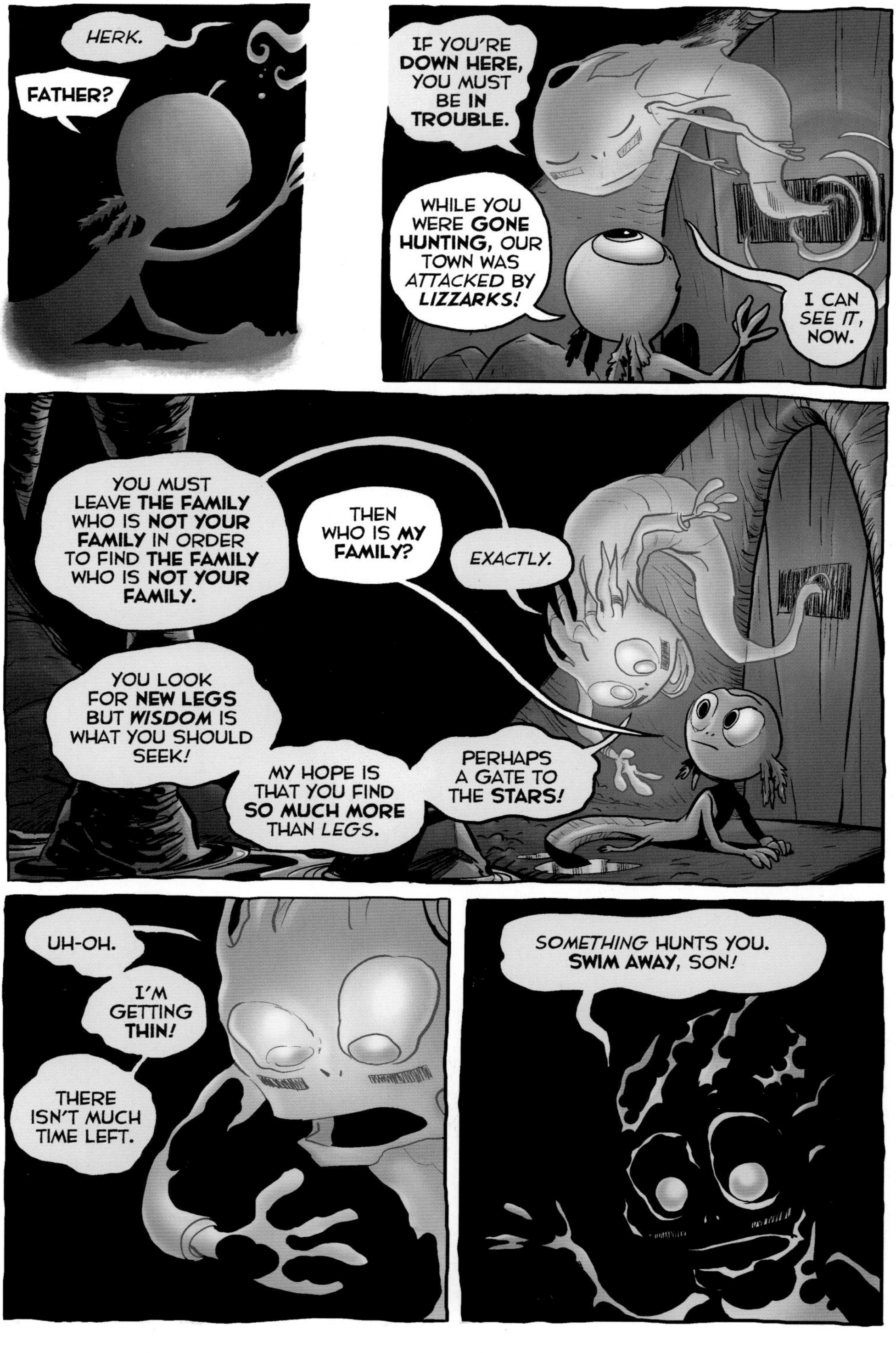
HERK.
FATHER?
IF YOU'RE DOWN HERE, YOU MUST BE IN TROUBLE.
WHILE YOU WERE GONE HUNTING, OUR TOWN WAS ATTACKED BY LIZZARKS!
I CAN SEE IT, NOW.
YOU MUST LEAVE THE FAMILY WHO IS NOT YOUR FAMILY IN ORDER TO FIND THE FAMILY WHO IS NOT YOUR FAMILY.
THEN WHO IS MY FAMILY?
EXACTLY.
YOU LOOK FOR NEW LEGS BUT WISDOM IS WHAT YOU SHOULD SEEK!
MY HOPE IS THAT YOU FIND SO MUCH MORE THAN LEGS.
PERHAPS A GATE TO THE STARS!
UH-OH.
I'M GETTING THIN!
THERE ISN'T MUCH TIME LEFT.
SOMETHING HUNTS YOU. SWIM AWAY, SON!

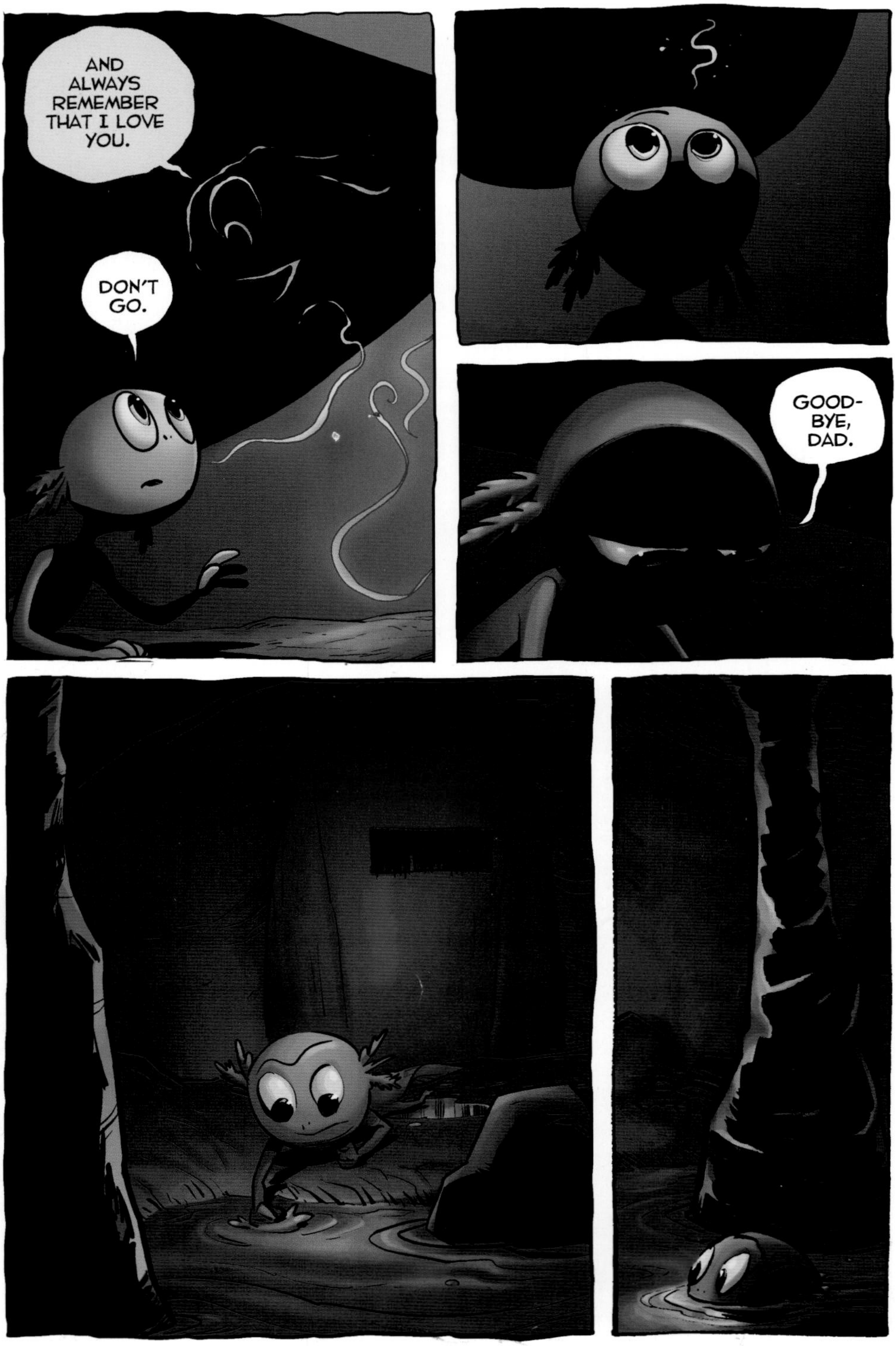
AND ALWAYS REMEMBER THAT I LOVE YOU.
DON'T GO.
GOOD-BYE, DAD.

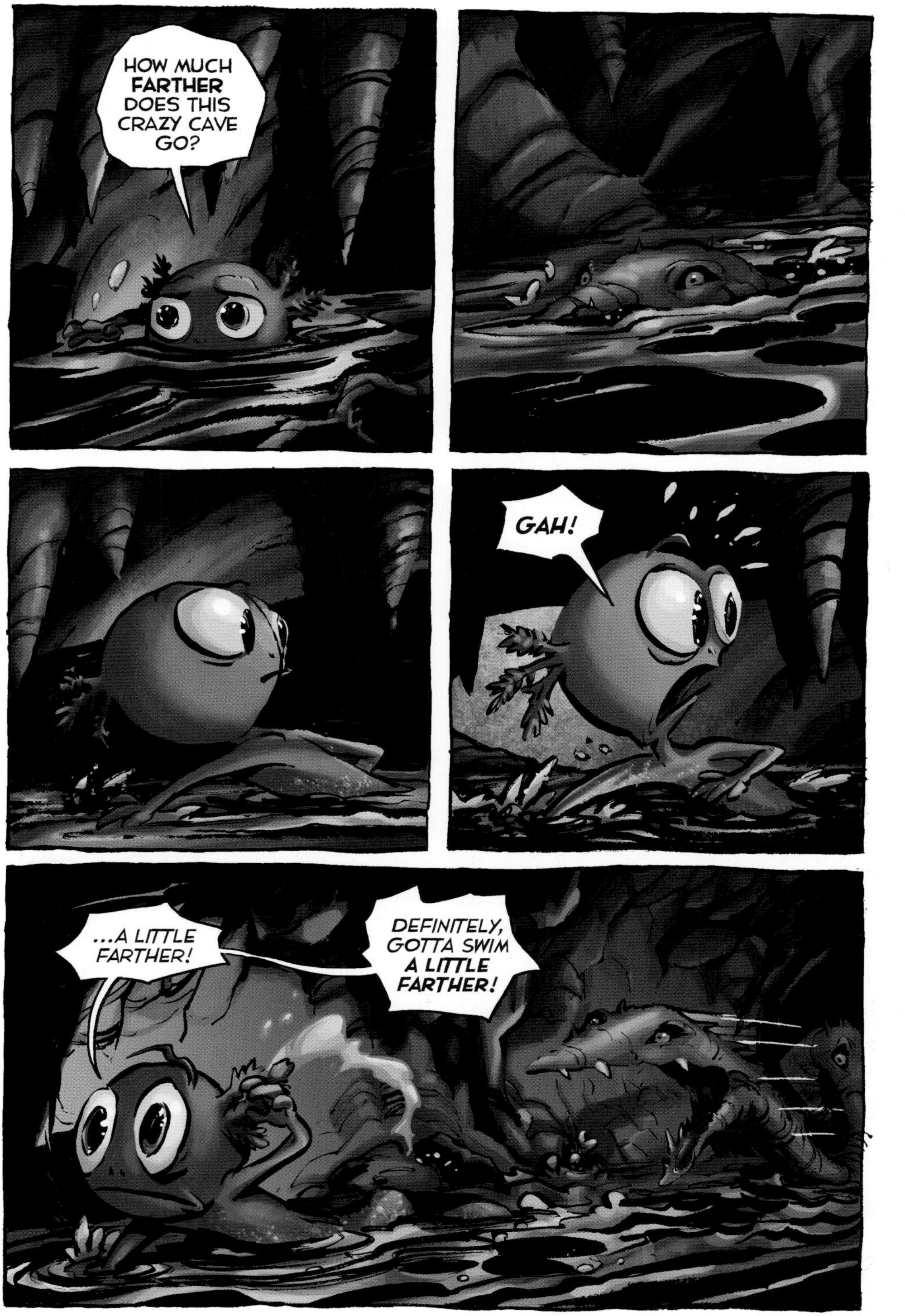
HOW MUCH FARTHER DOES THIS CRAZY CAVE GO?
GAH!
...A LITTLE FARTHER!
DEFINITELY, GOTTA SWIM A LITTLE FARTHER!

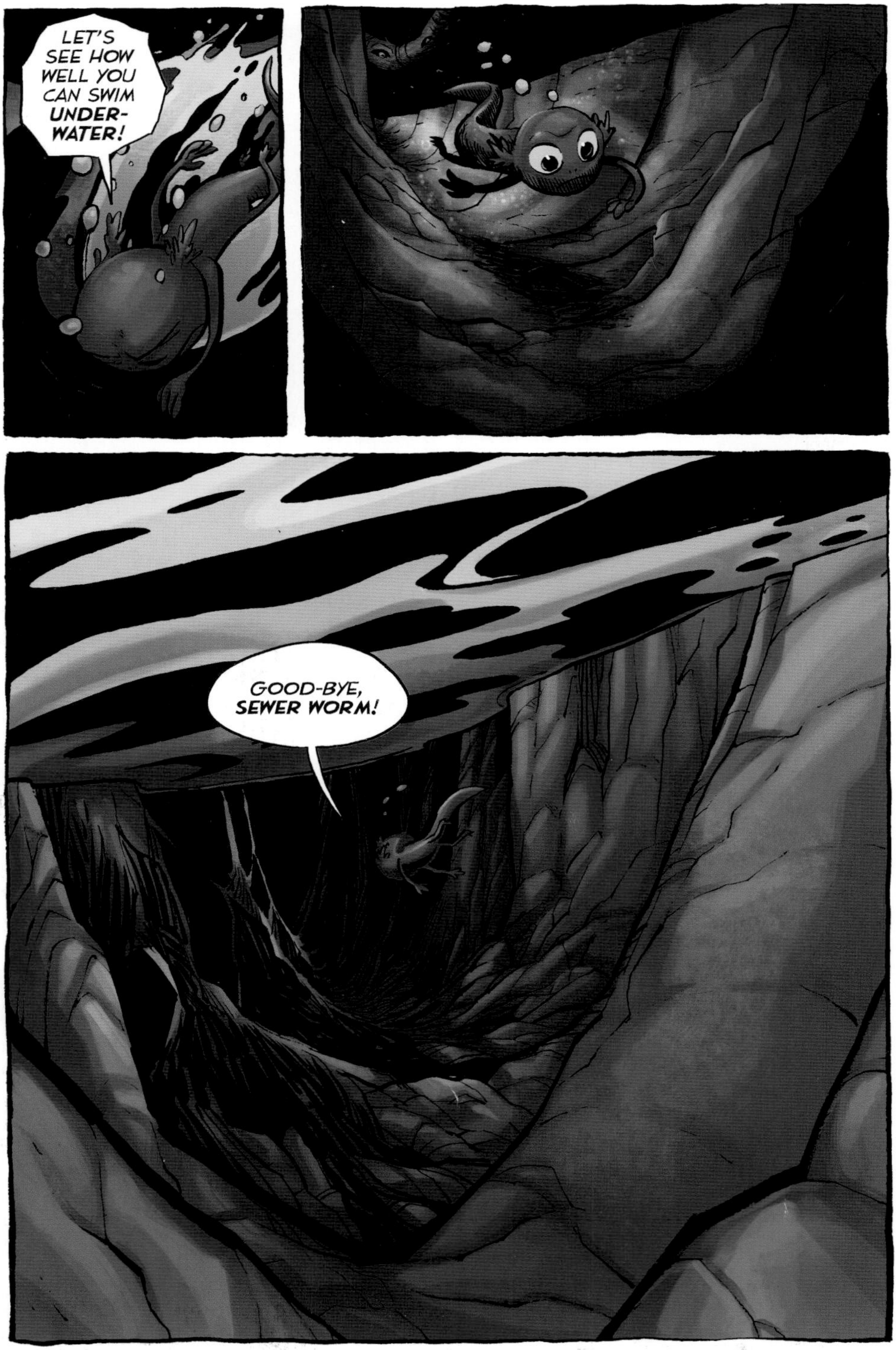
LET'S SEE HOW WELL YOU CAN SWIM UNDER-WATER!
GOOD-BYE, SEWER WORM!

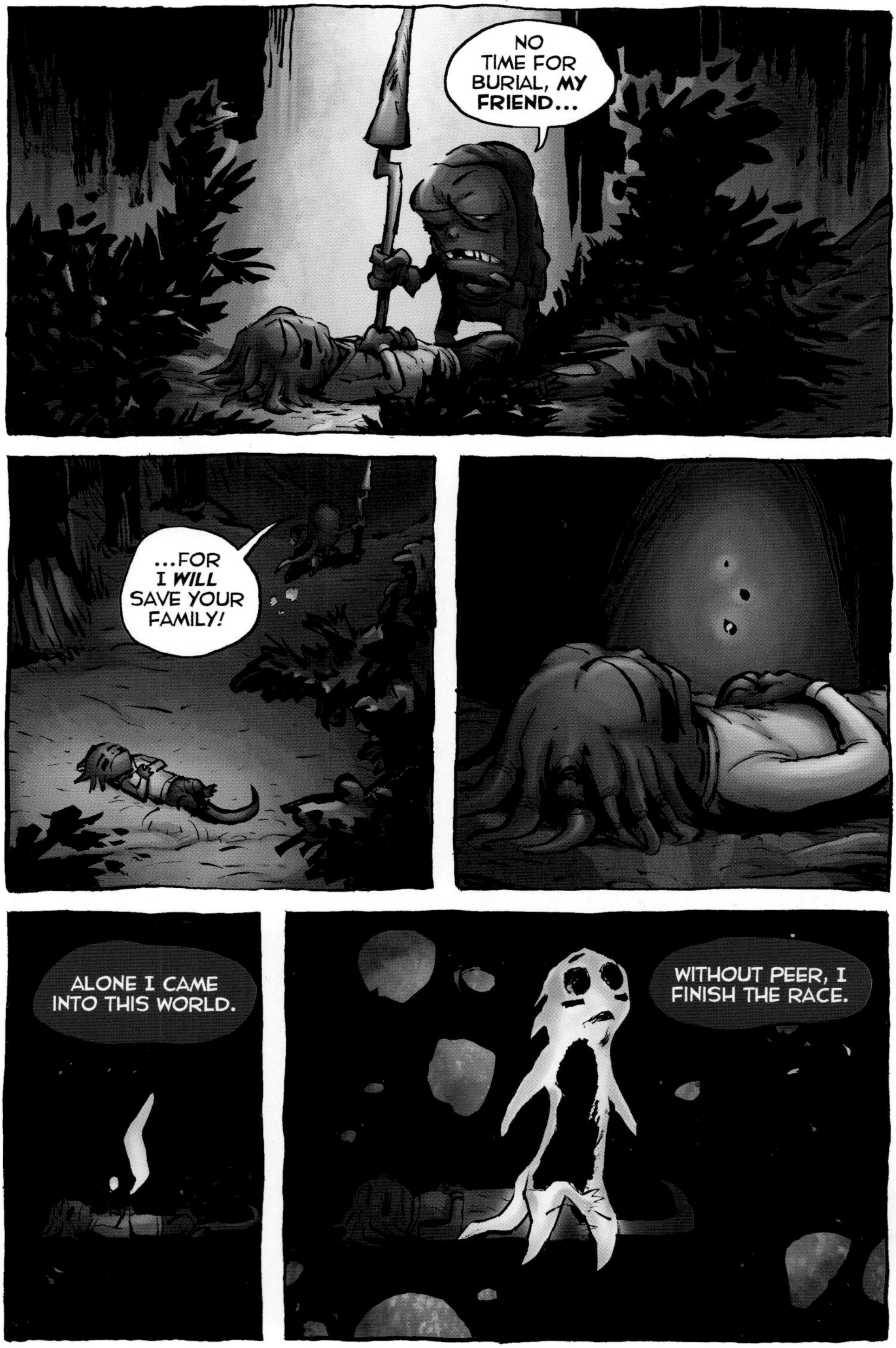
NO TIME FOR BURIAL, **MY FRIEND...**
...FOR I ***WILL*** SAVE YOUR FAMILY!
ALONE I CAME INTO THIS WORLD.
WITHOUT PEER, I FINISH THE RACE.

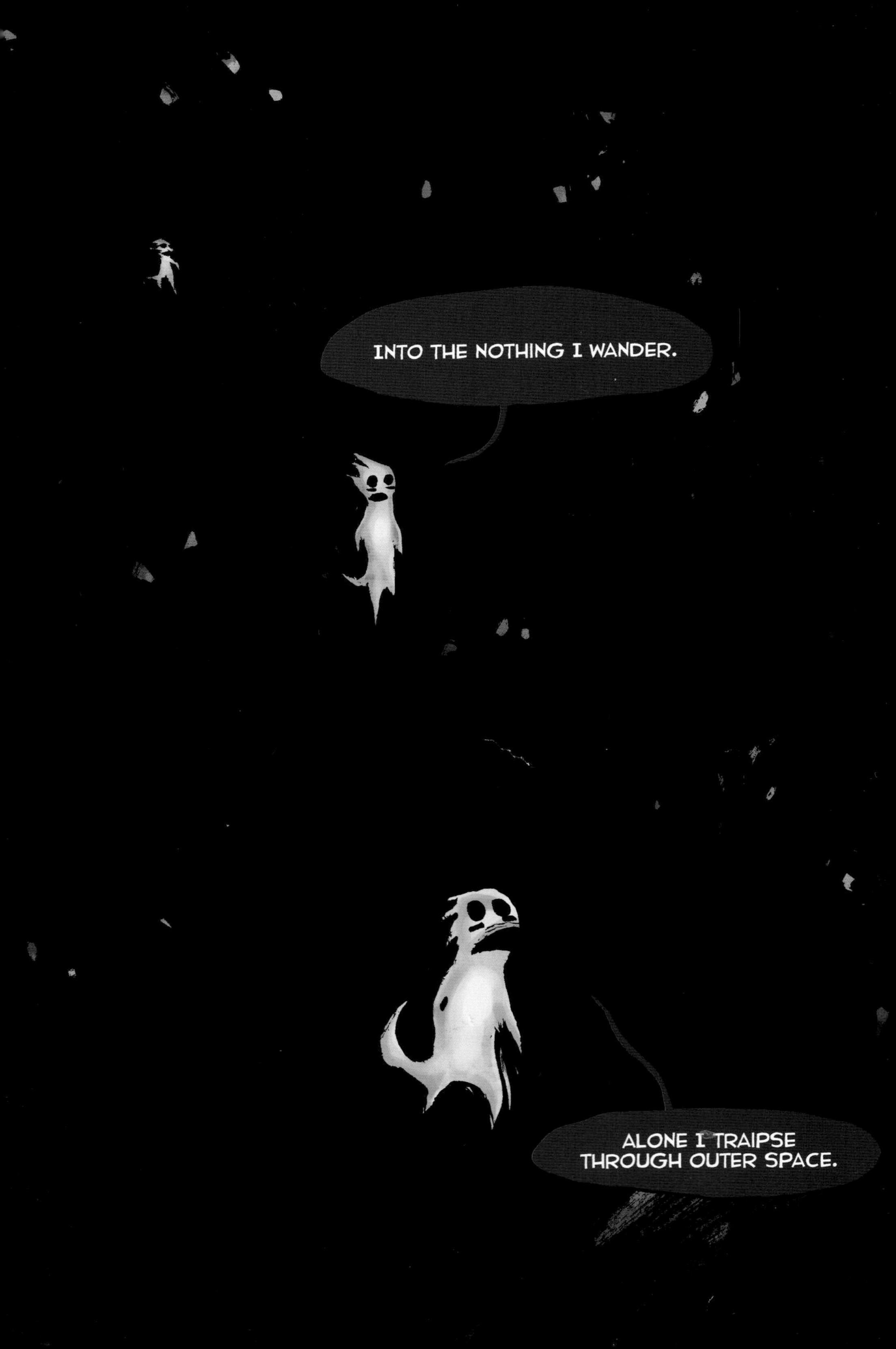
INTO THE NOTHING I WANDER.
ALONE I TRAIPSE THROUGH OUTER SPACE.

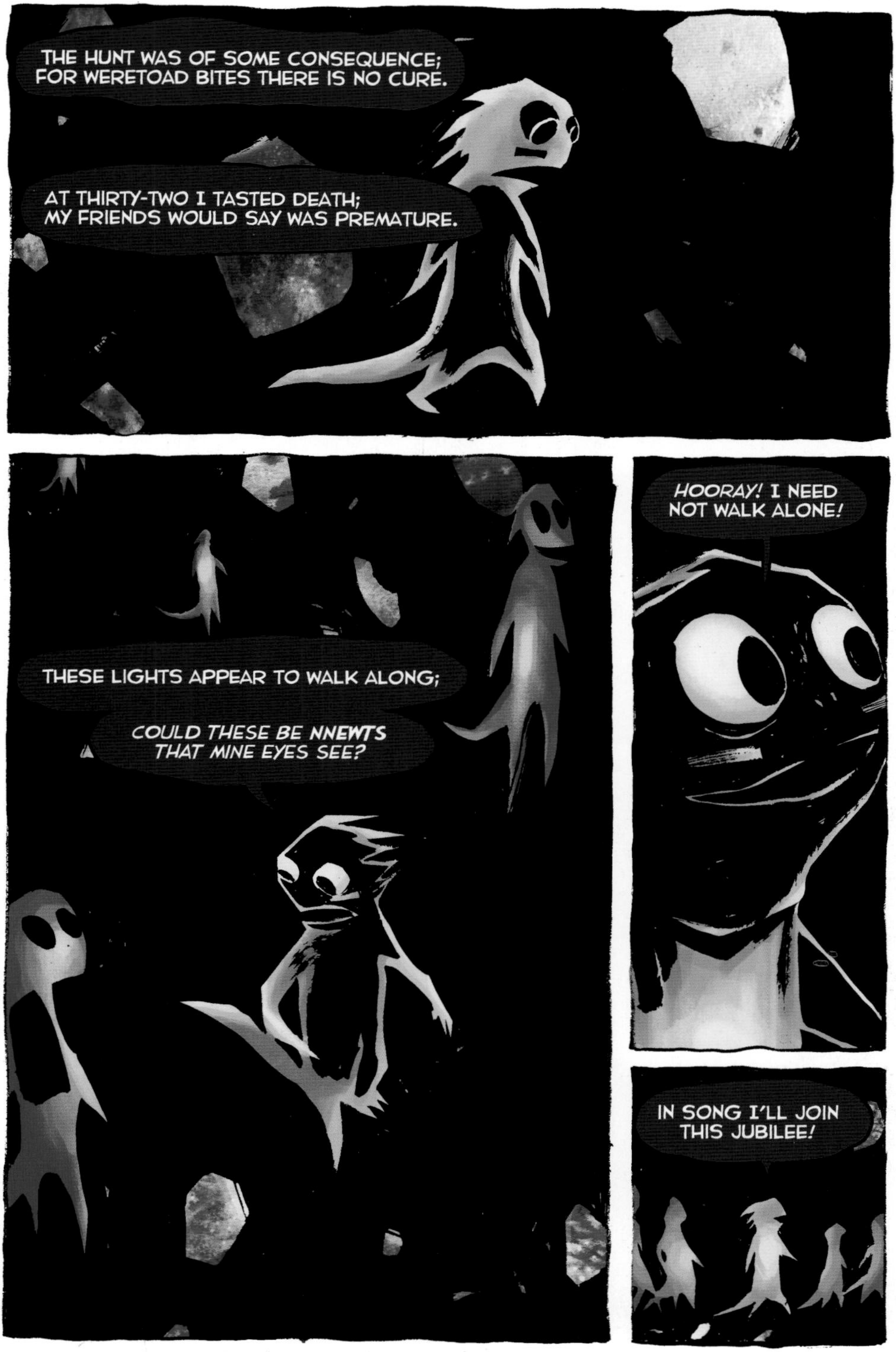
THE HUNT WAS OF SOME CONSEQUENCE; FOR WERETOAD BITES THERE IS NO CURE.
AT THIRTY-TWO I TASTED DEATH; MY FRIENDS WOULD SAY WAS PREMATURE.
THESE LIGHTS APPEAR TO WALK ALONG;
*COULD THESE BE **NNEWTS** THAT MINE EYES SEE?*
HOORAY! I NEED NOT WALK ALONE!
IN SONG I'LL JOIN THIS JUBILEE!

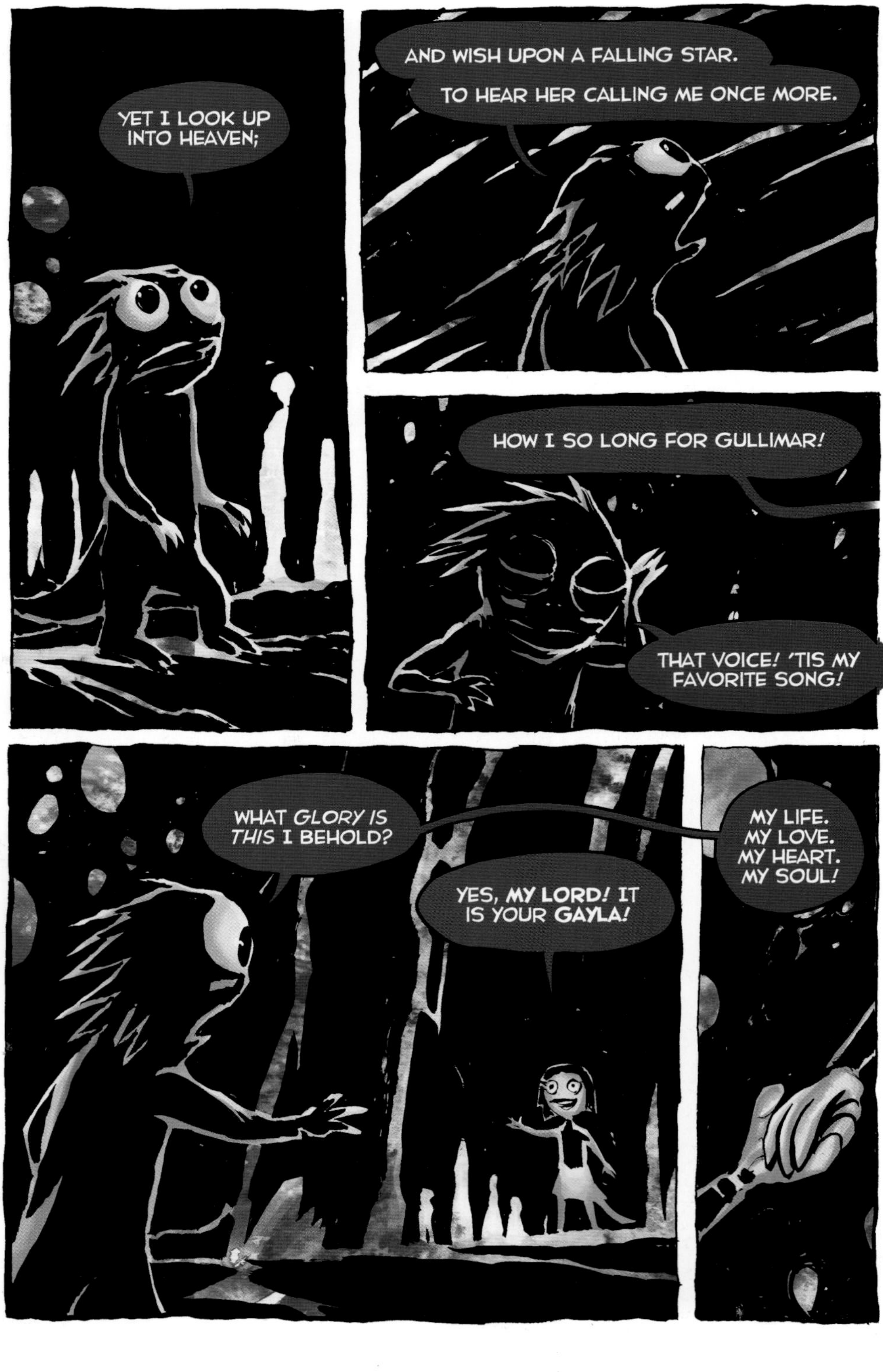
YET I LOOK UP INTO HEAVEN;
AND WISH UPON A FALLING STAR.
TO HEAR HER CALLING ME ONCE MORE.
HOW I SO LONG FOR GULLIMAR!
THAT VOICE! 'TIS MY FAVORITE SONG!
WHAT GLORY IS THIS I BEHOLD?
MY LIFE. MY LOVE. MY HEART. MY SOUL!
YES, MY LORD! IT IS YOUR GAYLA!

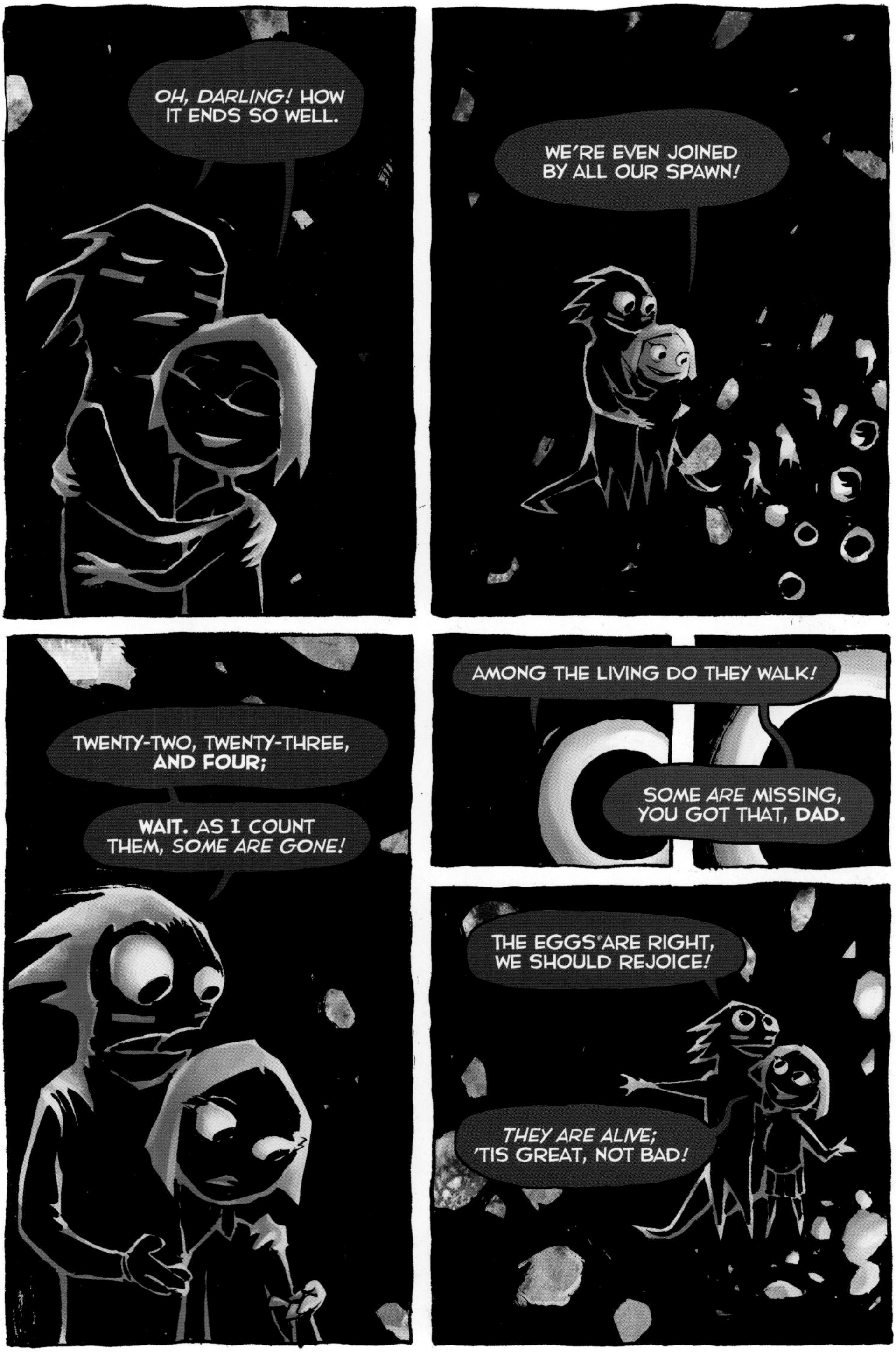
OH, DARLING! HOW IT ENDS SO WELL.
WE'RE EVEN JOINED BY ALL OUR SPAWN!
TWENTY-TWO, TWENTY-THREE, AND FOUR;
WAIT. AS I COUNT THEM, SOME ARE GONE!
AMONG THE LIVING DO THEY WALK!
SOME ARE MISSING, YOU GOT THAT, DAD.
THE EGGS ARE RIGHT, WE SHOULD REJOICE!
THEY ARE ALIVE; 'TIS GREAT, NOT BAD!

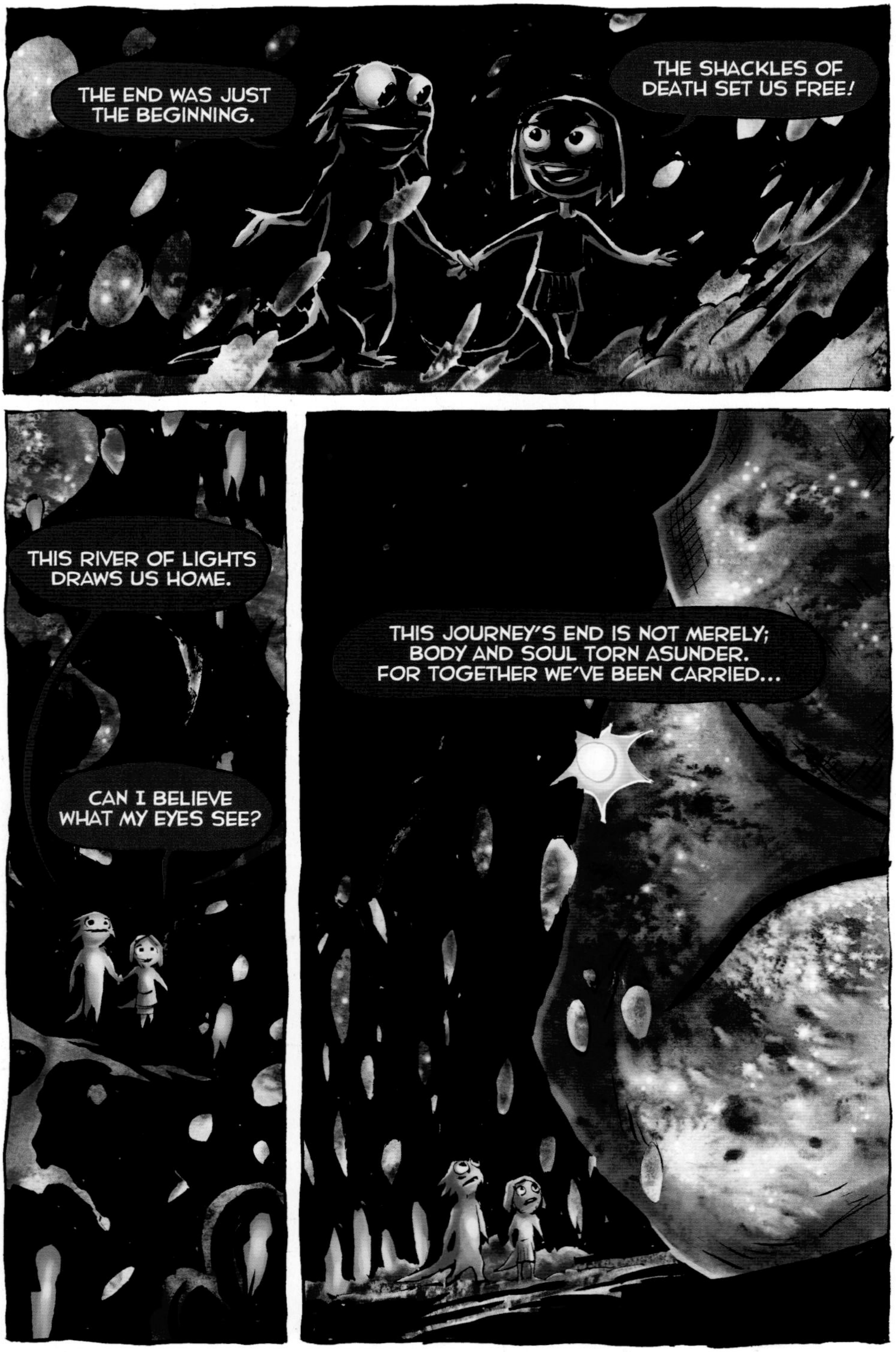
THE END WAS JUST THE BEGINNING.
THE SHACKLES OF DEATH SET US FREE!
THIS RIVER OF LIGHTS DRAWS US HOME.
CAN I BELIEVE WHAT MY EYES SEE?
THIS JOURNEY'S END IS NOT MERELY; BODY AND SOUL TORN ASUNDER. FOR TOGETHER WE'VE BEEN CARRIED...

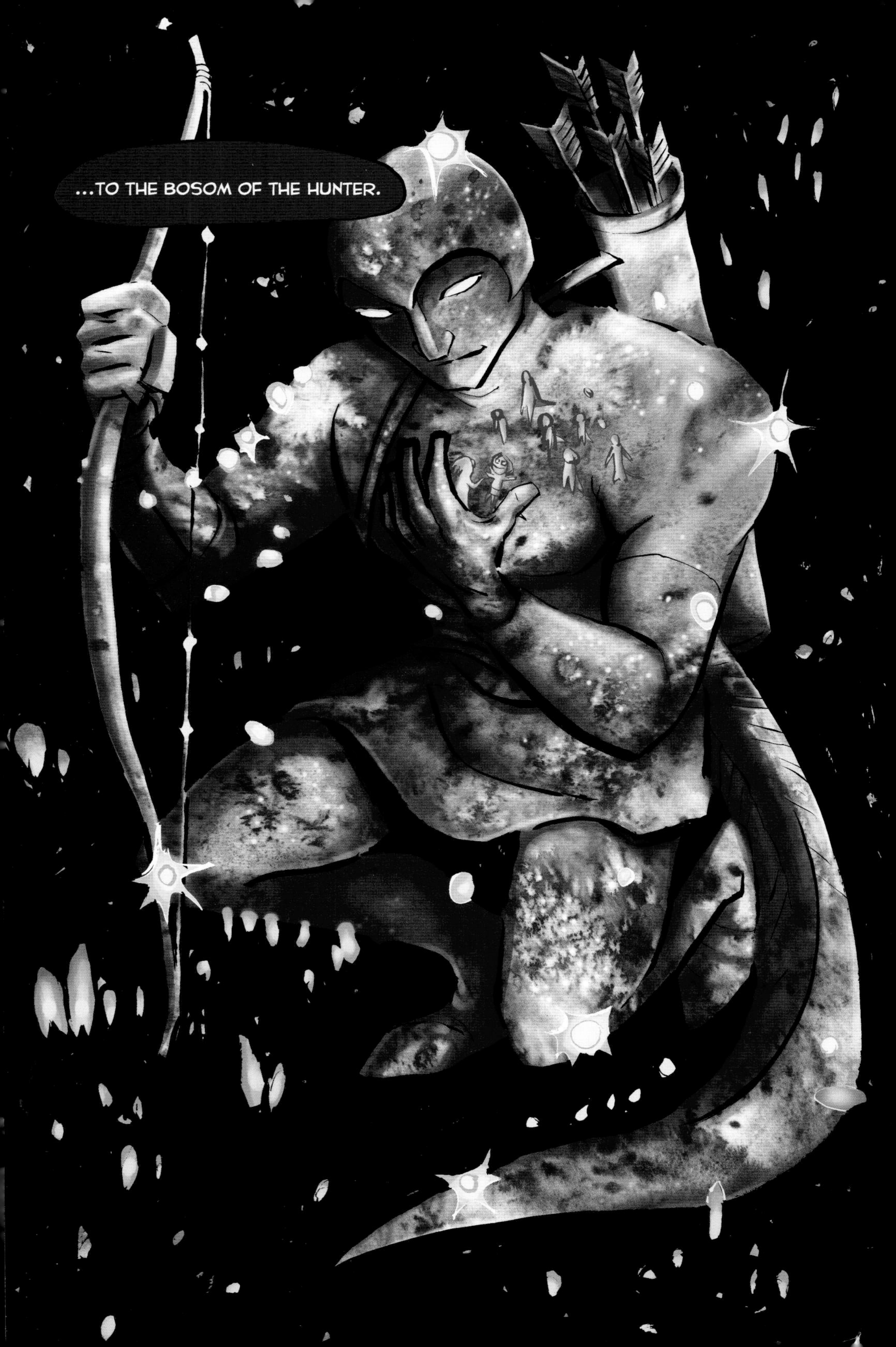
...TO THE BOSOM OF THE HUNTER.

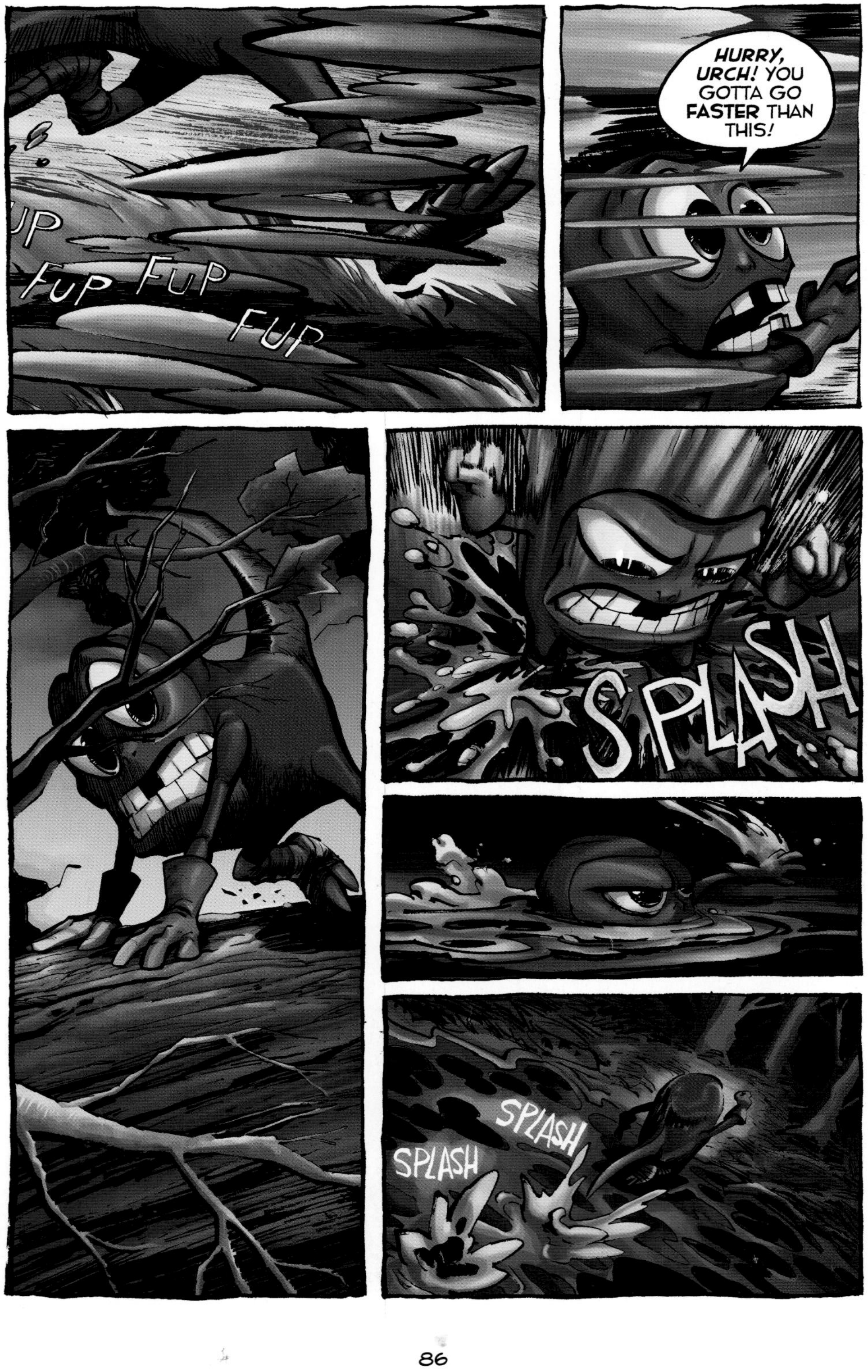
FUP
FUP FUP
FUP
HURRY, URCH! YOU GOTTA GO FASTER THAN THIS!
SPLASH
SPLASH
SPLASH

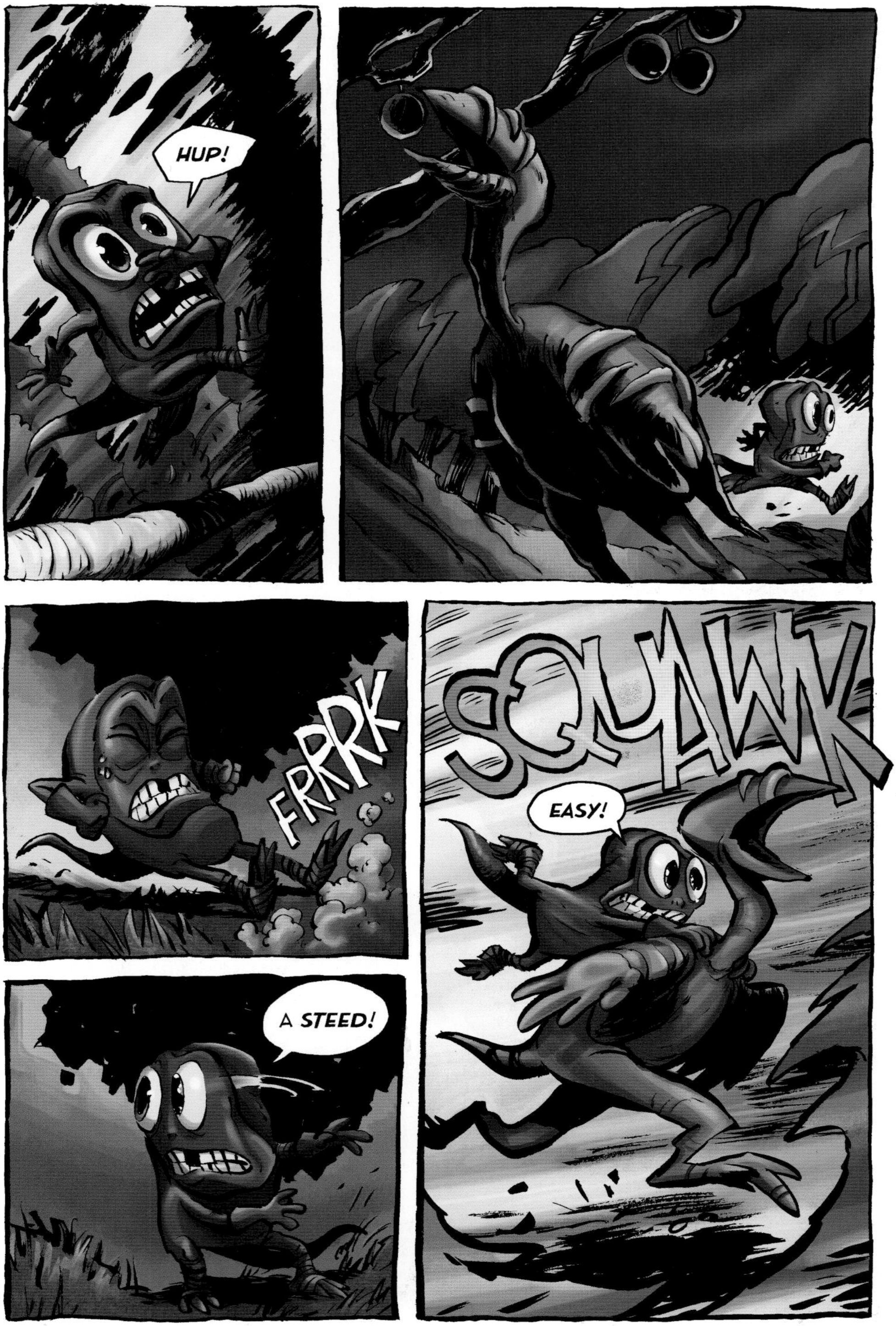
HUP!
FRRRK
A STEED!
SQUAWK
EASY!

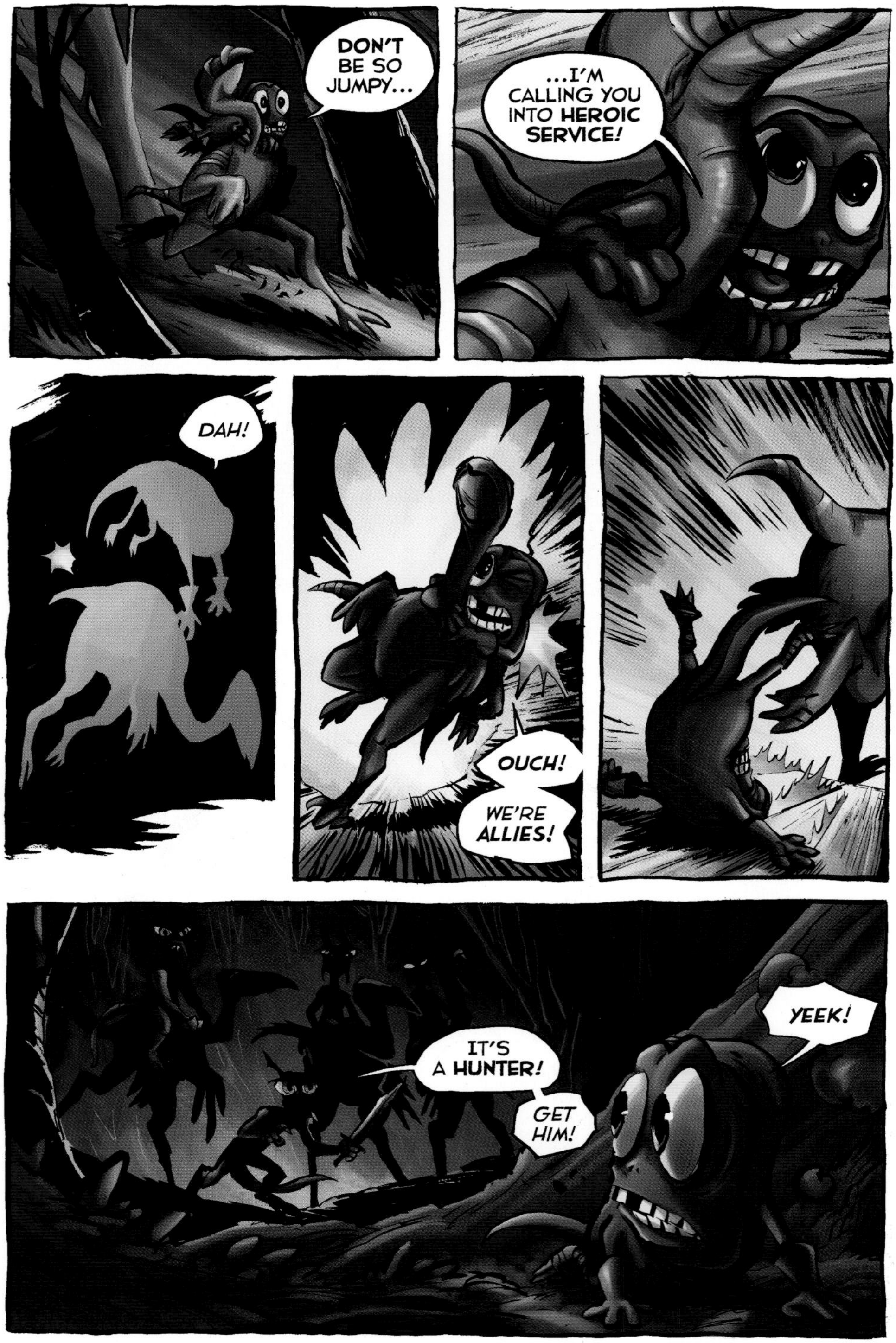
DON'T BE SO JUMPY...
...I'M CALLING YOU INTO HEROIC SERVICE!
DAH!
OUCH!
WE'RE ALLIES!
IT'S A HUNTER!
GET HIM!
YEEK!

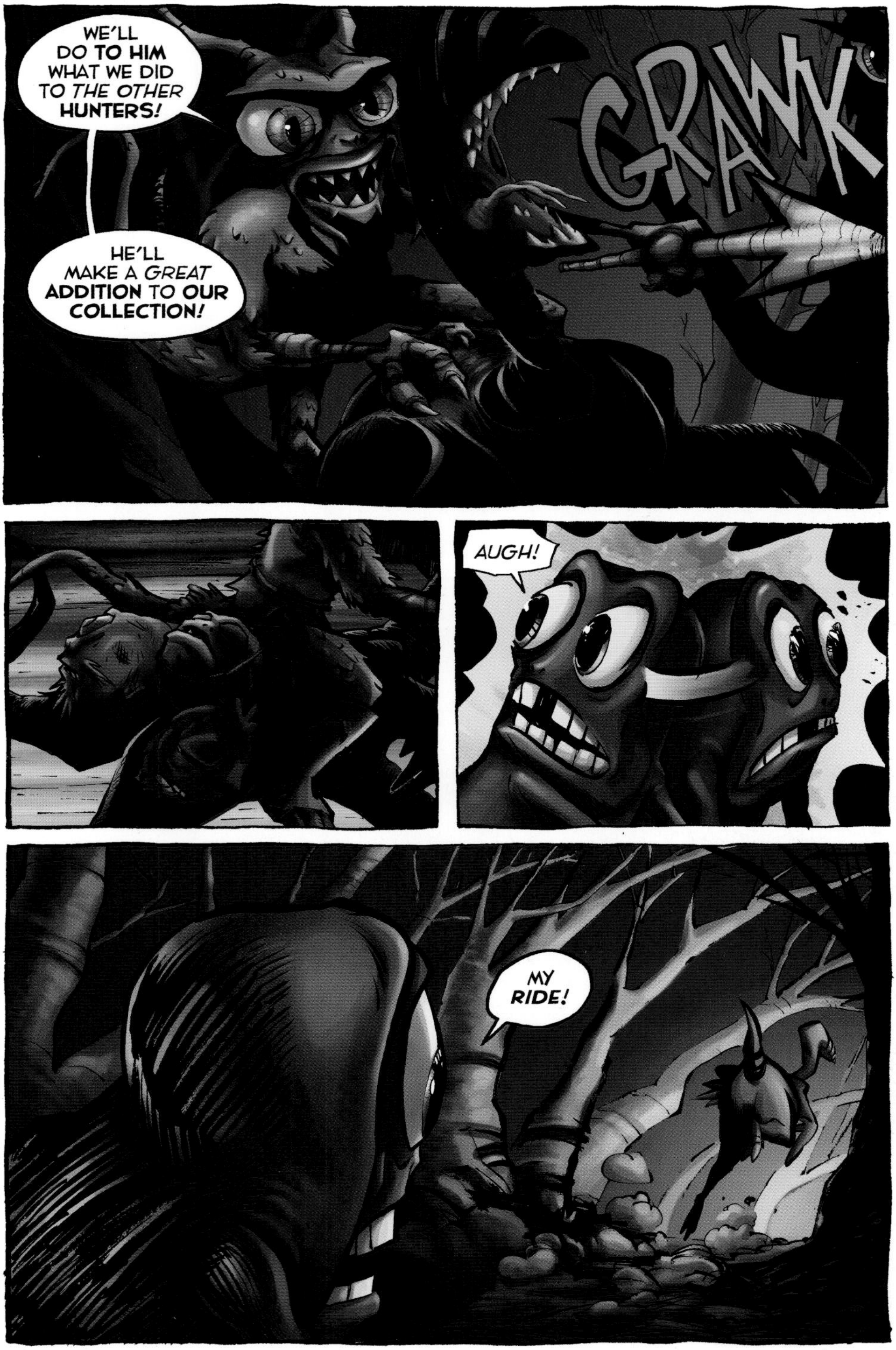
WE'LL DO TO HIM WHAT WE DID TO THE OTHER HUNTERS!
HE'LL MAKE A GREAT ADDITION TO OUR COLLECTION!
GRAWK
AUGH!
MY RIDE!

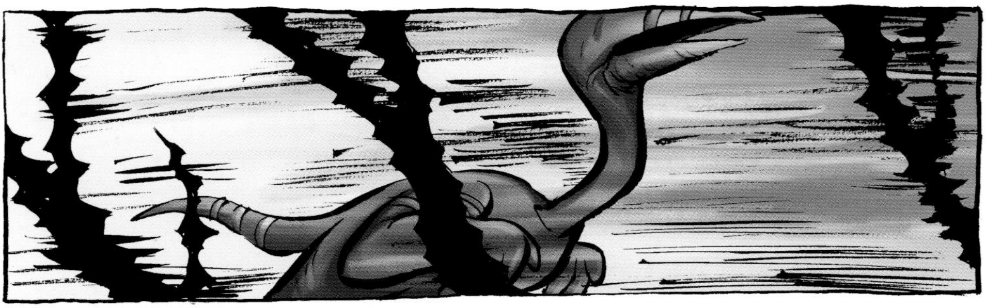

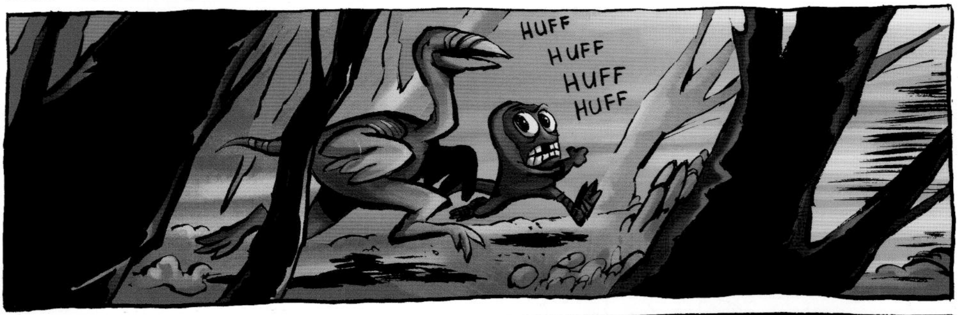
HUFF
HUFF
HUFF
HUFF

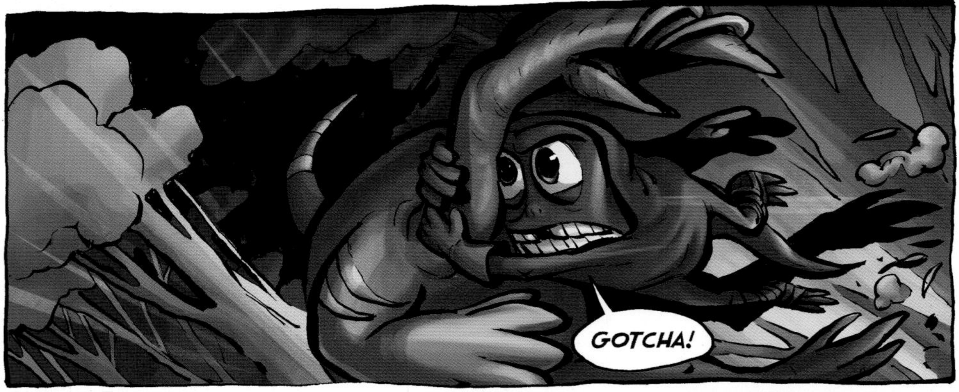
GOTCHA!

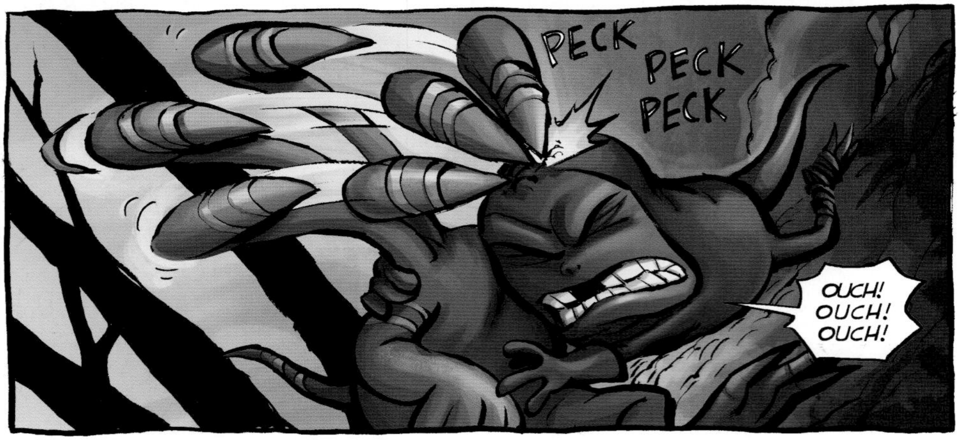
PECK
PECK
PECK
OUCH!
OUCH!
OUCH!

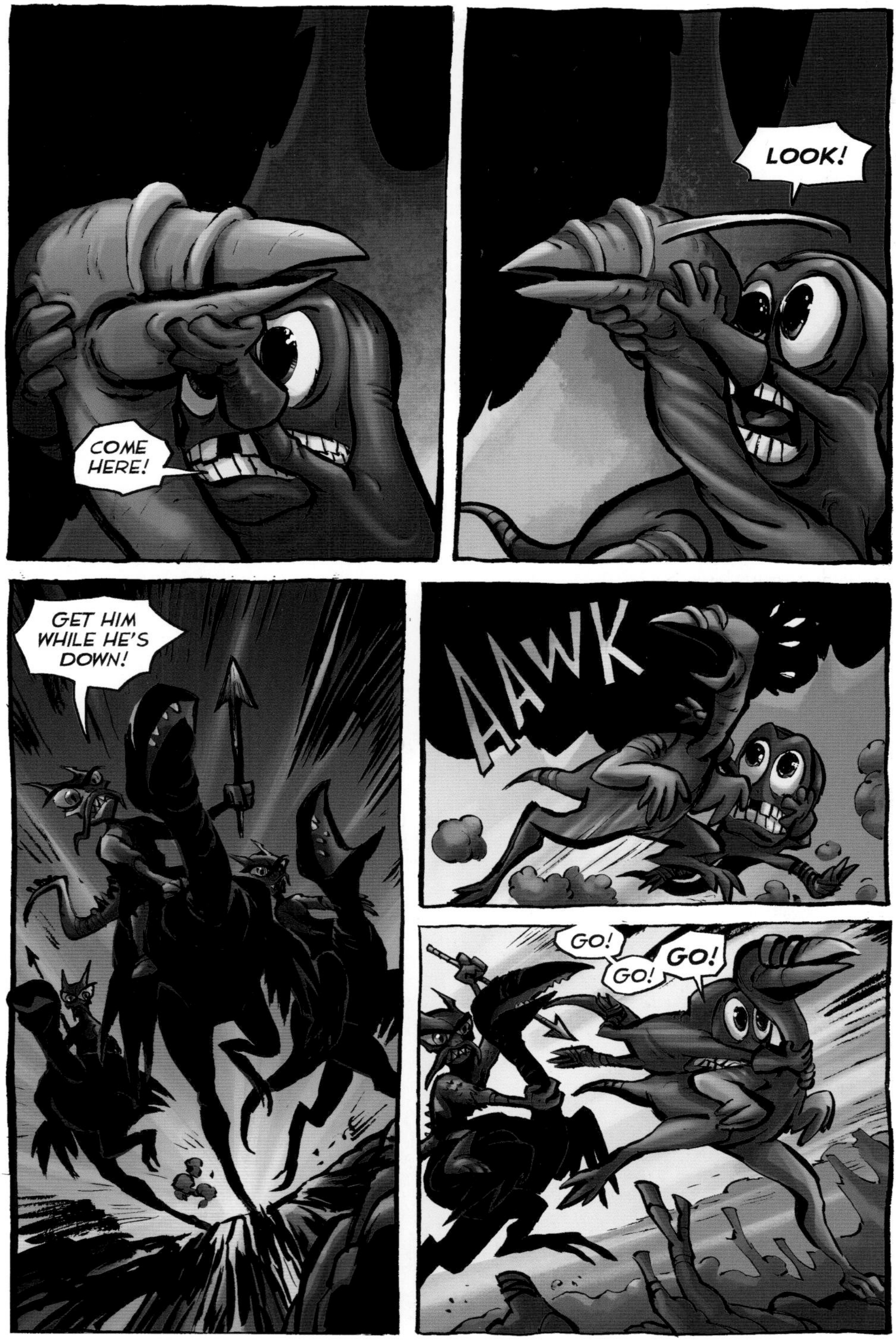
COME HERE!
LOOK!
GET HIM WHILE HE'S DOWN!
AAWK
GO!
GO!
GO!

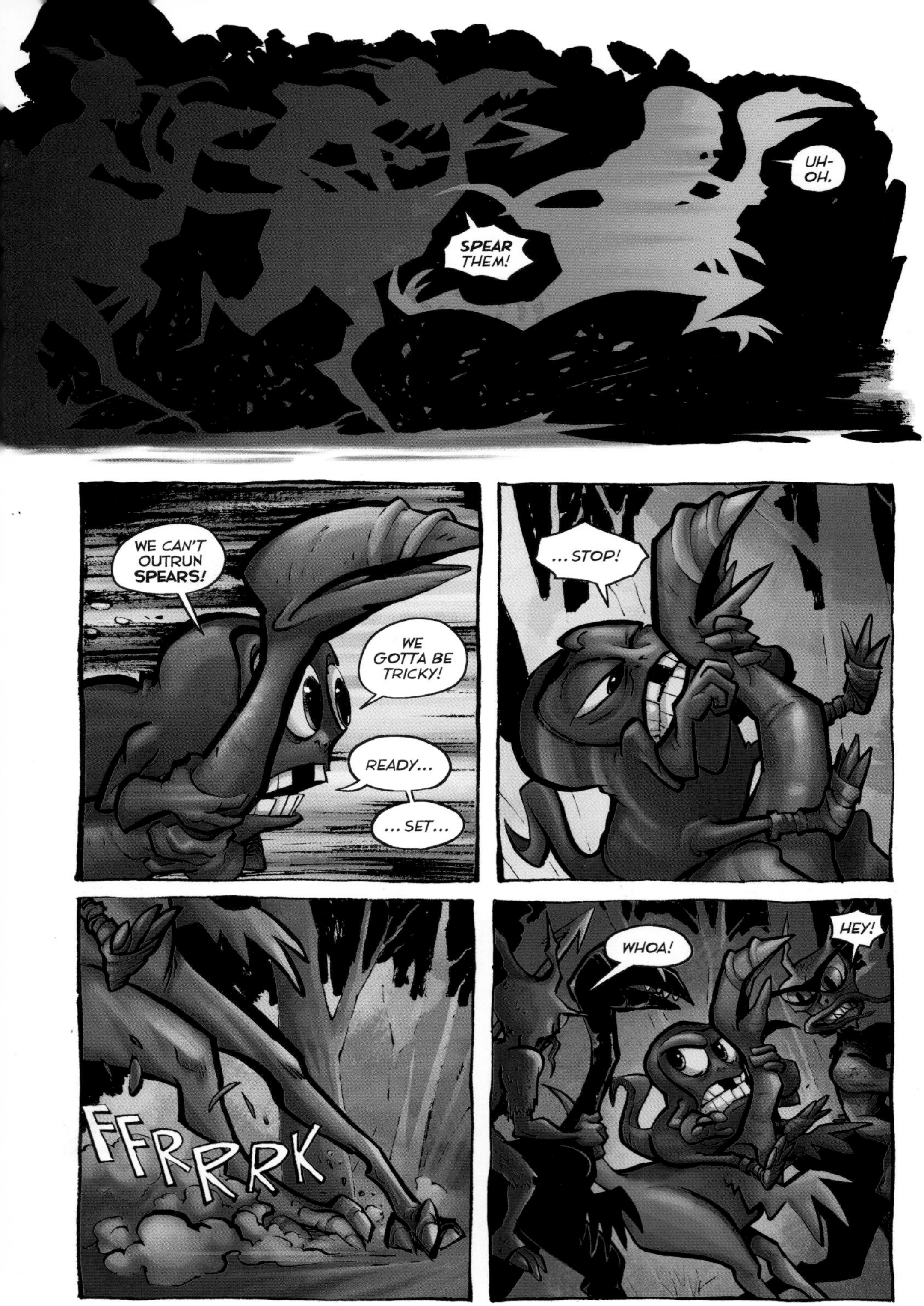
UH-OH.
SPEAR THEM!
WE CAN'T OUTRUN SPEARS!
WE GOTTA BE TRICKY!
READY...
...SET...
...STOP!
FFRRRK
WHOA!
HEY!

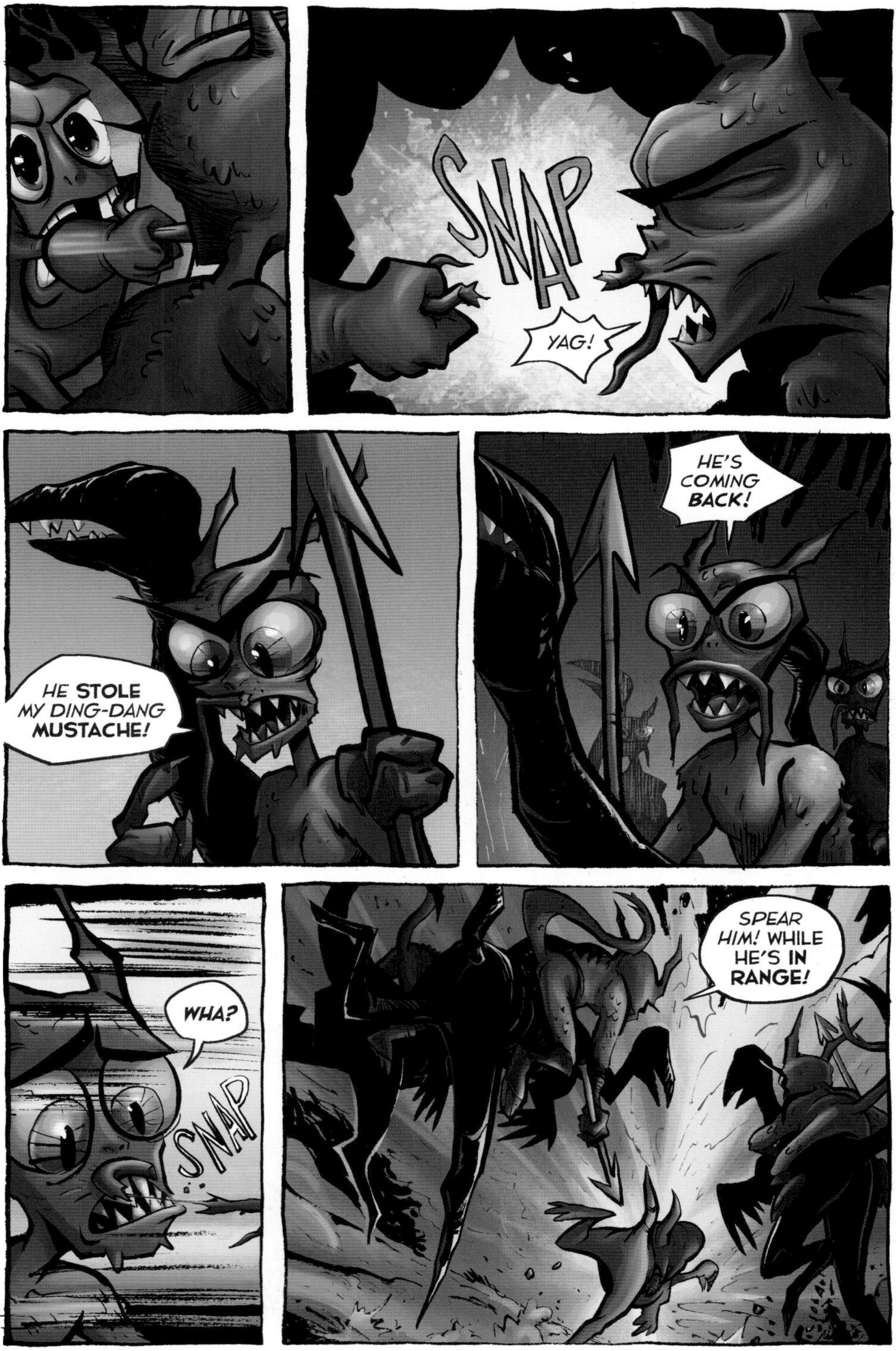
SNAP
YAG!
HE STOLE MY DING-DANG MUSTACHE!
HE'S COMING BACK!
WHA?
SNAP
SPEAR HIM! WHILE HE'S IN RANGE!

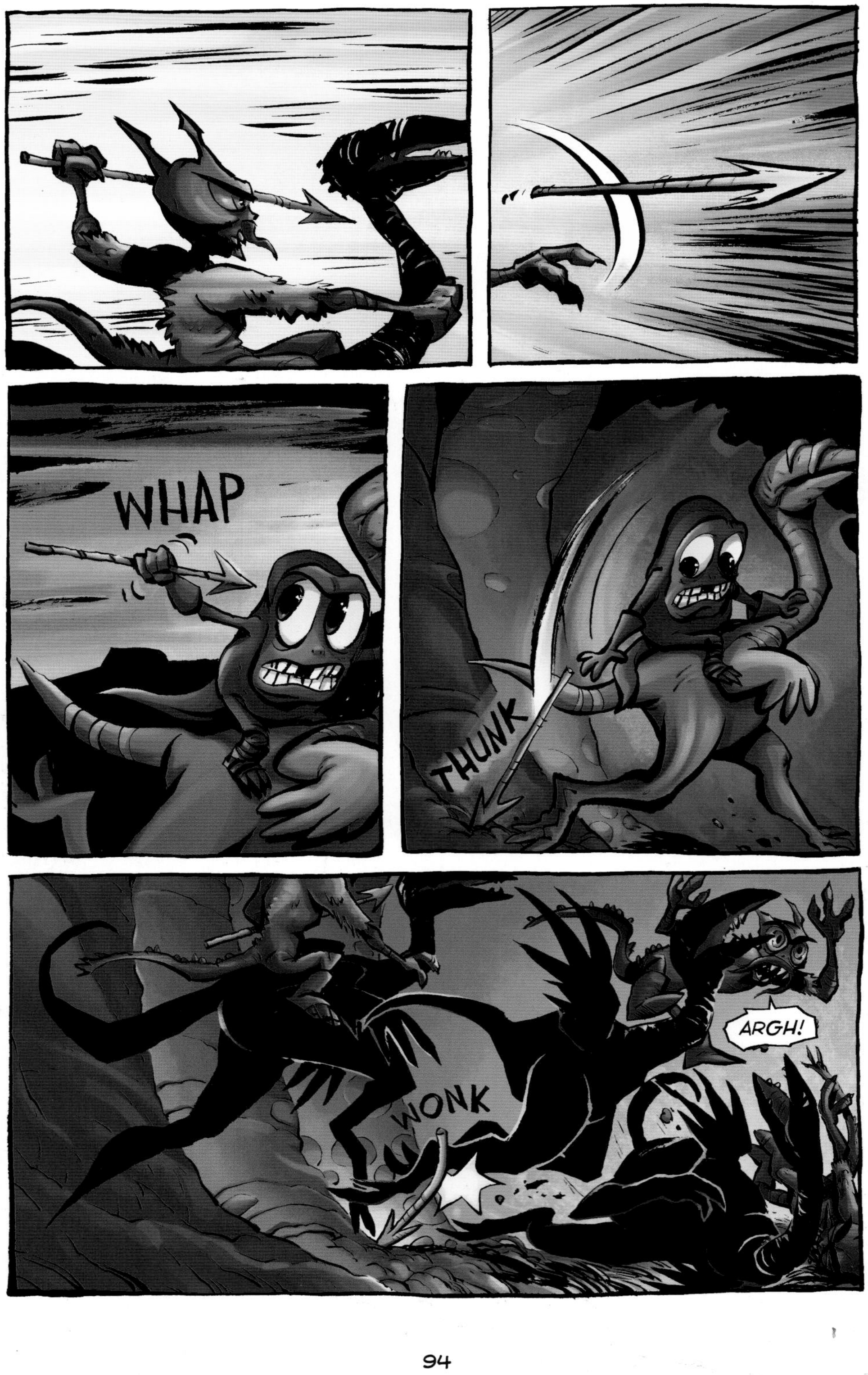
WHAP
THUNK
ARGH!
WONK

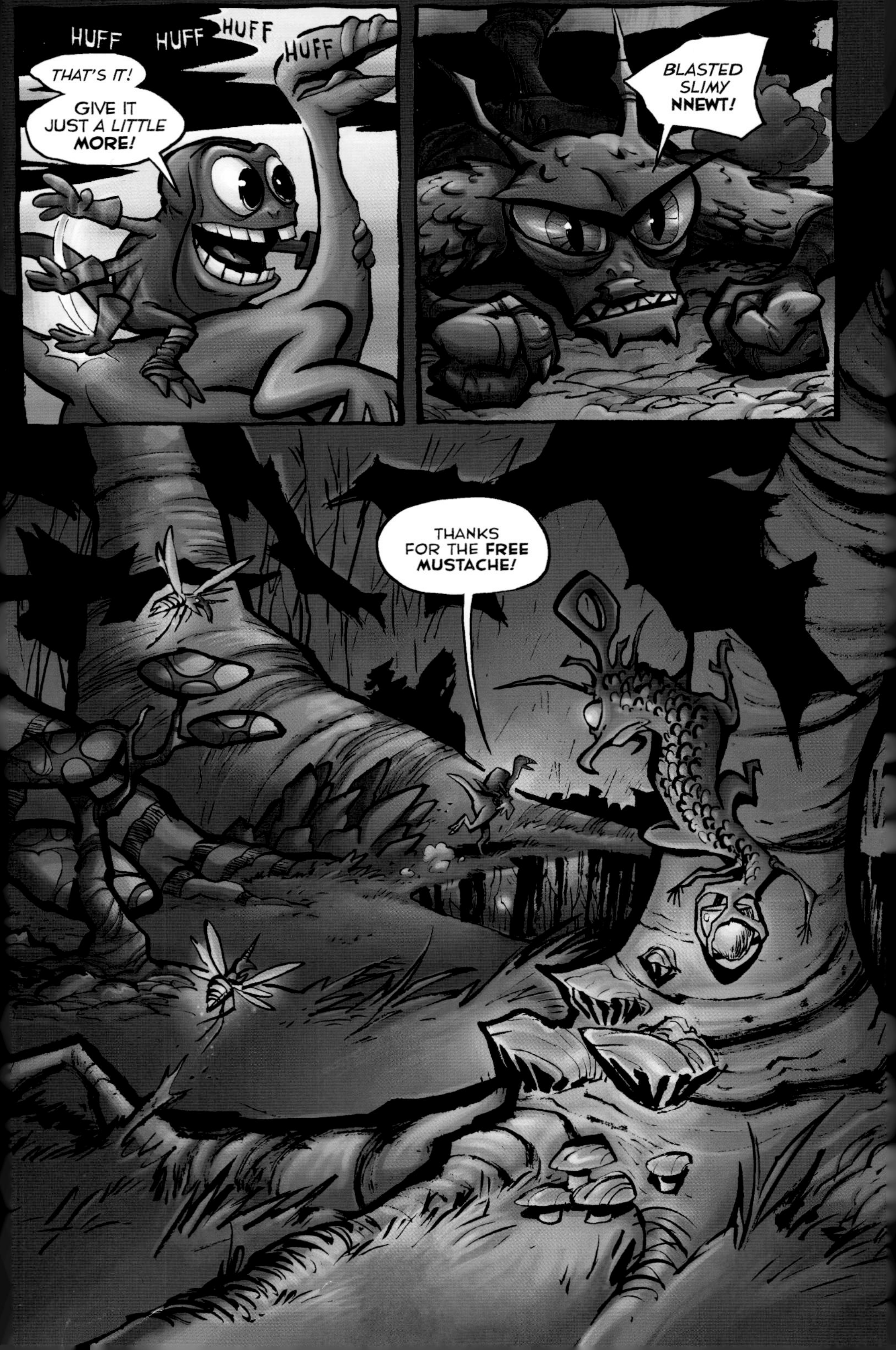
HUFF HUFF HUFF HUFF
THAT'S IT!
GIVE IT JUST A *LITTLE* **MORE!**
BLASTED SLIMY **NNEWT!**
THANKS FOR THE **FREE MUSTACHE!**

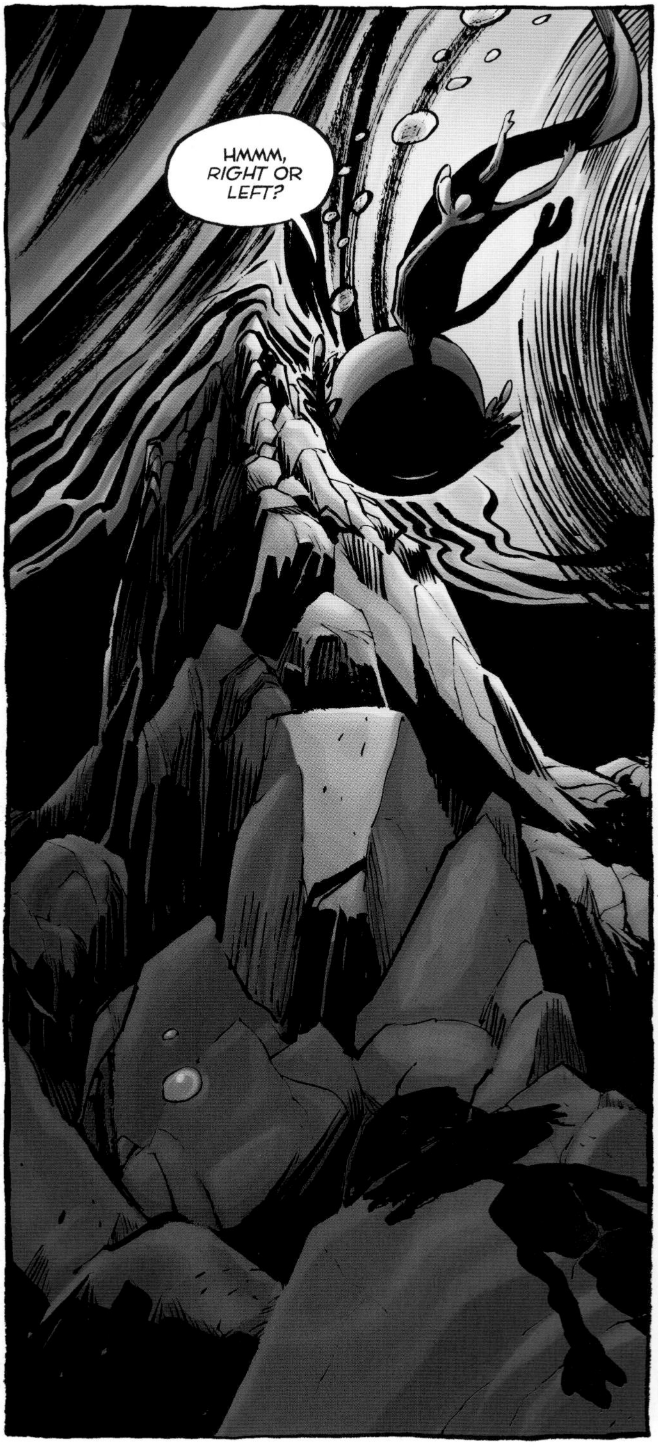
HMMM, RIGHT OR LEFT?

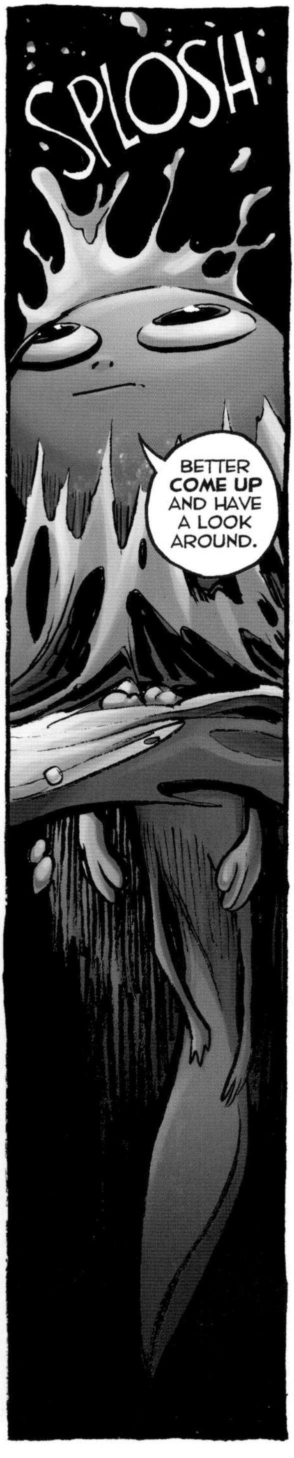
SPLOSH
BETTER COME UP AND HAVE A LOOK AROUND.

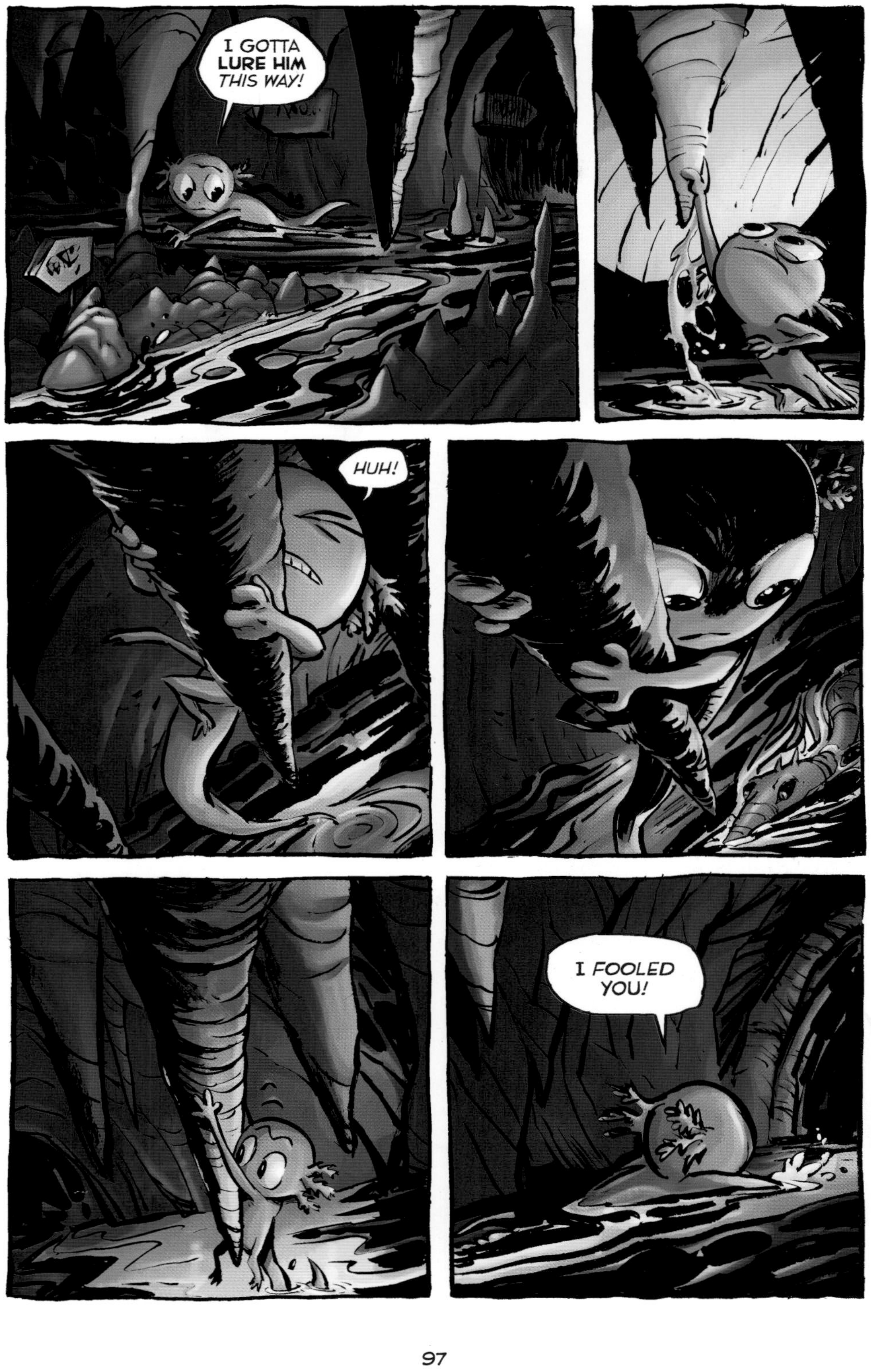
I GOTTA **LURE HIM** *THIS WAY!*
HUH!
I *FOOLED* *YOU!*

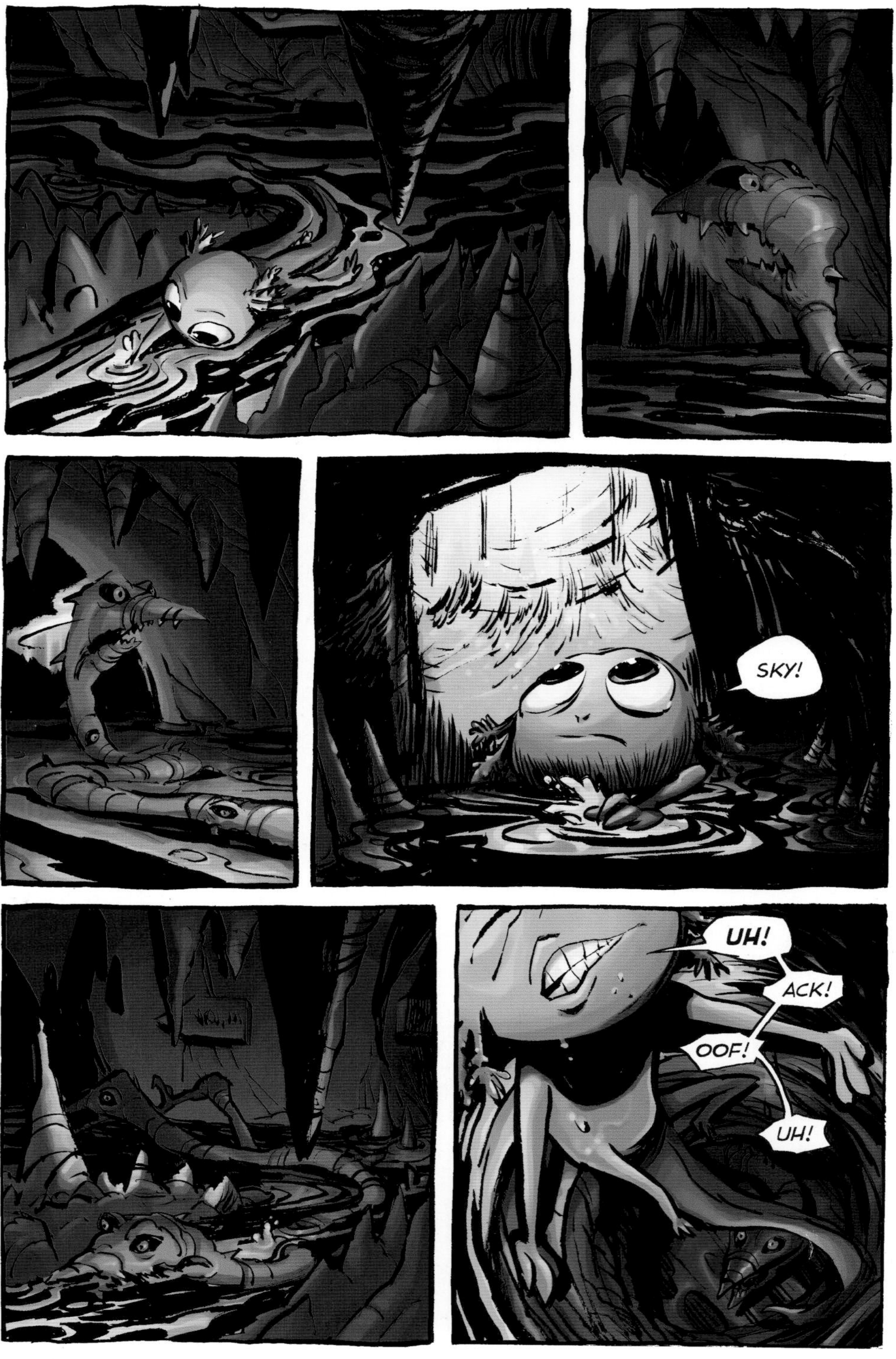
SKY!
UH!
ACK!
OOF!
UH!

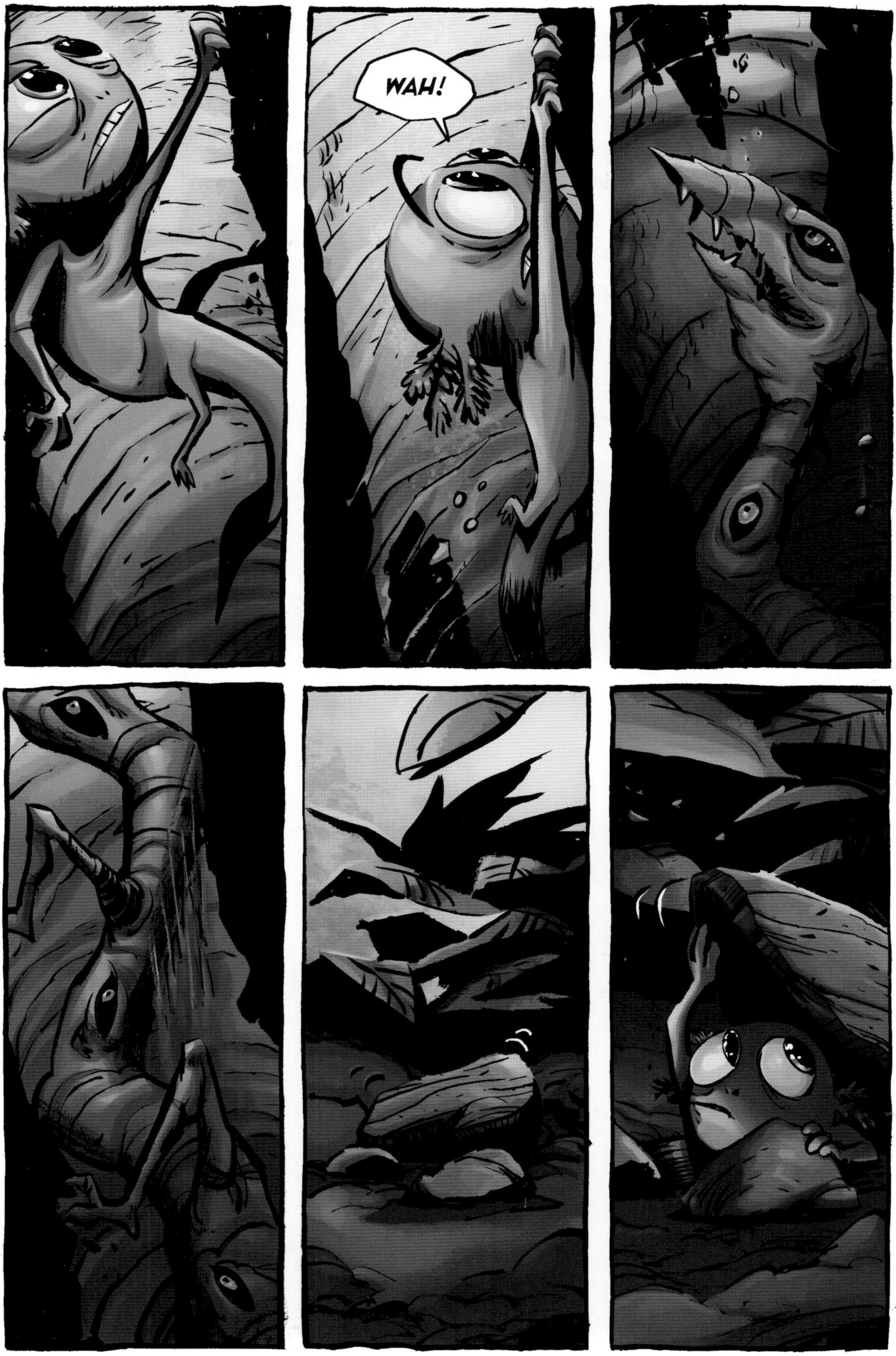
WAH!

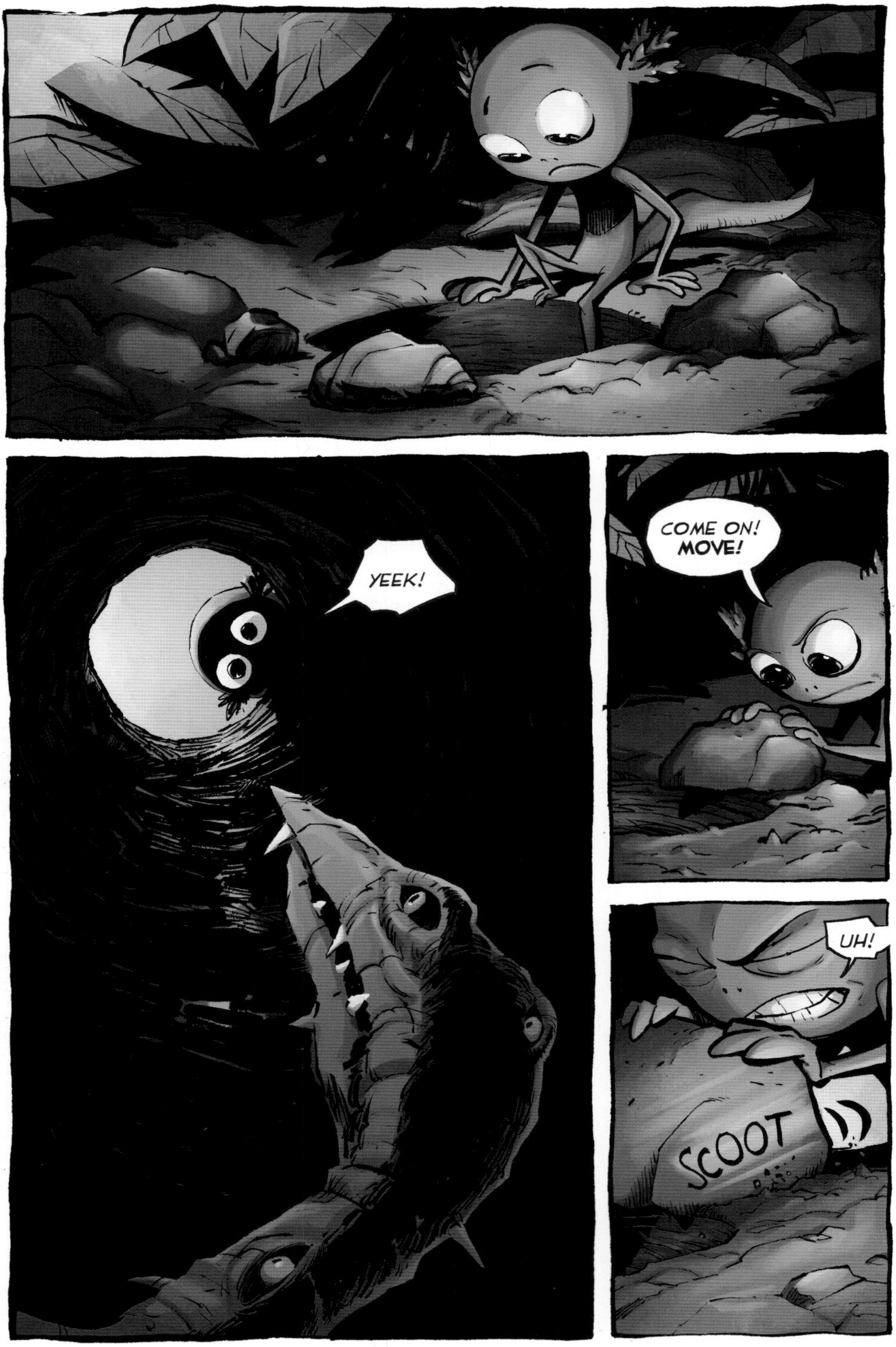

YEEK!
COME ON! MOVE!
UH!
SCOOT

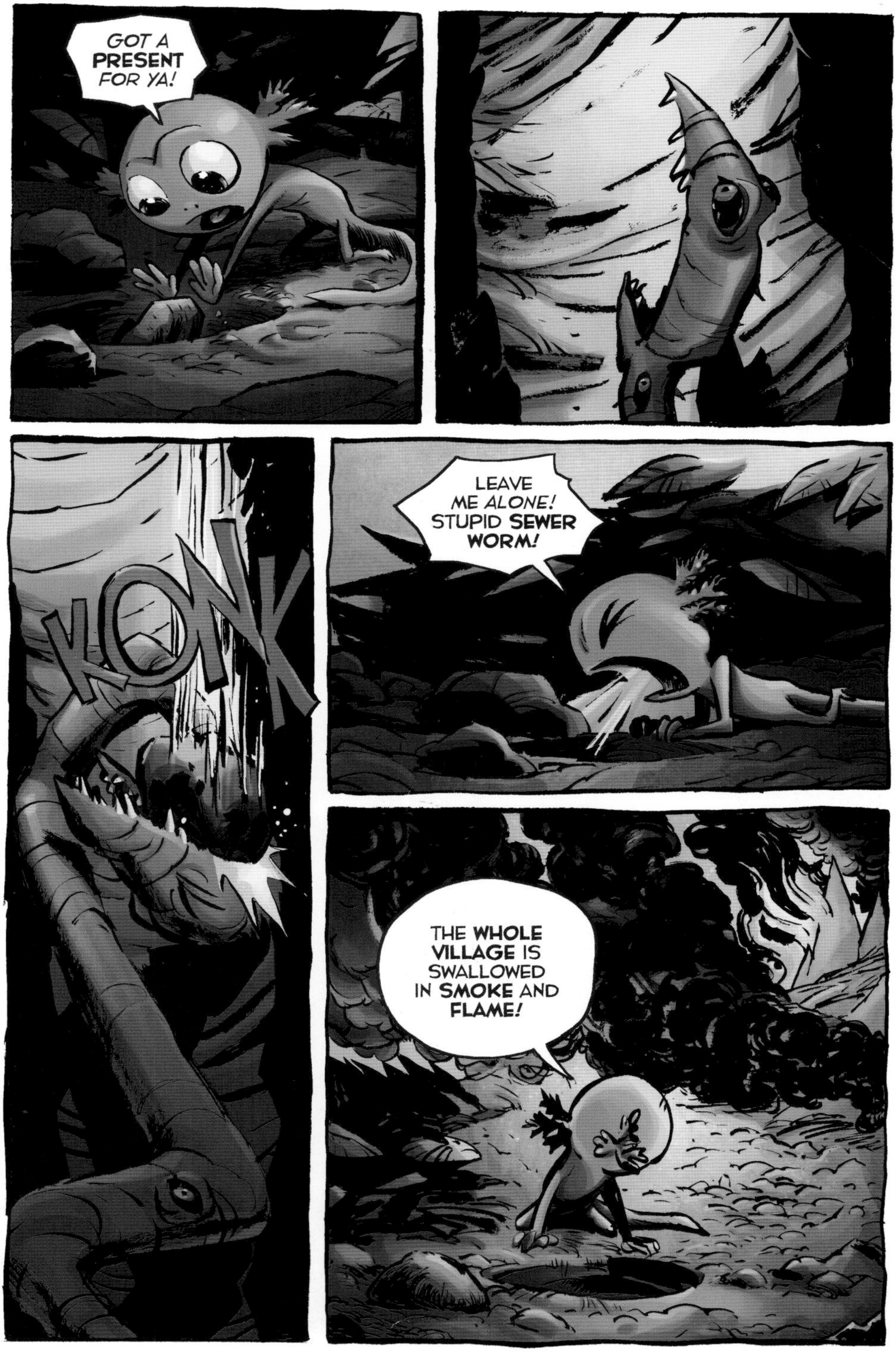
GOT A PRESENT FOR YA!
KONK
LEAVE ME ALONE! STUPID SEWER WORM!
THE WHOLE VILLAGE IS SWALLOWED IN SMOKE AND FLAME!

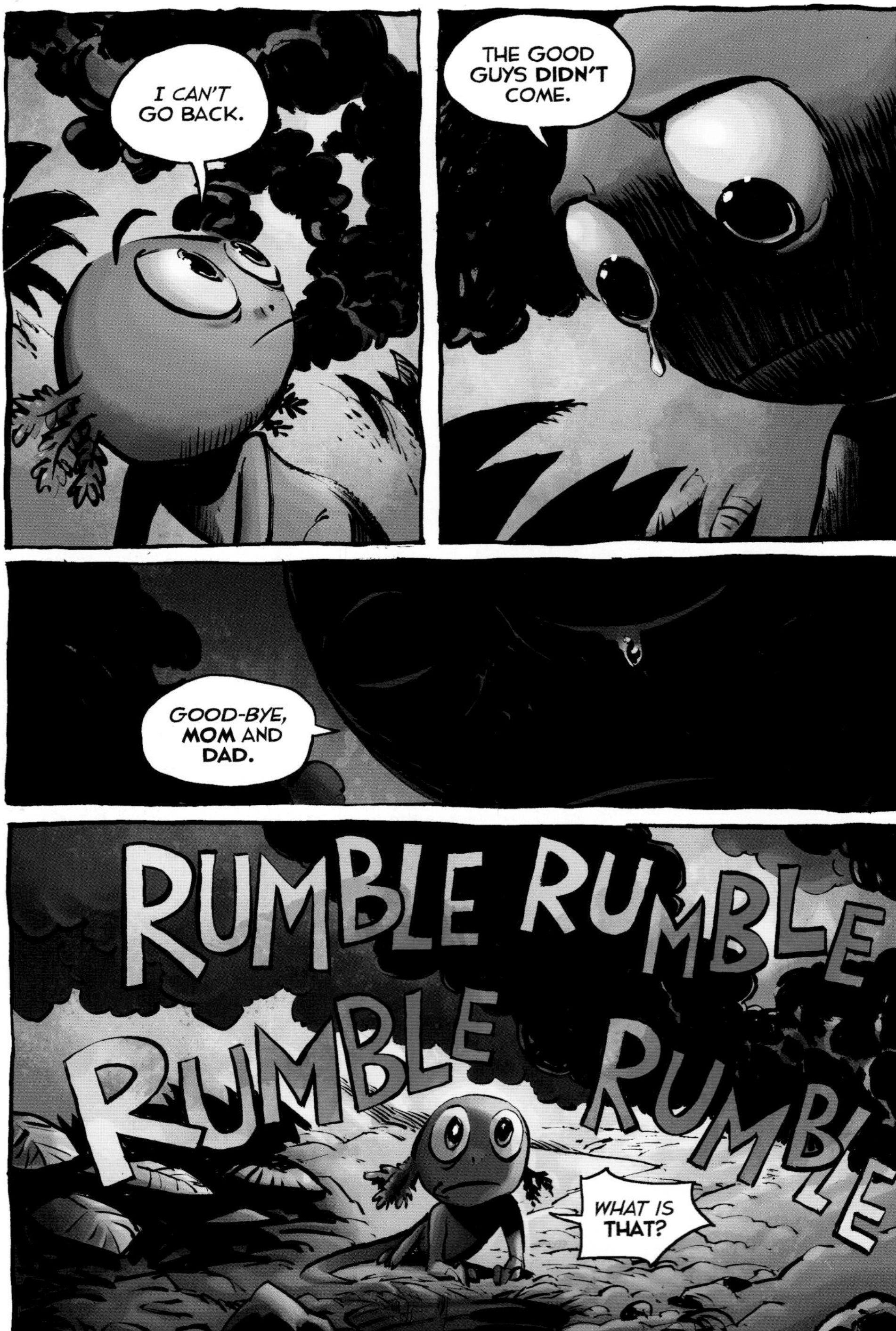
I CAN'T GO BACK.
THE GOOD GUYS **DIDN'T** COME.
GOOD-BYE, **MOM** AND **DAD.**
RUMBLE RUMBLE
RUMBLE RUMBLE
WHAT IS **THAT?**

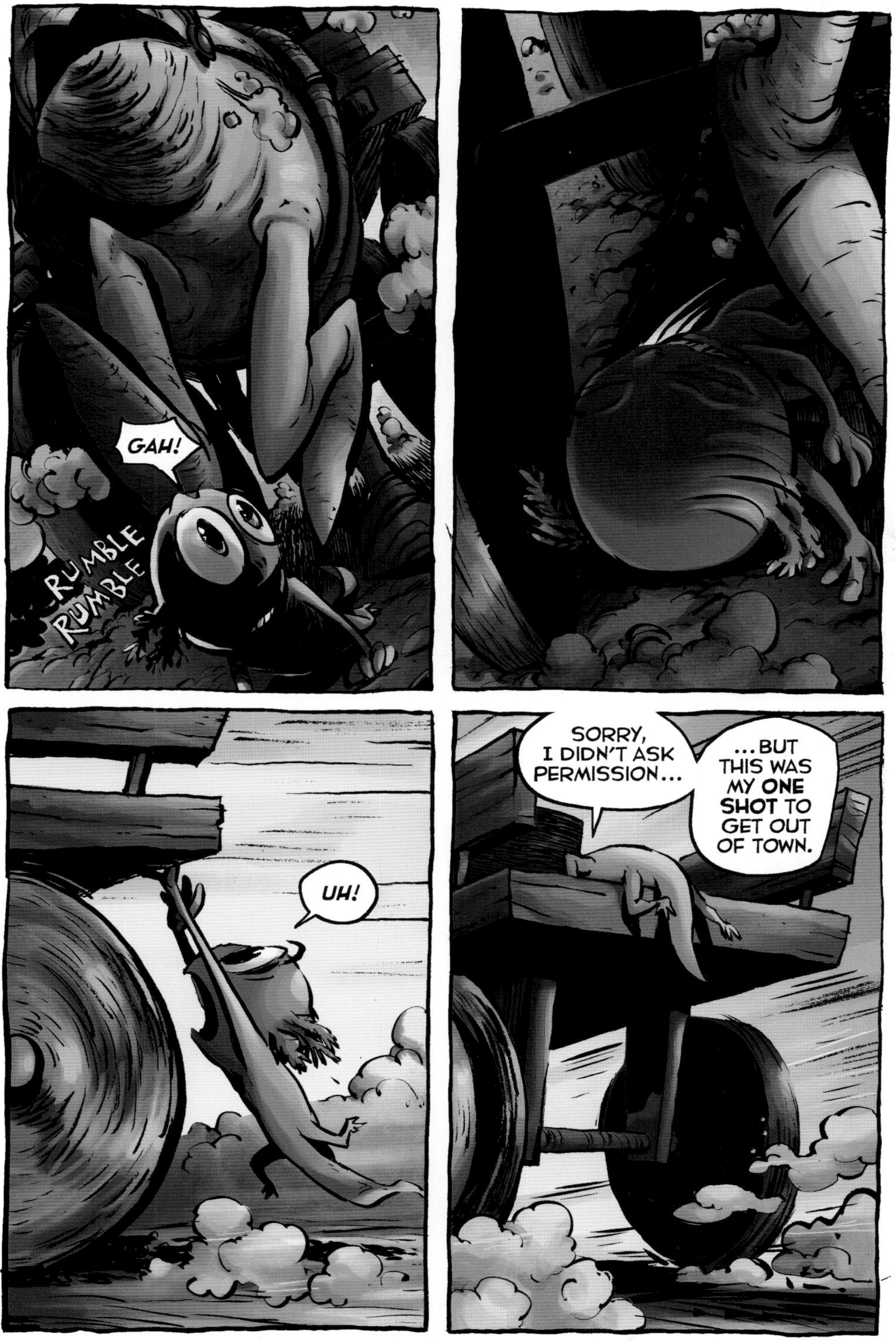
GAH!
RUMBLE RUMBLE
UH!
SORRY, I DIDN'T ASK PERMISSION...
...BUT THIS WAS MY **ONE SHOT** TO GET OUT OF TOWN.

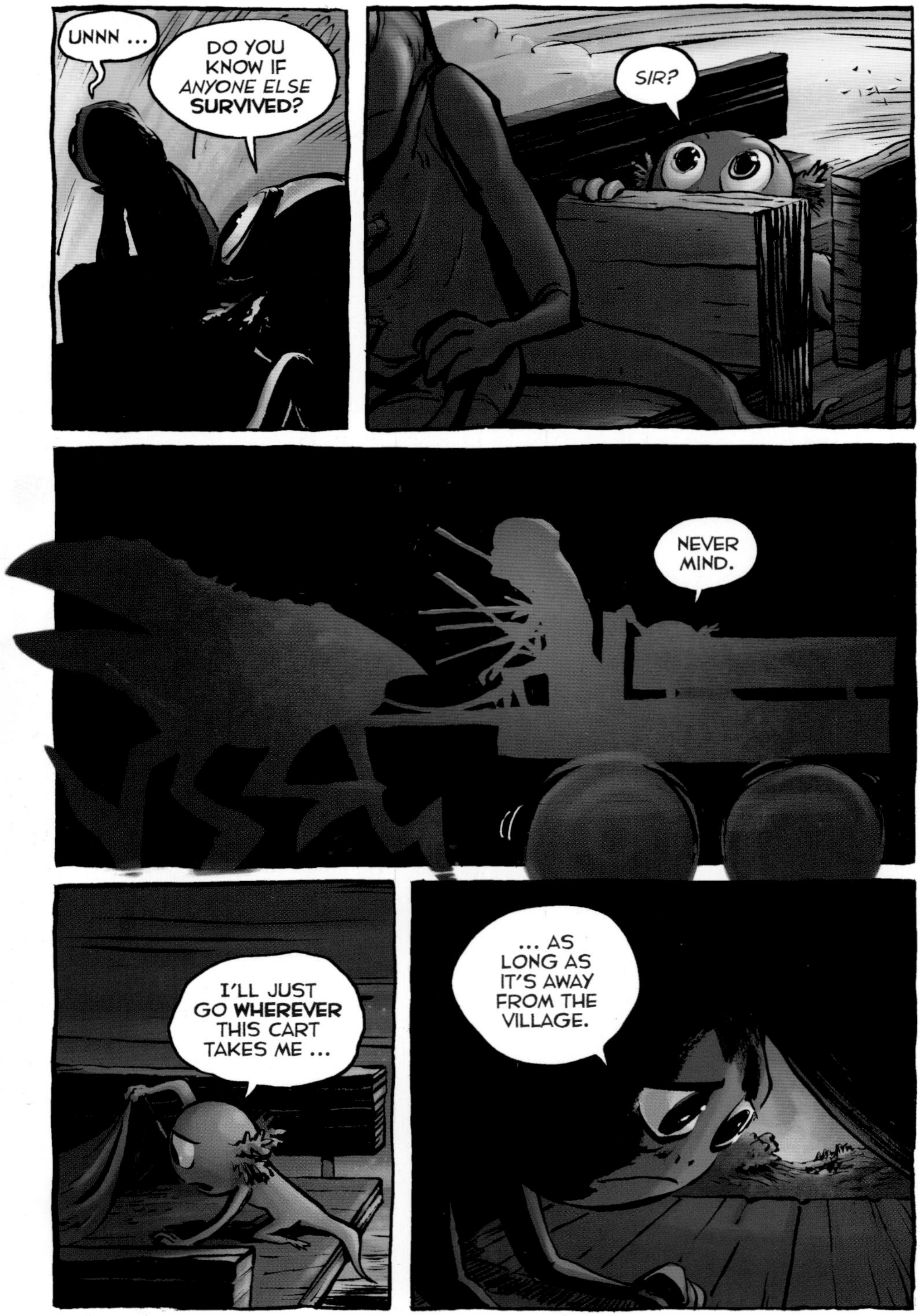
UNNN ...
DO YOU KNOW IF *ANYONE ELSE* **SURVIVED?**
SIR?
NEVER MIND.
I'LL JUST GO **WHEREVER** THIS CART TAKES ME ...
... AS LONG AS IT'S AWAY FROM THE VILLAGE.

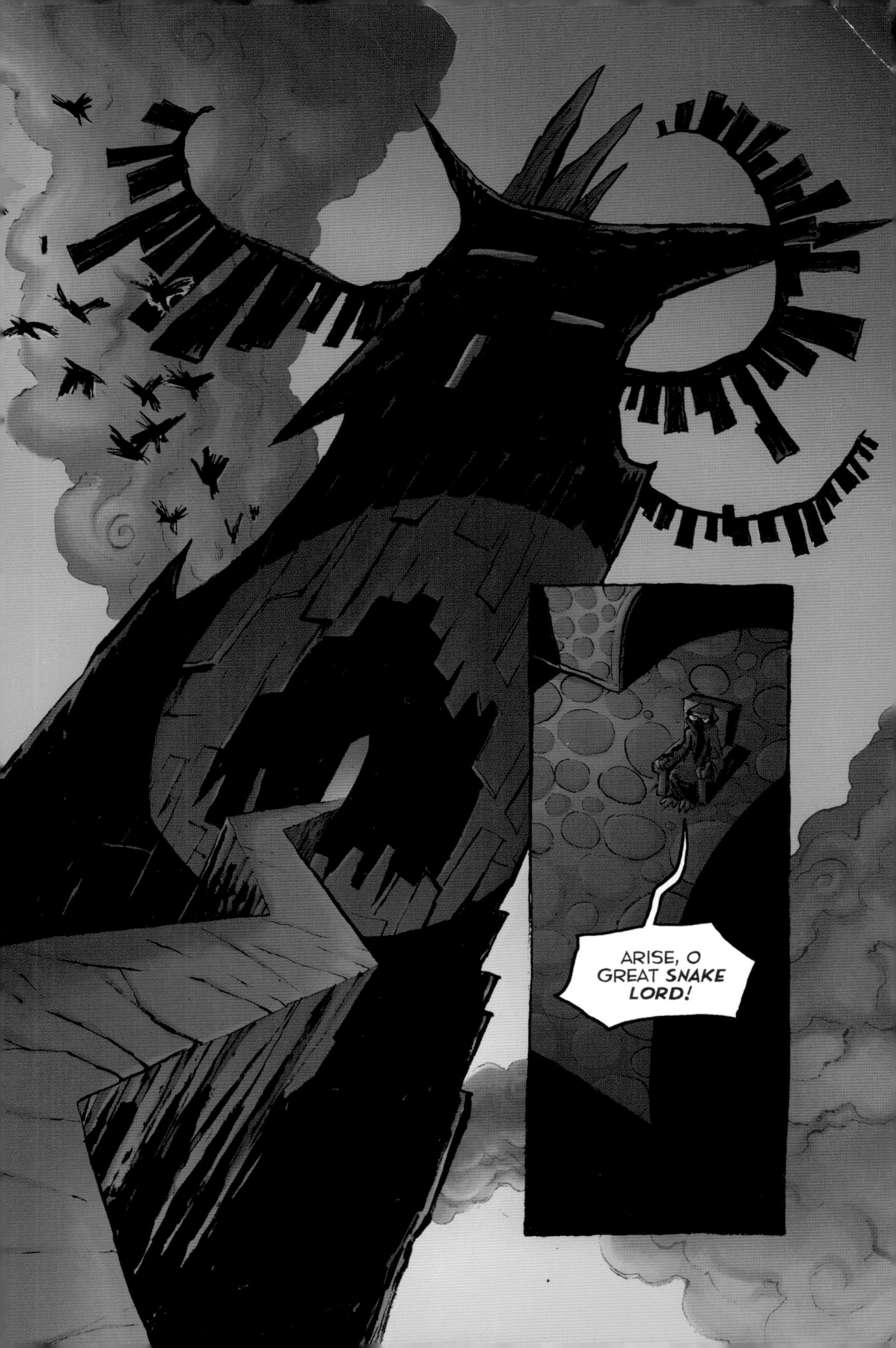
ARISE, O GREAT **SNAKE LORD!**

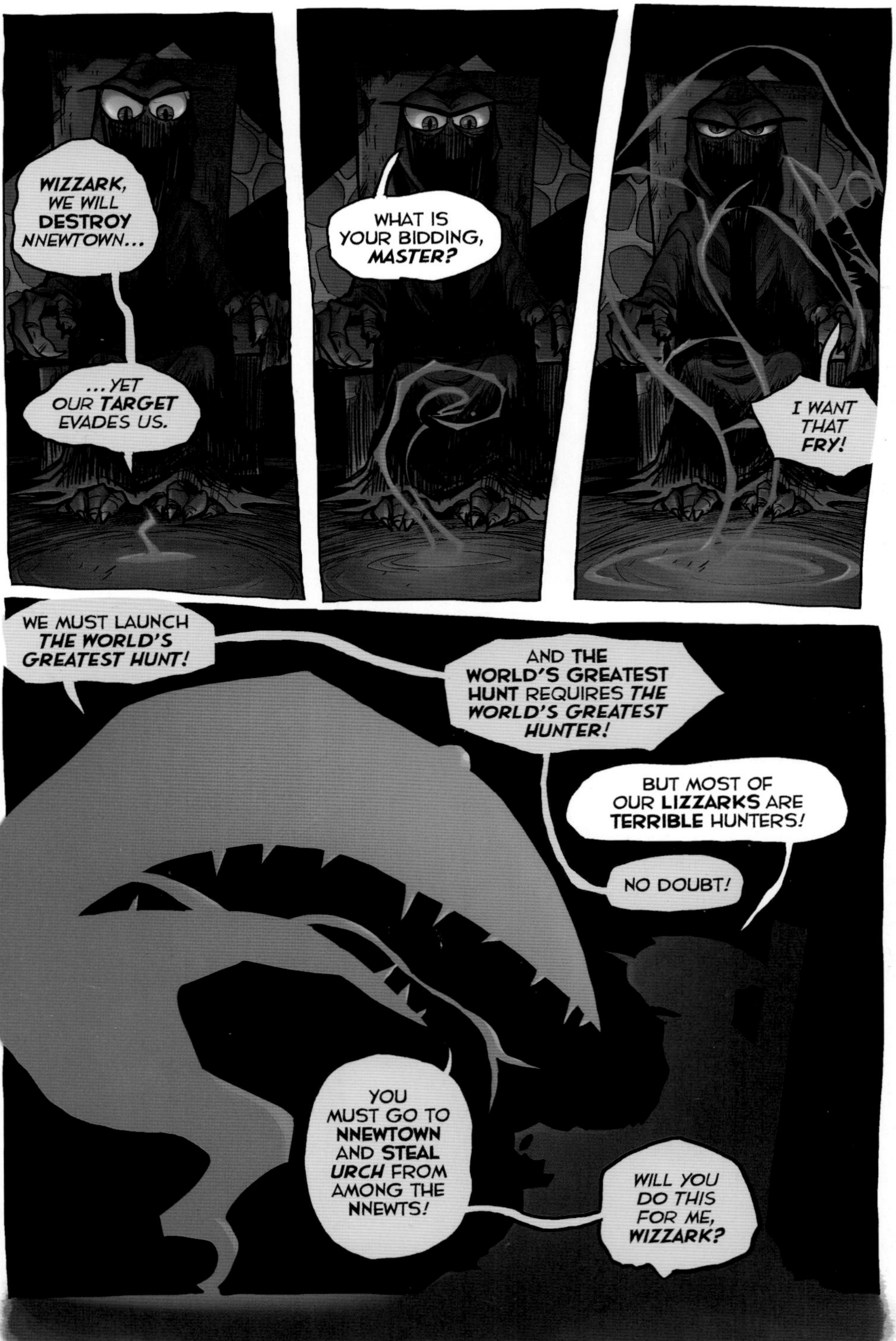
WIZZARK, WE WILL DESTROY NNEWTOWN...
...YET OUR TARGET EVADES US.
WHAT IS YOUR BIDDING, MASTER?
I WANT THAT FRY!
WE MUST LAUNCH THE WORLD'S GREATEST HUNT!
AND THE WORLD'S GREATEST HUNT REQUIRES THE WORLD'S GREATEST HUNTER!
BUT MOST OF OUR LIZZARKS ARE TERRIBLE HUNTERS!
NO DOUBT!
YOU MUST GO TO NNEWTOWN AND STEAL URCH FROM AMONG THE NNEWTS!
WILL YOU DO THIS FOR ME, WIZZARK?

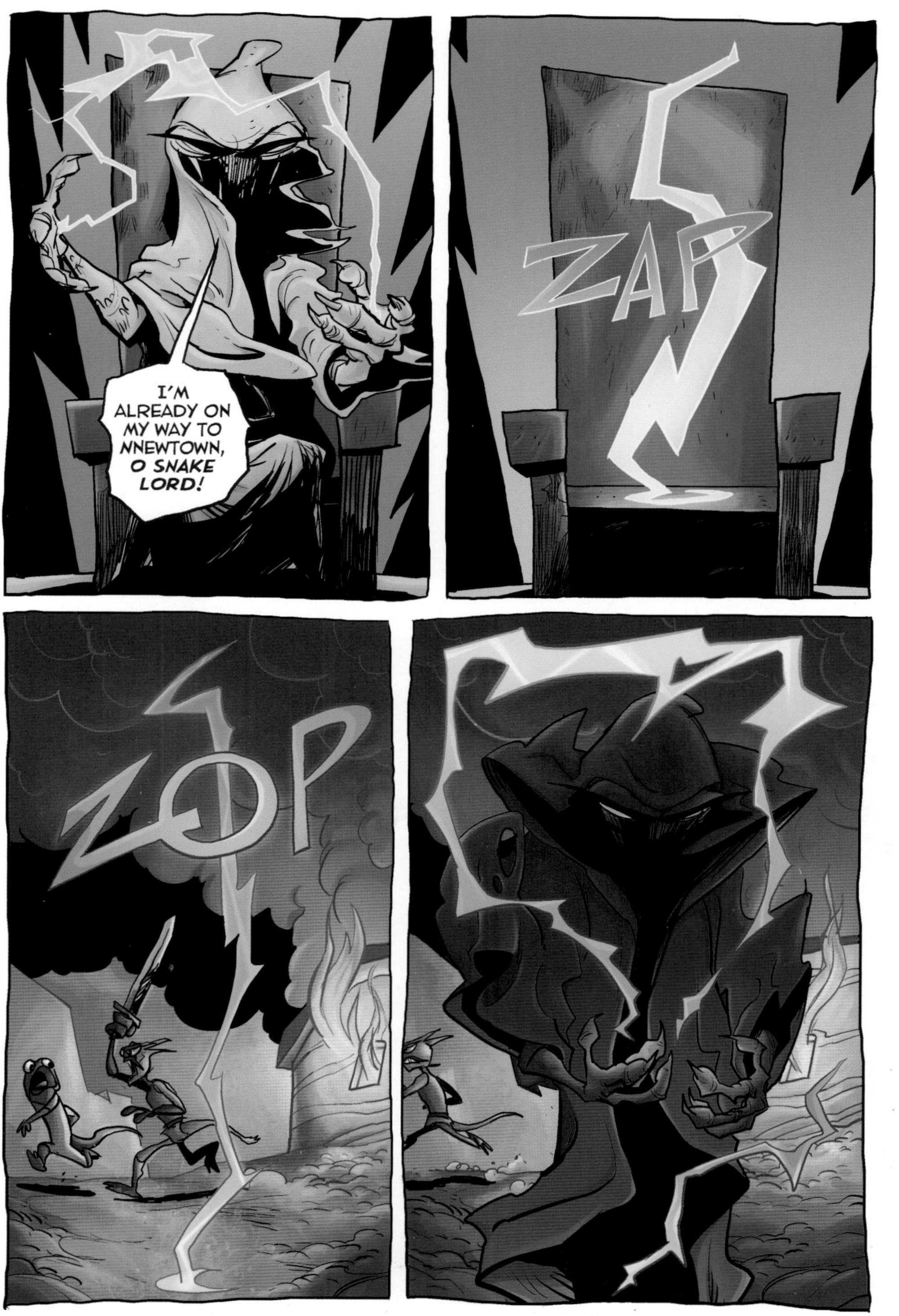
I'M ALREADY ON MY WAY TO NNEWTOWN, O SNAKE LORD!
ZAP
ZOP

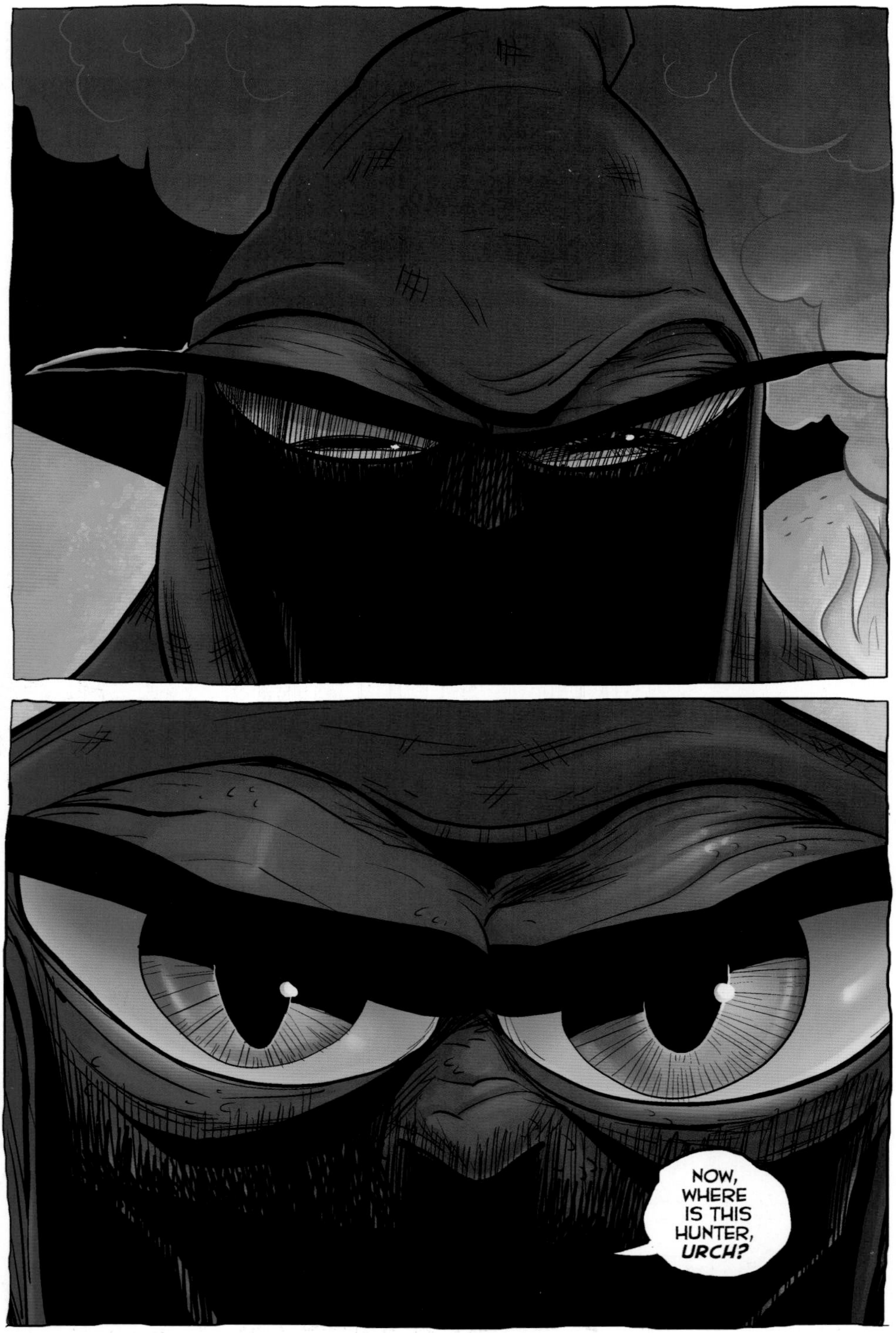
NOW, WHERE IS THIS HUNTER, *URCH?*

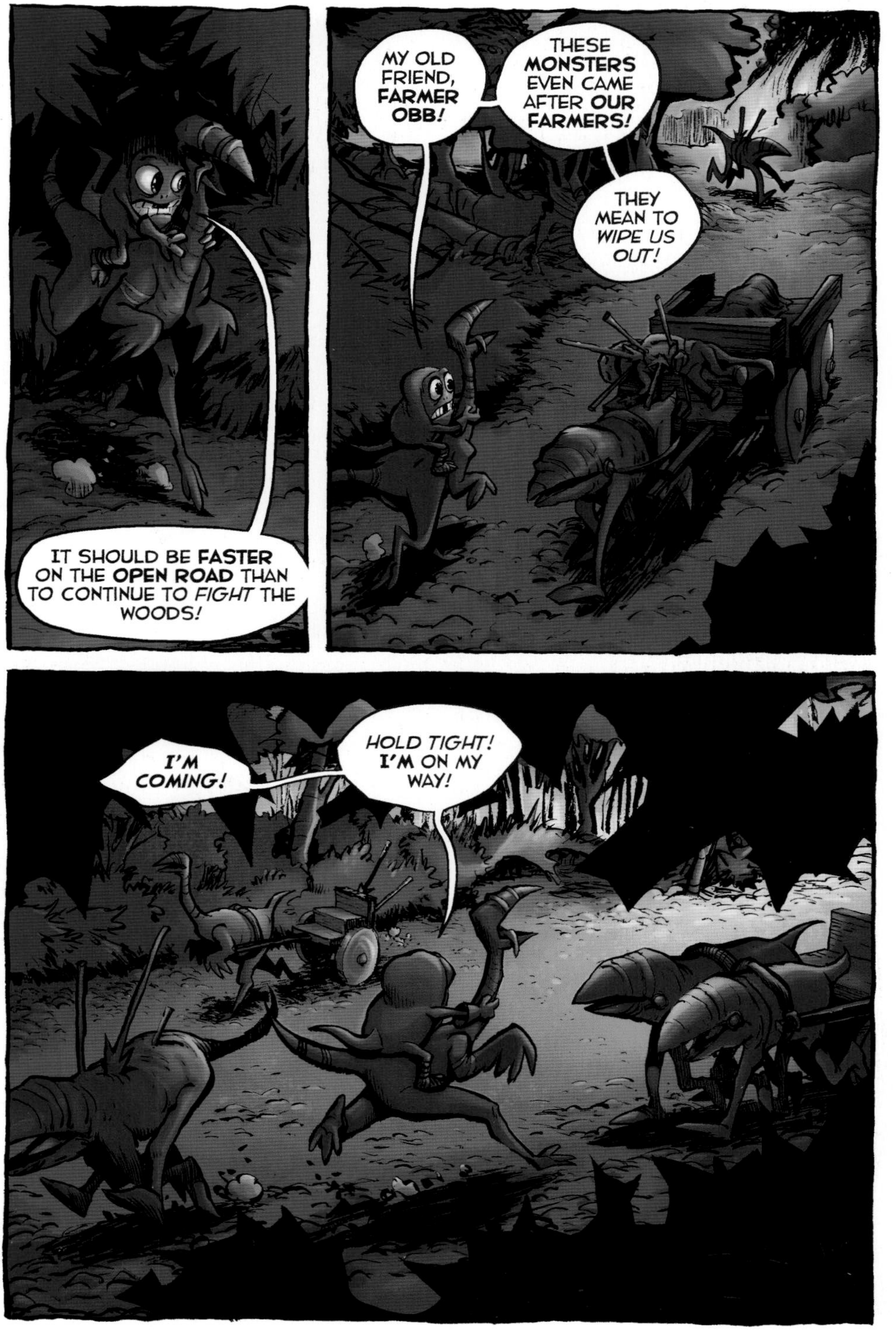
IT SHOULD BE FASTER ON THE OPEN ROAD THAN TO CONTINUE TO FIGHT THE WOODS!
MY OLD FRIEND, FARMER OBB!
THESE MONSTERS EVEN CAME AFTER OUR FARMERS!
THEY MEAN TO WIPE US OUT!
I'M COMING!
HOLD TIGHT! I'M ON MY WAY!

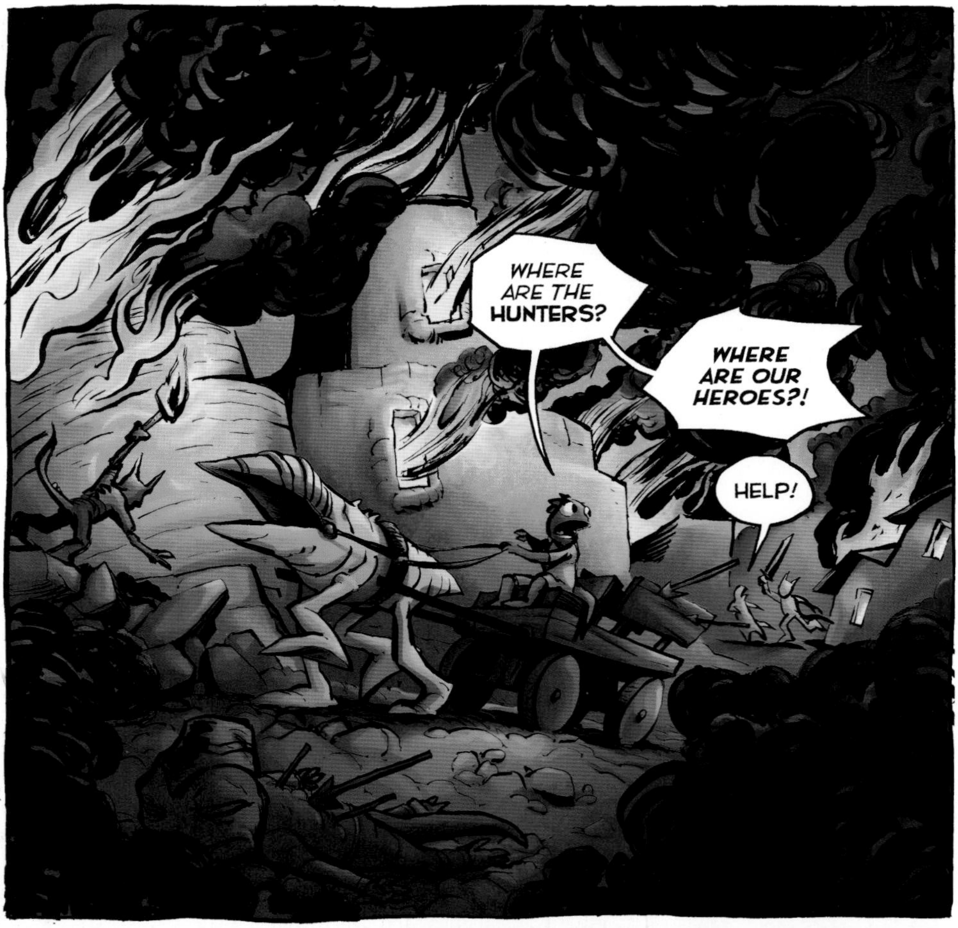
WHERE ARE THE HUNTERS?
WHERE ARE OUR HEROES?!
HELP!

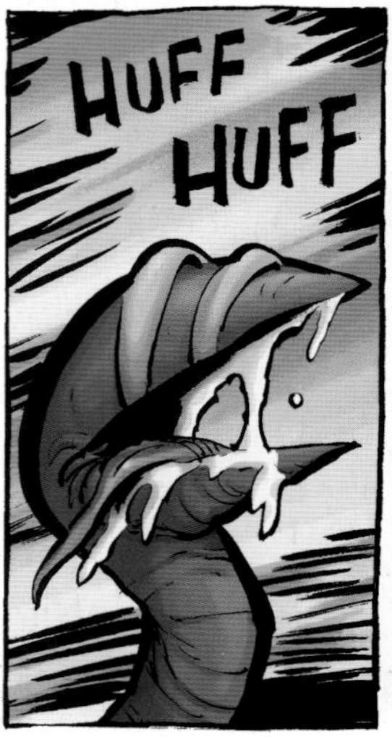
HUFF HUFF

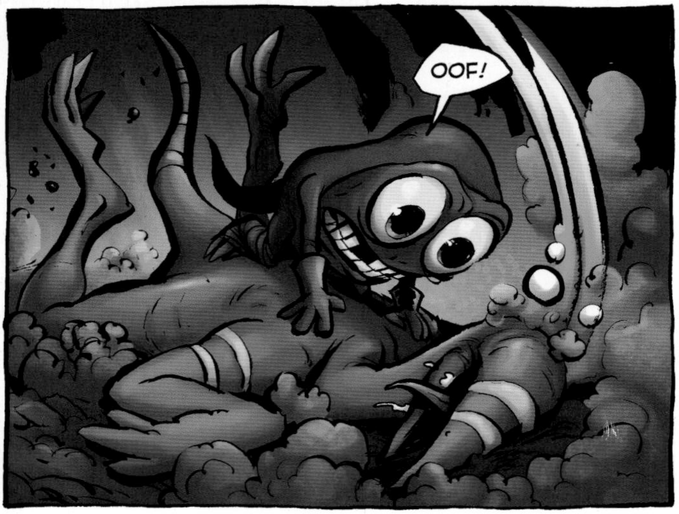
OOF!

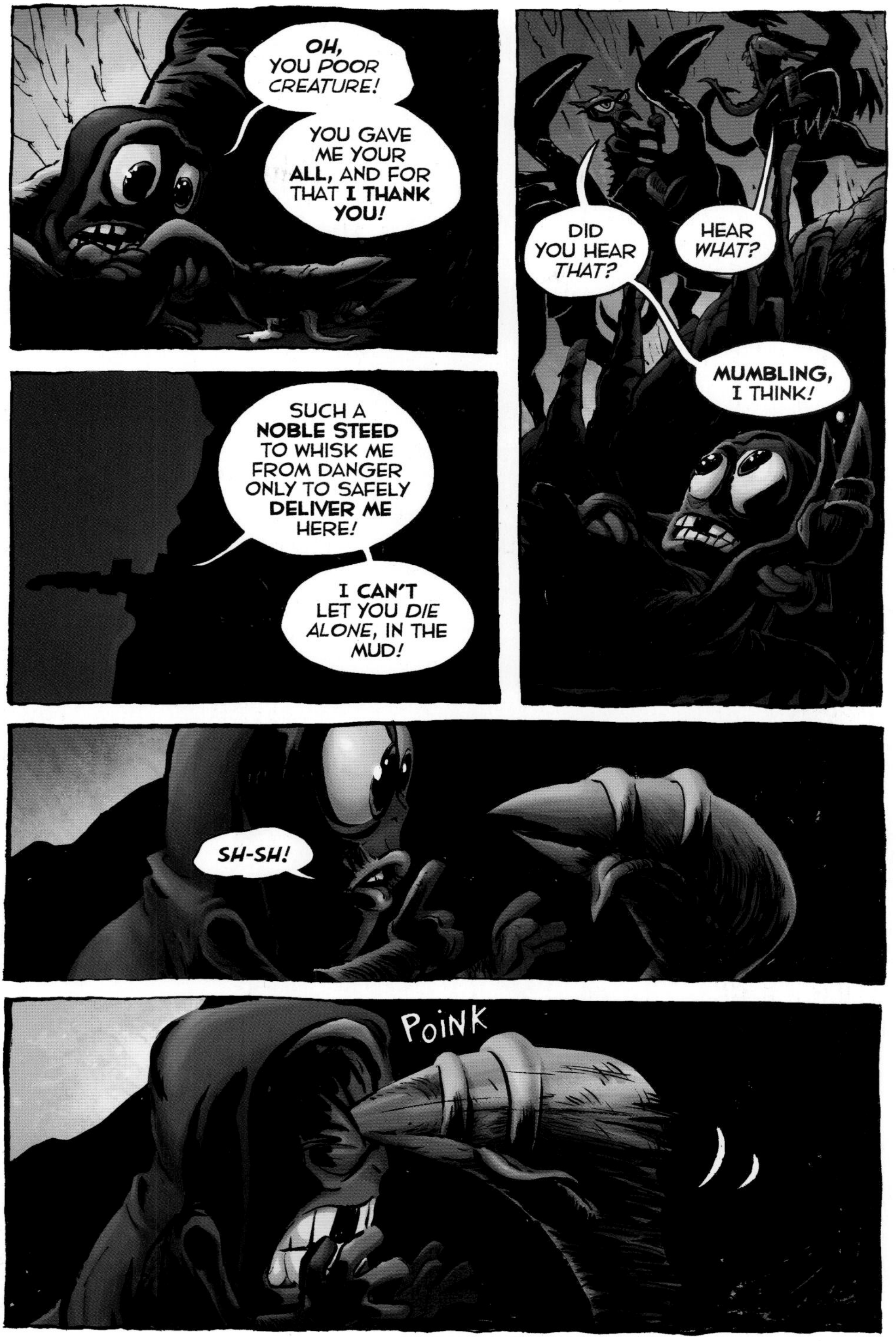
OH, YOU POOR CREATURE!
YOU GAVE ME YOUR ALL, AND FOR THAT I THANK YOU!
DID YOU HEAR THAT?
HEAR WHAT?
MUMBLING, I THINK!
SUCH A NOBLE STEED TO WHISK ME FROM DANGER ONLY TO SAFELY DELIVER ME HERE!
I CAN'T LET YOU DIE ALONE, IN THE MUD!
SH-SH!
POINK

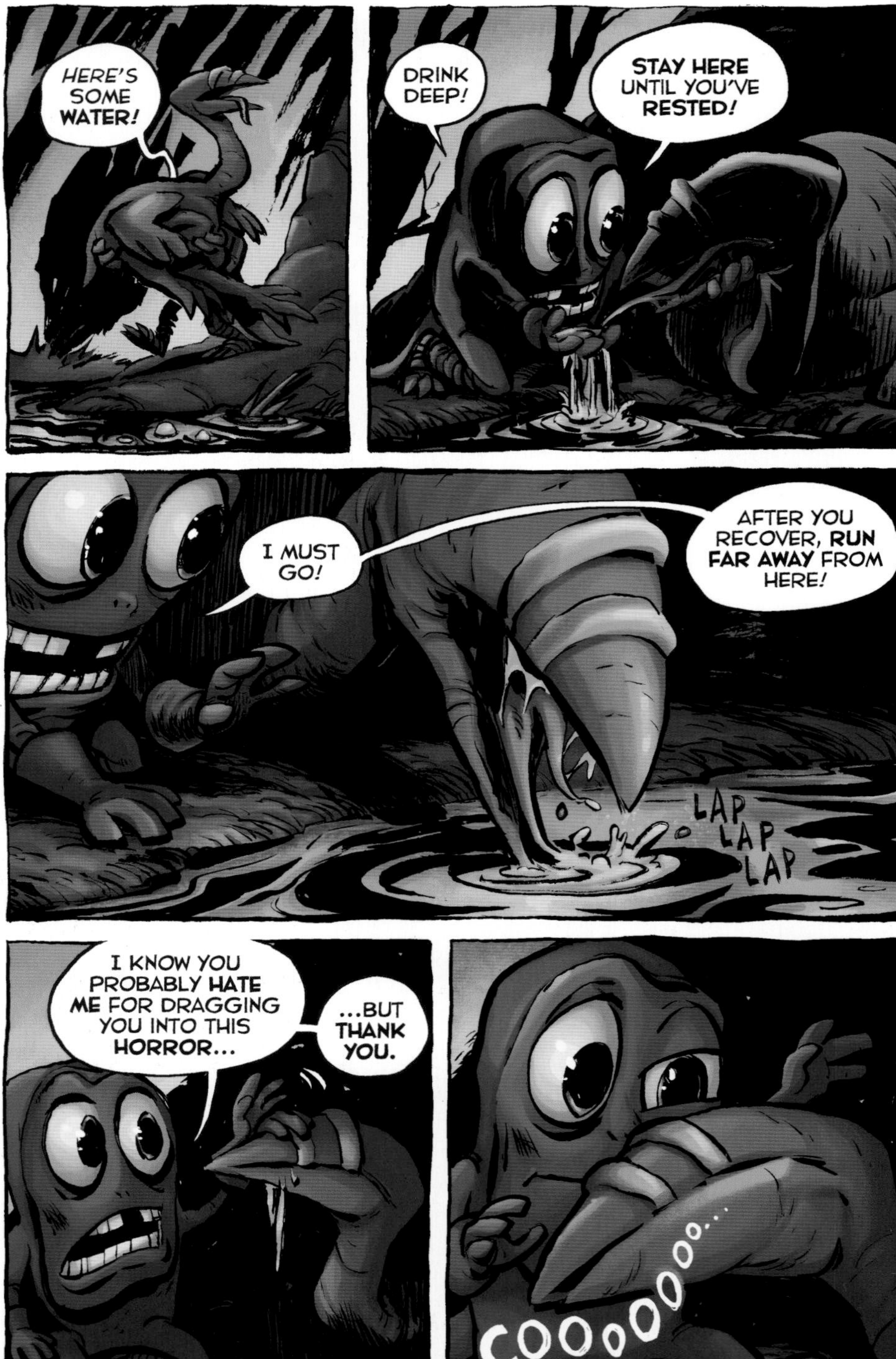
HERE'S SOME WATER!
DRINK DEEP!
STAY HERE UNTIL YOU'VE RESTED!
I MUST GO!
AFTER YOU RECOVER, RUN FAR AWAY FROM HERE!
LAP LAP LAP
I KNOW YOU PROBABLY HATE ME FOR DRAGGING YOU INTO THIS HORROR...
...BUT THANK YOU.
COOOOOOOOOO...

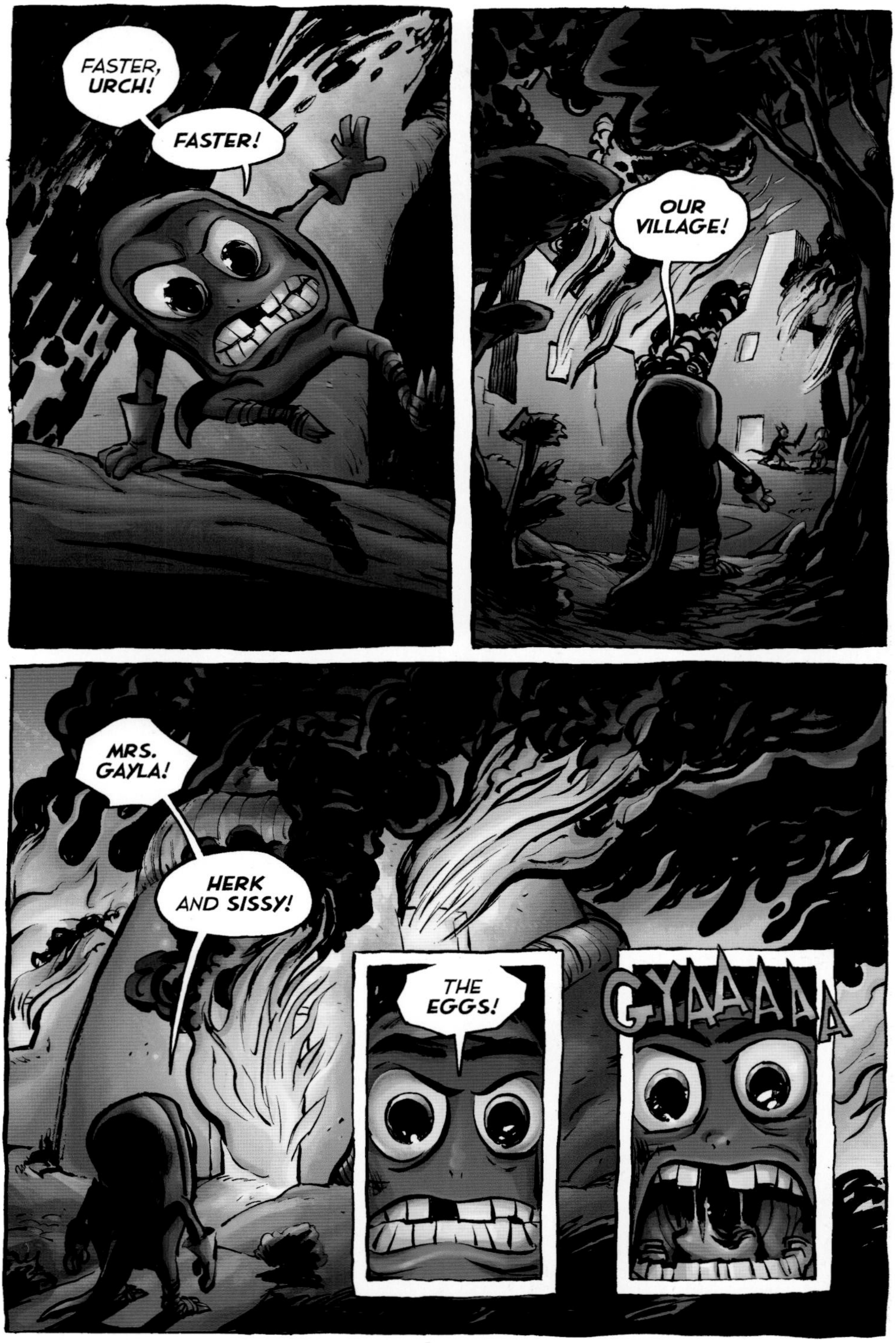
FASTER, URCH!
FASTER!
OUR VILLAGE!
MRS. GAYLA!
HERK AND SISSY!
THE EGGS!
GYAAAAA

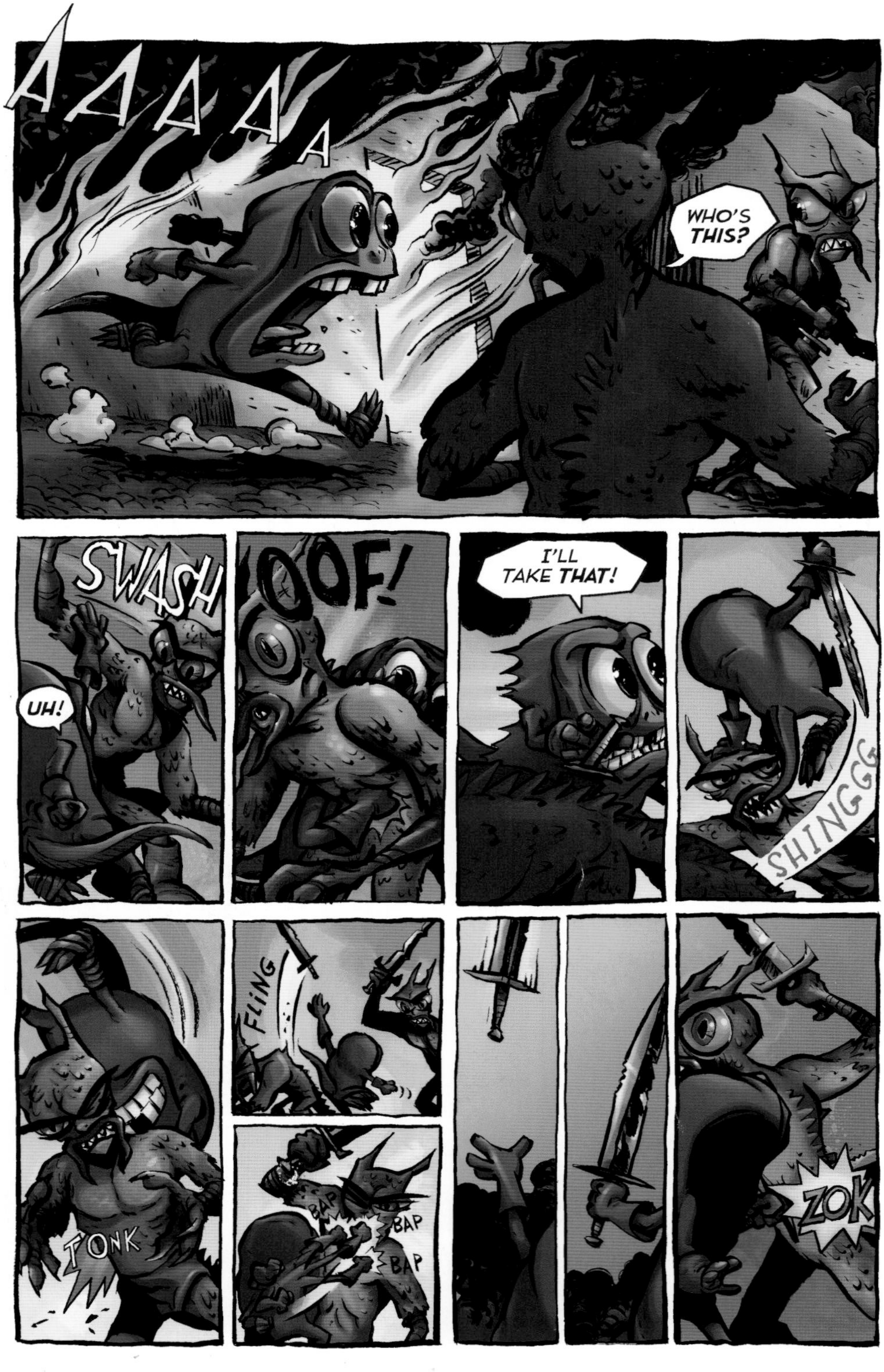

AAAAAA
WHO'S THIS?
SWASH
UH!
OOF!
I'LL TAKE THAT!
SHINGGG
TONK
FLING
BAP
BAP
BAP
ZOK

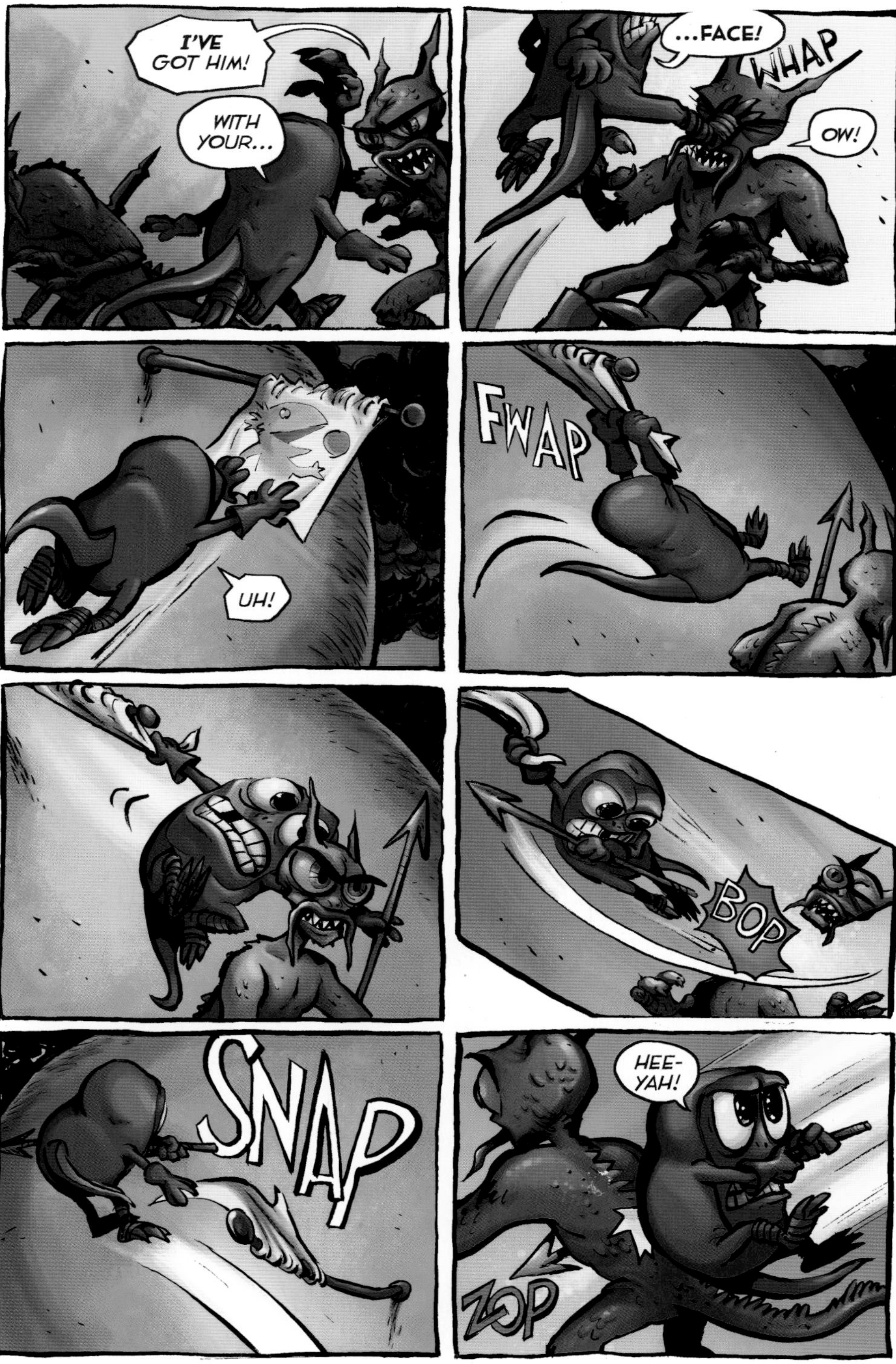
I'VE GOT HIM!
WITH YOUR...
...FACE!
WHAP
OW!
UH!
FWAP
BOP
SNAP
HEE-YAH!
ZOP

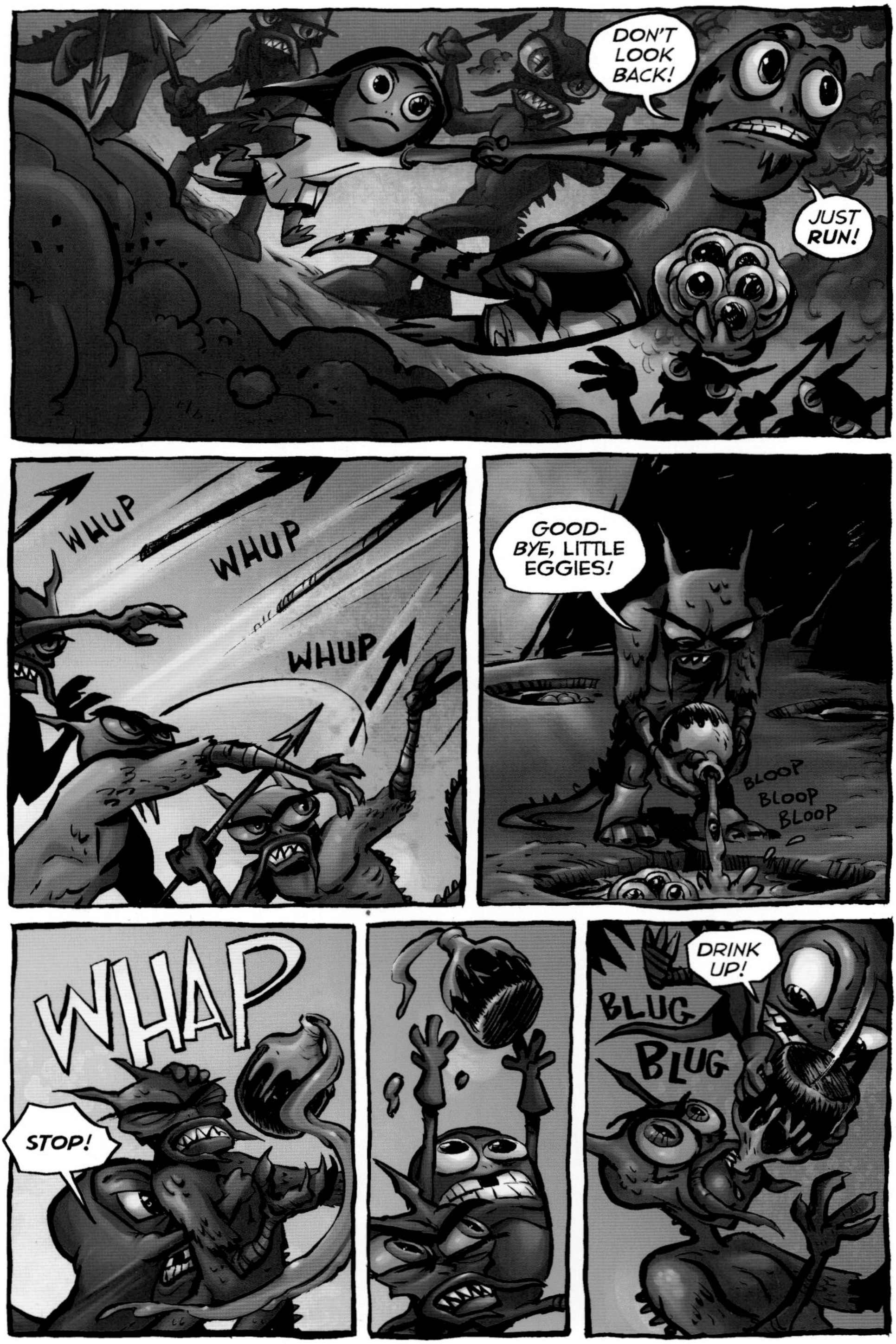
DON'T LOOK BACK!
JUST RUN!
WHUP
WHUP
WHUP
GOOD-BYE, LITTLE EGGIES!
BLOOP BLOOP BLOOP
WHAP
STOP!
DRINK UP!
BLUG
BLUG

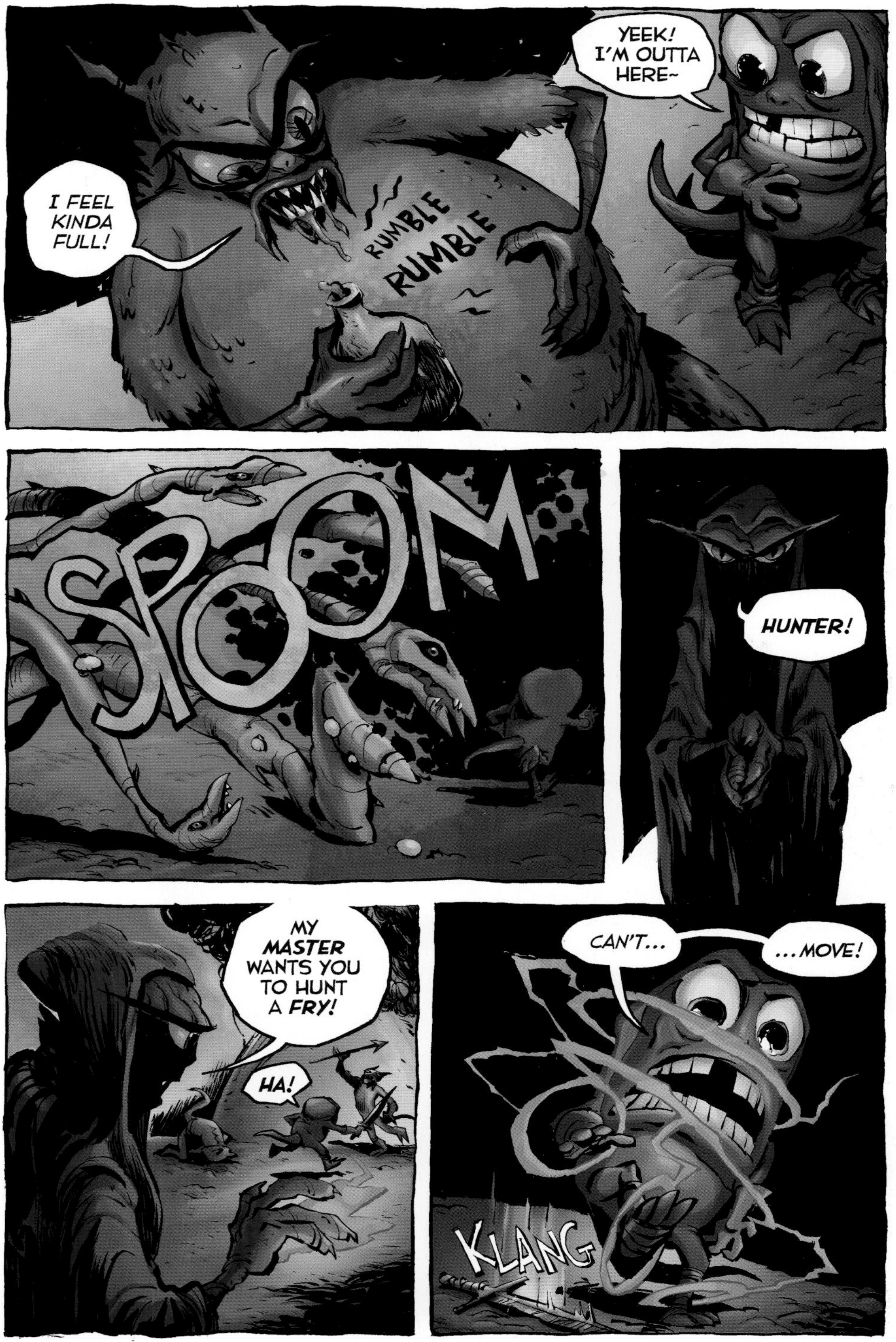
YEEK! I'M OUTTA HERE~
I FEEL KINDA FULL!
RUMBLE RUMBLE
SPOOOM
HUNTER!
MY MASTER WANTS YOU TO HUNT A FRY!
HA!
CAN'T...
...MOVE!
KLANG

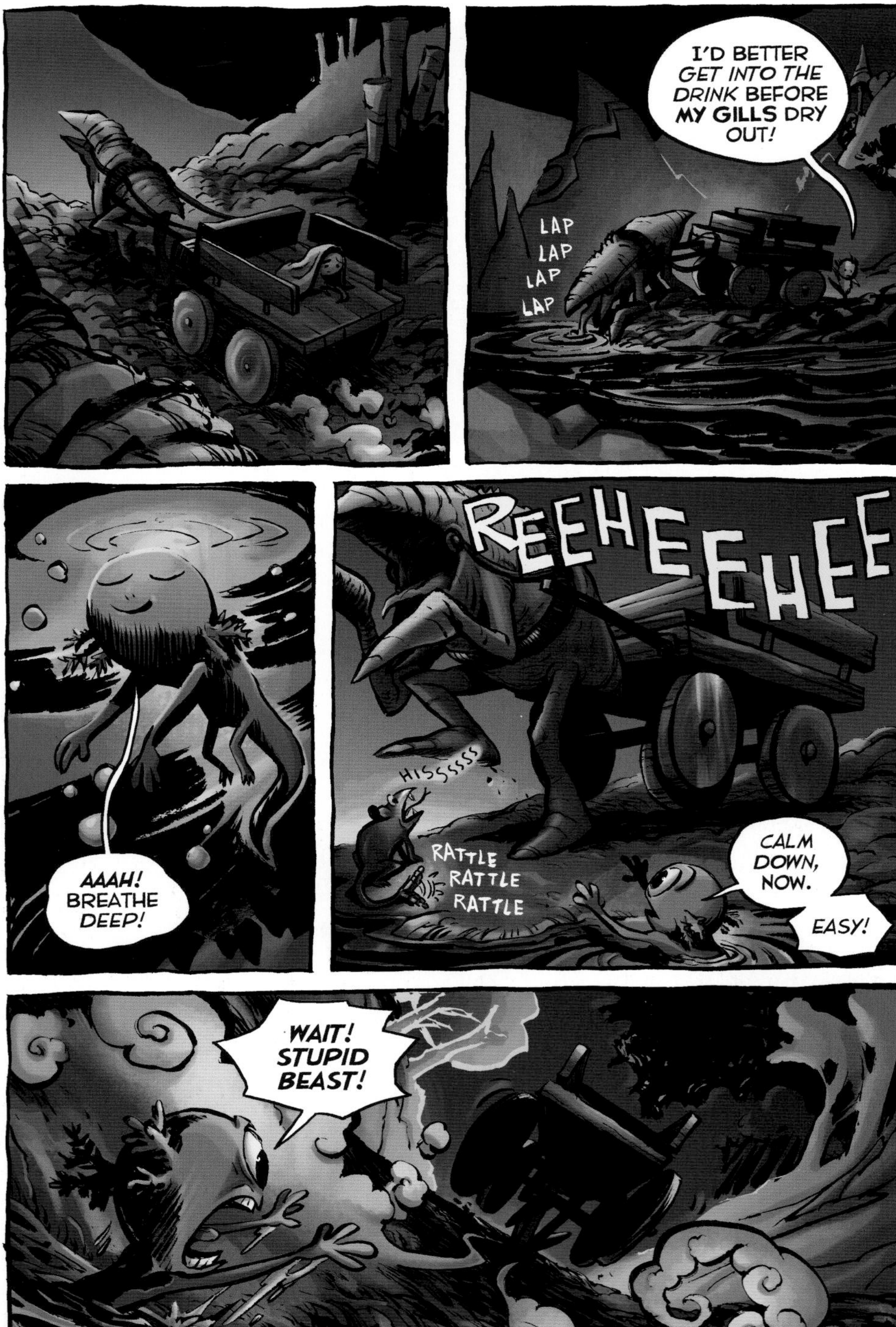
I'D BETTER GET INTO THE DRINK BEFORE MY GILLS DRY OUT!
LAP LAP LAP LAP
AAAH! BREATHE DEEP!
REEHEEEHEE
HISSSSS
RATTLE RATTLE RATTLE
CALM DOWN, NOW.
EASY!
WAIT! STUPID BEAST!

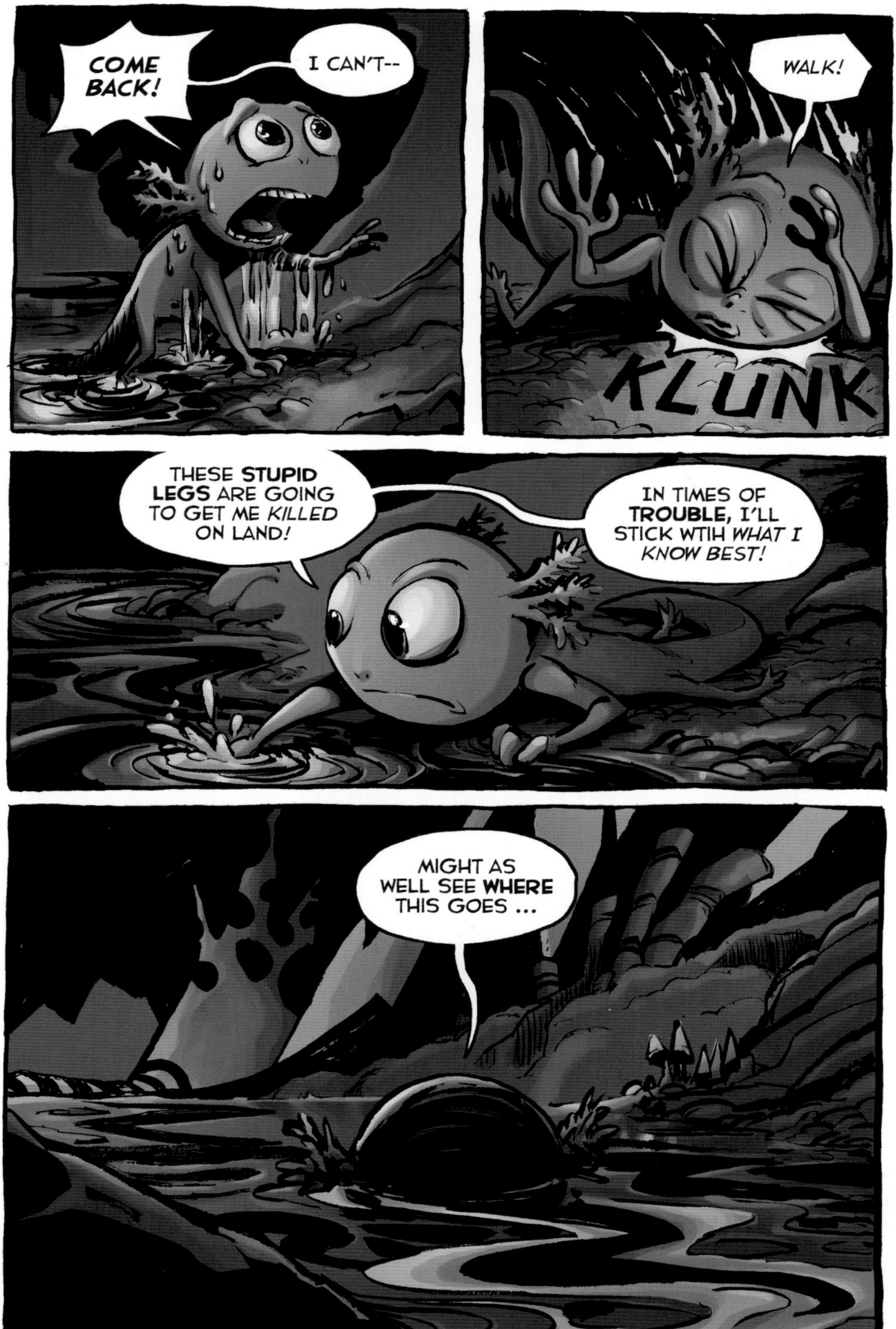
COME BACK!
I CAN'T--
WALK!
KLUNK
THESE **STUPID LEGS** ARE GOING TO GET ME *KILLED* ON LAND!
IN TIMES OF **TROUBLE,** I'LL STICK WTIH *WHAT I KNOW BEST!*
MIGHT AS WELL SEE **WHERE** THIS GOES ...

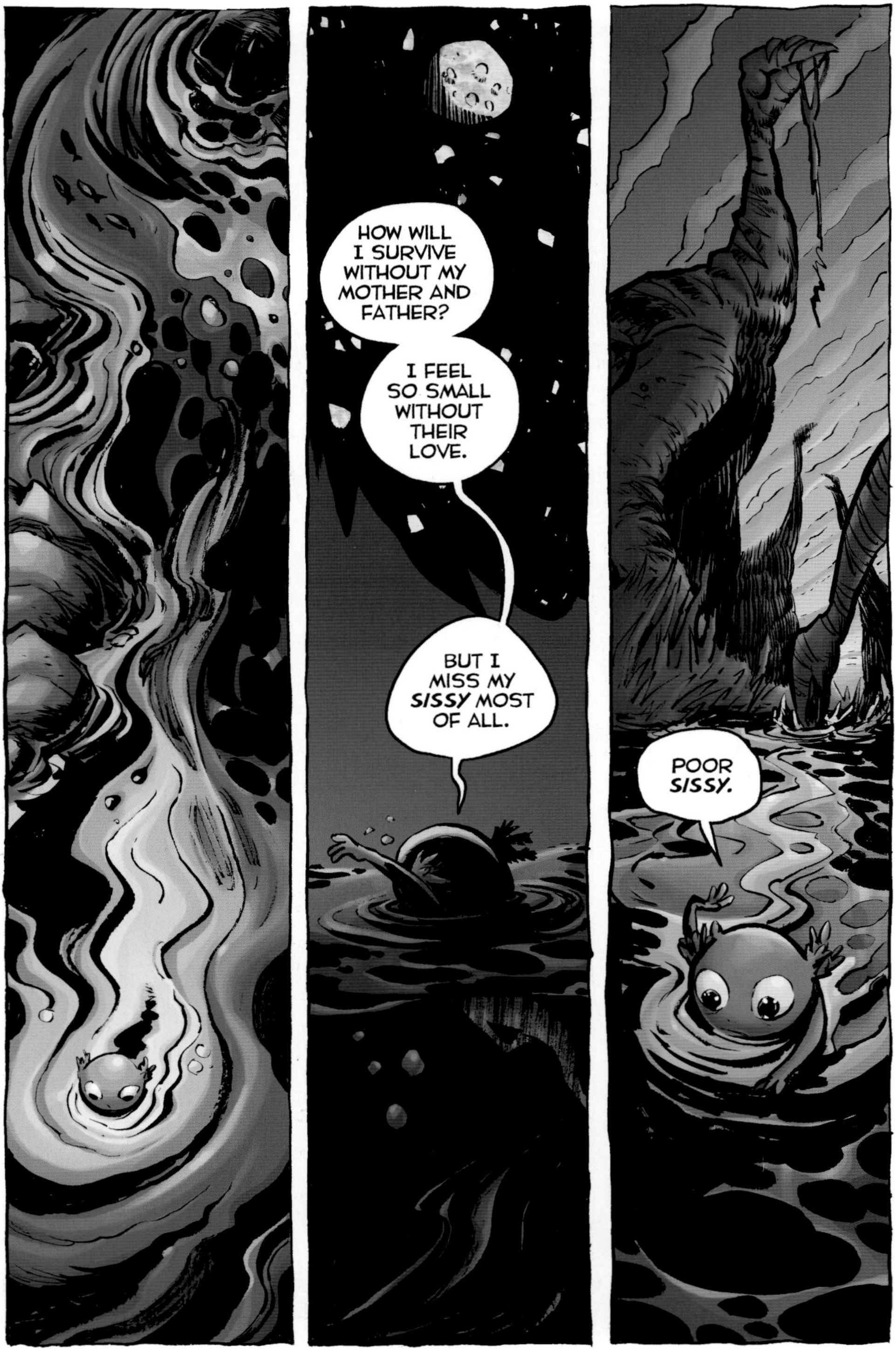
HOW WILL I SURVIVE WITHOUT MY MOTHER AND FATHER?
I FEEL SO SMALL WITHOUT THEIR LOVE.
BUT I MISS MY *SISSY* MOST OF ALL.
POOR *SISSY*.

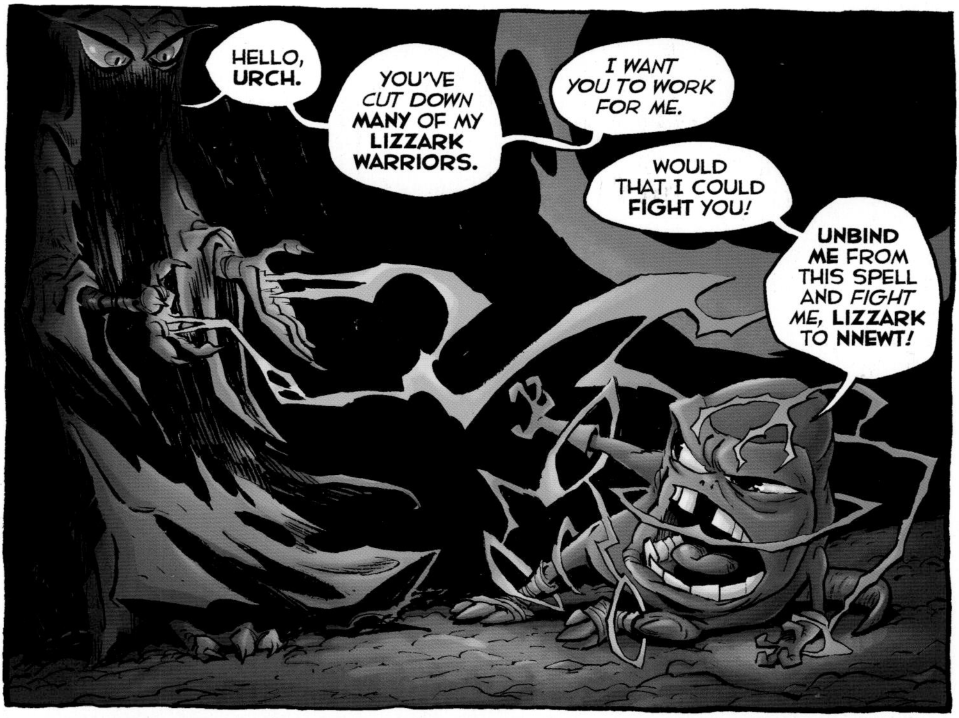
HELLO, URCH.
YOU'VE CUT DOWN MANY OF MY LIZZARK WARRIORS.
I WANT YOU TO WORK FOR ME.
WOULD THAT I COULD FIGHT YOU!
UNBIND ME FROM THIS SPELL AND FIGHT ME, LIZZARK TO NNEWT!

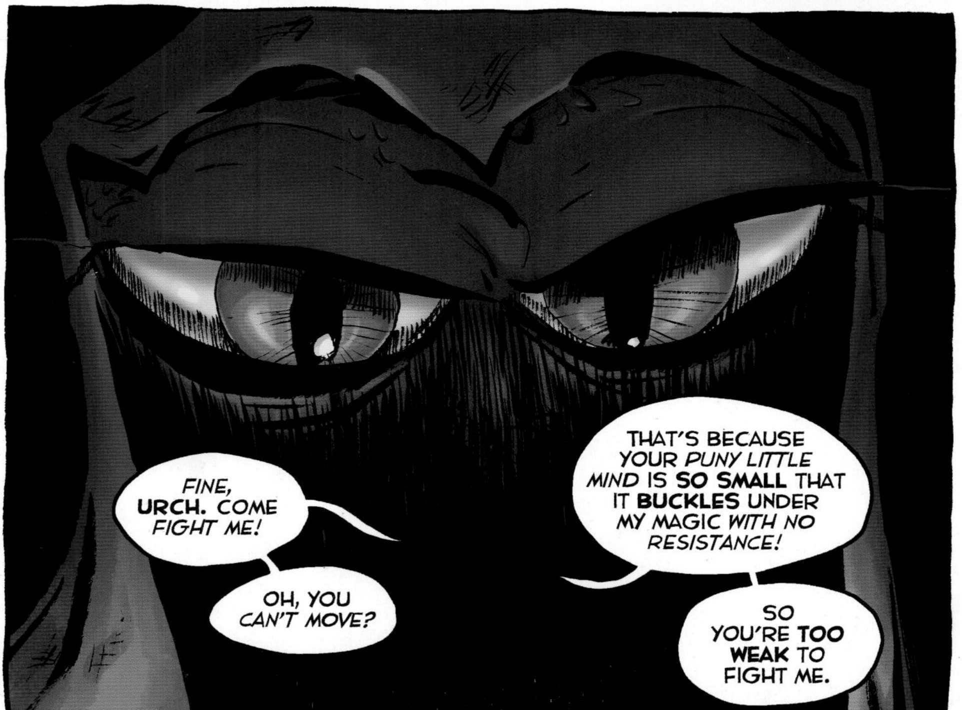
FINE, URCH. COME FIGHT ME!
OH, YOU CAN'T MOVE?
THAT'S BECAUSE YOUR PUNY LITTLE MIND IS SO SMALL THAT IT BUCKLES UNDER MY MAGIC WITH NO RESISTANCE!
SO YOU'RE TOO WEAK TO FIGHT ME.

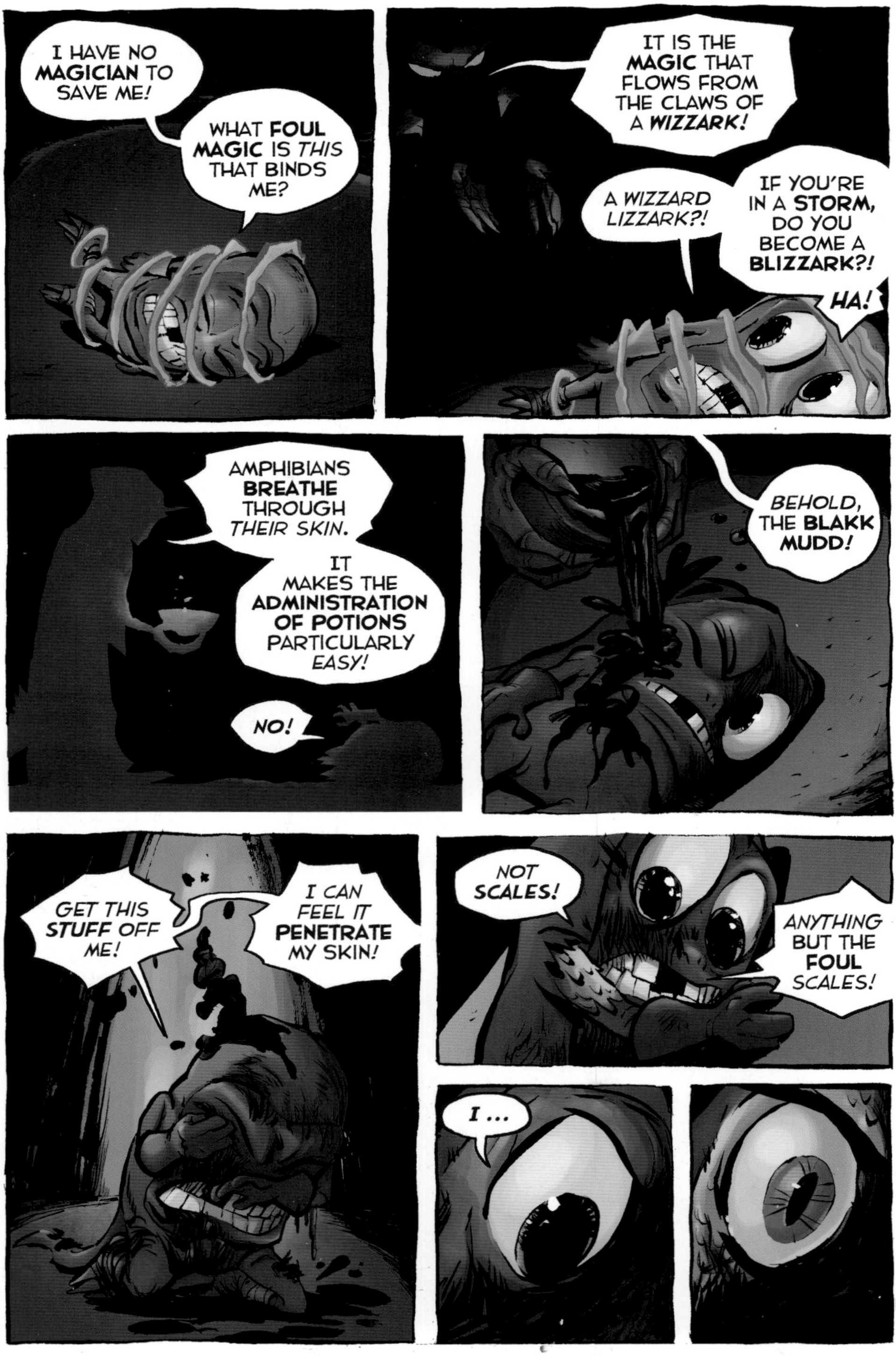
I HAVE NO MAGICIAN TO SAVE ME!
WHAT FOUL MAGIC IS THIS THAT BINDS ME?
IT IS THE MAGIC THAT FLOWS FROM THE CLAWS OF A WIZZARK!
A WIZZARD LIZZARK?!
IF YOU'RE IN A STORM, DO YOU BECOME A BLIZZARK?!
HA!
AMPHIBIANS BREATHE THROUGH THEIR SKIN.
IT MAKES THE ADMINISTRATION OF POTIONS PARTICULARLY EASY!
NO!
BEHOLD, THE BLAKK MUDD!
GET THIS STUFF OFF ME!
I CAN FEEL IT PENETRATE MY SKIN!
NOT SCALES!
ANYTHING BUT THE FOUL SCALES!
I ...

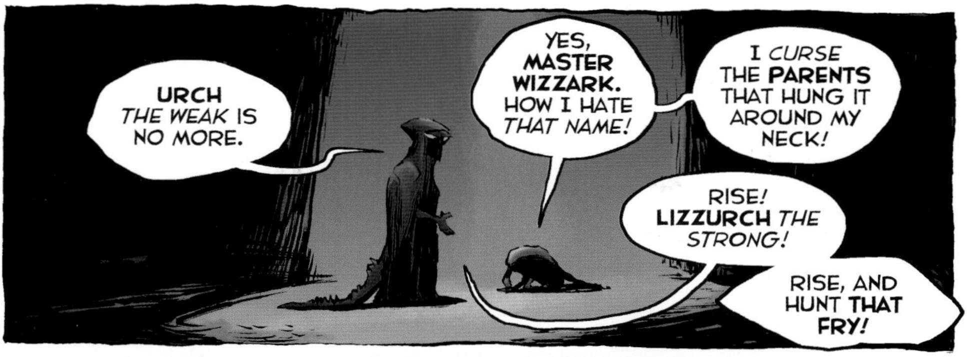
URCH THE WEAK IS NO MORE.
YES, MASTER WIZZARK. HOW I HATE THAT NAME!
I CURSE THE PARENTS THAT HUNG IT AROUND MY NECK!
RISE! LIZZURCH THE STRONG!
RISE, AND HUNT THAT FRY!

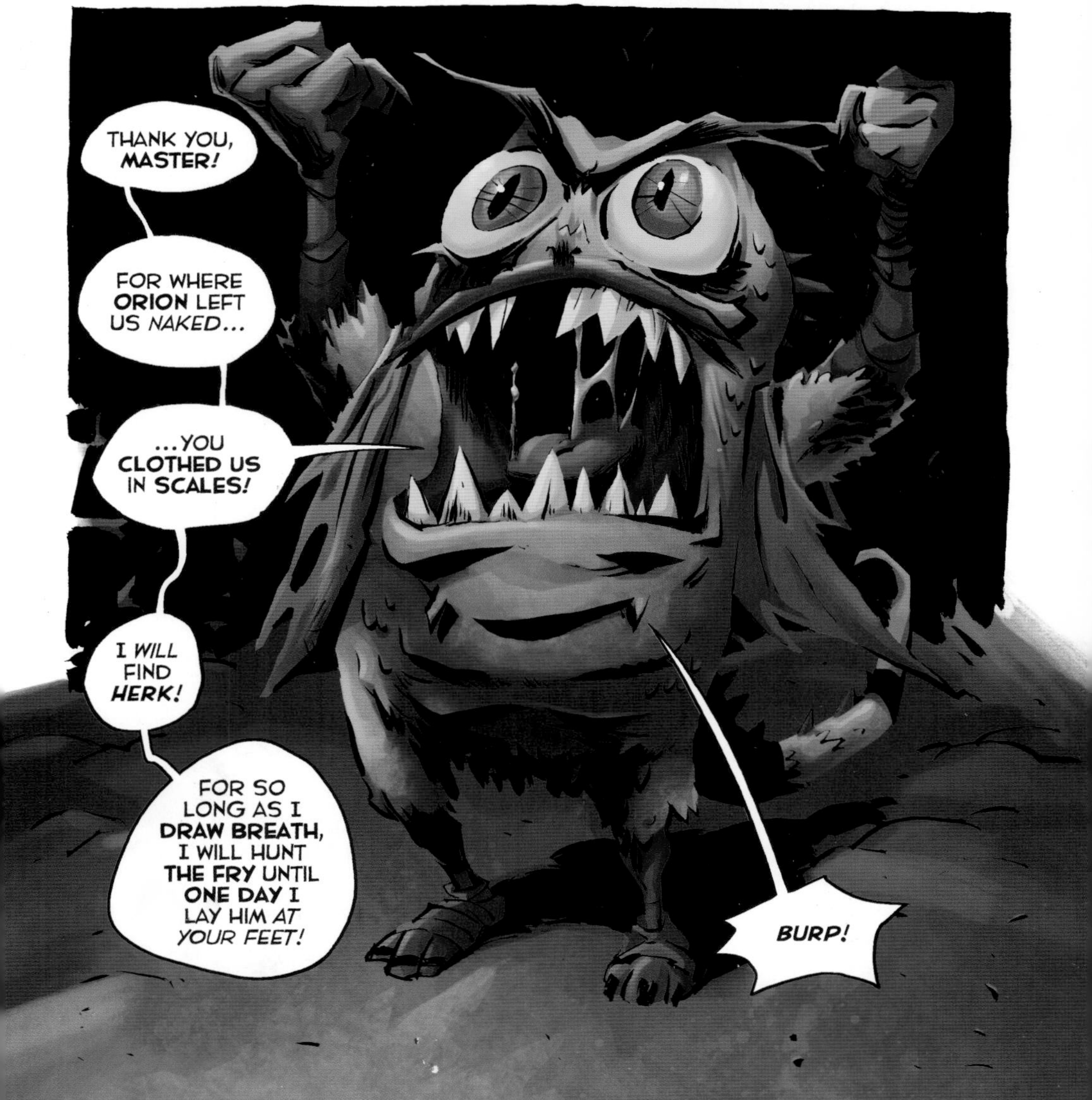
THANK YOU, MASTER!
FOR WHERE ORION LEFT US NAKED...
...YOU CLOTHED US IN SCALES!
I WILL FIND HERK!
FOR SO LONG AS I DRAW BREATH, I WILL HUNT THE FRY UNTIL ONE DAY I LAY HIM AT YOUR FEET!
BURP!

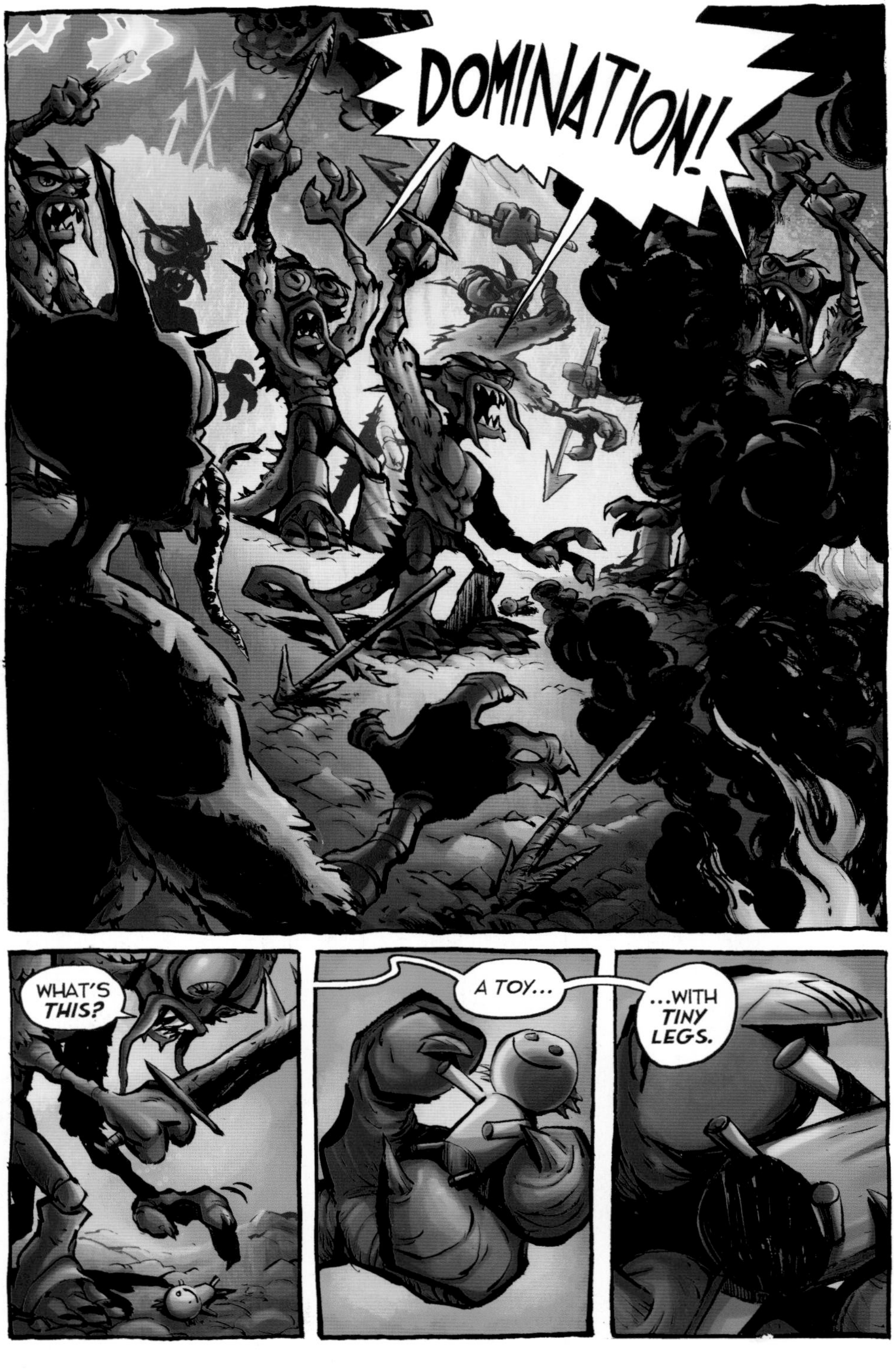
DOMINATION!
WHAT'S THIS?
A TOY...
...WITH TINY LEGS.

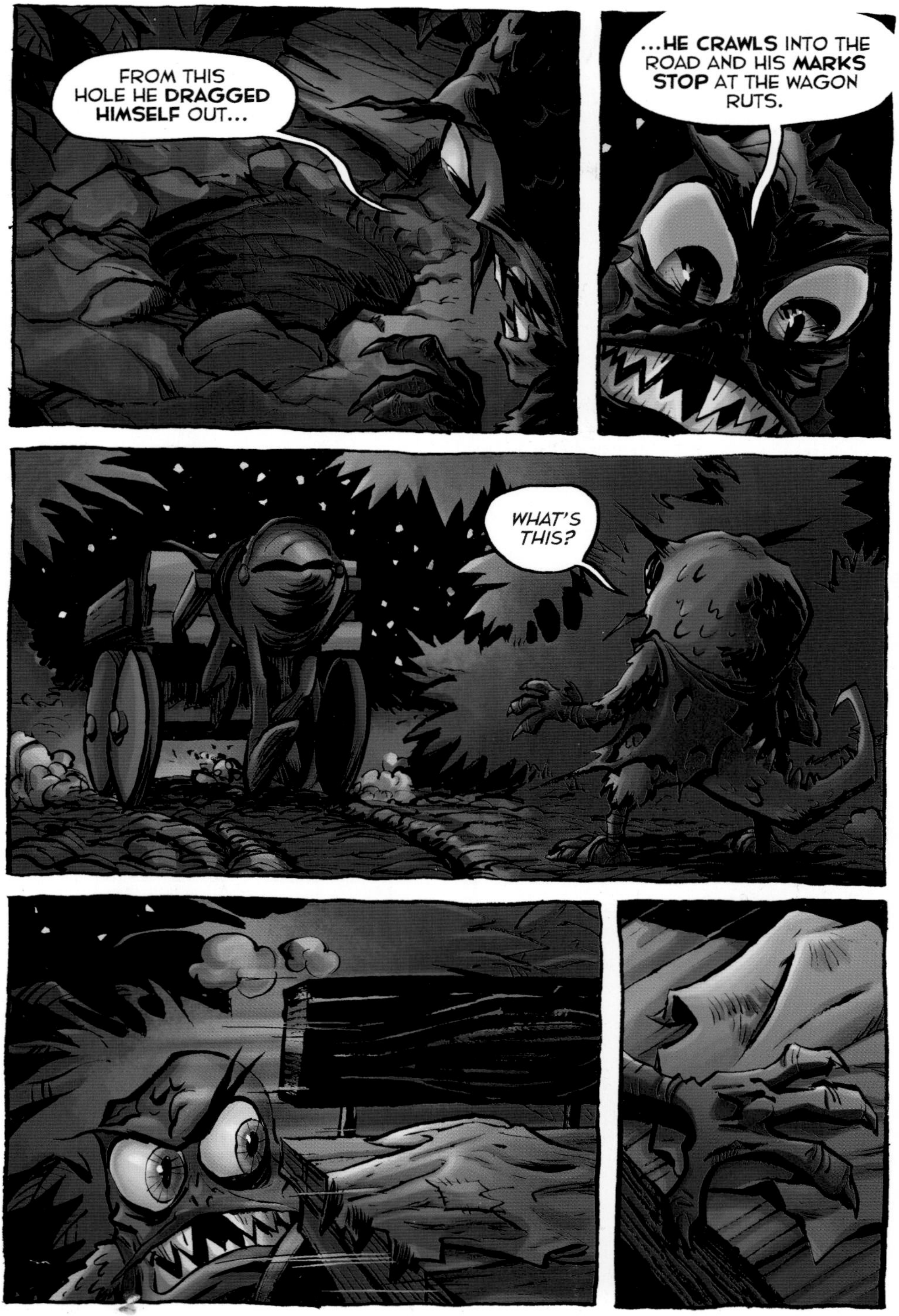
FROM THIS HOLE HE DRAGGED HIMSELF OUT...
...HE CRAWLS INTO THE ROAD AND HIS MARKS STOP AT THE WAGON RUTS.
WHAT'S THIS?

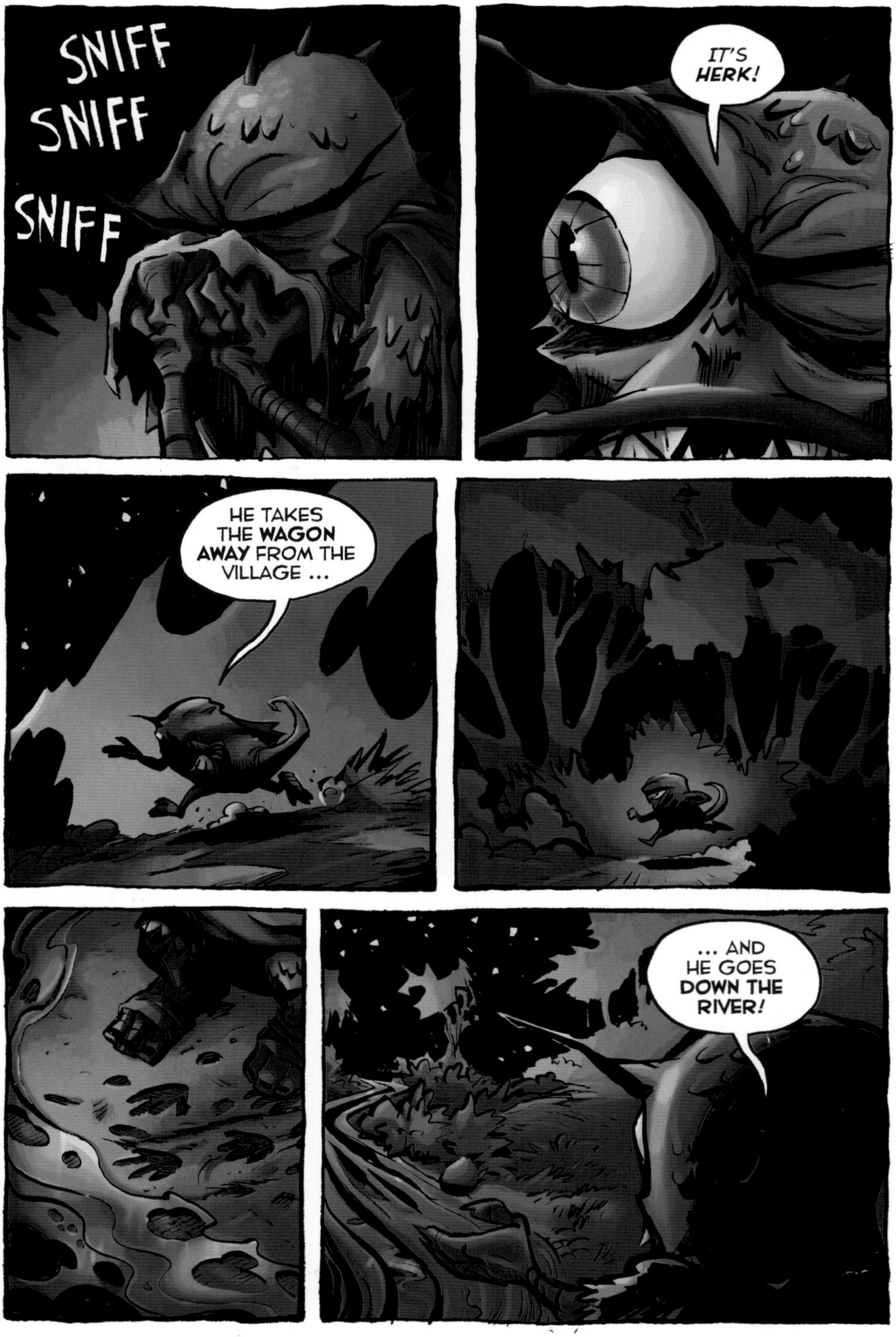
SNIFF
SNIFF
SNIFF
IT'S HERK!
HE TAKES THE WAGON AWAY FROM THE VILLAGE ...
... AND HE GOES DOWN THE RIVER!

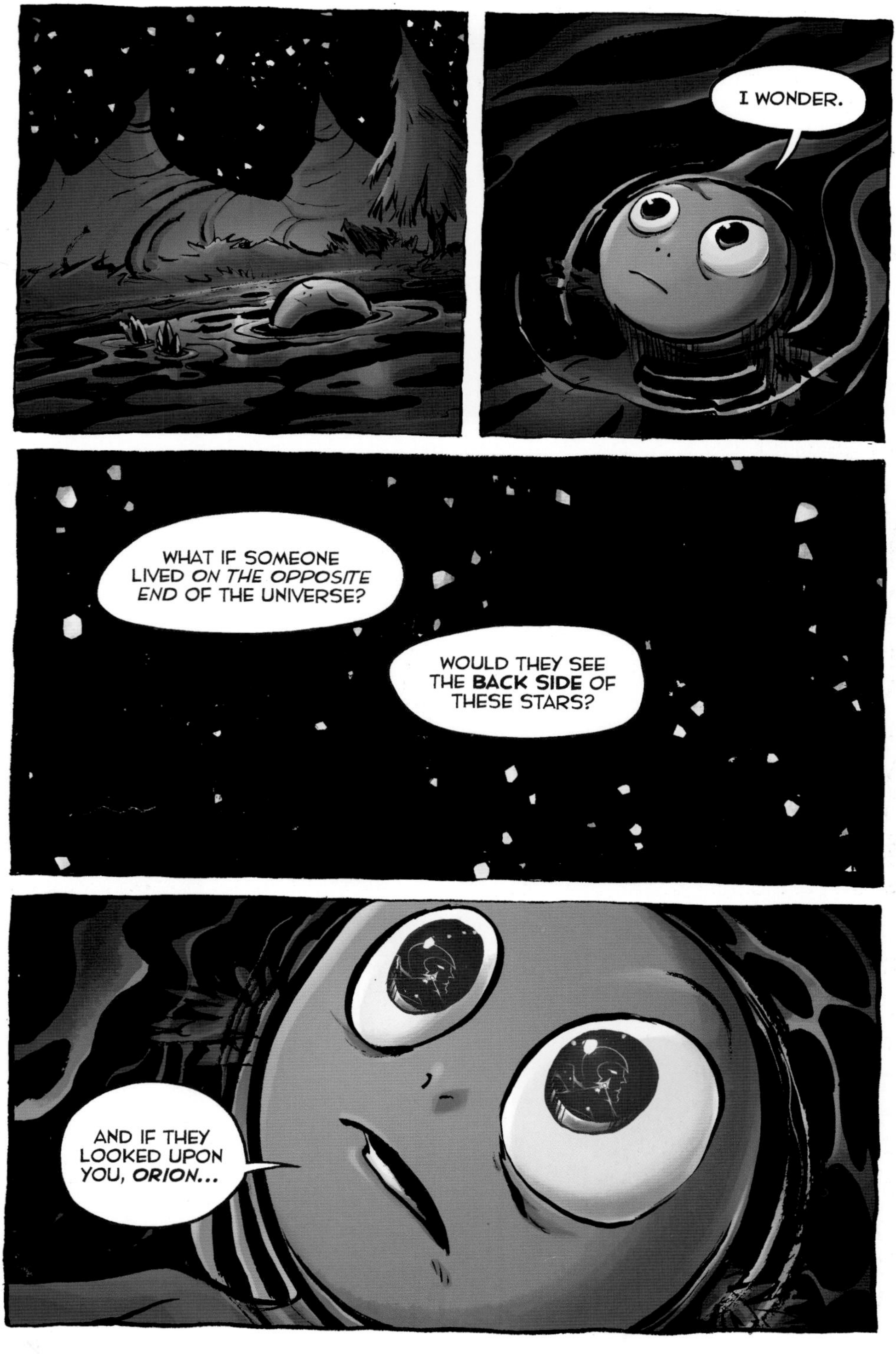
I WONDER.
WHAT IF SOMEONE LIVED *ON THE OPPOSITE END* OF THE UNIVERSE?
WOULD THEY SEE THE **BACK SIDE** OF THESE STARS?
AND IF THEY LOOKED UPON YOU, ***ORION...***

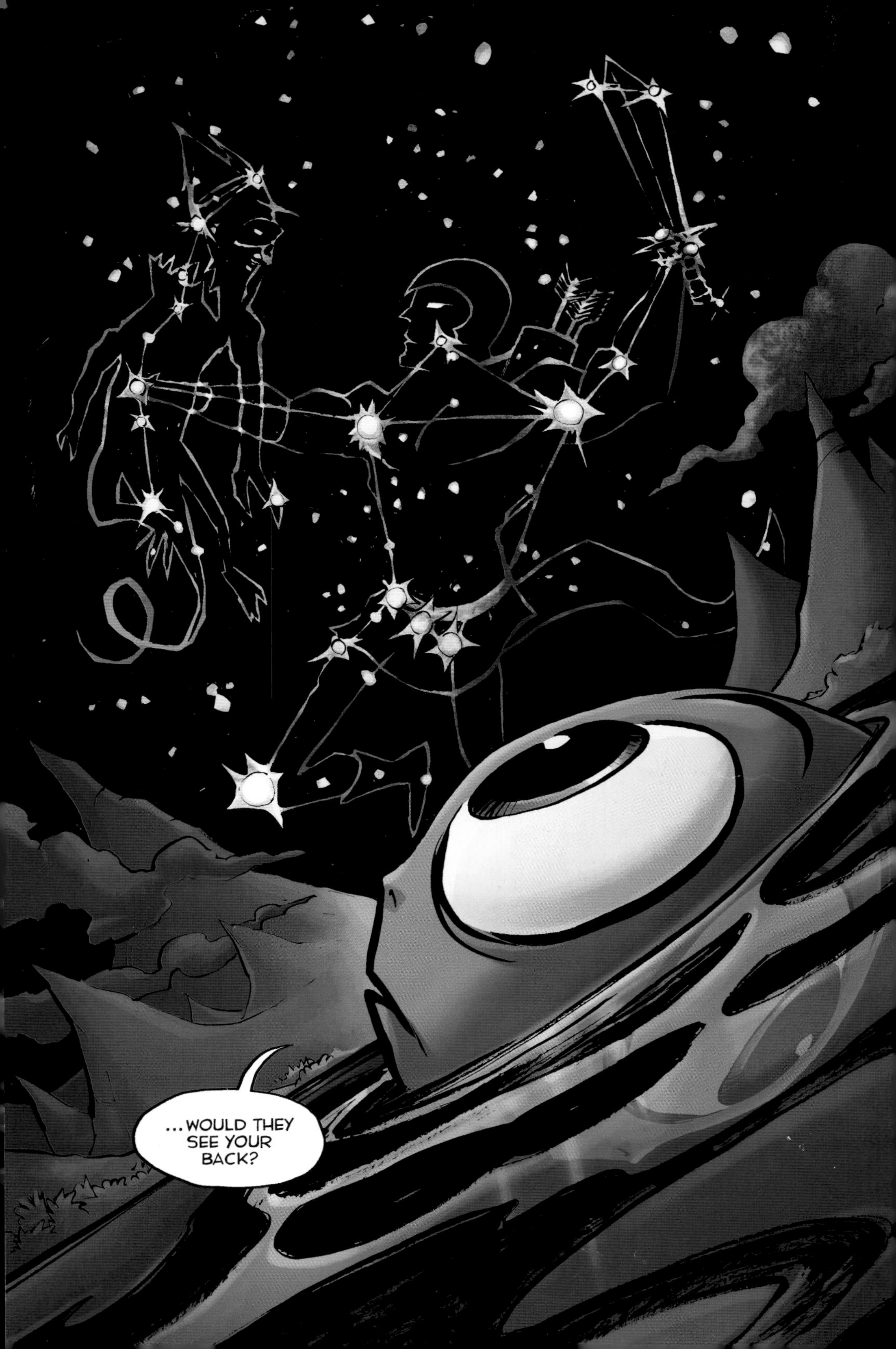
...WOULD THEY SEE YOUR BACK?

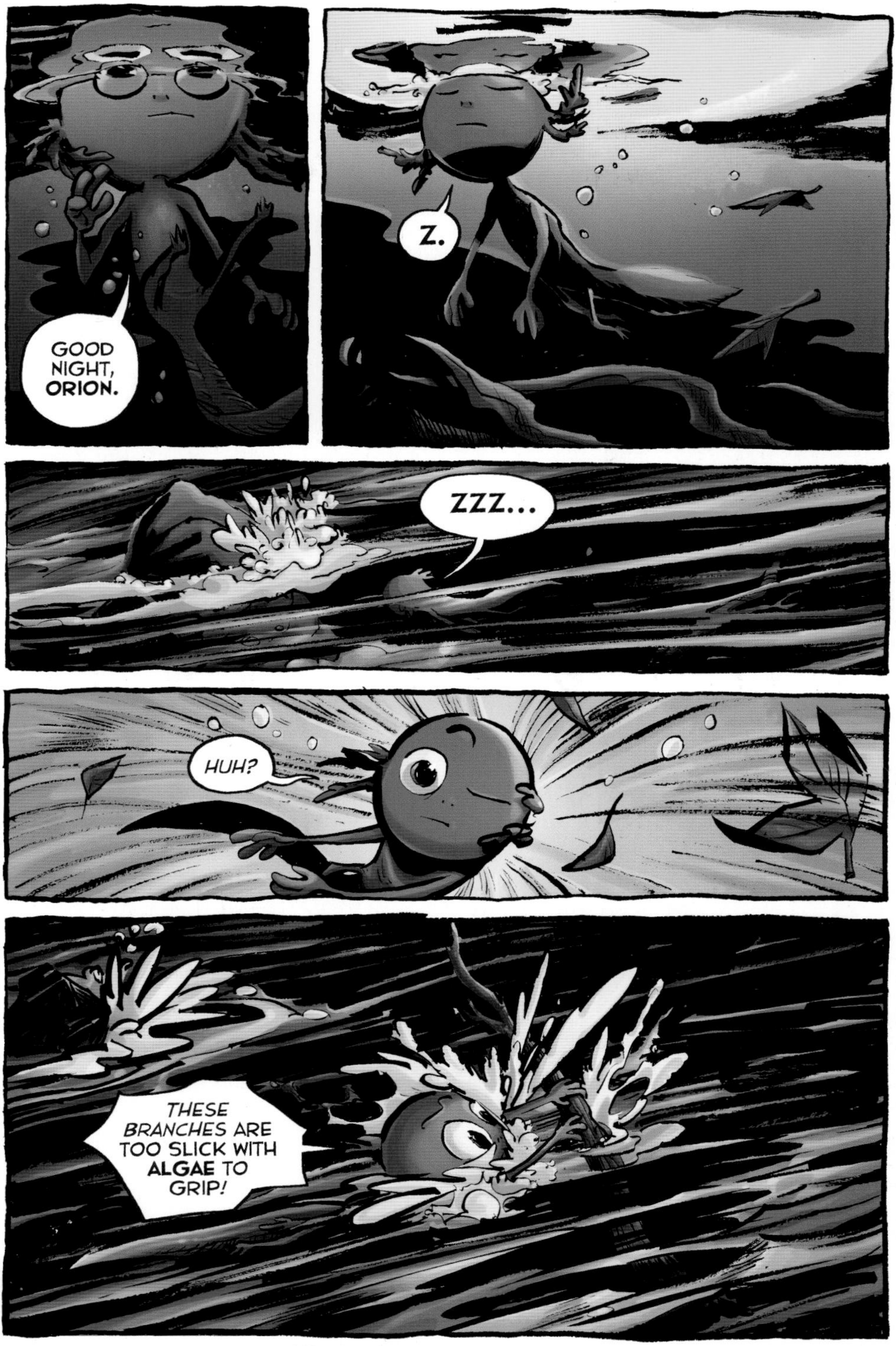
GOOD NIGHT, ORION.
Z.
ZZZ...
HUH?
THESE BRANCHES ARE TOO SLICK WITH ALGAE TO GRIP!

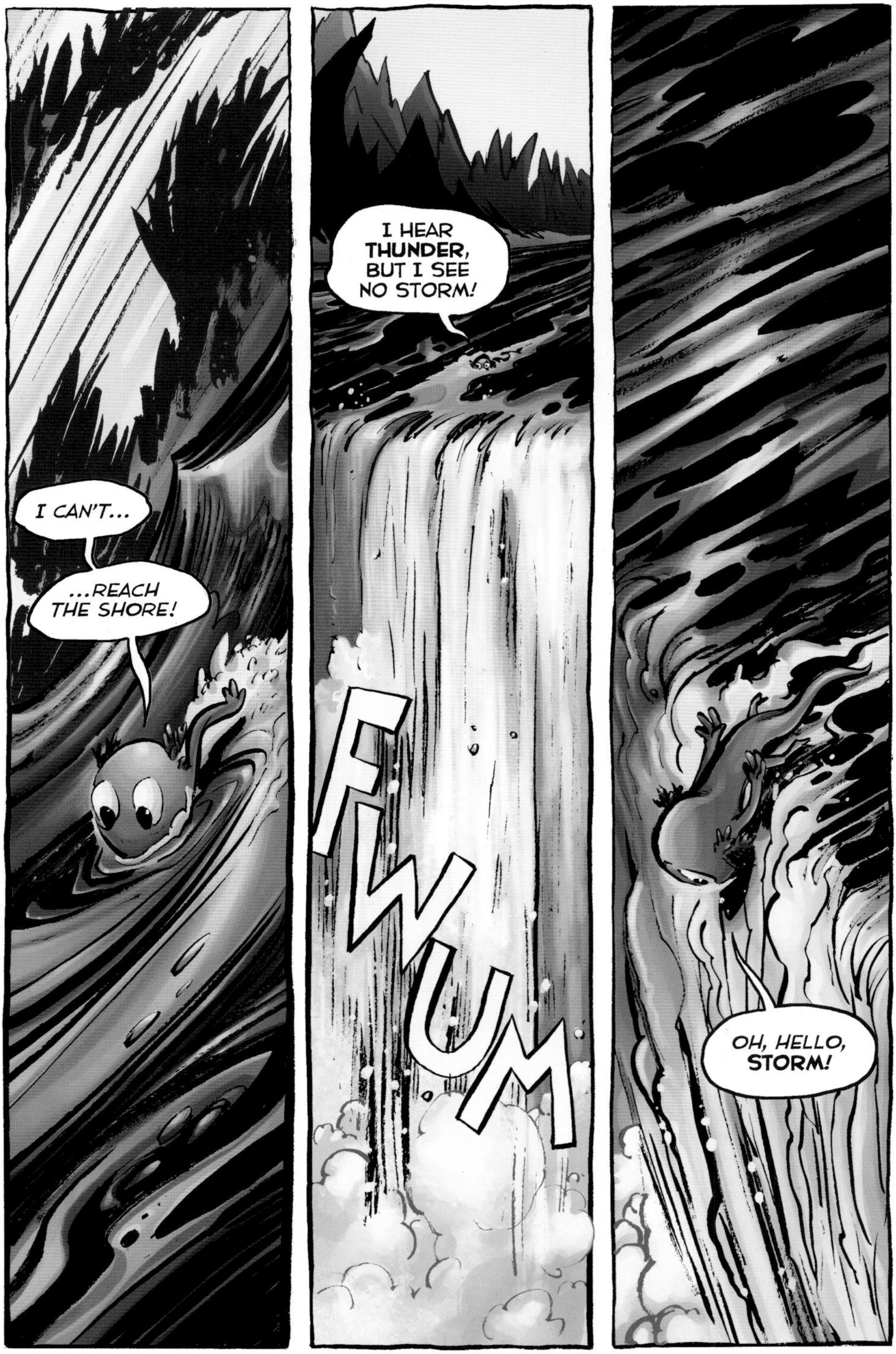
I CAN'T...
...REACH THE SHORE!
I HEAR THUNDER, BUT I SEE NO STORM!
FWUM
OH, HELLO, STORM!

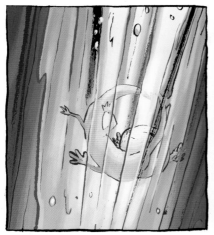

I'M ALIVE!

I CAN'T SEE **ANYTHING** IN THIS CHURN!

TIME TO GO DEEP.

MUCH BETTER.

NO LONGER DOES THE **SEA GRASS** *BEND*...

...THE WATER IS AT A NEAR **STANDSTILL.**

A BOAT!

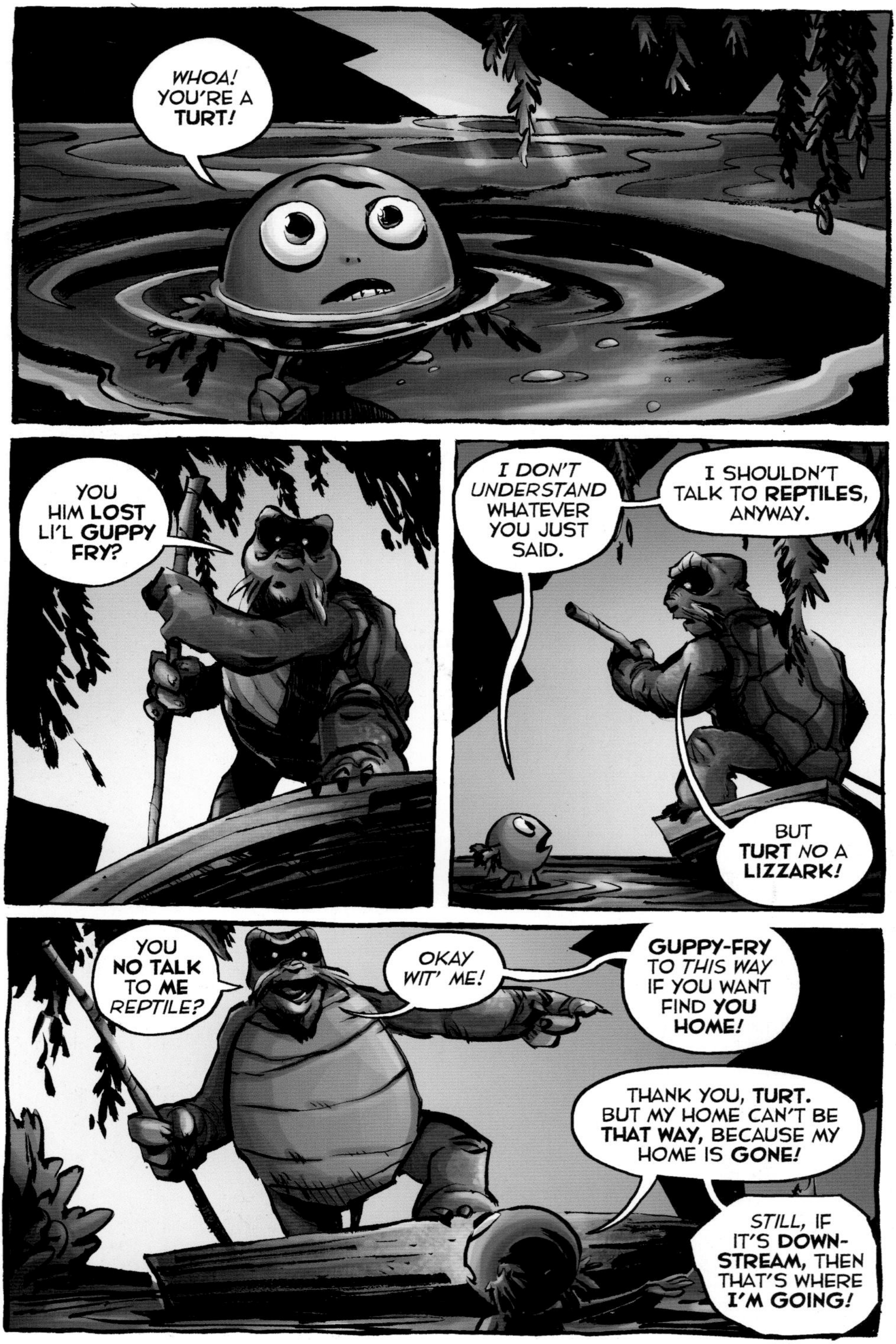
WHOA! YOU'RE A TURT!
YOU HIM LOST LI'L GUPPY FRY?
I DON'T UNDERSTAND WHATEVER YOU JUST SAID.
I SHOULDN'T TALK TO REPTILES, ANYWAY.
BUT TURT NO A LIZZARK!
YOU NO TALK TO ME REPTILE?
OKAY WIT' ME!
GUPPY-FRY TO THIS WAY IF YOU WANT FIND YOU HOME!
THANK YOU, TURT. BUT MY HOME CAN'T BE THAT WAY, BECAUSE MY HOME IS GONE!
STILL, IF IT'S DOWN-STREAM, THEN THAT'S WHERE I'M GOING!

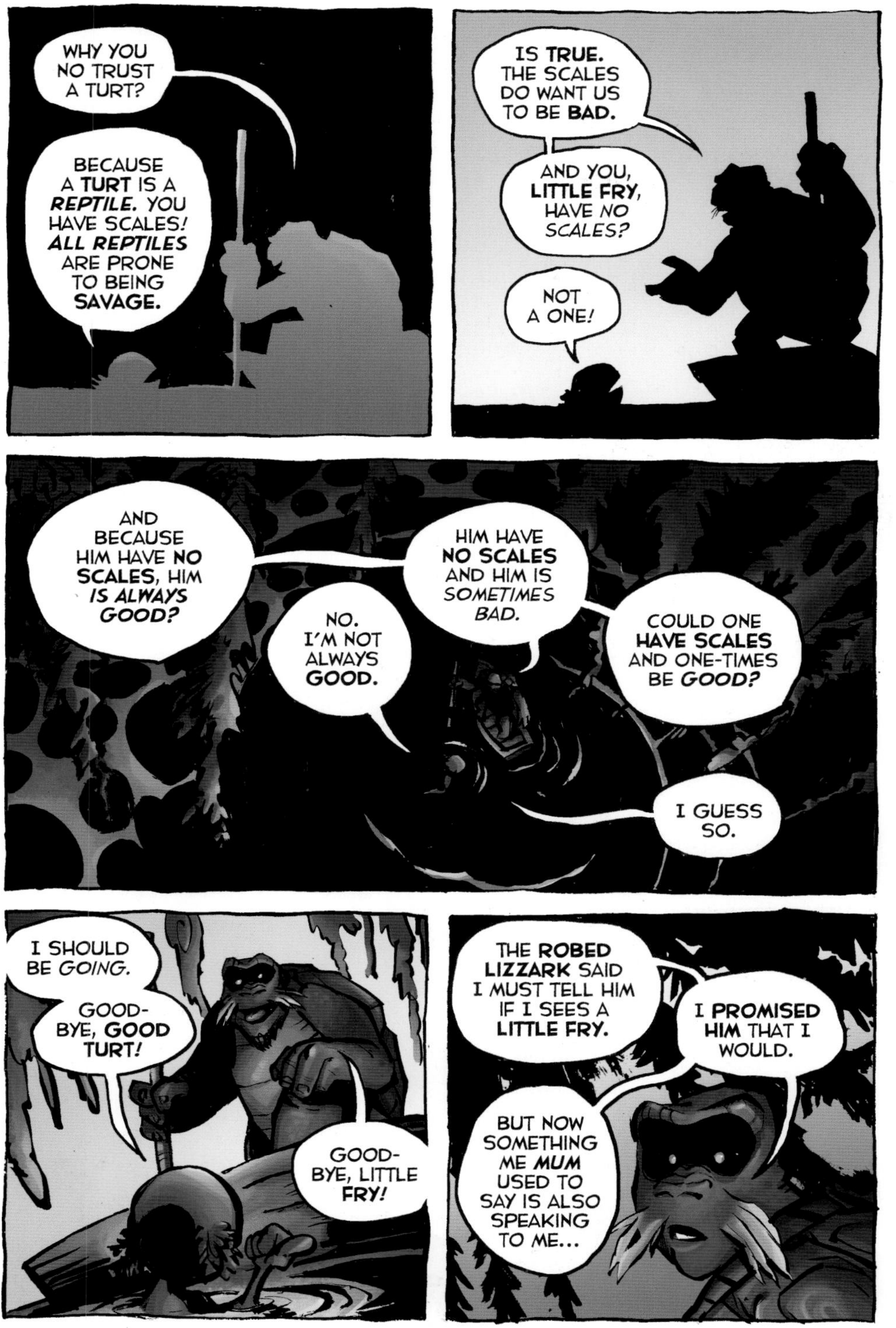
WHY YOU NO TRUST A TURT?
BECAUSE A TURT IS A REPTILE. YOU HAVE SCALES! ALL REPTILES ARE PRONE TO BEING SAVAGE.
IS TRUE. THE SCALES DO WANT US TO BE BAD.
AND YOU, LITTLE FRY, HAVE NO SCALES?
NOT A ONE!
AND BECAUSE HIM HAVE NO SCALES, HIM IS ALWAYS GOOD?
NO. I'M NOT ALWAYS GOOD.
HIM HAVE NO SCALES AND HIM IS SOMETIMES BAD.
COULD ONE HAVE SCALES AND ONE-TIMES BE GOOD?
I GUESS SO.
I SHOULD BE GOING.
GOOD-BYE, GOOD TURT!
GOOD-BYE, LITTLE FRY!
THE ROBED LIZZARK SAID I MUST TELL HIM IF I SEES A LITTLE FRY.
I PROMISED HIM THAT I WOULD.
BUT NOW SOMETHING ME MUM USED TO SAY IS ALSO SPEAKING TO ME...

...SHE SAY,
"*HIM IS LOW WHO HAS NO HEART,
HIM IS HIGH WHO HELPS THE GUY.
IN THIS EVIL TAKE NO PART,
NEVER HARM A LITTLE FRY.*"

I NO WILL TELL THE **ROBED LIZZARK** WHAT I FOUND.

SPLISH
SPLASH

SHOULD I **TRUST** THE WORDS OF A *REPTILE*?

SPLISH
SPLASH
SPLISH
SPLISH
SPLISH
SPLASH
SPLISH

MAYBE I SHOULD GO IN *THE OPPOSITE* DIRECTION!

SPLASH
SPLISH
SPLASH
SPLISH
SPLASH

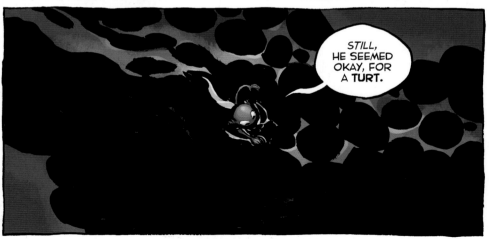

STILL, HE SEEMED OKAY, FOR A **TURT.**

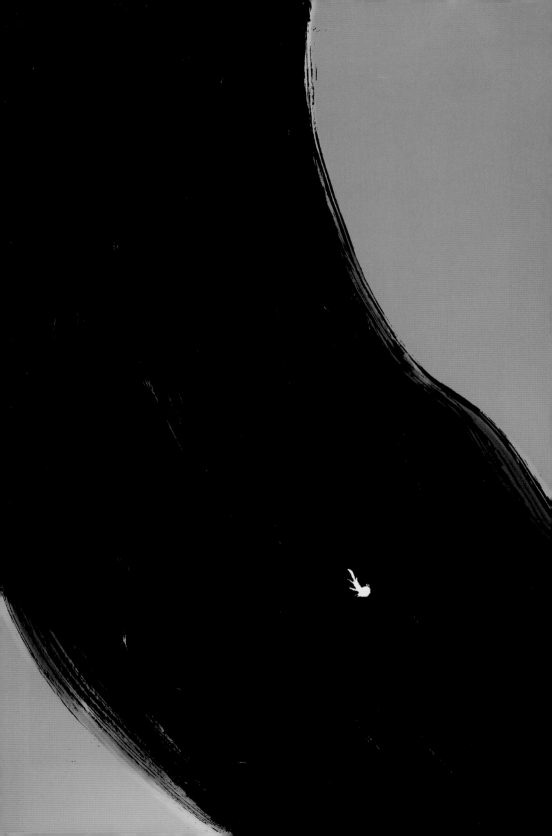

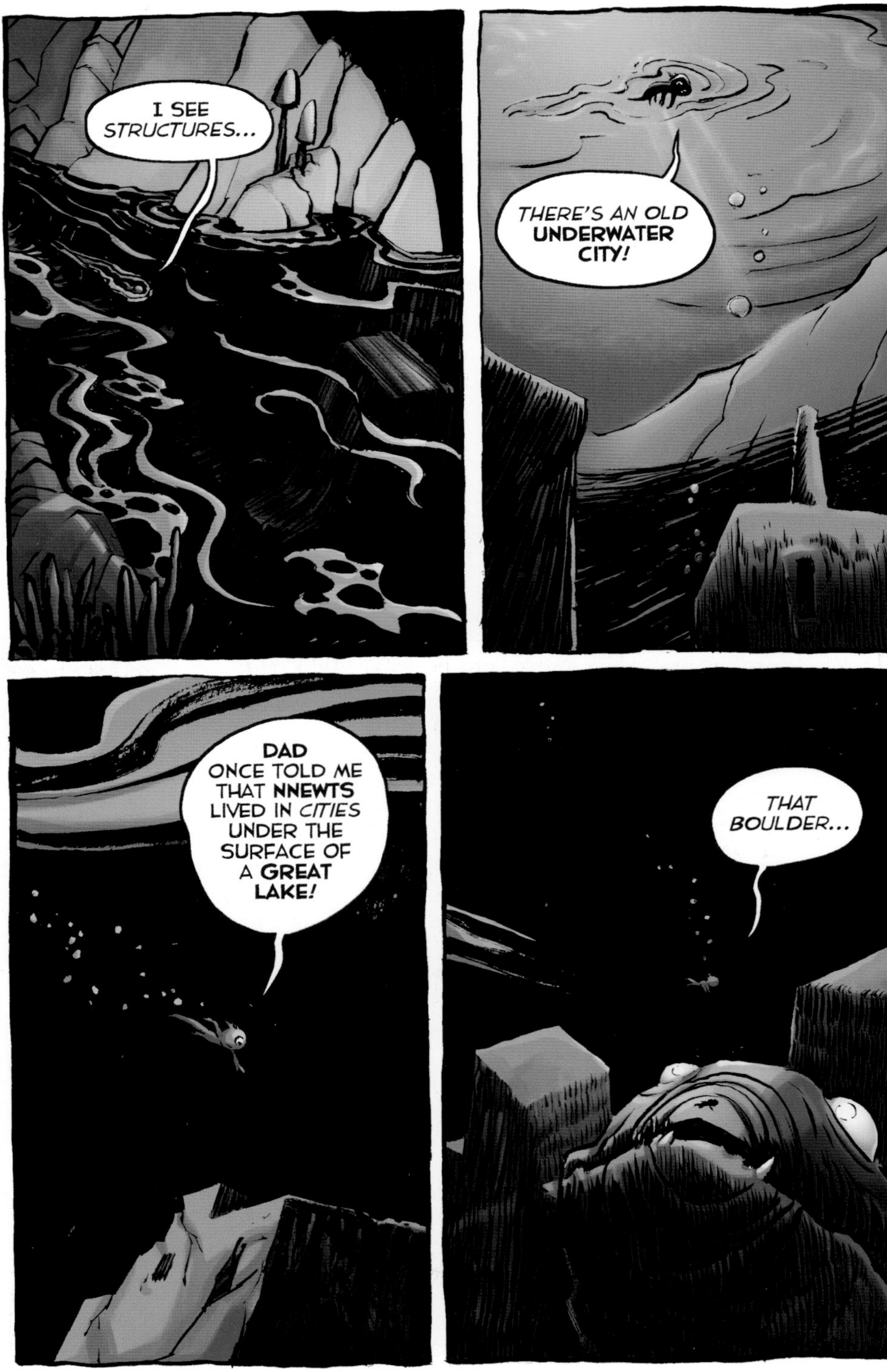
I SEE STRUCTURES...
THERE'S AN OLD UNDERWATER CITY!
DAD ONCE TOLD ME THAT NNEWTS LIVED IN CITIES UNDER THE SURFACE OF A GREAT LAKE!
THAT BOULDER...

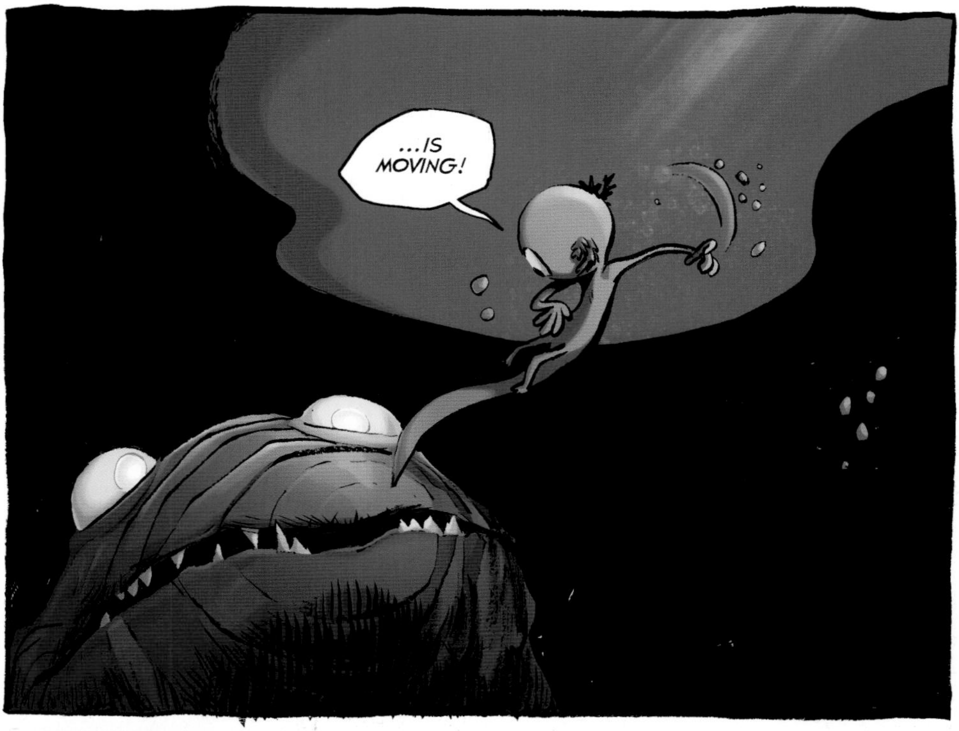
...IS MOVING!

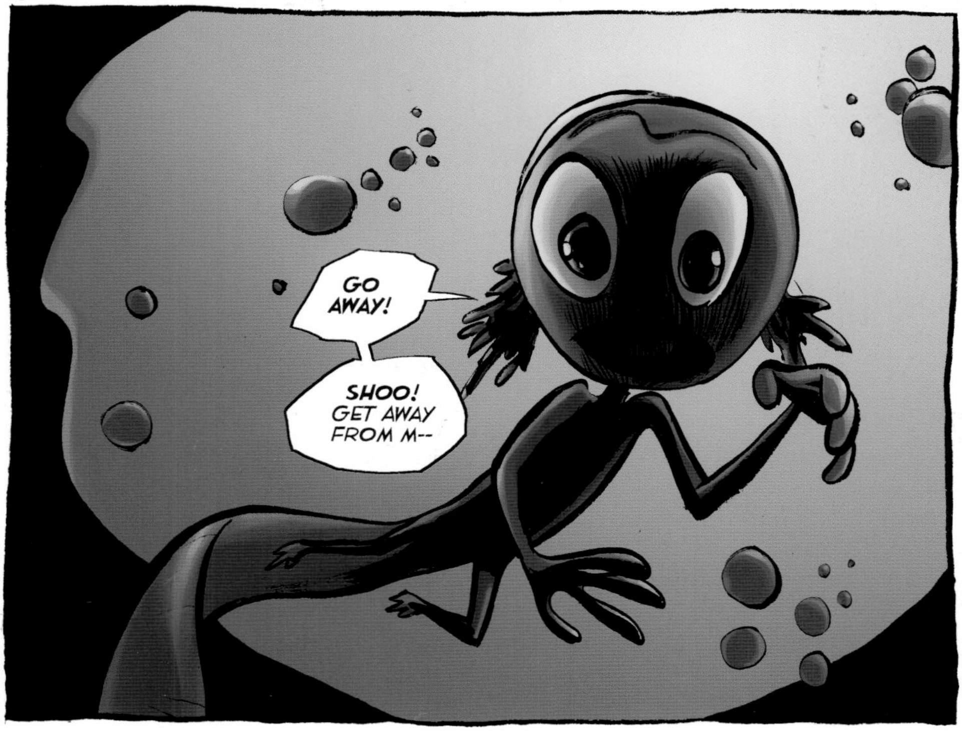
GO AWAY!
SHOO! GET AWAY FROM M--

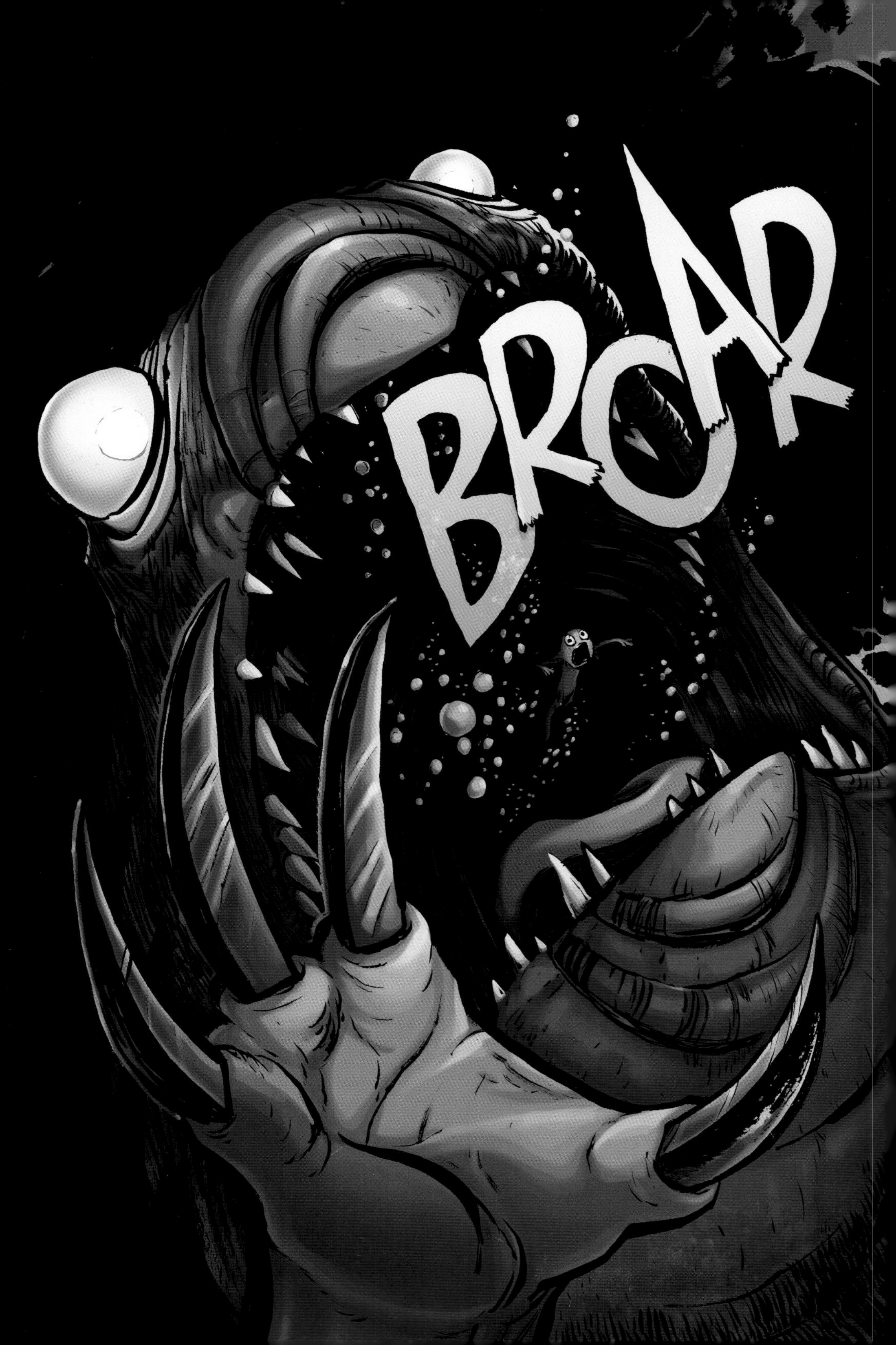
BROAR

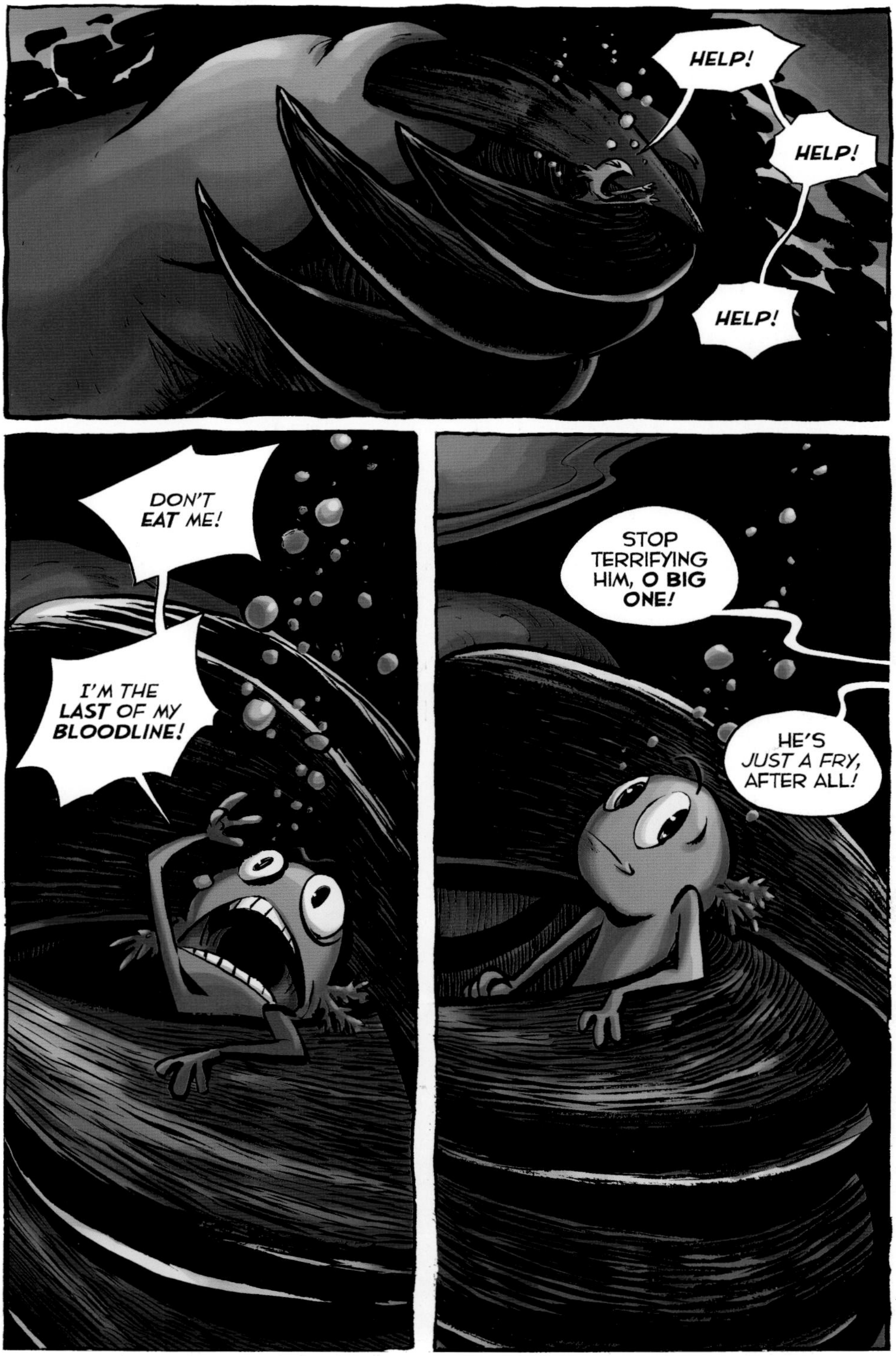
HELP!
HELP!
HELP!
DON'T EAT ME!
I'M THE LAST OF MY BLOODLINE!
STOP TERRIFYING HIM, O BIG ONE!
HE'S JUST A FRY, AFTER ALL!

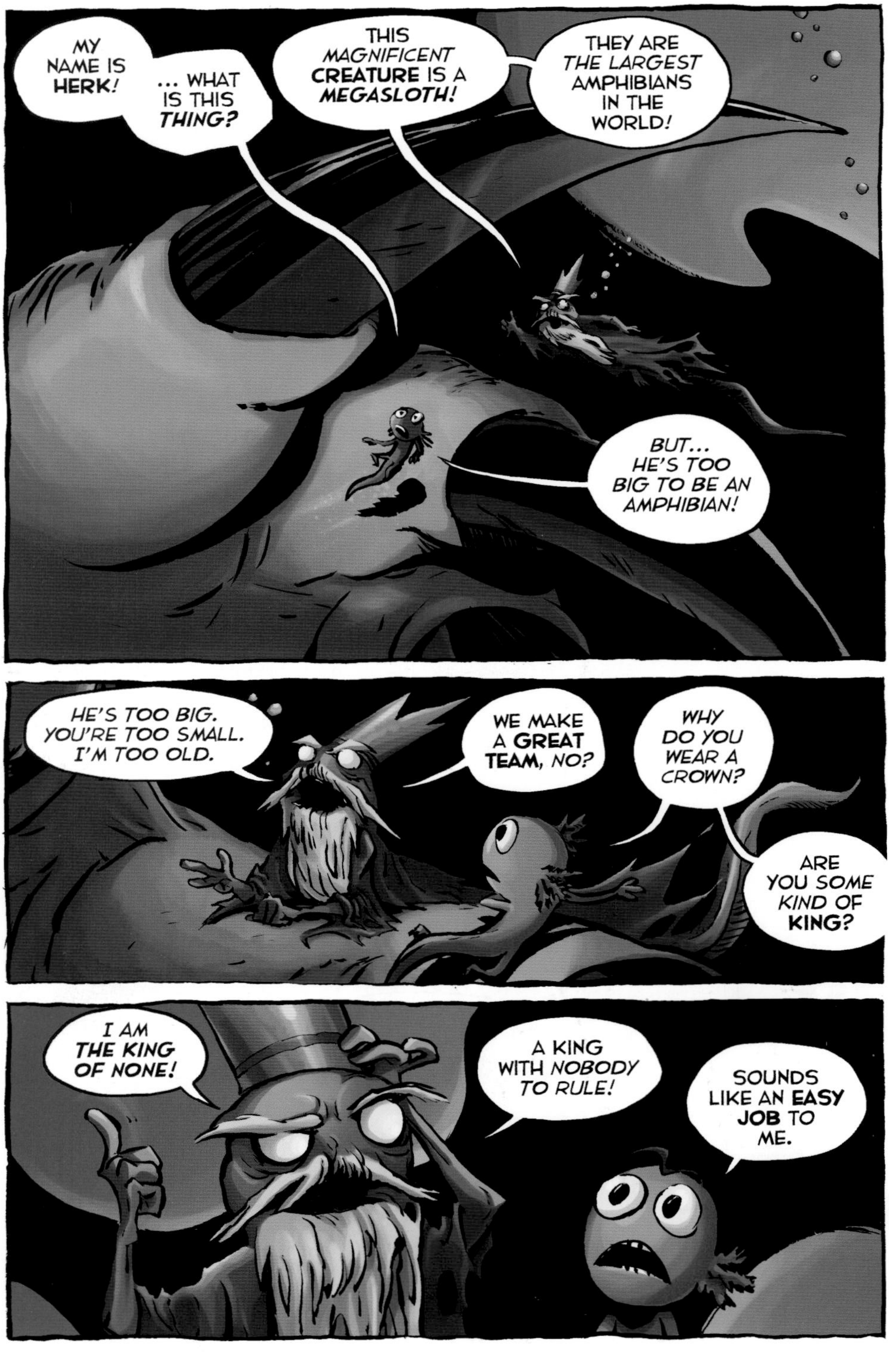

MY NAME IS **HERK**!
... WHAT IS THIS *THING?*
THIS *MAGNIFICENT* **CREATURE** IS A *MEGASLOTH!*
THEY ARE *THE LARGEST* AMPHIBIANS IN THE WORLD!
BUT... HE'S TOO BIG TO BE AN AMPHIBIAN!
HE'S TOO BIG. YOU'RE TOO SMALL. I'M TOO OLD.
WE MAKE A **GREAT TEAM,** *NO?*
WHY DO YOU WEAR A CROWN?
ARE YOU SOME *KIND OF* **KING?**
I AM **THE KING OF NONE!**
A KING WITH *NOBODY TO RULE!*
SOUNDS LIKE AN **EASY JOB** TO ME.

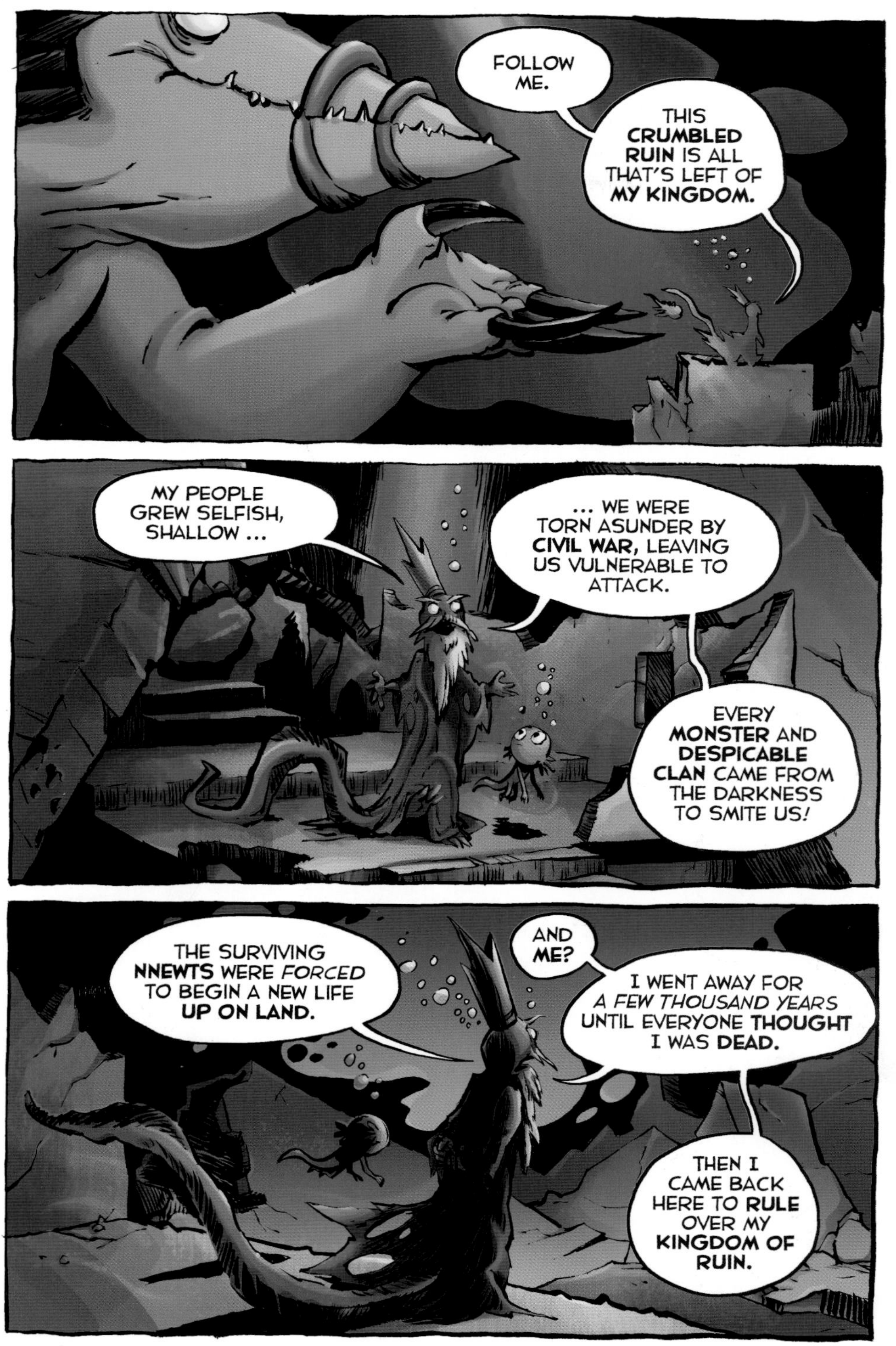
FOLLOW ME.
THIS CRUMBLED RUIN IS ALL THAT'S LEFT OF MY KINGDOM.
MY PEOPLE GREW SELFISH, SHALLOW ...
... WE WERE TORN ASUNDER BY CIVIL WAR, LEAVING US VULNERABLE TO ATTACK.
EVERY MONSTER AND DESPICABLE CLAN CAME FROM THE DARKNESS TO SMITE US!
THE SURVIVING NNEWTS WERE FORCED TO BEGIN A NEW LIFE UP ON LAND.
AND ME?
I WENT AWAY FOR A FEW THOUSAND YEARS UNTIL EVERYONE THOUGHT I WAS DEAD.
THEN I CAME BACK HERE TO RULE OVER MY KINGDOM OF RUIN.

WE COULD **REBUILD** THIS PLACE!

BLESS YOU, **HERK!**

YOU CAN **SEE** IT! *CAN'T YOU?*

THIS IS WHY I'LL **NEVER** GIVE UP ON **MY KINGDOM!**

... I'M **OBSESSED** WITH **HOPE!**

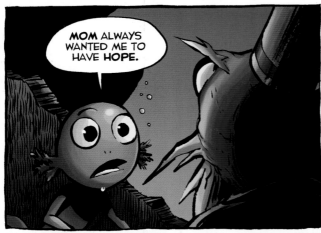

MOM ALWAYS WANTED ME TO HAVE **HOPE.**

I NEVER *REALLY* UNDERSTOOD WHAT **HOPE** WAS ABOUT UNTIL I LOST *EVERYTHING.*

NOW IT'S ALL I'VE GOT.

WELL ...

... LET'S HAVE SOME **LUNCH!**

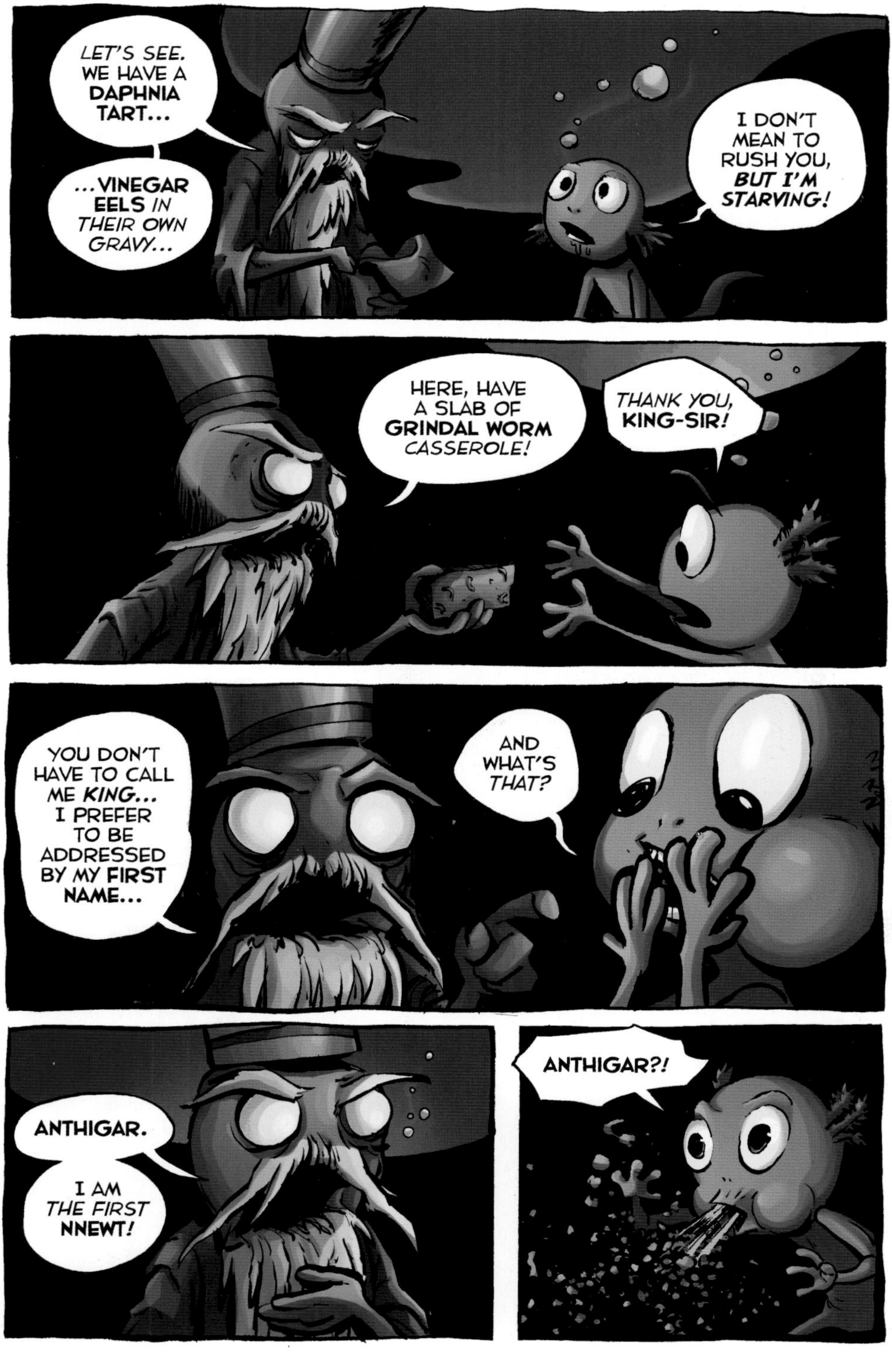
LET'S SEE. WE HAVE A DAPHNIA TART...
...VINEGAR EELS IN THEIR OWN GRAVY...
I DON'T MEAN TO RUSH YOU, BUT I'M STARVING!
HERE, HAVE A SLAB OF GRINDAL WORM CASSEROLE!
THANK YOU, KING-SIR!
YOU DON'T HAVE TO CALL ME KING... I PREFER TO BE ADDRESSED BY MY FIRST NAME...
AND WHAT'S THAT?
ANTHIGAR.
I AM THE FIRST NNEWT!
ANTHIGAR?!

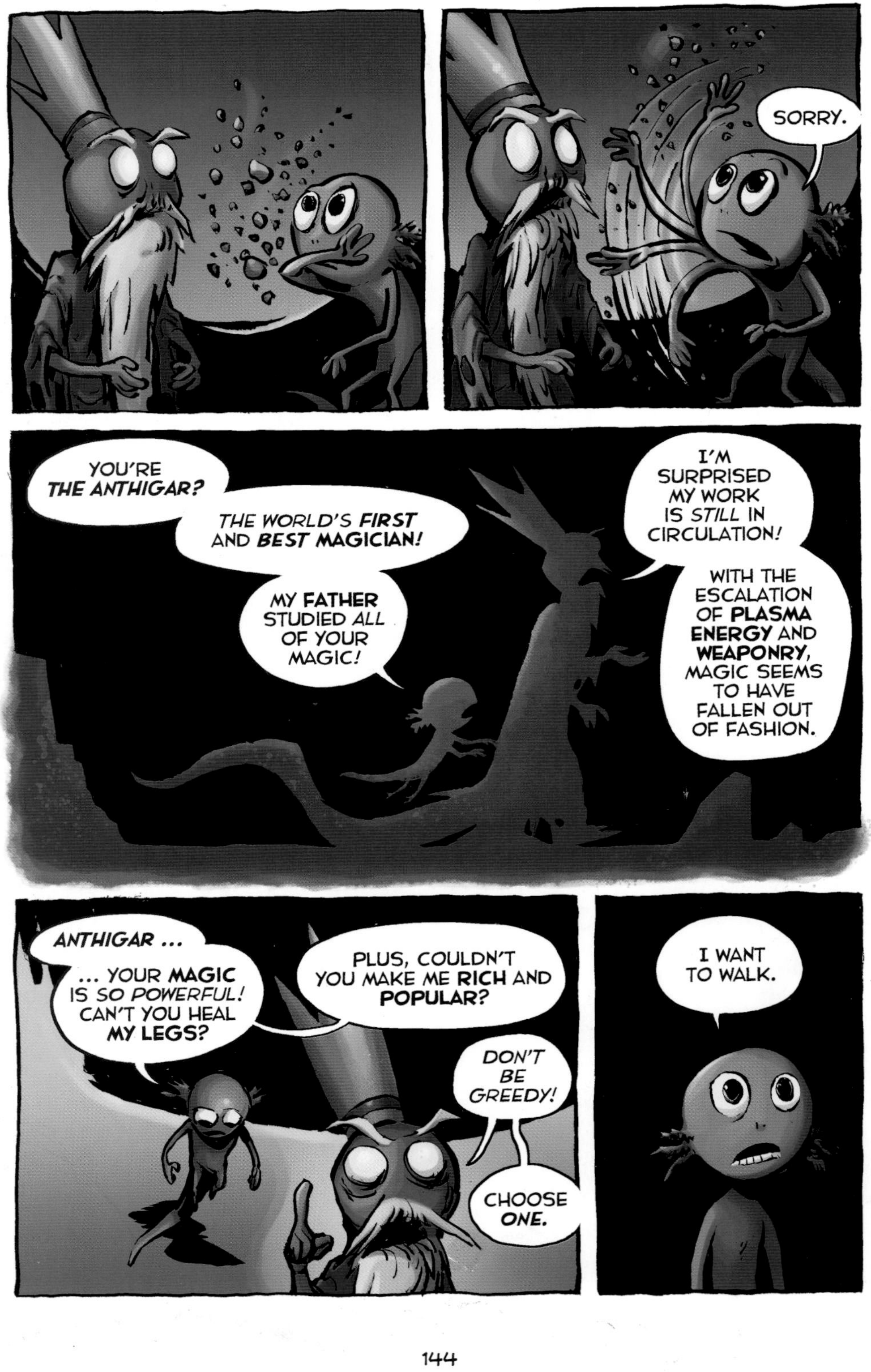
SORRY.
YOU'RE THE ANTHIGAR?
THE WORLD'S FIRST AND BEST MAGICIAN!
MY FATHER STUDIED ALL OF YOUR MAGIC!
I'M SURPRISED MY WORK IS STILL IN CIRCULATION!
WITH THE ESCALATION OF PLASMA ENERGY AND WEAPONRY, MAGIC SEEMS TO HAVE FALLEN OUT OF FASHION.
ANTHIGAR ...
... YOUR MAGIC IS SO POWERFUL! CAN'T YOU HEAL MY LEGS?
PLUS, COULDN'T YOU MAKE ME RICH AND POPULAR?
DON'T BE GREEDY!
CHOOSE ONE.
I WANT TO WALK.

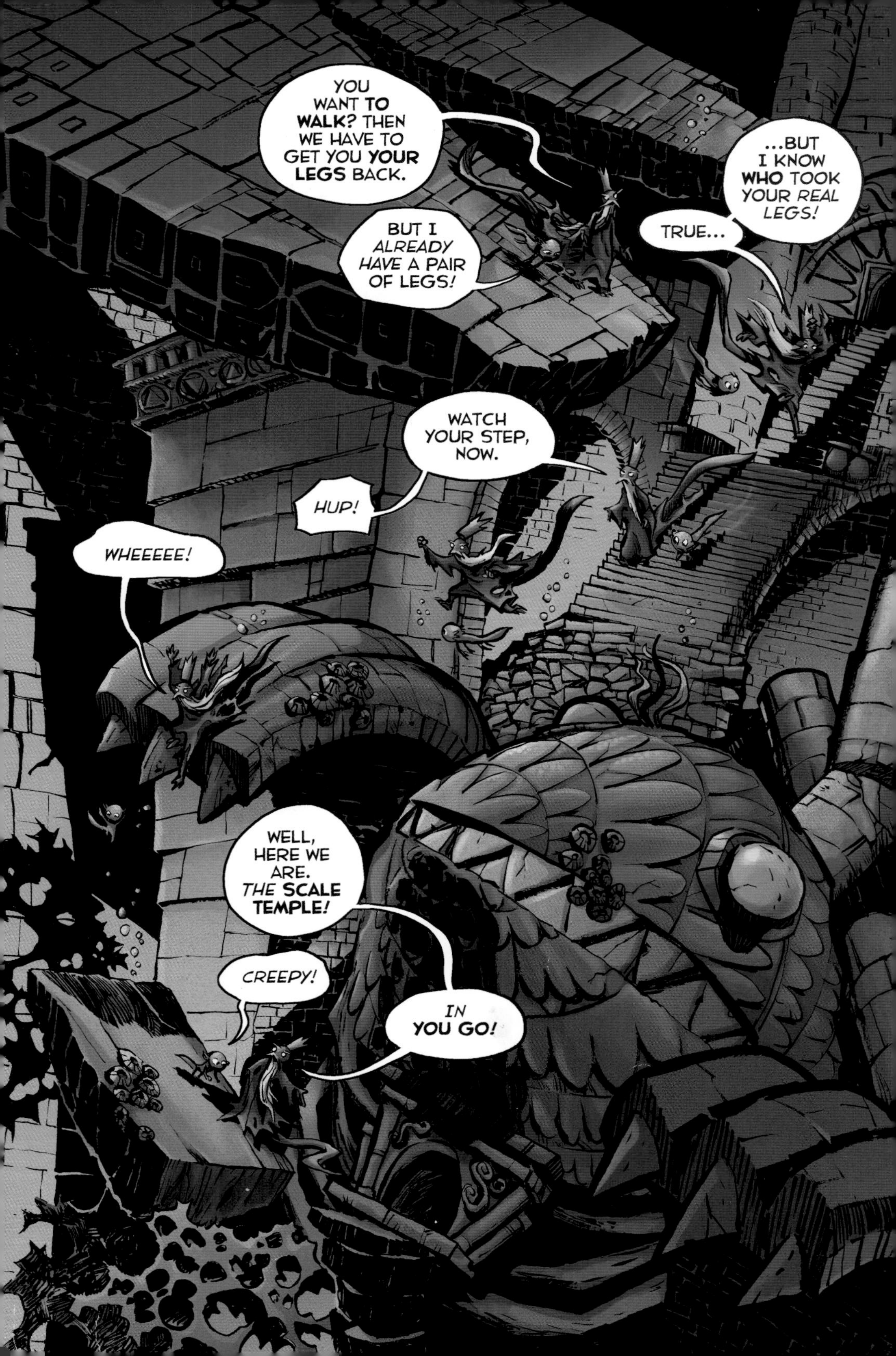
YOU WANT TO WALK? THEN WE HAVE TO GET YOU YOUR LEGS BACK.
BUT I ALREADY HAVE A PAIR OF LEGS!
TRUE...
...BUT I KNOW WHO TOOK YOUR REAL LEGS!
WATCH YOUR STEP, NOW.
HUP!
WHEEEEE!
WELL, HERE WE ARE. THE SCALE TEMPLE!
CREEPY!
IN YOU GO!

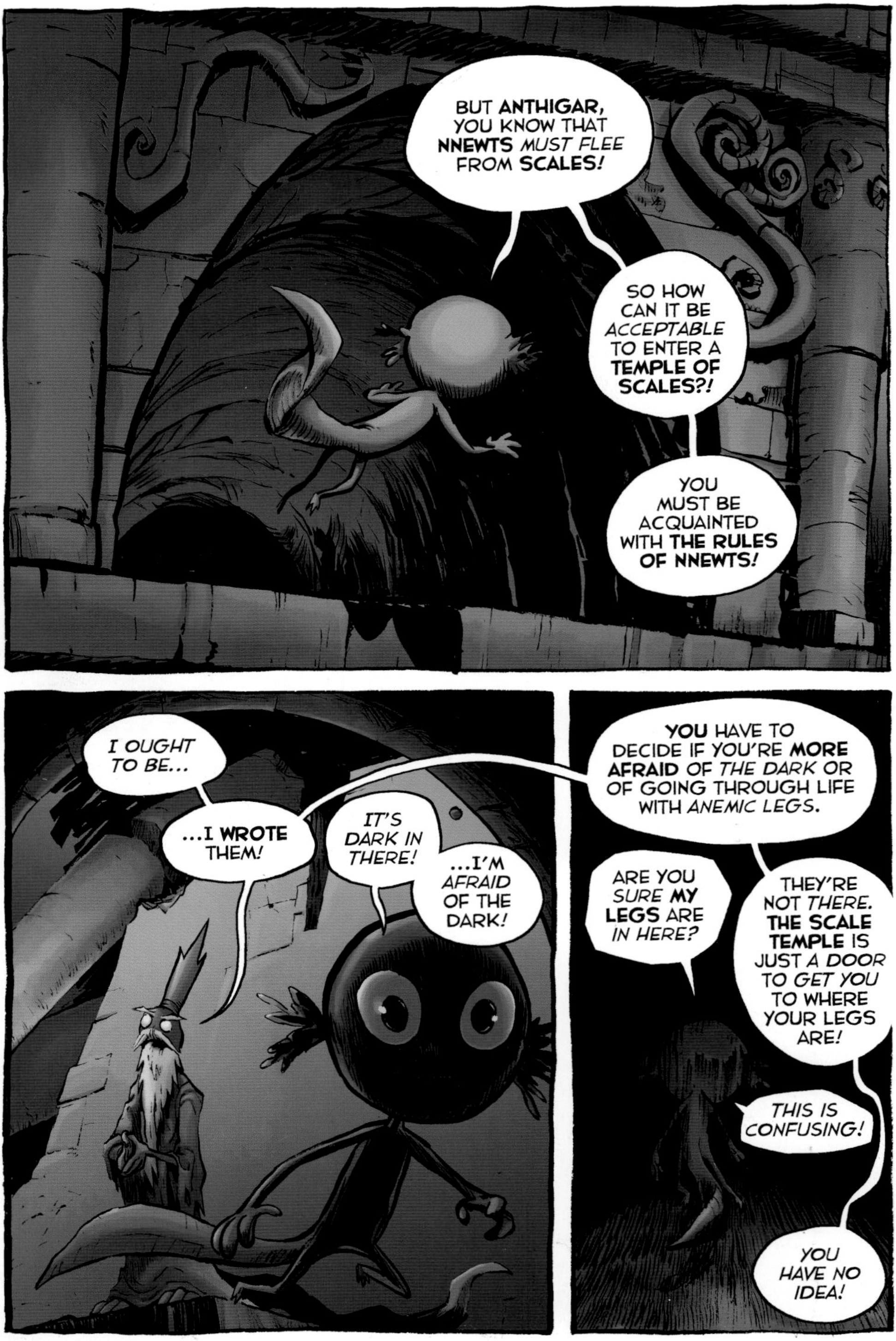
BUT ANTHIGAR, YOU KNOW THAT NNEWTS MUST FLEE FROM SCALES!
SO HOW CAN IT BE ACCEPTABLE TO ENTER A TEMPLE OF SCALES?!
YOU MUST BE ACQUAINTED WITH THE RULES OF NNEWTS!
I OUGHT TO BE...
...I WROTE THEM!
IT'S DARK IN THERE!
...I'M AFRAID OF THE DARK!
YOU HAVE TO DECIDE IF YOU'RE MORE AFRAID OF THE DARK OR OF GOING THROUGH LIFE WITH ANEMIC LEGS.
ARE YOU SURE MY LEGS ARE IN HERE?
THEY'RE NOT THERE. THE SCALE TEMPLE IS JUST A DOOR TO GET YOU TO WHERE YOUR LEGS ARE!
THIS IS CONFUSING!
YOU HAVE NO IDEA!

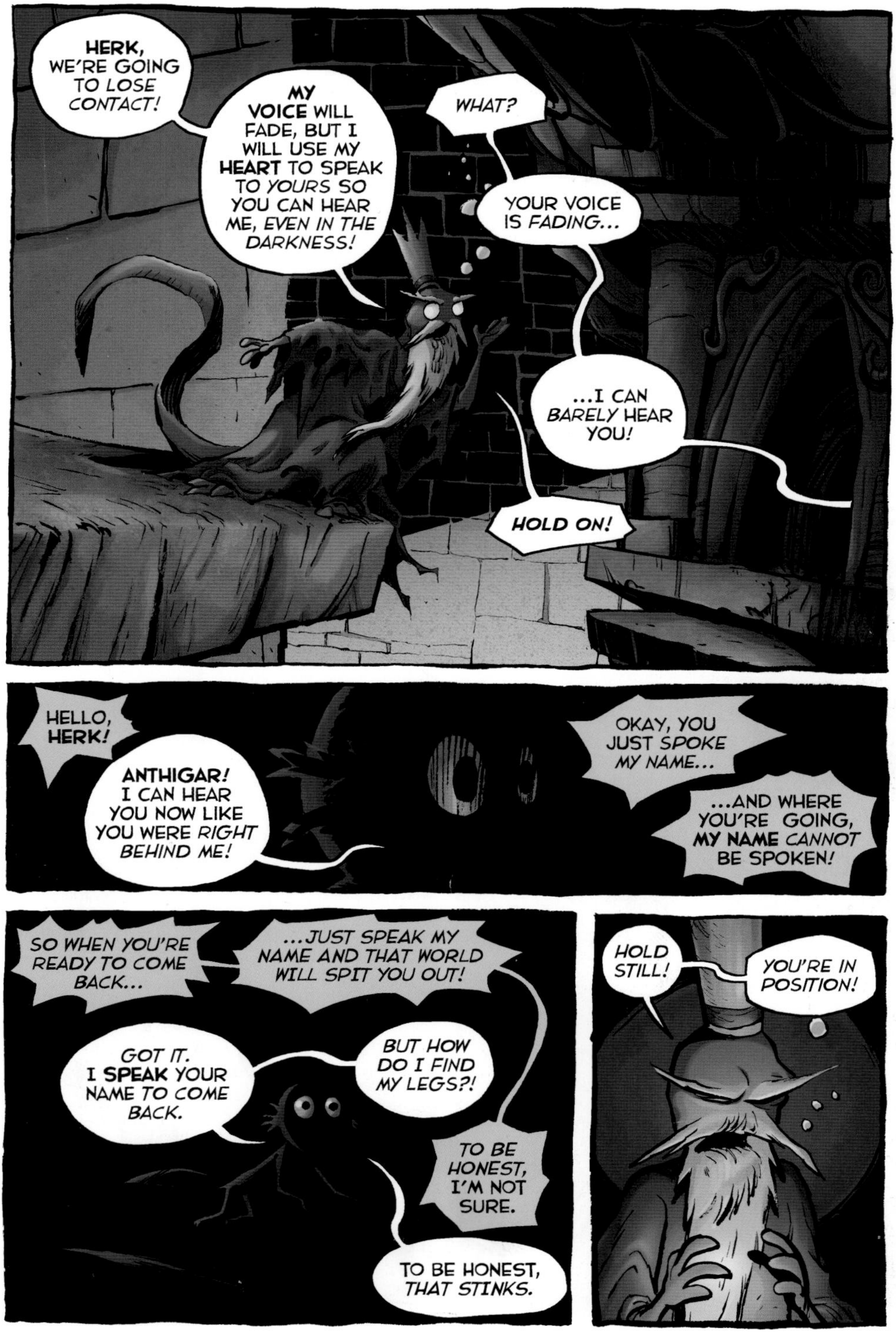
HERK, WE'RE GOING TO LOSE CONTACT!
MY VOICE WILL FADE, BUT I WILL USE MY HEART TO SPEAK TO YOURS SO YOU CAN HEAR ME, EVEN IN THE DARKNESS!
WHAT?
YOUR VOICE IS FADING...
...I CAN BARELY HEAR YOU!
HOLD ON!
HELLO, HERK!
ANTHIGAR! I CAN HEAR YOU NOW LIKE YOU WERE RIGHT BEHIND ME!
OKAY, YOU JUST SPOKE MY NAME...
...AND WHERE YOU'RE GOING, MY NAME CANNOT BE SPOKEN!
SO WHEN YOU'RE READY TO COME BACK...
...JUST SPEAK MY NAME AND THAT WORLD WILL SPIT YOU OUT!
GOT IT. I SPEAK YOUR NAME TO COME BACK.
BUT HOW DO I FIND MY LEGS?!
TO BE HONEST, I'M NOT SURE.
TO BE HONEST, THAT STINKS.
HOLD STILL!
YOU'RE IN POSITION!

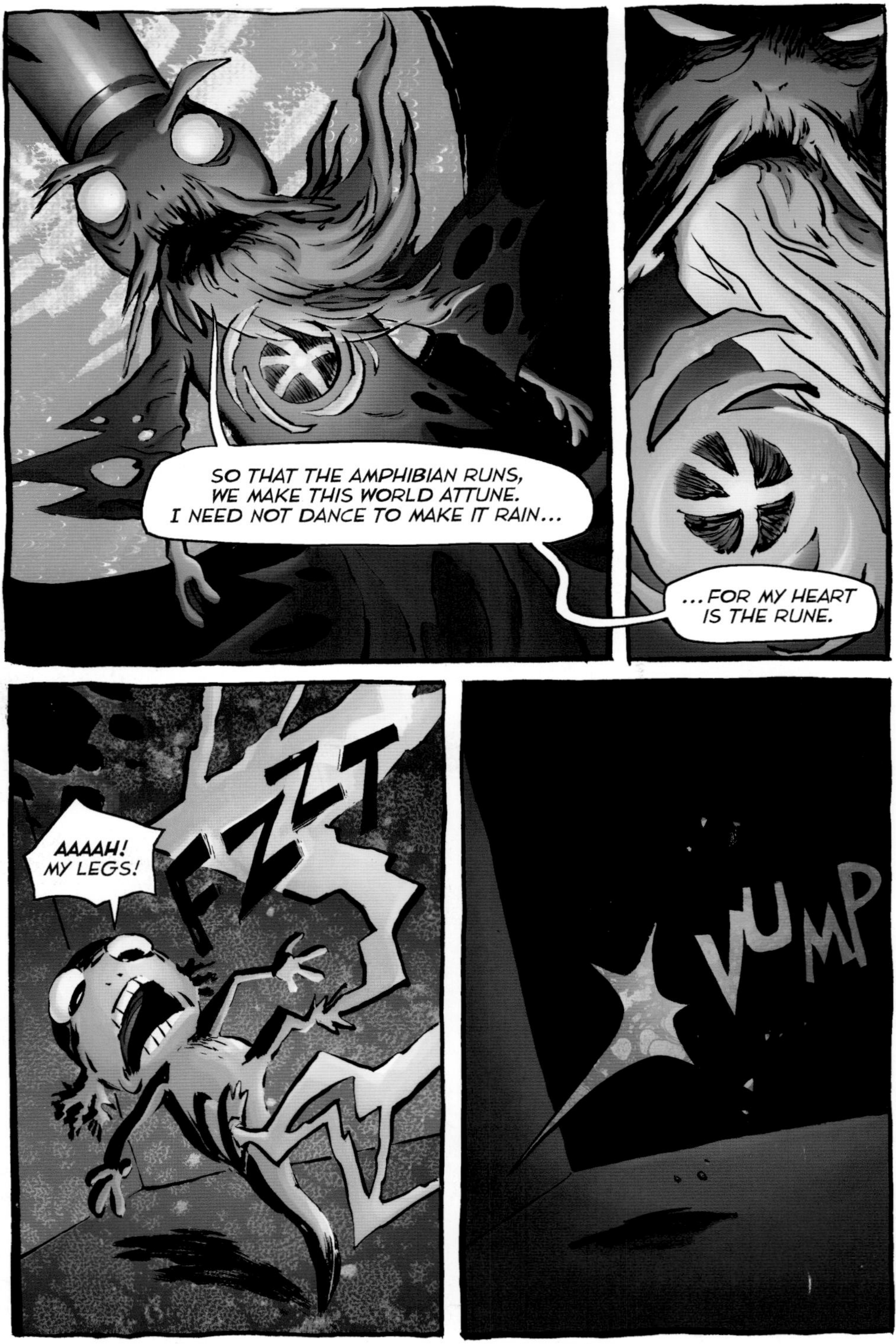
SO THAT THE AMPHIBIAN RUNS,
WE MAKE THIS WORLD ATTUNE.
I NEED NOT DANCE TO MAKE IT RAIN...
...FOR MY HEART
IS THE RUNE.
AAAAH!
MY LEGS!
FZZT
VUMP

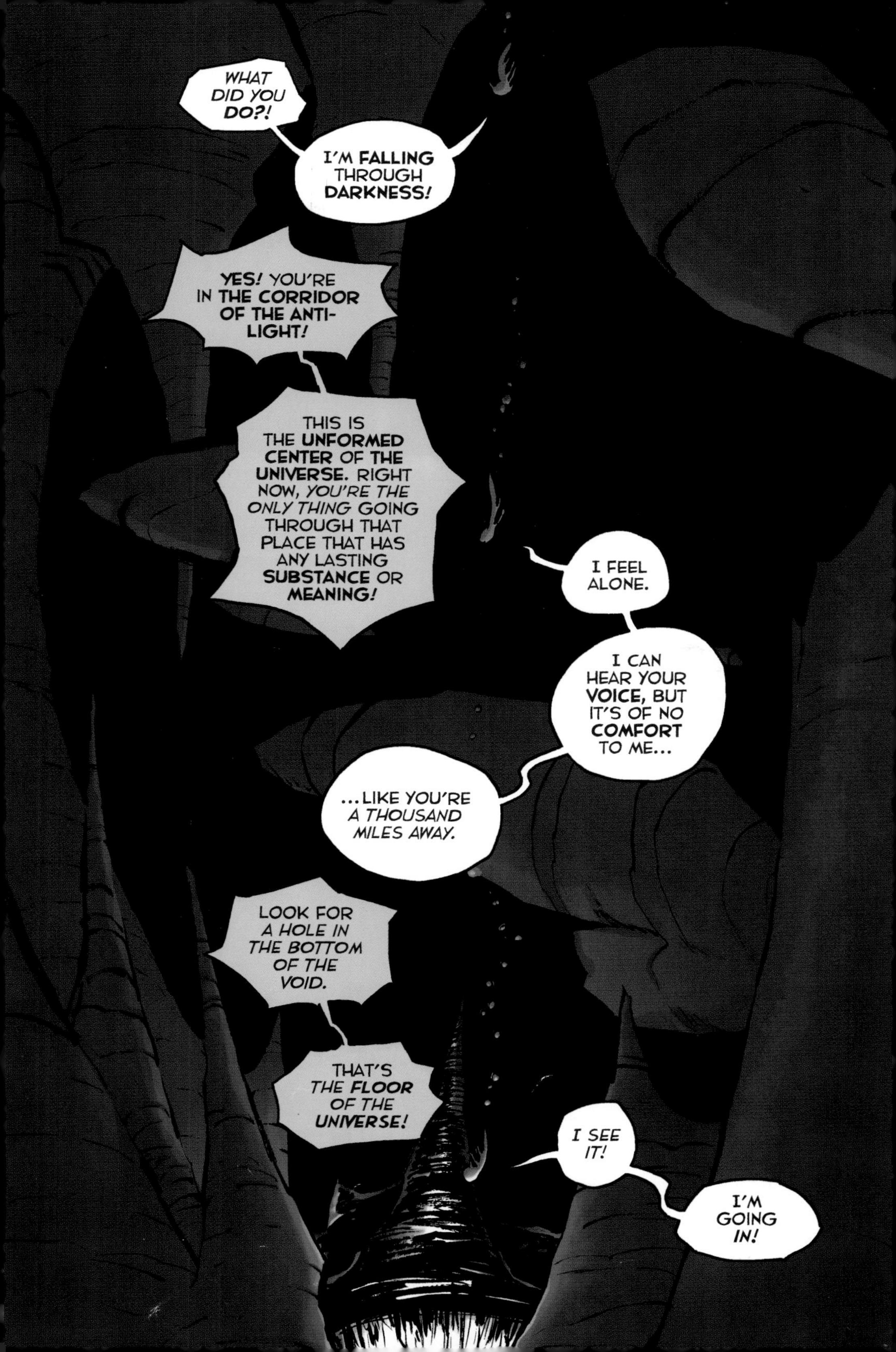
WHAT DID YOU DO?!
I'M FALLING THROUGH DARKNESS!
YES! YOU'RE IN THE CORRIDOR OF THE ANTI-LIGHT!
THIS IS THE UNFORMED CENTER OF THE UNIVERSE. RIGHT NOW, YOU'RE THE ONLY THING GOING THROUGH THAT PLACE THAT HAS ANY LASTING SUBSTANCE OR MEANING!
I FEEL ALONE.
I CAN HEAR YOUR VOICE, BUT IT'S OF NO COMFORT TO ME...
...LIKE YOU'RE A THOUSAND MILES AWAY.
LOOK FOR A HOLE IN THE BOTTOM OF THE VOID.
THAT'S THE FLOOR OF THE UNIVERSE!
I SEE IT!
I'M GOING IN!

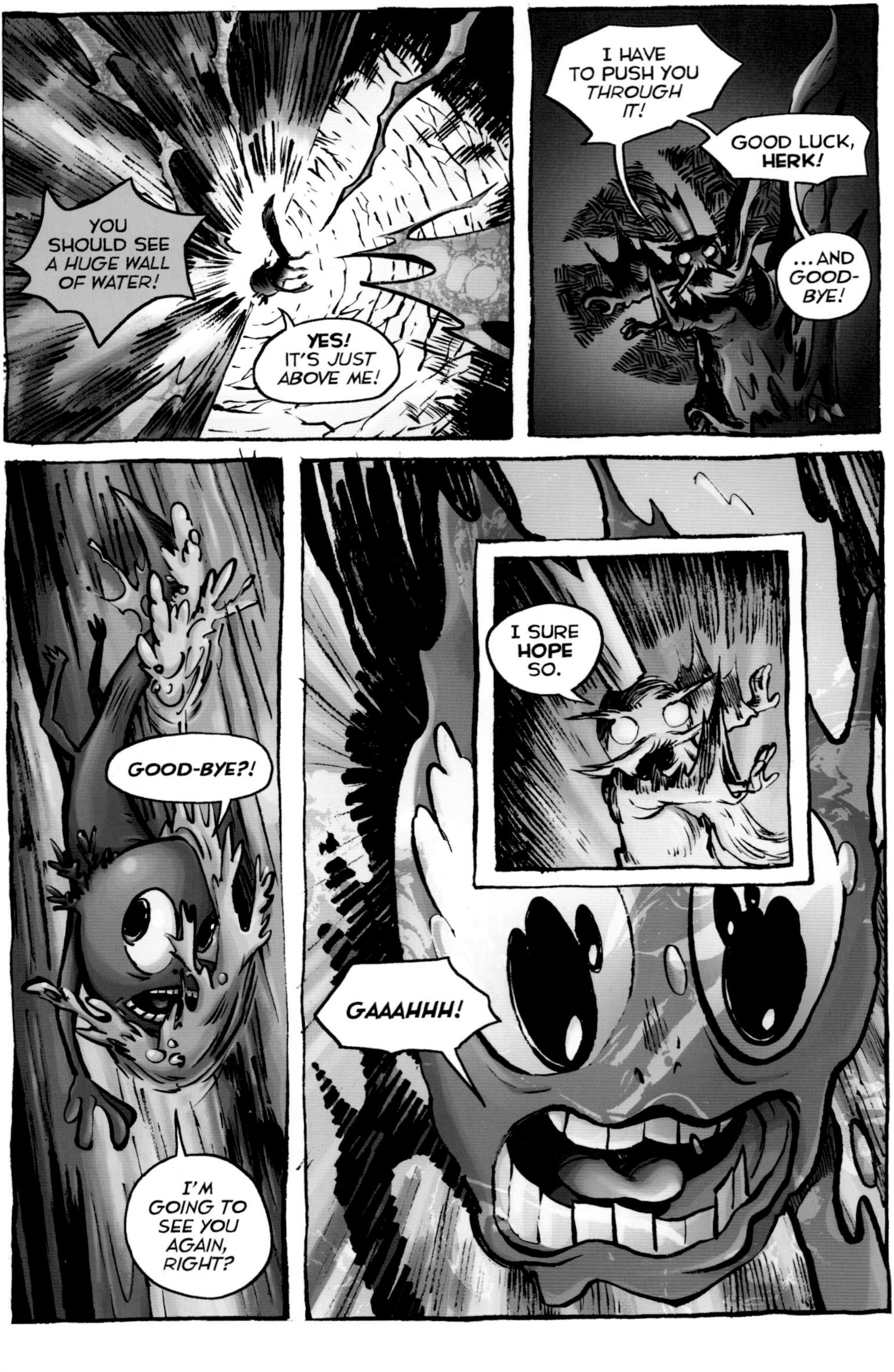
YOU SHOULD SEE A *HUGE WALL OF WATER!*
YES! IT'S JUST *ABOVE ME!*
I HAVE TO PUSH YOU *THROUGH* IT!
GOOD LUCK, **HERK!**
...AND GOOD-BYE!
GOOD-BYE?!
I'M GOING TO SEE YOU AGAIN, RIGHT?
I SURE **HOPE** SO.
GAAAHHH!

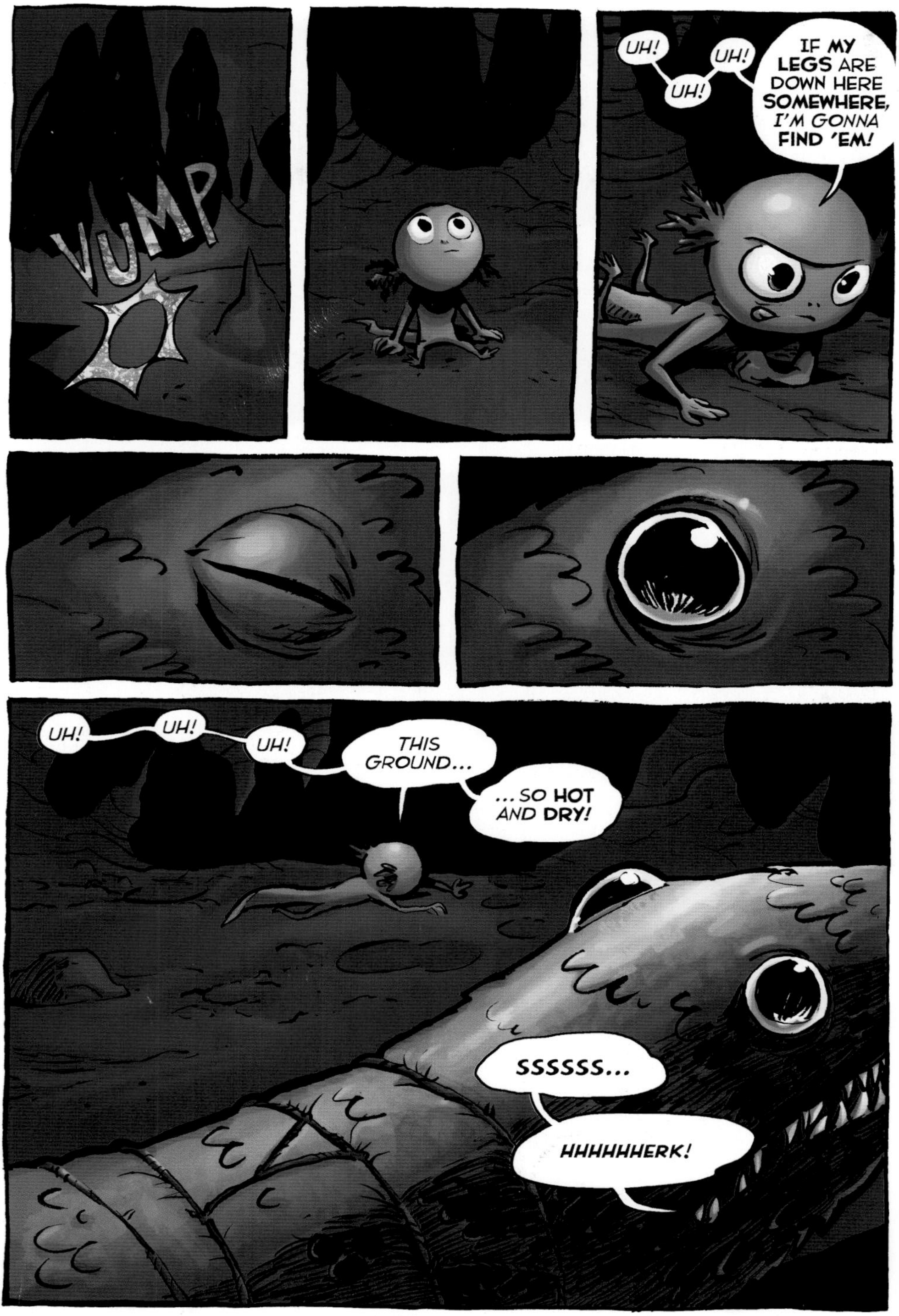
VUMP
UH!
UH!
UH!
IF MY LEGS ARE DOWN HERE SOMEWHERE, I'M GONNA FIND 'EM!
UH!
UH!
UH!
THIS GROUND...
...SO HOT AND DRY!
SSSSSS...
HHHHHHERK!

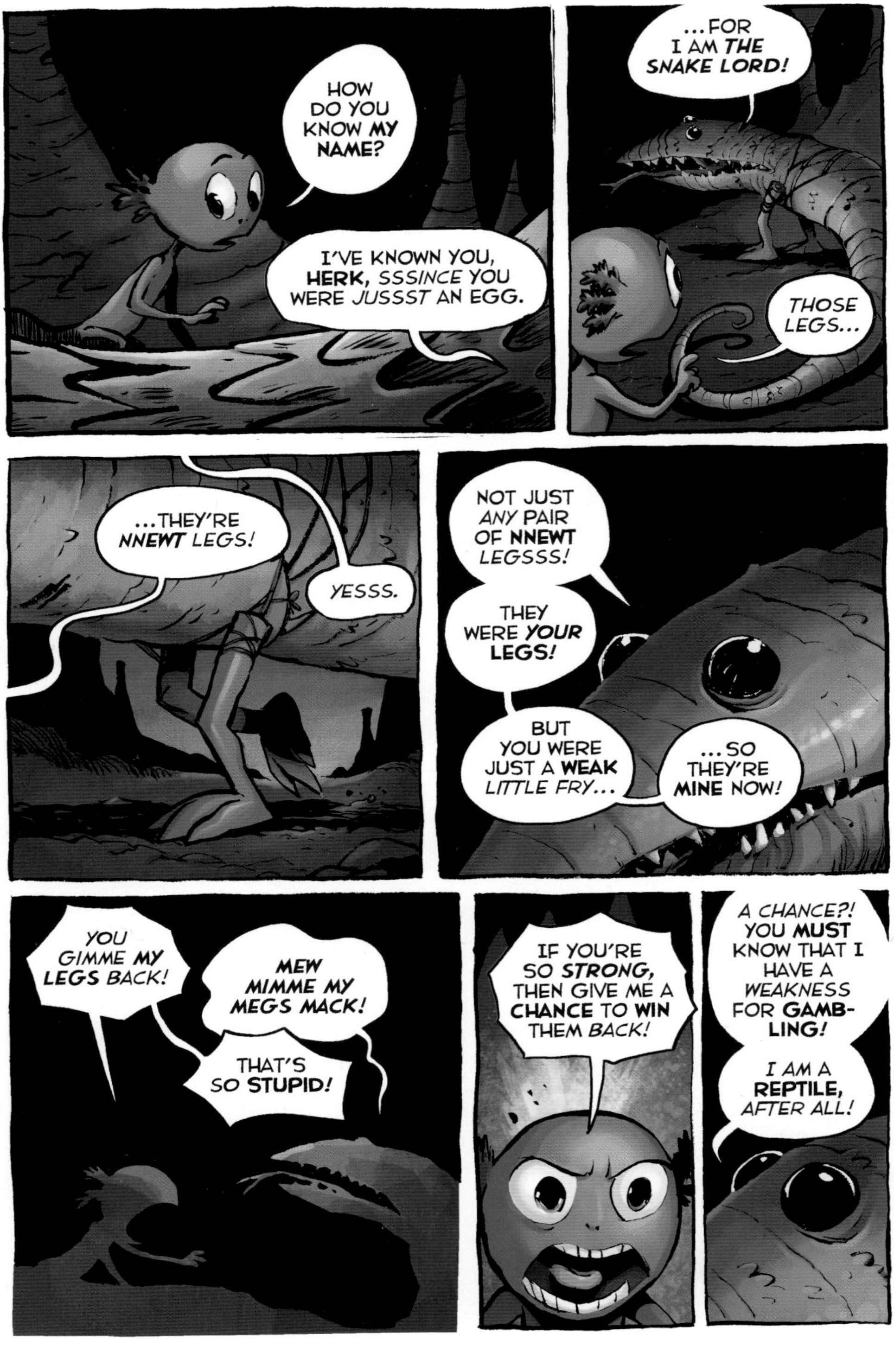
HOW DO YOU KNOW MY NAME?
I'VE KNOWN YOU, HERK, SSSINCE YOU WERE JUSSST AN EGG.
...FOR I AM THE SNAKE LORD!
THOSE LEGS...
...THEY'RE NNEWT LEGS!
YESSS.
NOT JUST ANY PAIR OF NNEWT LEGSSS!
THEY WERE YOUR LEGS!
BUT YOU WERE JUST A WEAK LITTLE FRY...
...SO THEY'RE MINE NOW!
YOU GIMME MY LEGS BACK!
MEW MIMME MY MEGS MACK!
THAT'S SO STUPID!
IF YOU'RE SO STRONG, THEN GIVE ME A CHANCE TO WIN THEM BACK!
A CHANCE?! YOU MUST KNOW THAT I HAVE A WEAKNESS FOR GAMB-LING!
I AM A REPTILE, AFTER ALL!

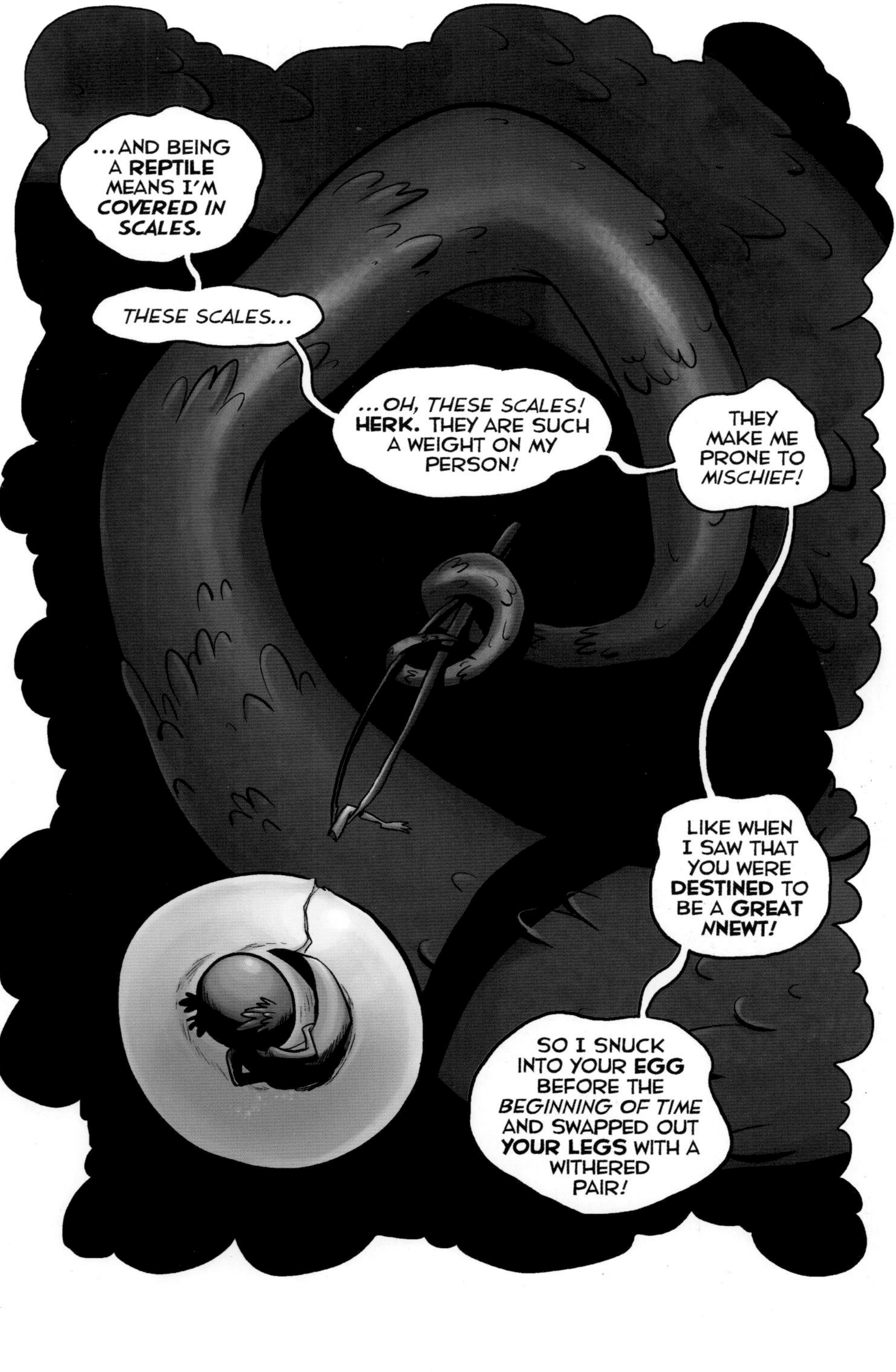

...AND BEING A **REPTILE** MEANS I'M ***COVERED IN SCALES.***
THESE SCALES...
...OH, THESE SCALES! **HERK.** THEY ARE SUCH A WEIGHT ON MY PERSON!
THEY MAKE ME PRONE TO *MISCHIEF!*
LIKE WHEN I SAW THAT YOU WERE **DESTINED** TO BE A **GREAT *NNEWT!***
SO I SNUCK INTO *YOUR* **EGG** BEFORE THE *BEGINNING OF TIME* AND SWAPPED OUT **YOUR LEGS** WITH A WITHERED PAIR!

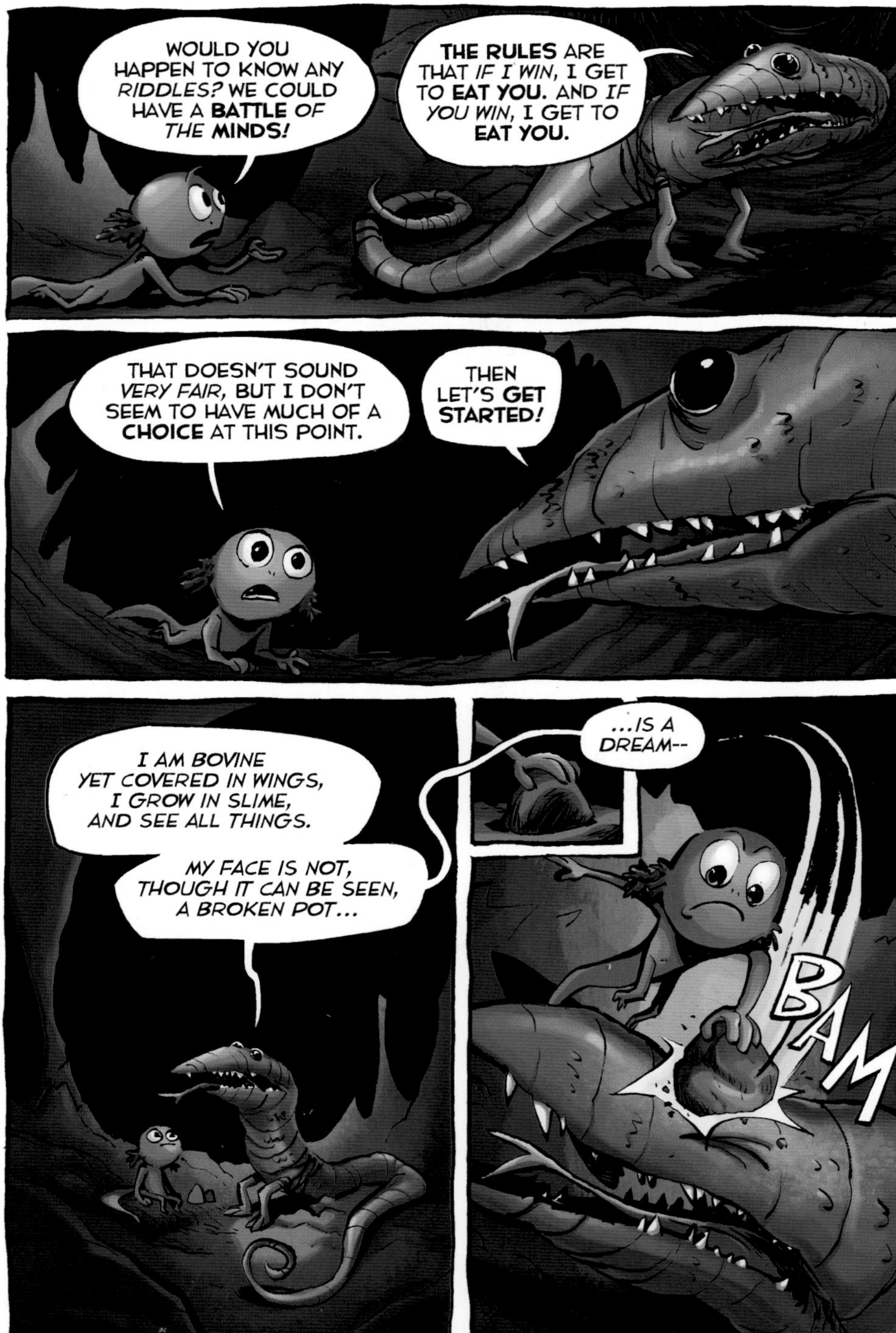
WOULD YOU HAPPEN TO KNOW ANY RIDDLES? WE COULD HAVE A BATTLE OF THE MINDS!
THE RULES ARE THAT IF I WIN, I GET TO EAT YOU. AND IF YOU WIN, I GET TO EAT YOU.
THAT DOESN'T SOUND VERY FAIR, BUT I DON'T SEEM TO HAVE MUCH OF A CHOICE AT THIS POINT.
THEN LET'S GET STARTED!
I AM BOVINE YET COVERED IN WINGS, I GROW IN SLIME, AND SEE ALL THINGS.
MY FACE IS NOT, THOUGH IT CAN BE SEEN, A BROKEN POT...
...IS A DREAM--
BAM

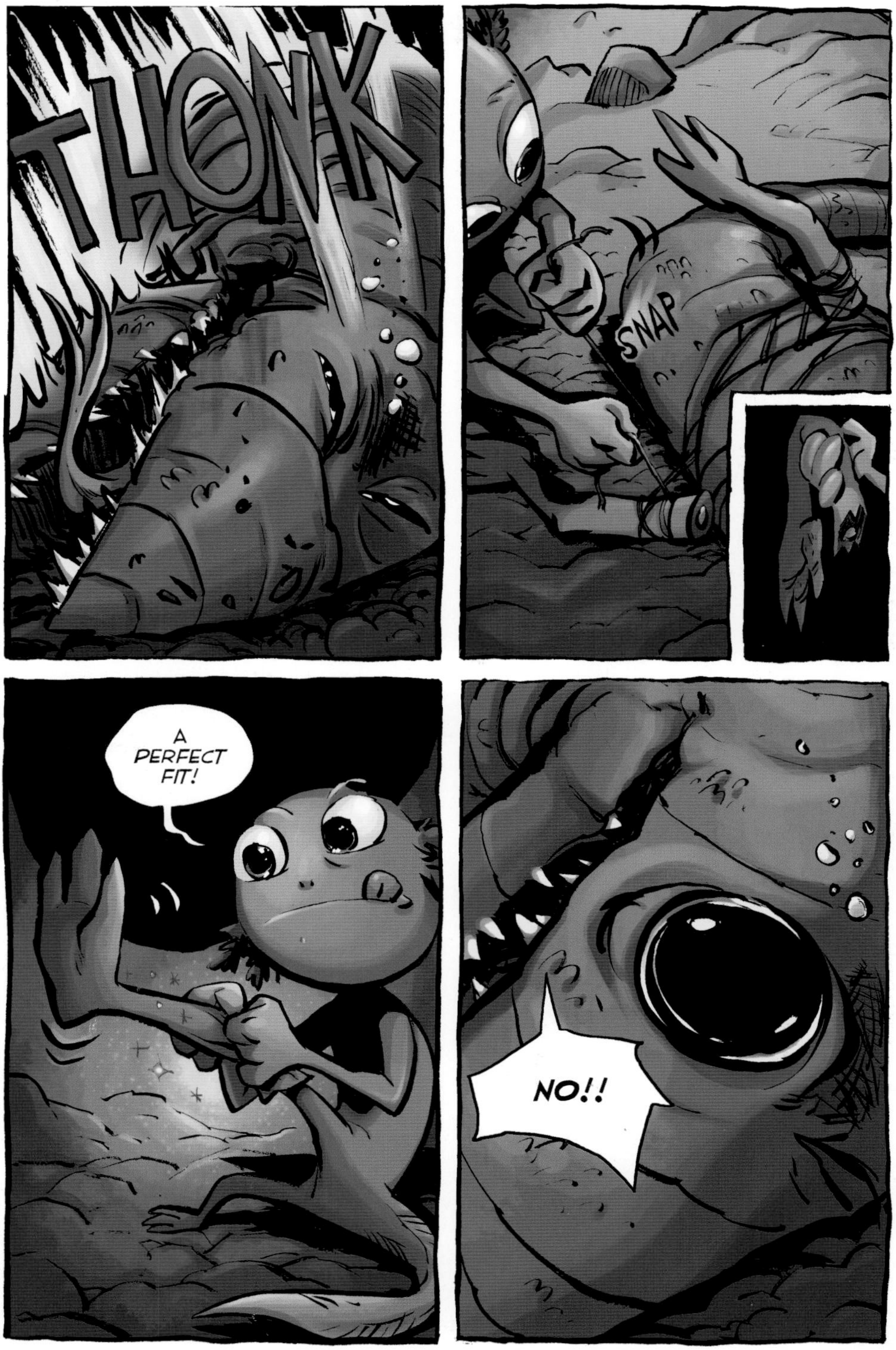
THONK
SNAP
A PERFECT FIT!
NO!!

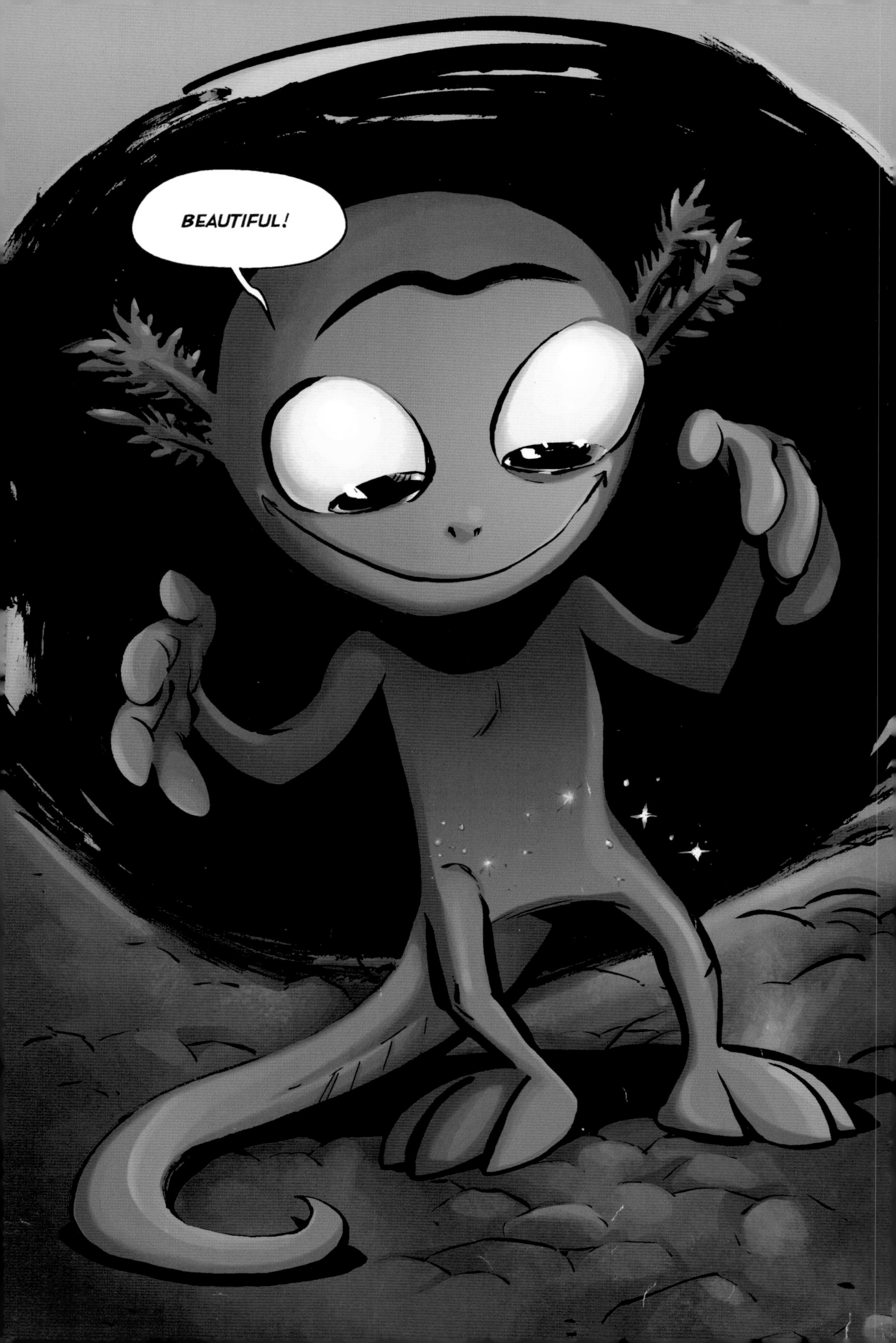
BEAUTIFUL!

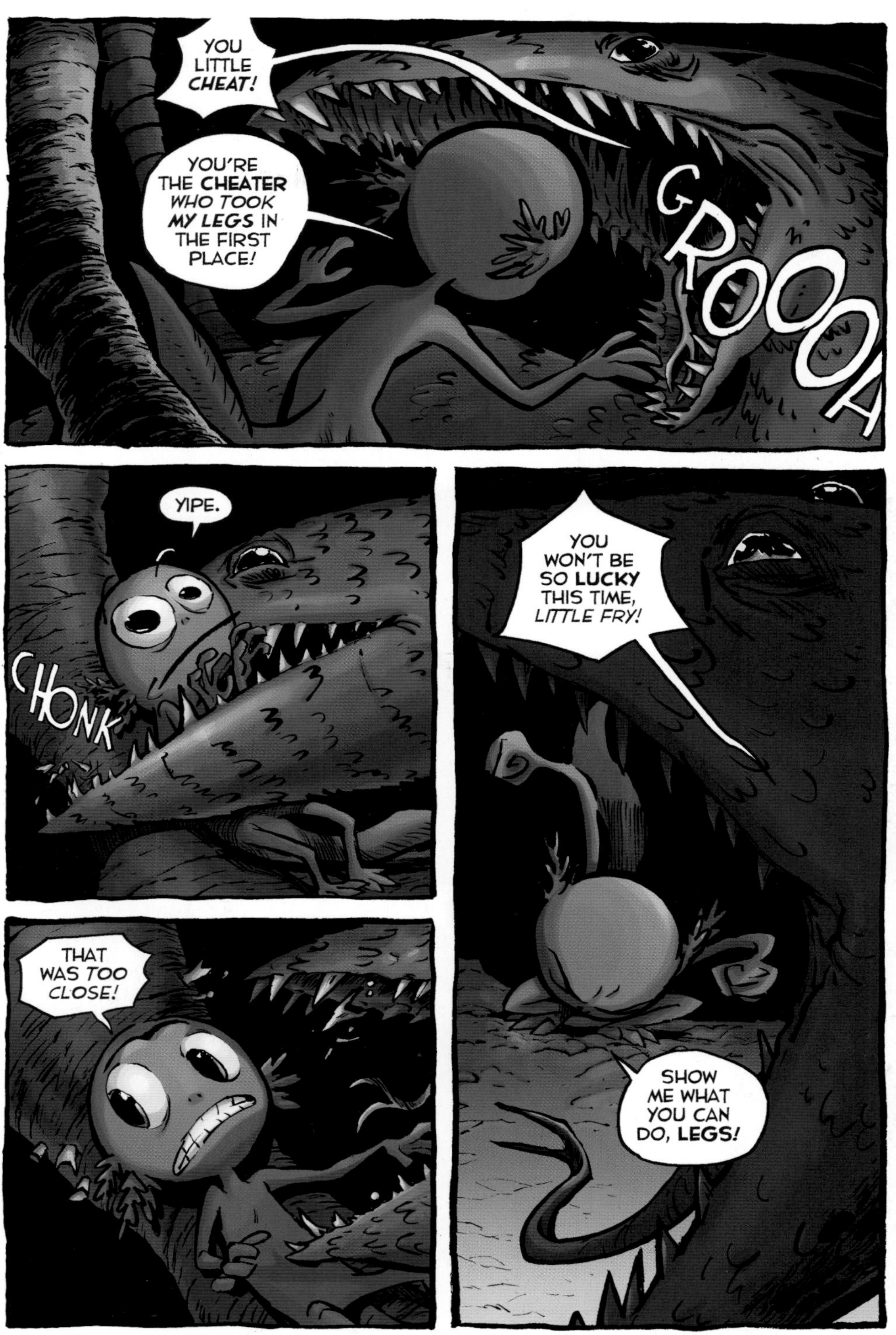
YOU LITTLE CHEAT!
YOU'RE THE CHEATER WHO TOOK MY LEGS IN THE FIRST PLACE!
GROOOOA
YIPE.
CHONK
YOU WON'T BE SO LUCKY THIS TIME, LITTLE FRY!
THAT WAS TOO CLOSE!
SHOW ME WHAT YOU CAN DO, LEGS!

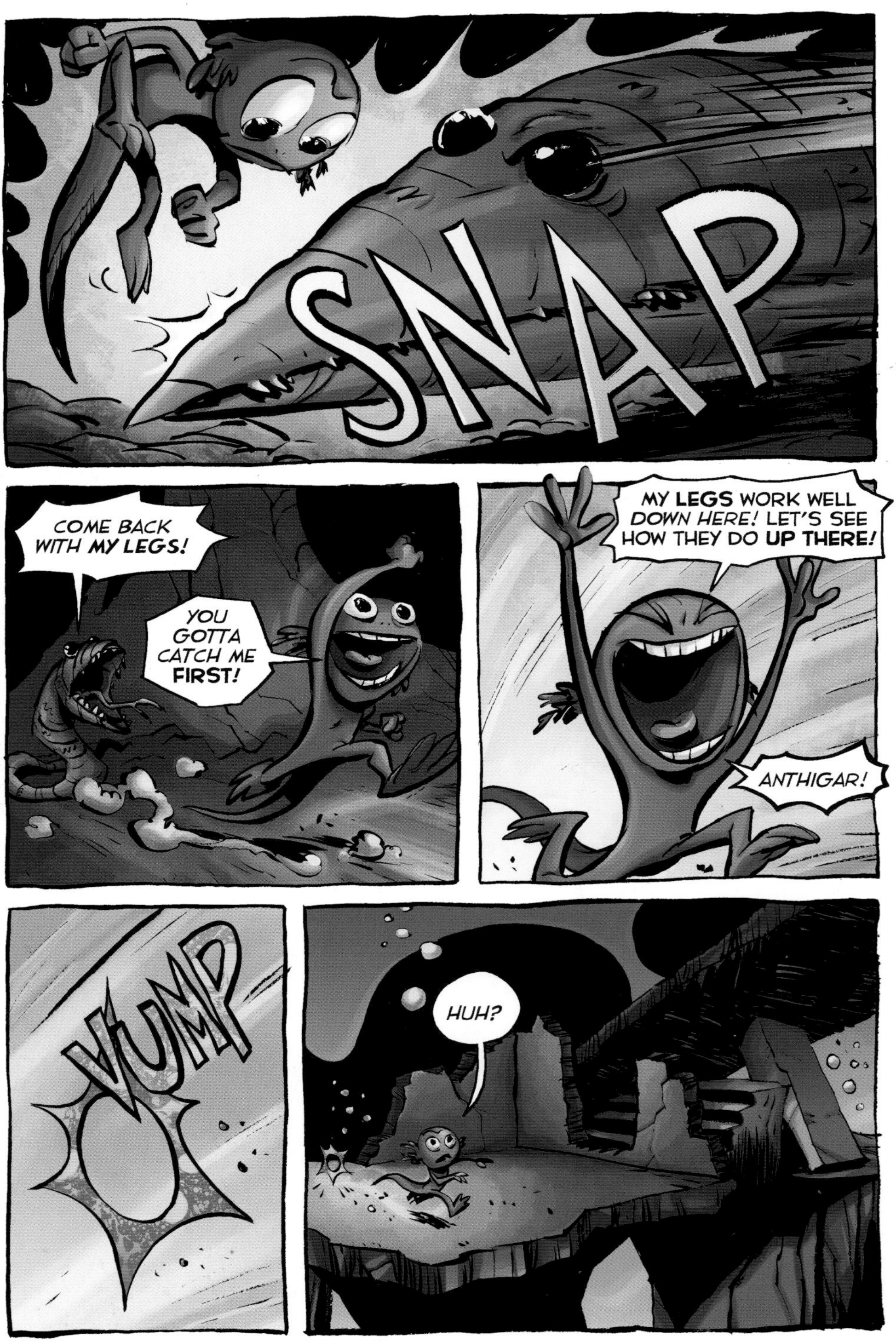
SNAP
COME BACK WITH MY LEGS!
YOU GOTTA CATCH ME FIRST!
MY LEGS WORK WELL DOWN HERE! LET'S SEE HOW THEY DO UP THERE!
ANTHIGAR!
VUMP
HUH?

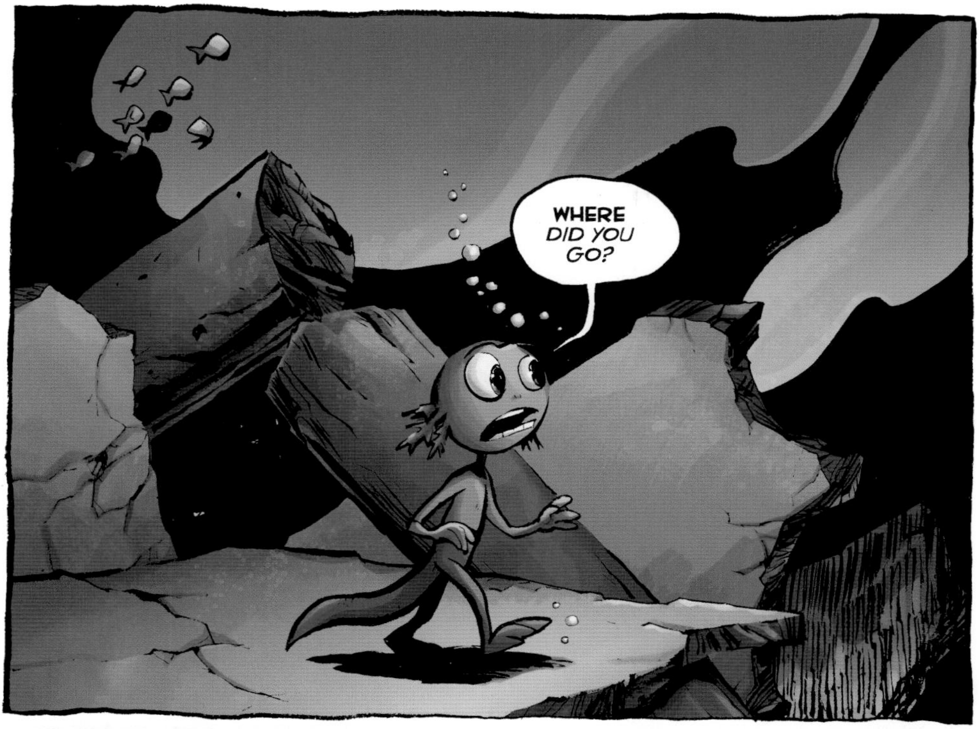
WHERE DID YOU GO?

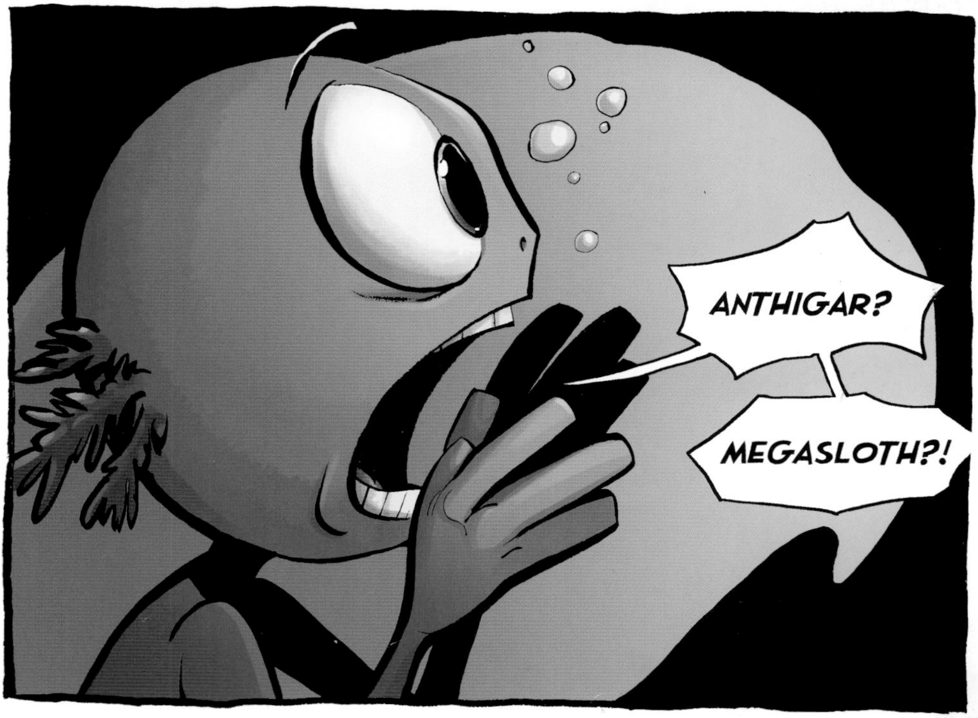
ANTHIGAR?
MEGASLOTH?!

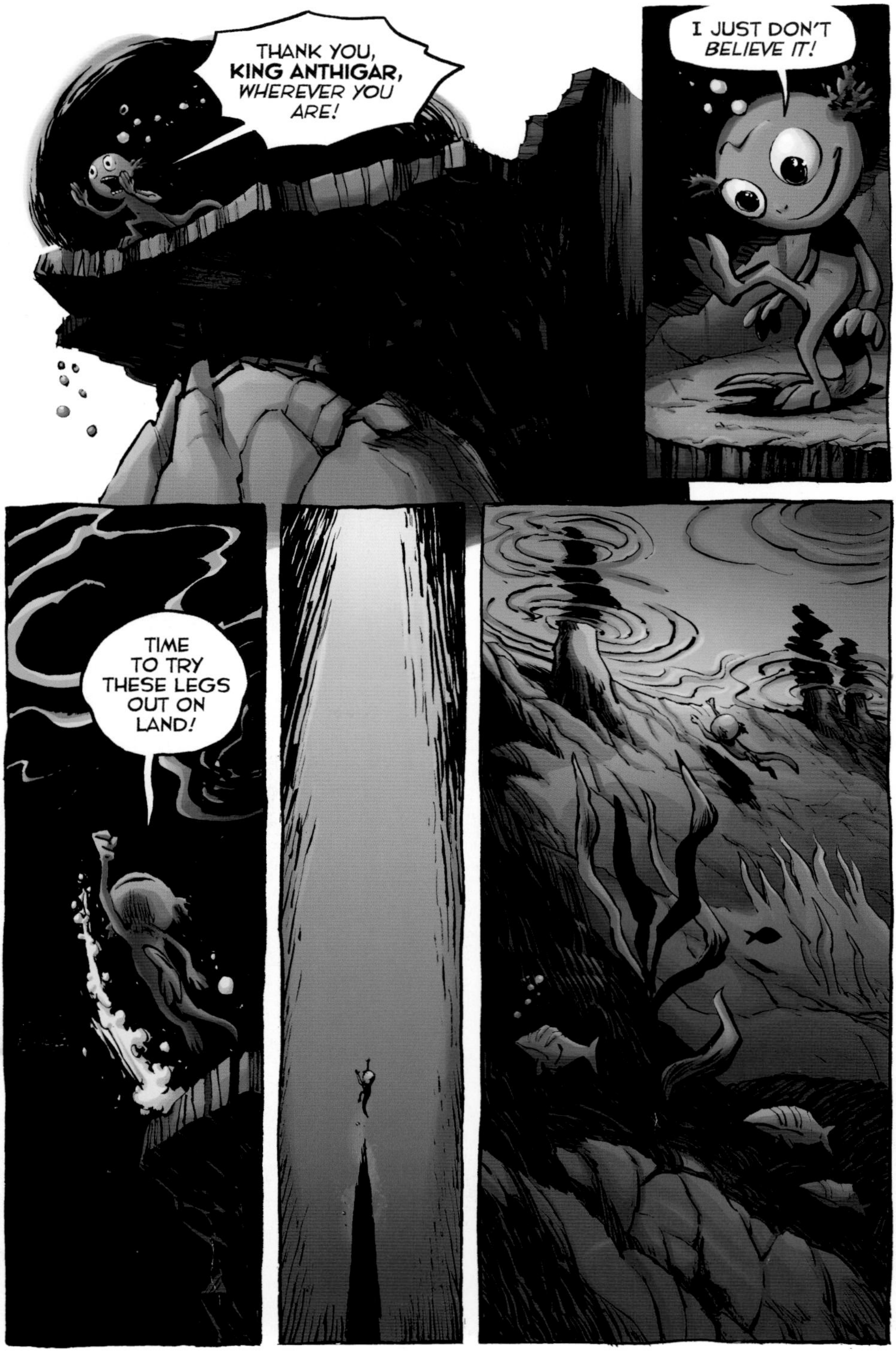
THANK YOU, **KING ANTHIGAR,** *WHEREVER YOU ARE!*
I JUST DON'T *BELIEVE IT!*
TIME TO TRY THESE LEGS OUT ON LAND!

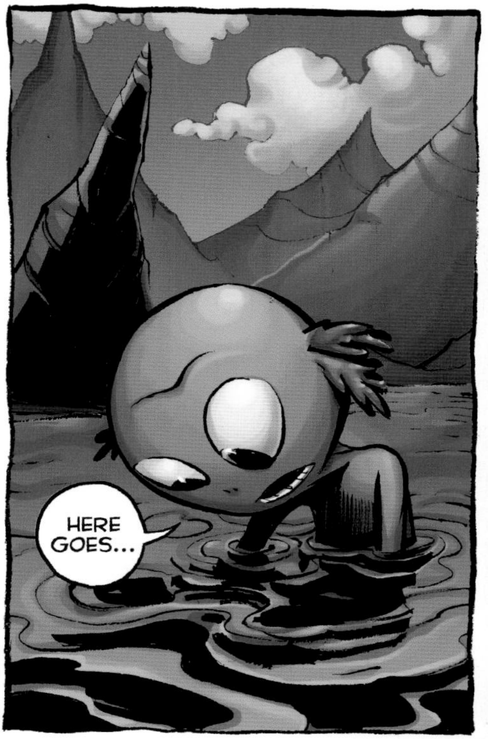
HERE GOES...

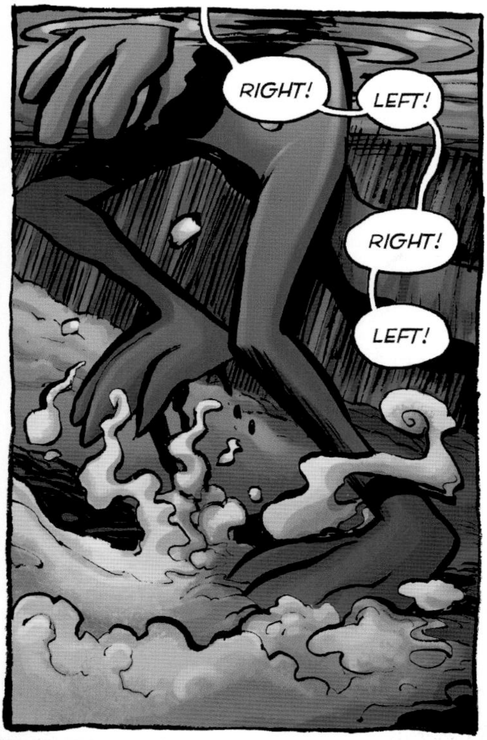
RIGHT!
LEFT!
RIGHT!
LEFT!

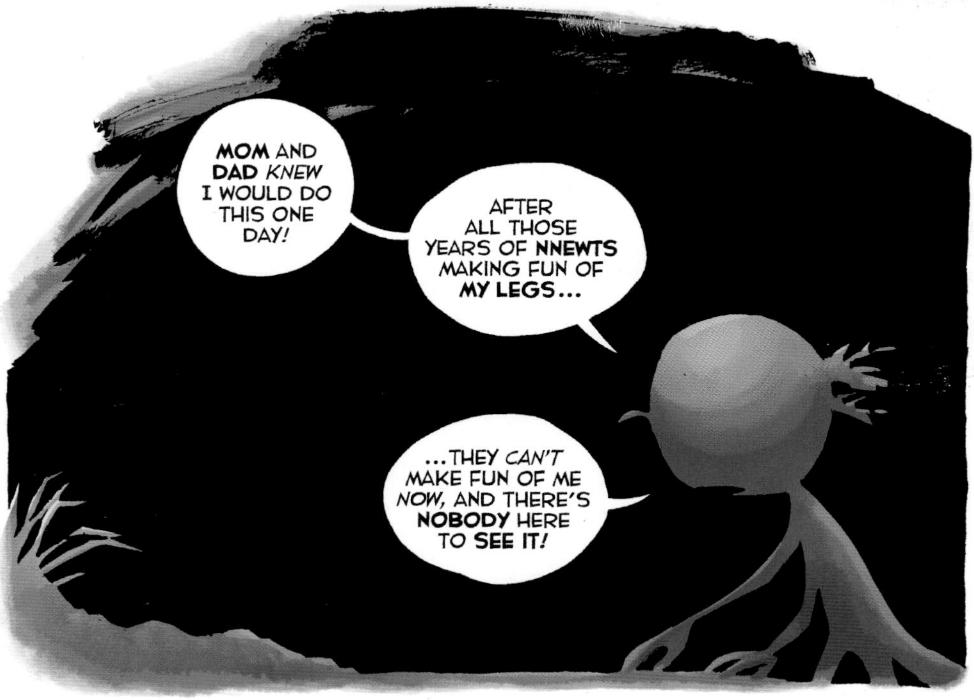
MOM AND **DAD** *KNEW* I WOULD DO THIS ONE DAY!
AFTER ALL THOSE YEARS OF **NNEWTS** MAKING FUN OF **MY LEGS**...
...THEY *CAN'T* MAKE FUN OF ME *NOW,* AND THERE'S **NOBODY** HERE TO **SEE IT**!

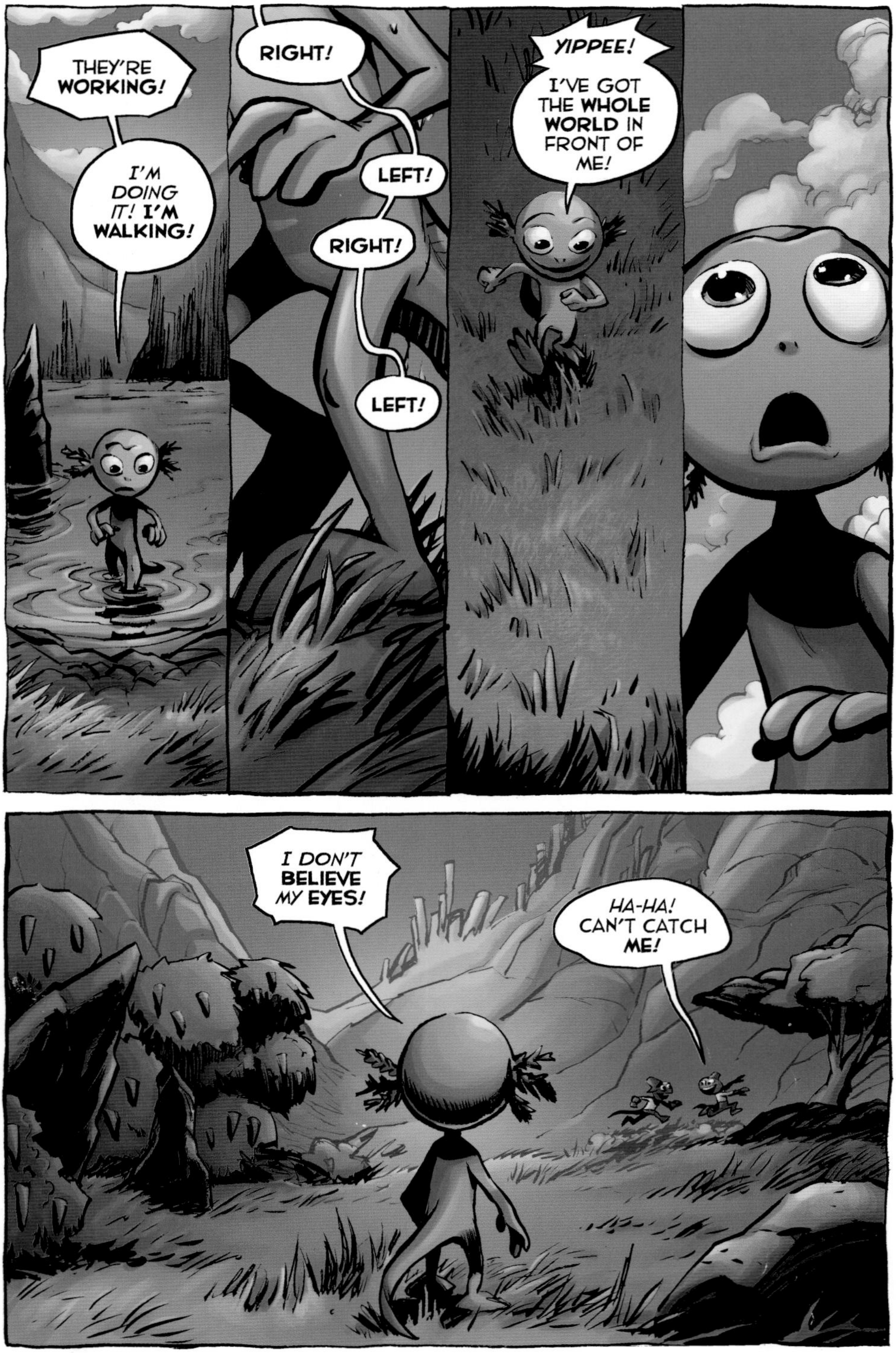
THEY'RE WORKING!
I'M DOING IT! I'M WALKING!
RIGHT!
LEFT!
RIGHT!
LEFT!
YIPPEE!
I'VE GOT THE WHOLE WORLD IN FRONT OF ME!
I DON'T BELIEVE MY EYES!
HA-HA! CAN'T CATCH ME!

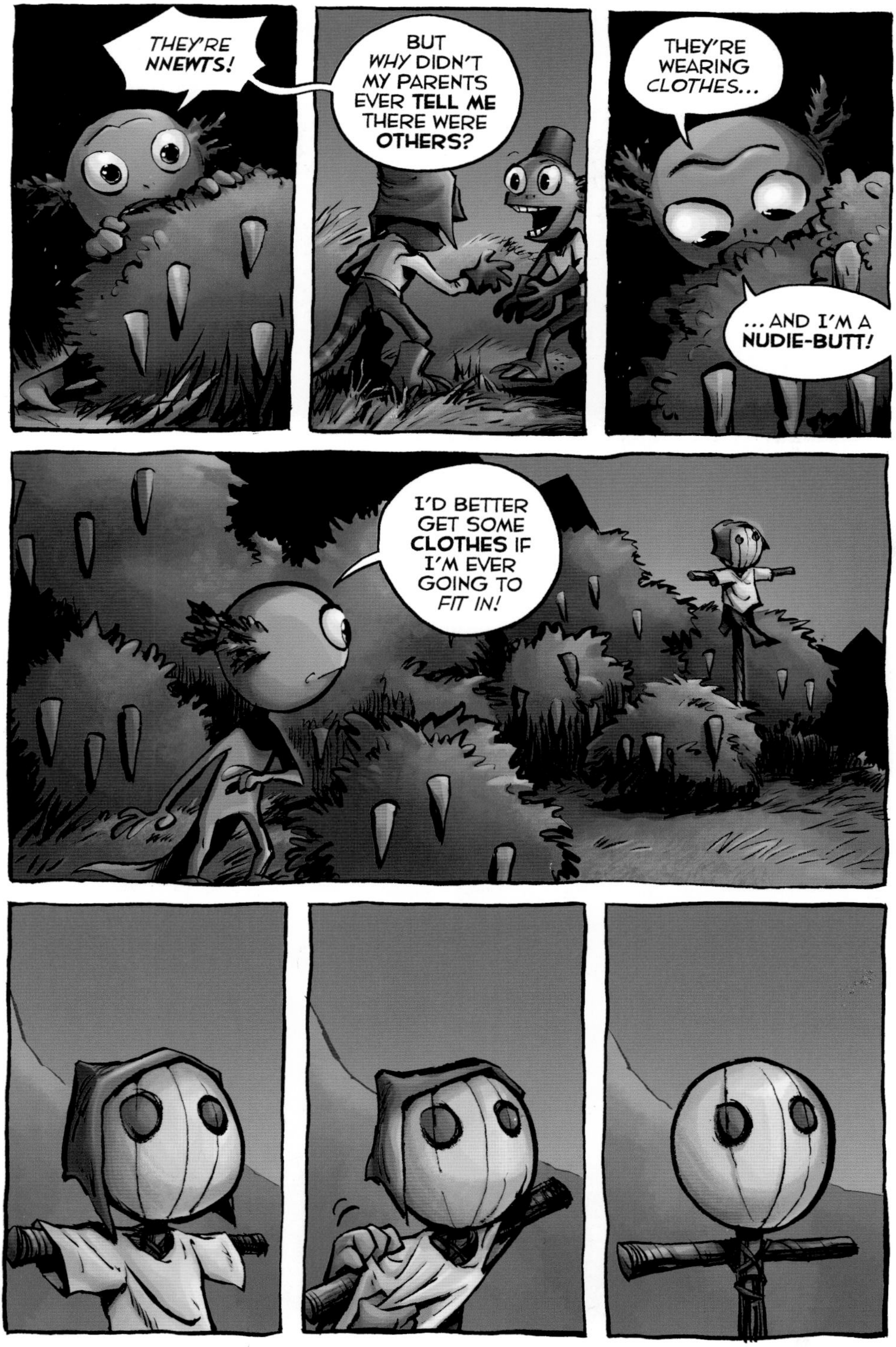
THEY'RE NNEWTS!
BUT WHY DIDN'T MY PARENTS EVER TELL ME THERE WERE OTHERS?
THEY'RE WEARING CLOTHES...
...AND I'M A NUDIE-BUTT!
I'D BETTER GET SOME CLOTHES IF I'M EVER GOING TO FIT IN!

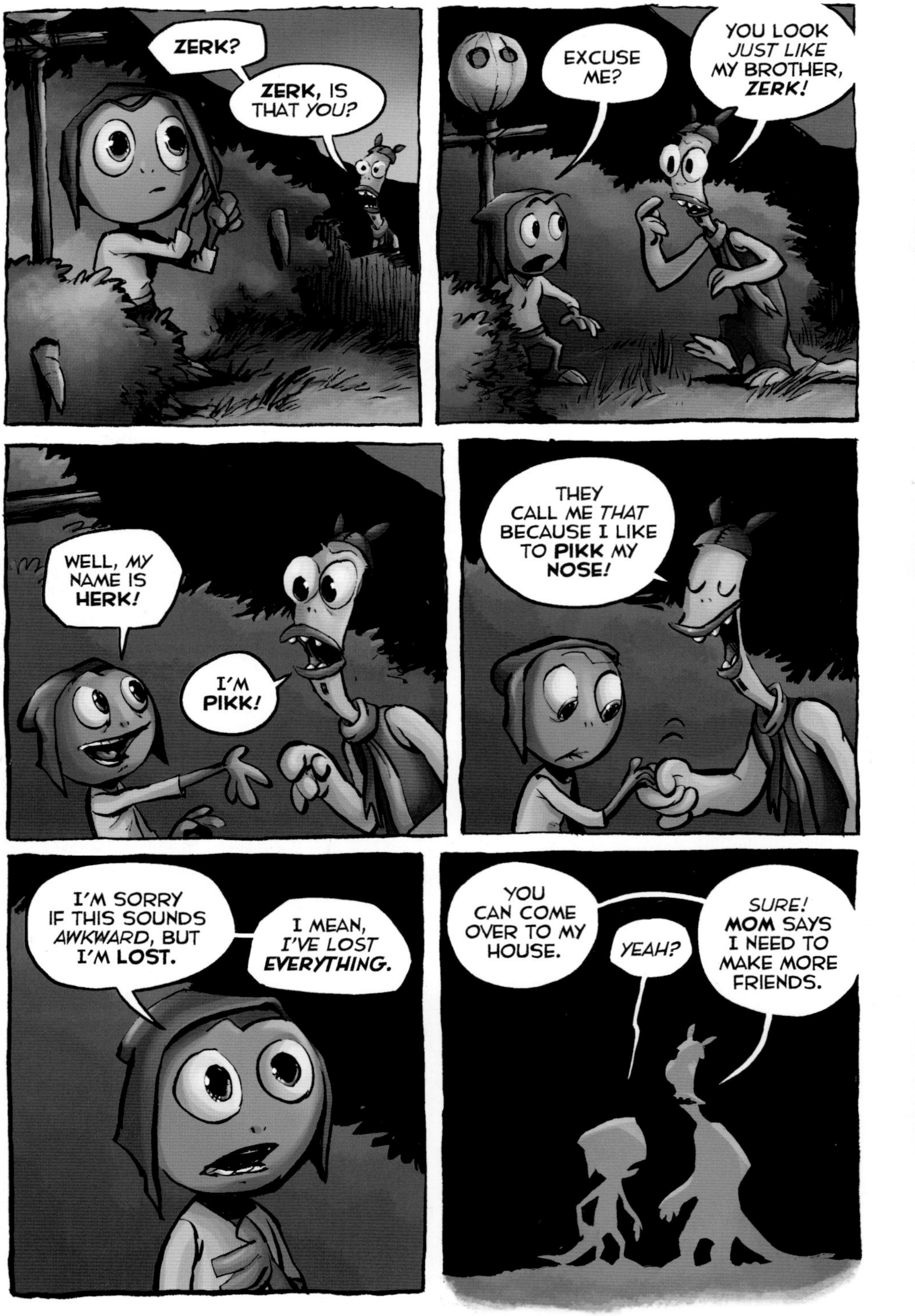
ZERK?
ZERK, IS THAT *YOU?*
EXCUSE ME?
YOU LOOK *JUST LIKE* MY BROTHER, ***ZERK!***
WELL, *MY* NAME IS **HERK!**
I'M **PIKK!**
THEY CALL ME *THAT* BECAUSE I LIKE TO **PIKK** MY **NOSE!**
I'M SORRY IF THIS SOUNDS *AWKWARD*, BUT I'M **LOST.**
I MEAN, *I'VE LOST* ***EVERYTHING.***
YOU CAN COME OVER TO MY HOUSE.
YEAH?
SURE! **MOM** SAYS I NEED TO MAKE MORE FRIENDS.

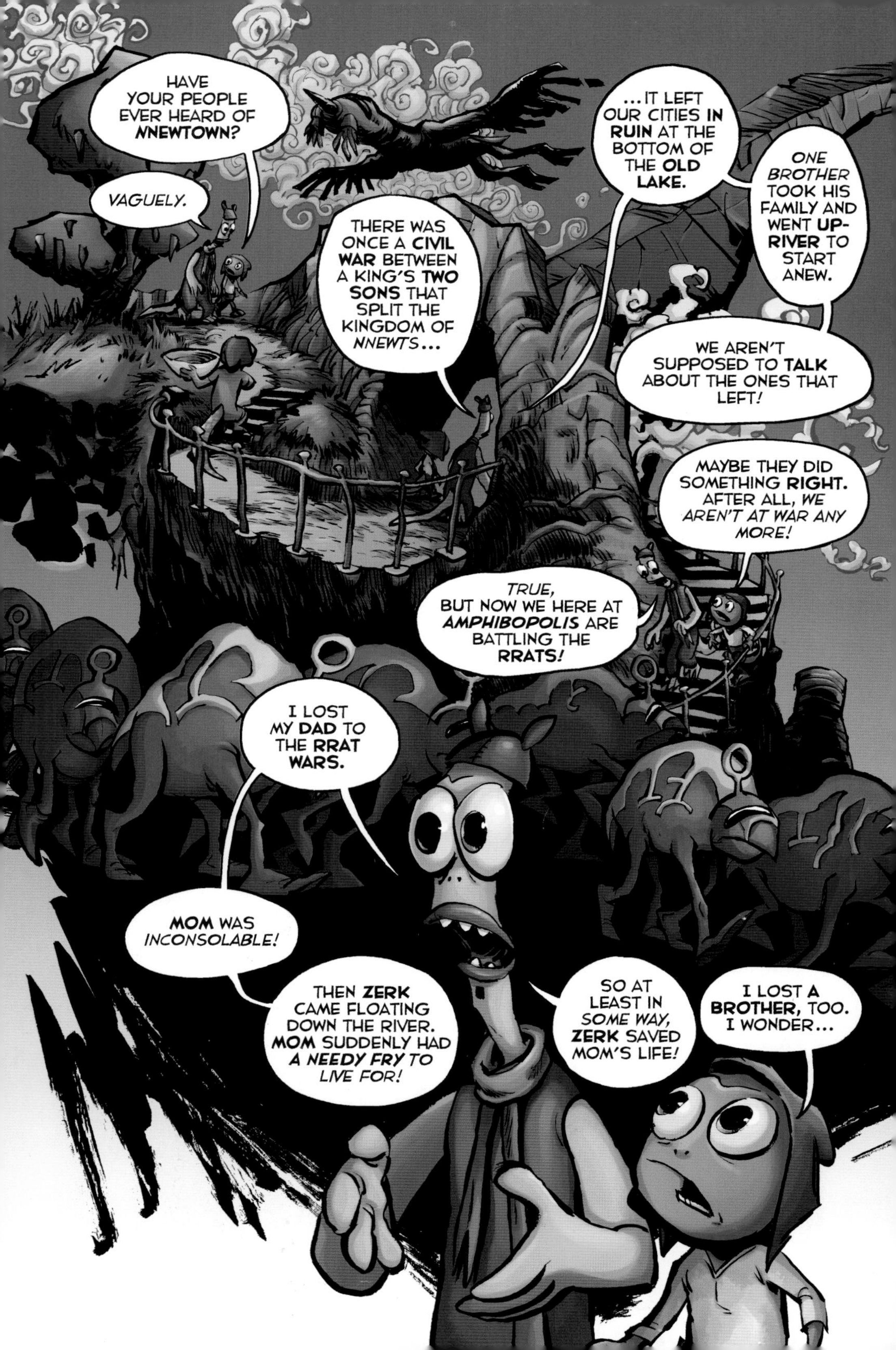
HAVE YOUR PEOPLE EVER HEARD OF NNEWTOWN?
VAGUELY.
THERE WAS ONCE A CIVIL WAR BETWEEN A KING'S TWO SONS THAT SPLIT THE KINGDOM OF NNEWTS...
...IT LEFT OUR CITIES IN RUIN AT THE BOTTOM OF THE OLD LAKE.
ONE BROTHER TOOK HIS FAMILY AND WENT UP-RIVER TO START ANEW.
WE AREN'T SUPPOSED TO TALK ABOUT THE ONES THAT LEFT!
MAYBE THEY DID SOMETHING RIGHT. AFTER ALL, WE AREN'T AT WAR ANY MORE!
TRUE, BUT NOW WE HERE AT AMPHIBOPOLIS ARE BATTLING THE RRATS!
I LOST MY DAD TO THE RRAT WARS.
MOM WAS INCONSOLABLE!
THEN ZERK CAME FLOATING DOWN THE RIVER. MOM SUDDENLY HAD A NEEDY FRY TO LIVE FOR!
SO AT LEAST IN SOME WAY, ZERK SAVED MOM'S LIFE!
I LOST A BROTHER, TOO. I WONDER...

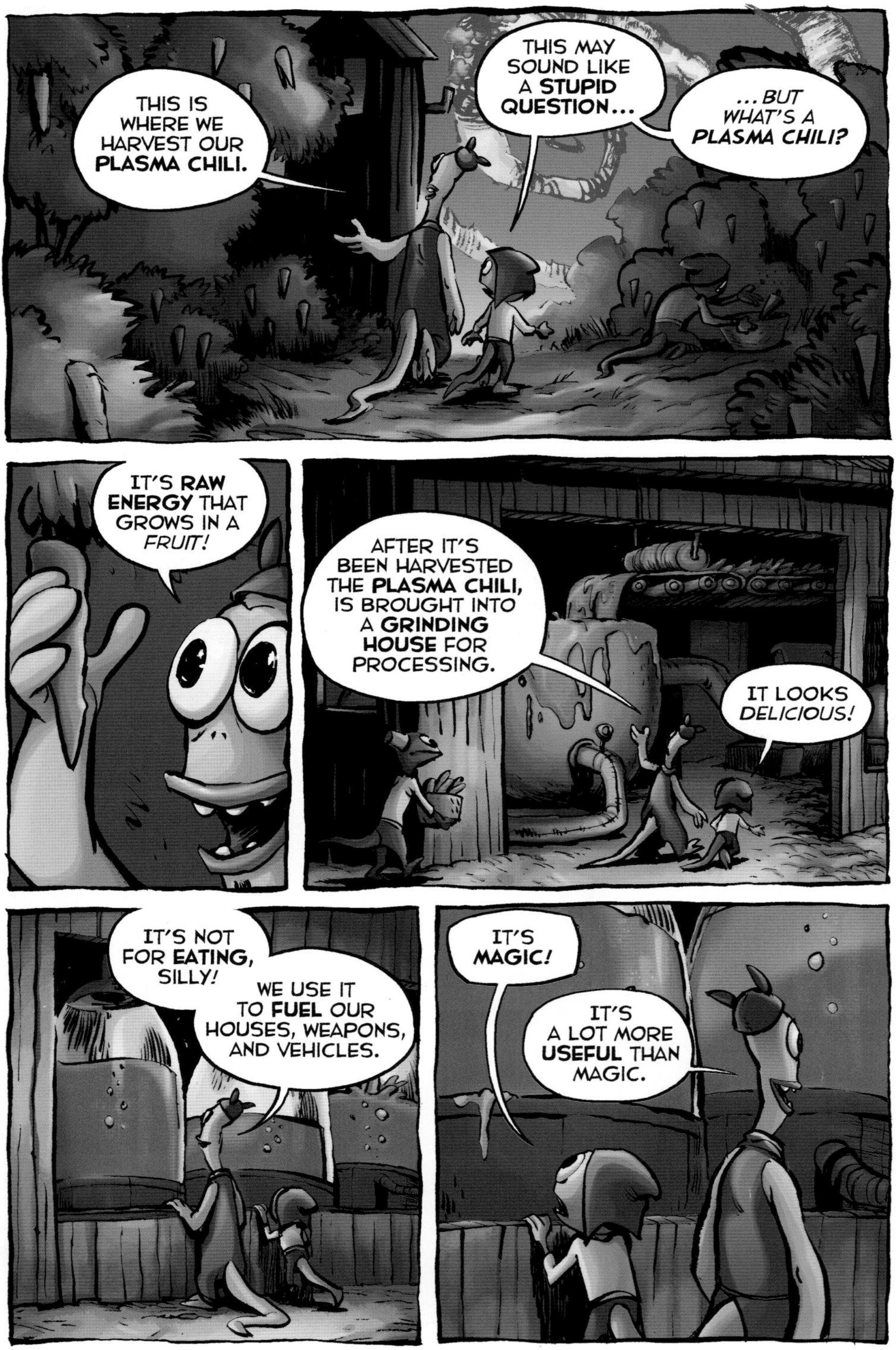
THIS IS WHERE WE HARVEST OUR PLASMA CHILI.
THIS MAY SOUND LIKE A STUPID QUESTION...
...BUT WHAT'S A PLASMA CHILI?
IT'S RAW ENERGY THAT GROWS IN A FRUIT!
AFTER IT'S BEEN HARVESTED THE PLASMA CHILI, IS BROUGHT INTO A GRINDING HOUSE FOR PROCESSING.
IT LOOKS DELICIOUS!
IT'S NOT FOR EATING, SILLY!
WE USE IT TO FUEL OUR HOUSES, WEAPONS, AND VEHICLES.
IT'S MAGIC!
IT'S A LOT MORE USEFUL THAN MAGIC.

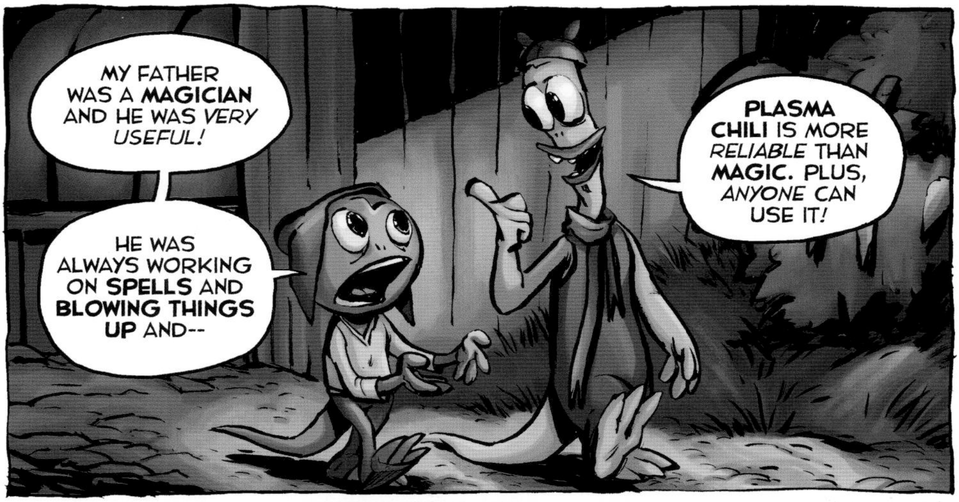
MY FATHER WAS A **MAGICIAN** AND HE WAS *VERY USEFUL!*
HE WAS ALWAYS WORKING ON **SPELLS** AND **BLOWING THINGS UP** AND--
PLASMA CHILI IS MORE *RELIABLE* THAN **MAGIC.** PLUS, *ANYONE* CAN USE IT*!*

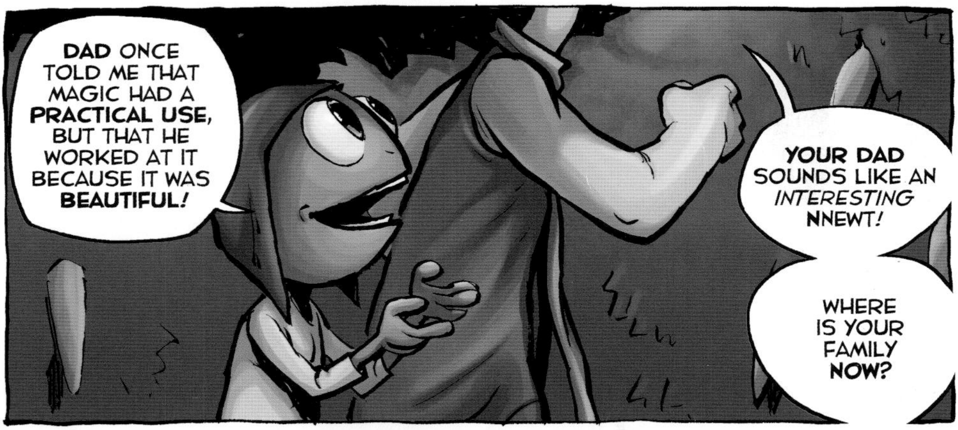
DAD ONCE TOLD ME THAT MAGIC HAD A **PRACTICAL USE,** BUT THAT HE WORKED AT IT BECAUSE IT WAS **BEAUTIFUL!**
YOUR DAD SOUNDS LIKE AN *INTERESTING* **N**NEWT*!*
WHERE IS YOUR FAMILY **NOW?**

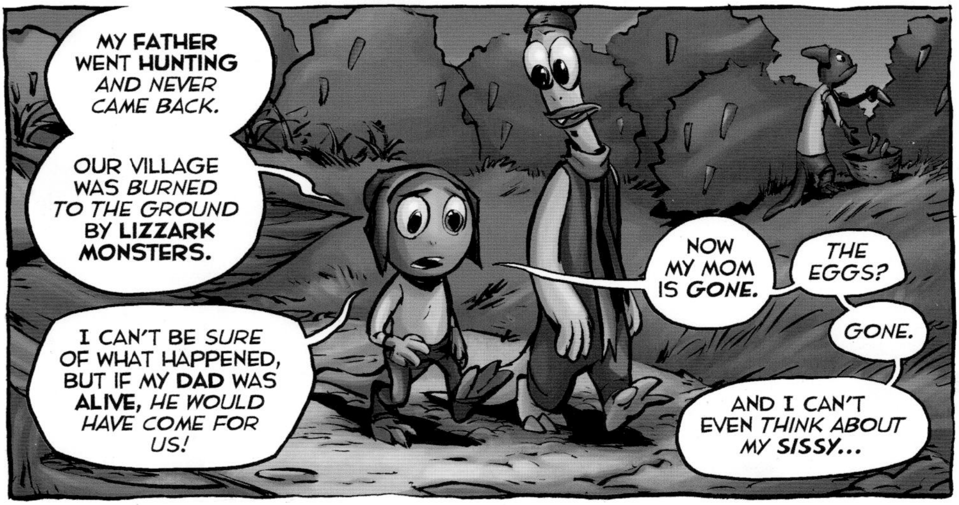
MY **FATHER** WENT **HUNTING** *AND NEVER CAME BACK.*
OUR VILLAGE WAS *BURNED TO THE GROUND* BY **LIZZARK MONSTERS.**
I CAN'T BE *SURE* OF WHAT HAPPENED, BUT IF MY **DAD** WAS **ALIVE,** *HE WOULD HAVE COME FOR US!*
NOW MY MOM IS ***GONE.***
THE EGGS?
GONE.
AND I CAN'T EVEN *THINK ABOUT* MY **SISSY...**

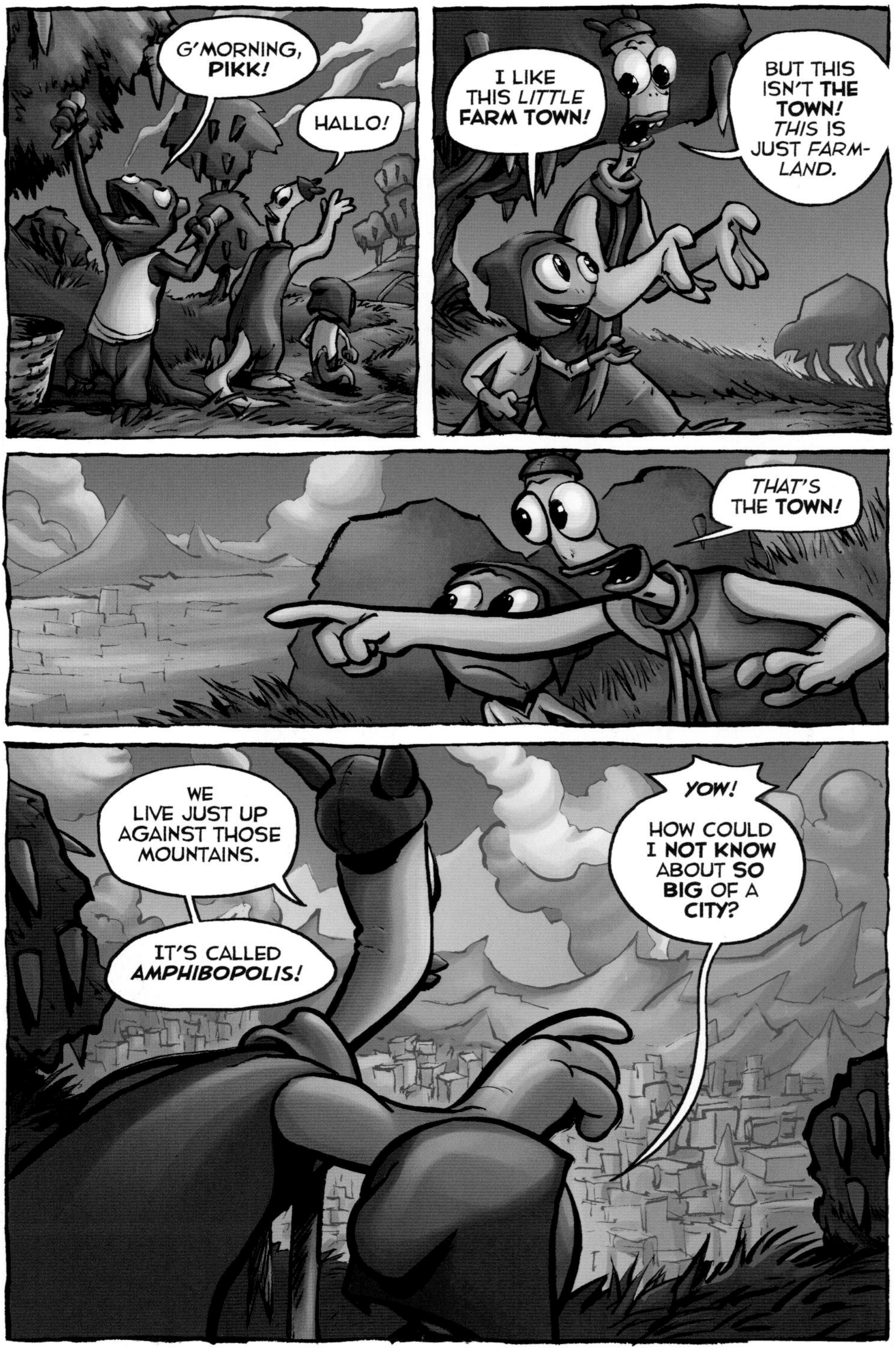
G'MORNING, **PIKK!**
HALLO!
I LIKE THIS *LITTLE* **FARM TOWN!**
BUT THIS ISN'T **THE TOWN!** *THIS* IS JUST *FARM-LAND.*
THAT'S THE **TOWN!**
WE LIVE JUST UP AGAINST THOSE MOUNTAINS.
IT'S CALLED **AMPHIBOPOLIS!**
YOW!
HOW COULD **I NOT KNOW** ABOUT **SO BIG** OF A **CITY?**

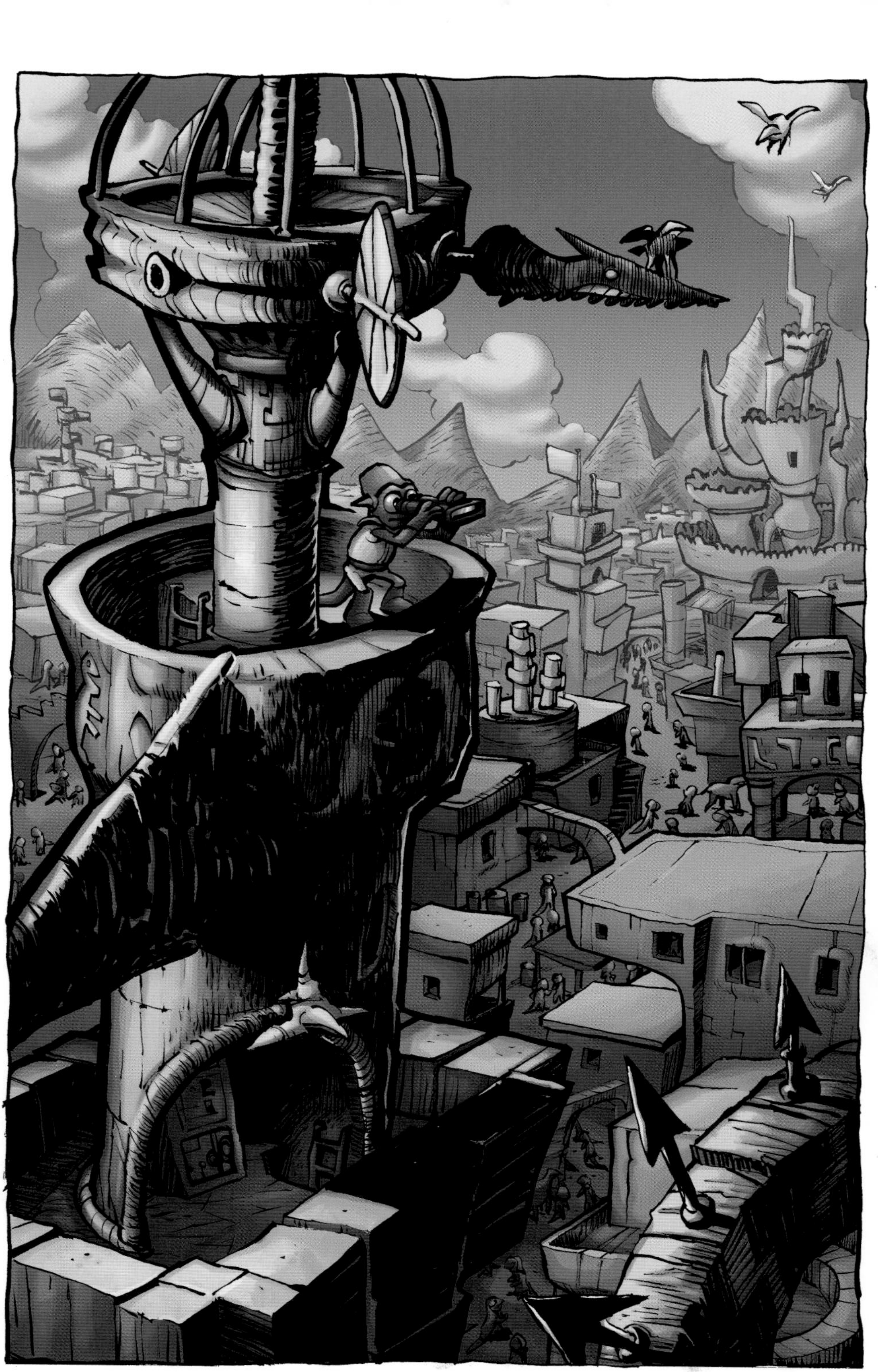

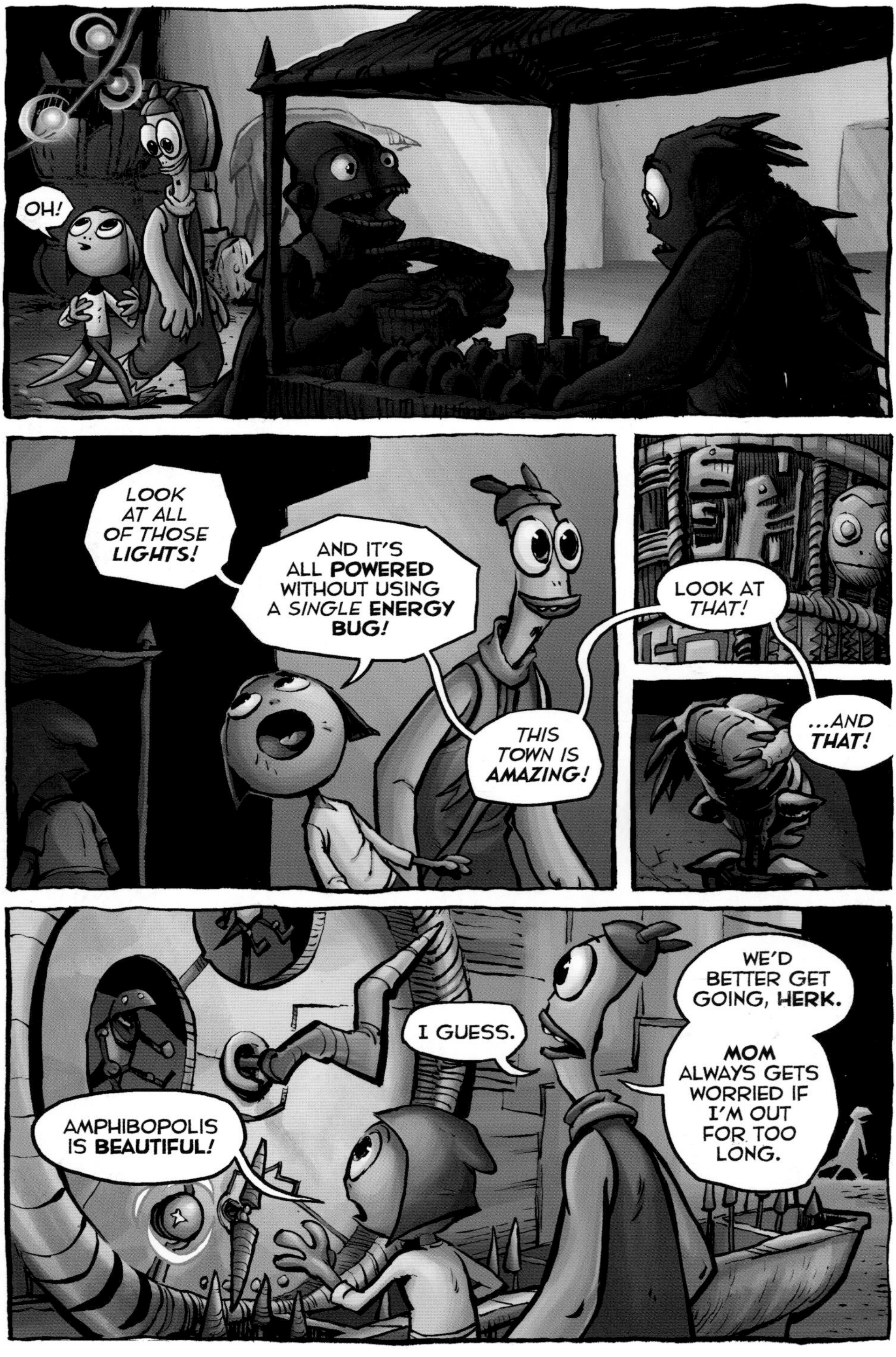
OH!
LOOK AT ALL OF THOSE LIGHTS!
AND IT'S ALL POWERED WITHOUT USING A SINGLE ENERGY BUG!
THIS TOWN IS AMAZING!
LOOK AT THAT!
...AND THAT!
AMPHIBOPOLIS IS BEAUTIFUL!
I GUESS.
WE'D BETTER GET GOING, HERK.
MOM ALWAYS GETS WORRIED IF I'M OUT FOR TOO LONG.

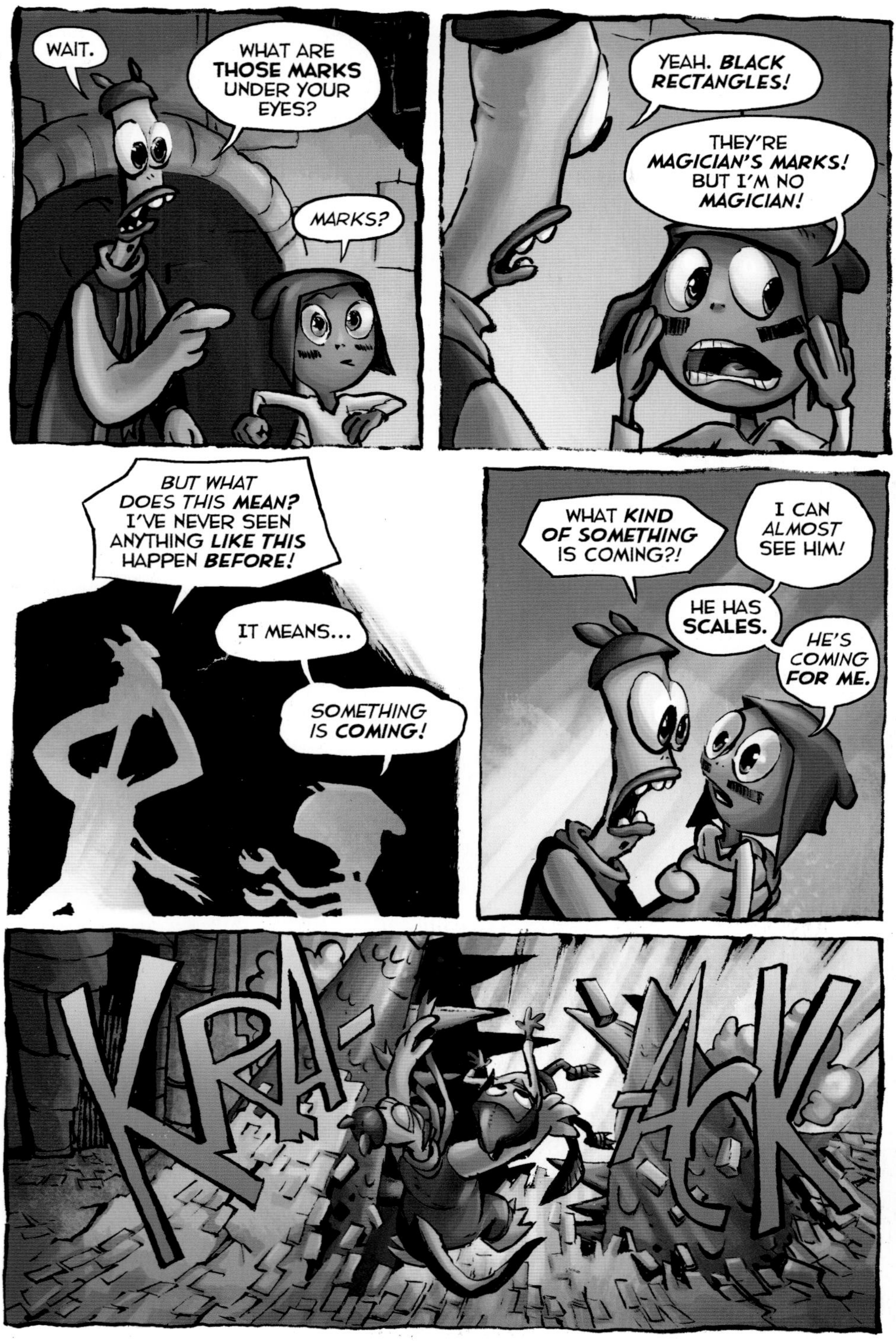
WAIT.
WHAT ARE THOSE MARKS UNDER YOUR EYES?
MARKS?
YEAH. BLACK RECTANGLES!
THEY'RE MAGICIAN'S MARKS! BUT I'M NO MAGICIAN!
BUT WHAT DOES THIS MEAN? I'VE NEVER SEEN ANYTHING LIKE THIS HAPPEN BEFORE!
IT MEANS...
SOMETHING IS COMING!
WHAT KIND OF SOMETHING IS COMING?!
I CAN ALMOST SEE HIM!
HE HAS SCALES.
HE'S COMING FOR ME.
KRA-ACK

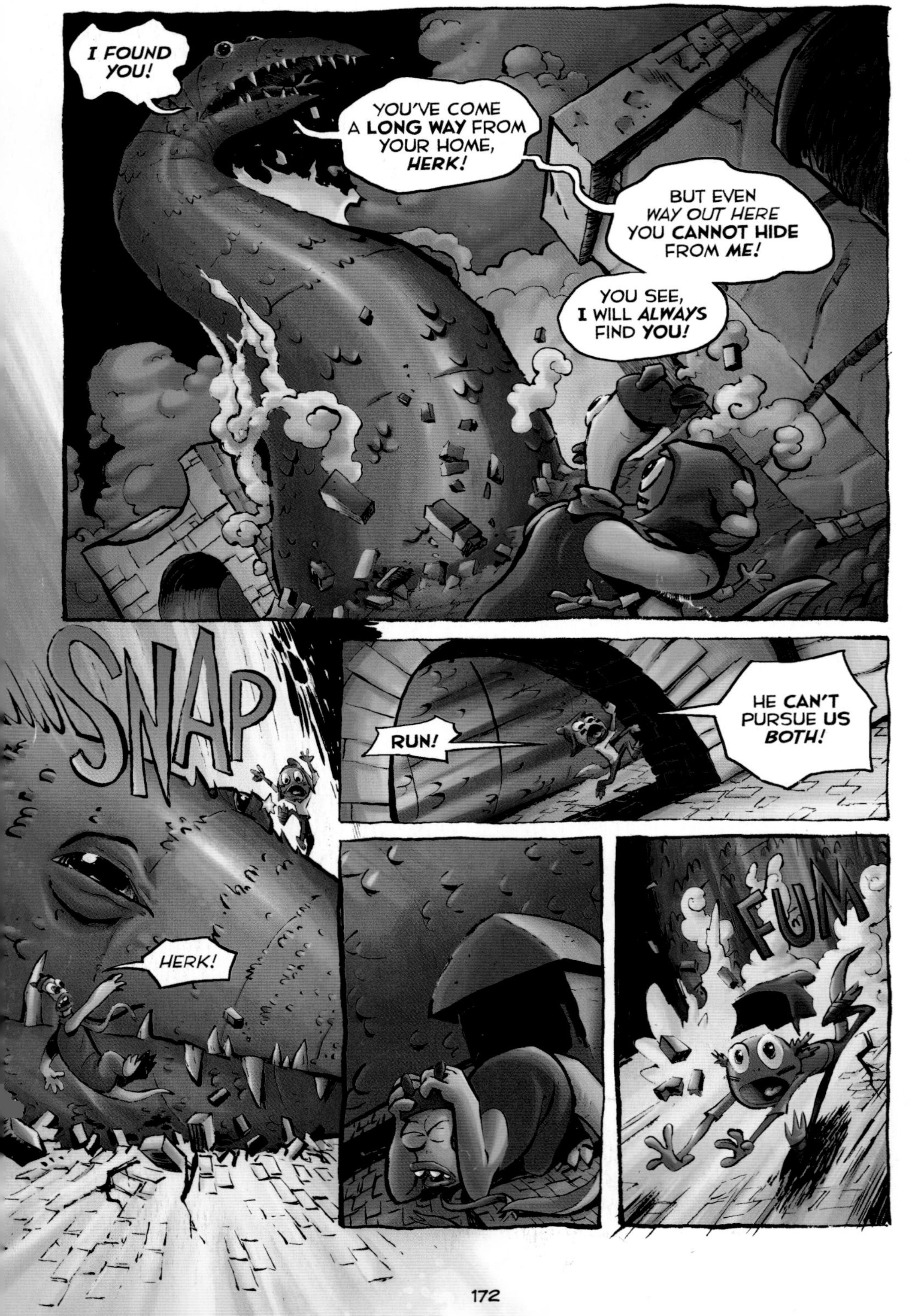
I FOUND YOU!
YOU'VE COME A **LONG WAY** FROM YOUR HOME, ***HERK!***
BUT EVEN *WAY OUT HERE* YOU **CANNOT HIDE** FROM ***ME!***
YOU SEE, **I WILL *ALWAYS*** FIND **YOU!**
SNAP
HERK!
RUN!
HE **CAN'T** PURSUE **US** ***BOTH!***
FUM

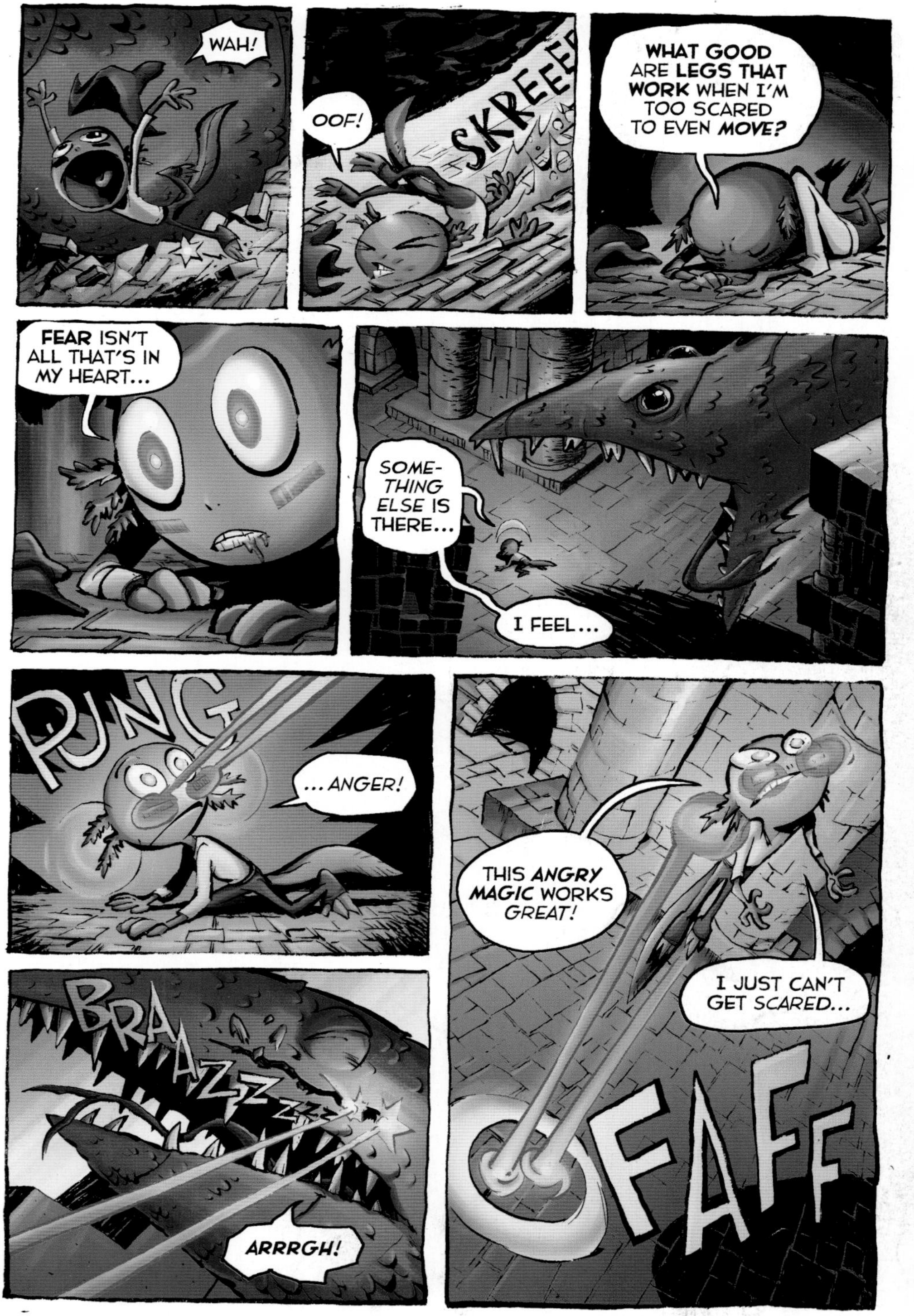
WAH!
OOF!
SKREEE
WHAT GOOD ARE LEGS THAT WORK WHEN I'M TOO SCARED TO EVEN MOVE?
FEAR ISN'T ALL THAT'S IN MY HEART...
SOME-THING ELSE IS THERE...
I FEEL...
PUNG
...ANGER!
THIS ANGRY MAGIC WORKS GREAT!
I JUST CAN'T GET SCARED...
FAFF
BRAAZZZZZ
ARRRGH!

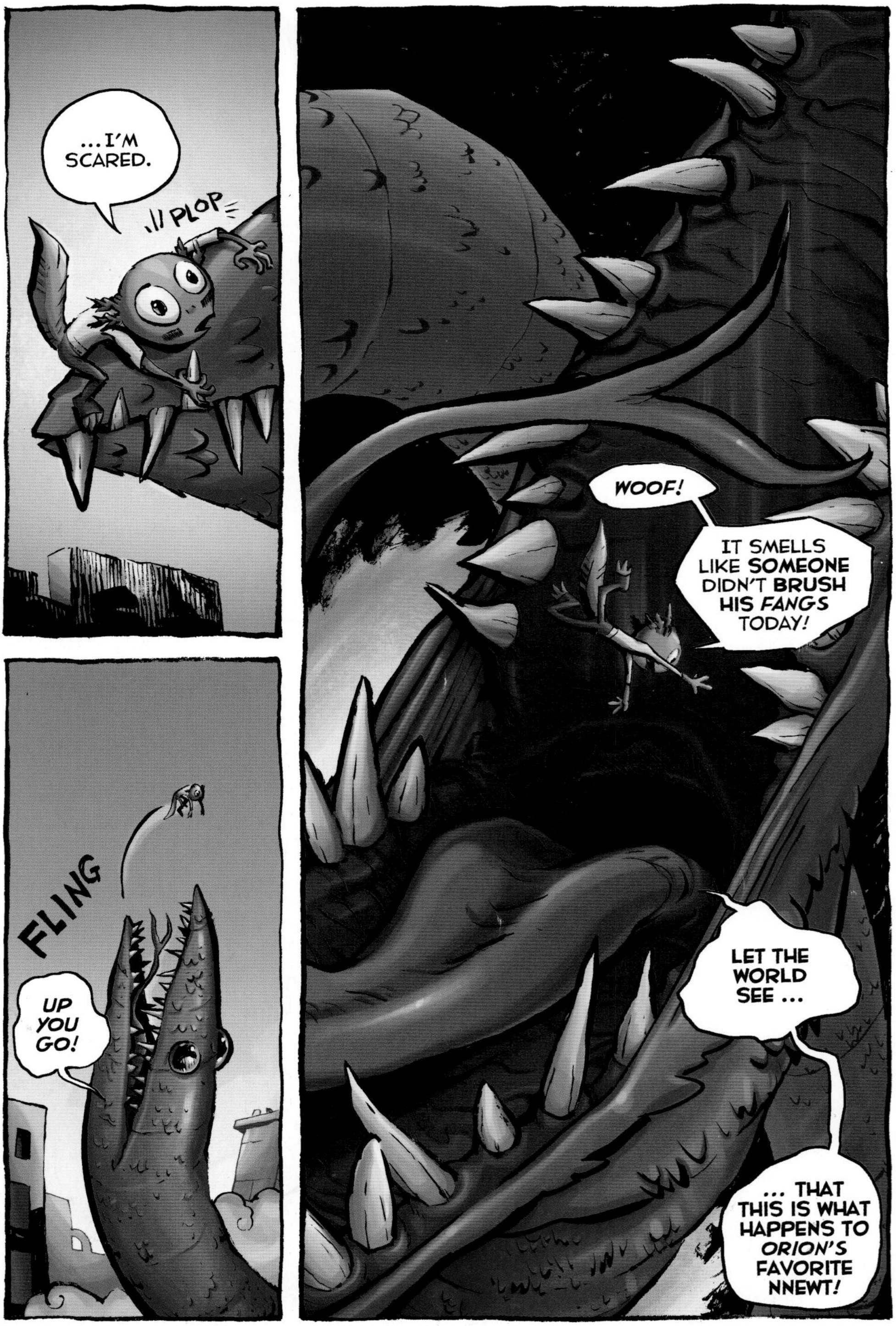
...I'M SCARED.
PLOP
FLING
UP YOU GO!
WOOF!
IT SMELLS LIKE SOMEONE DIDN'T BRUSH HIS *FANGS* TODAY!
LET THE WORLD SEE ...
... THAT THIS IS WHAT HAPPENS TO *ORION'S* FAVORITE NNEWT!

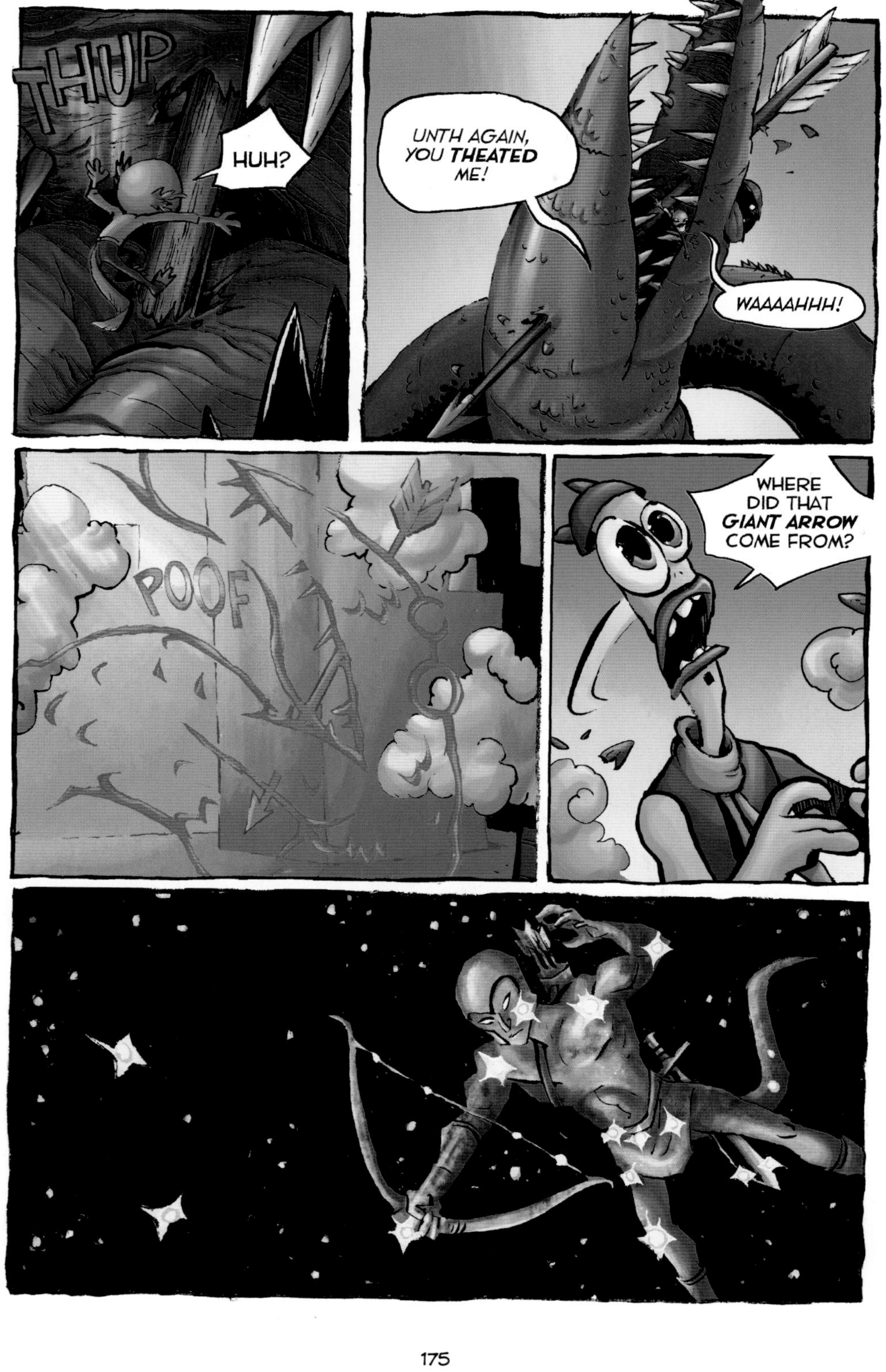
THUP
HUH?
UNTH AGAIN, YOU THEATED ME!
WAAAAHHH!
POOF
WHERE DID THAT GIANT ARROW COME FROM?

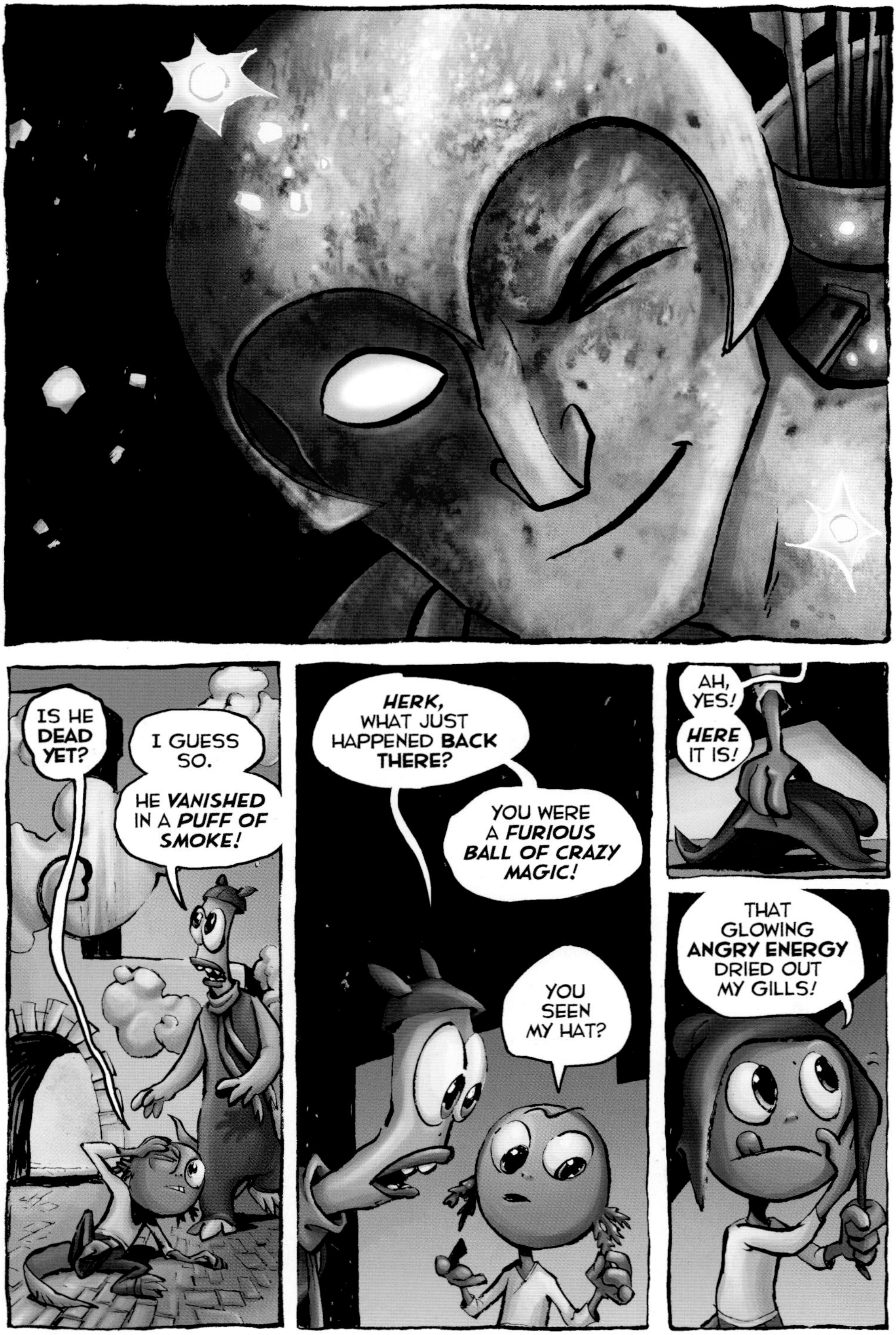
IS HE DEAD YET?
I GUESS SO.
HE VANISHED IN A PUFF OF SMOKE!
HERK, WHAT JUST HAPPENED BACK THERE?
YOU WERE A FURIOUS BALL OF CRAZY MAGIC!
YOU SEEN MY HAT?
AH, YES!
HERE IT IS!
THAT GLOWING ANGRY ENERGY DRIED OUT MY GILLS!

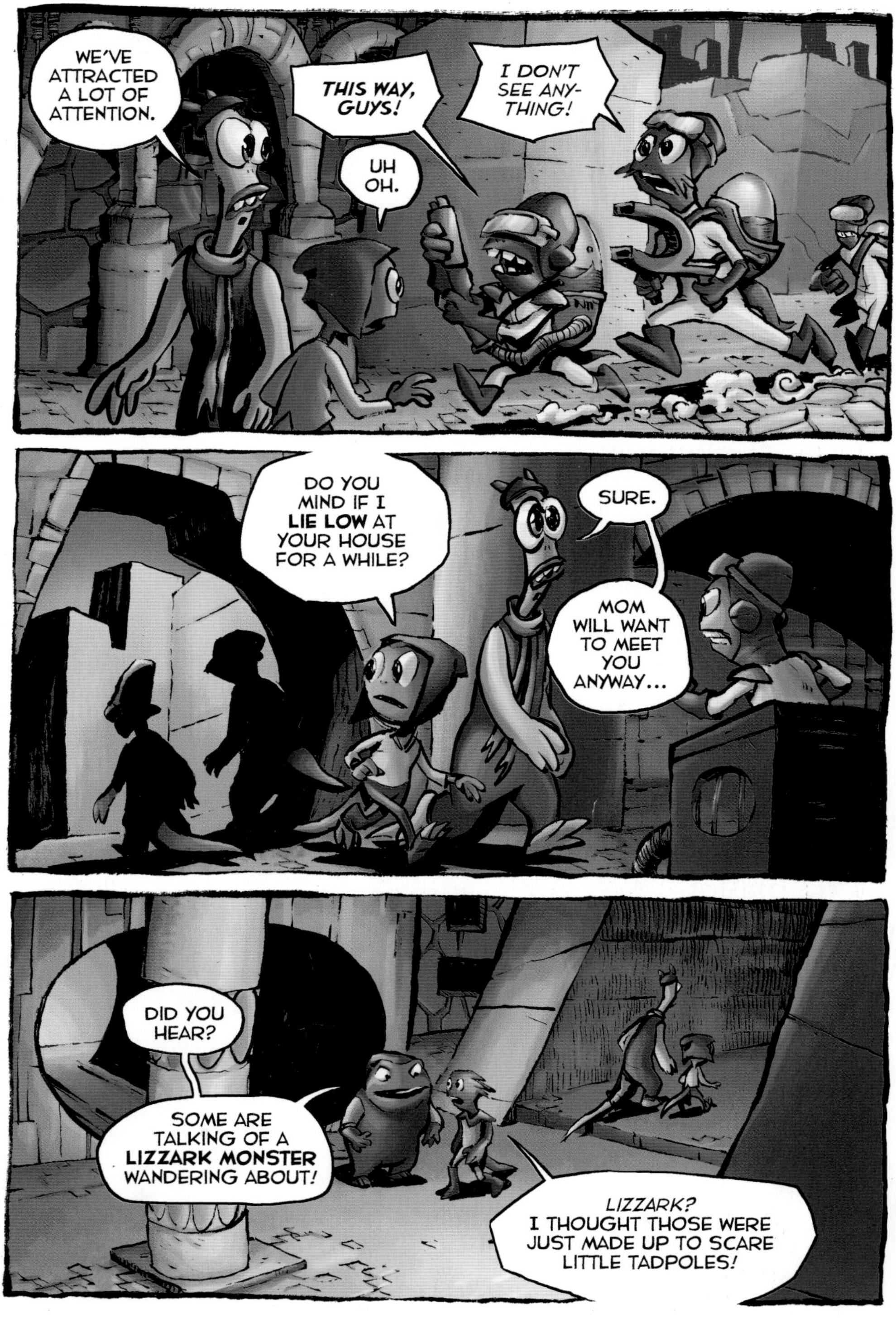
WE'VE ATTRACTED A LOT OF ATTENTION.
UH OH.
THIS WAY, GUYS!
I DON'T SEE ANY-THING!
DO YOU MIND IF I **LIE LOW** AT YOUR HOUSE FOR A WHILE?
SURE.
MOM WILL WANT TO MEET YOU ANYWAY...
DID YOU HEAR?
SOME ARE TALKING OF A **LIZZARK MONSTER** WANDERING ABOUT!
LIZZARK? I THOUGHT THOSE WERE JUST MADE UP TO SCARE LITTLE TADPOLES!

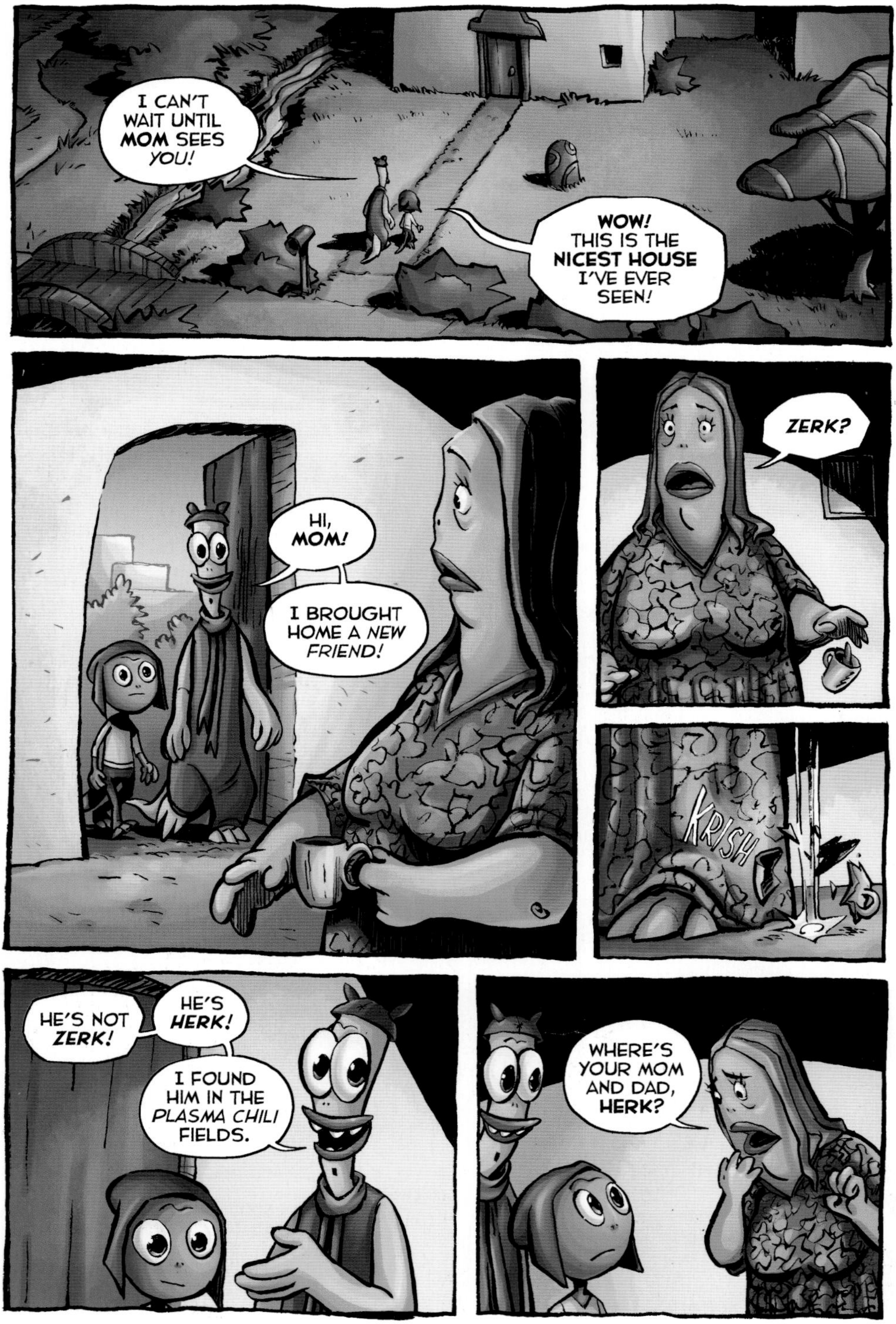
I CAN'T WAIT UNTIL MOM SEES YOU!
WOW! THIS IS THE NICEST HOUSE I'VE EVER SEEN!
HI, MOM!
I BROUGHT HOME A NEW FRIEND!
ZERK?
KRISH
HE'S NOT ZERK!
HE'S HERK!
I FOUND HIM IN THE PLASMA CHILI FIELDS.
WHERE'S YOUR MOM AND DAD, HERK?

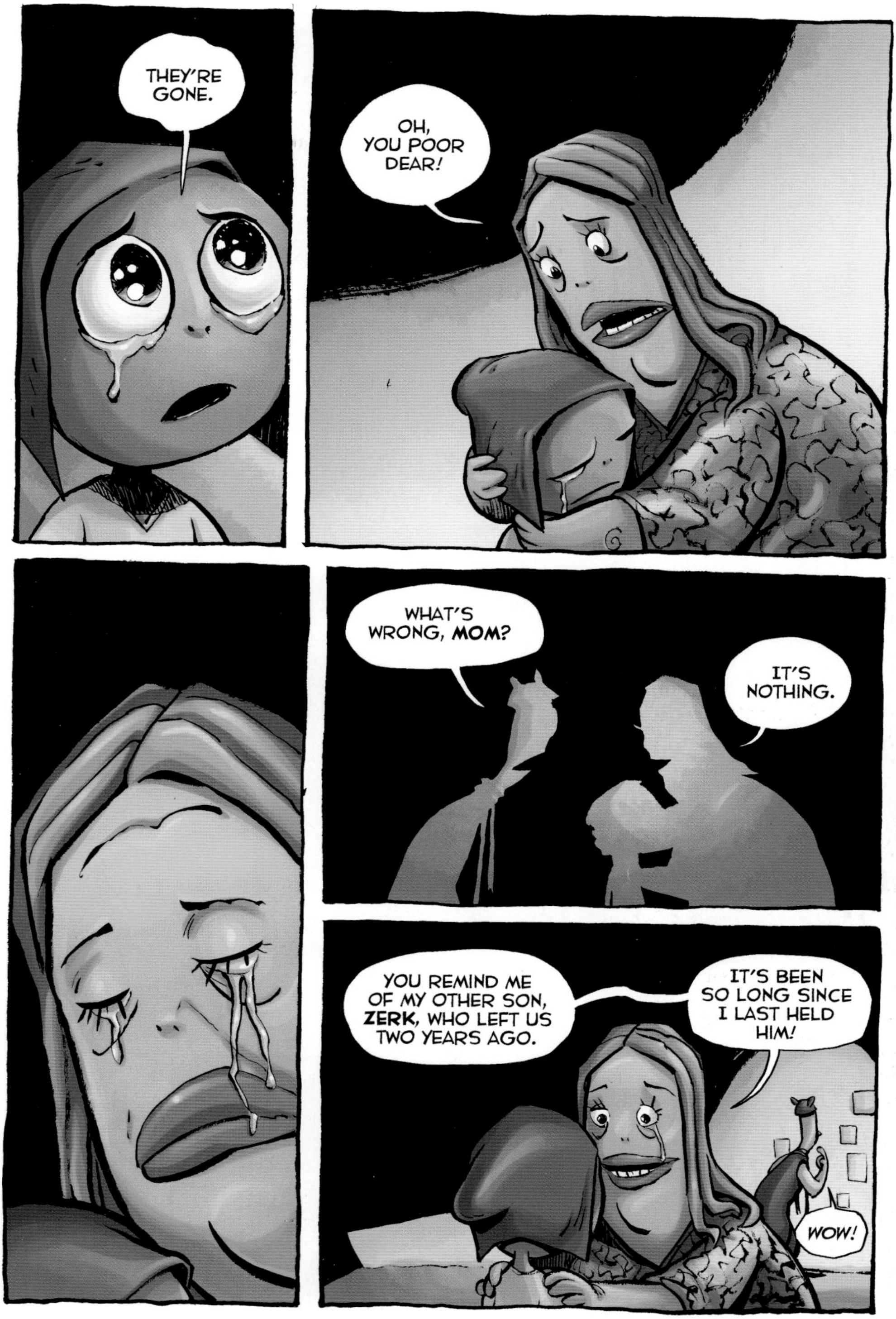
THEY'RE GONE.
OH, YOU POOR DEAR!
WHAT'S WRONG, **MOM**?
IT'S NOTHING.
YOU REMIND ME OF MY OTHER SON, **ZERK**, WHO LEFT US TWO YEARS AGO.
IT'S BEEN SO LONG SINCE I LAST HELD HIM!
WOW!

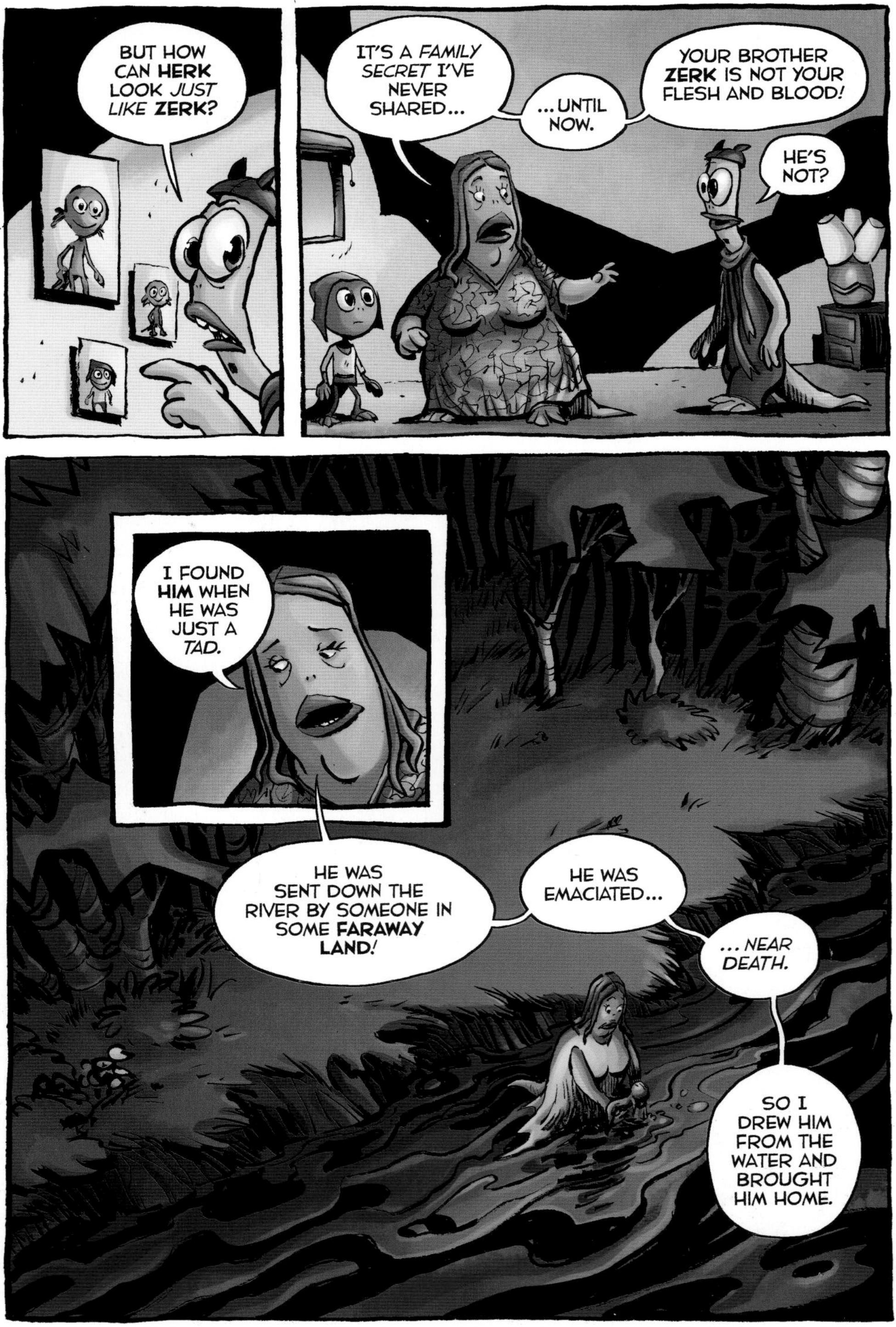
BUT HOW CAN HERK LOOK JUST LIKE ZERK?
IT'S A FAMILY SECRET I'VE NEVER SHARED...
...UNTIL NOW.
YOUR BROTHER ZERK IS NOT YOUR FLESH AND BLOOD!
HE'S NOT?
I FOUND HIM WHEN HE WAS JUST A TAD.
HE WAS SENT DOWN THE RIVER BY SOMEONE IN SOME FARAWAY LAND!
HE WAS EMACIATED...
...NEAR DEATH.
SO I DREW HIM FROM THE WATER AND BROUGHT HIM HOME.

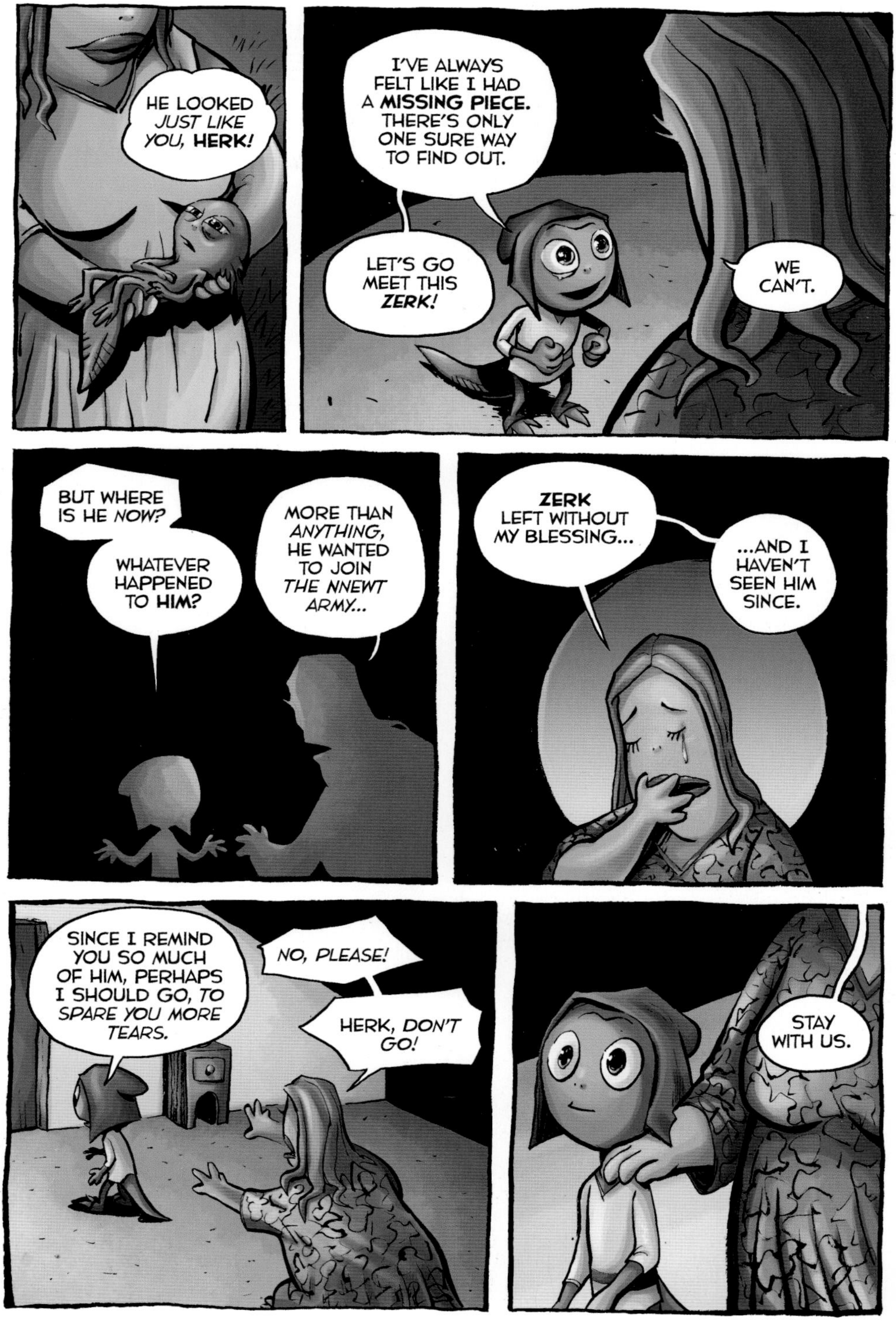
HE LOOKED *JUST LIKE YOU,* **HERK!**
I'VE ALWAYS FELT LIKE I HAD A **MISSING PIECE.** THERE'S ONLY ONE SURE WAY TO FIND OUT.
LET'S GO MEET THIS ***ZERK!***
WE CAN'T.
BUT WHERE IS HE *NOW?*
WHATEVER HAPPENED TO **HIM?**
MORE THAN *ANYTHING,* HE WANTED TO JOIN *THE NNEWT ARMY...*
ZERK LEFT WITHOUT MY BLESSING...
...AND I HAVEN'T SEEN HIM SINCE.
SINCE I REMIND YOU SO MUCH OF HIM, PERHAPS I SHOULD GO, *TO SPARE YOU MORE TEARS.*
NO, PLEASE!
HERK, *DON'T GO!*
STAY WITH US.

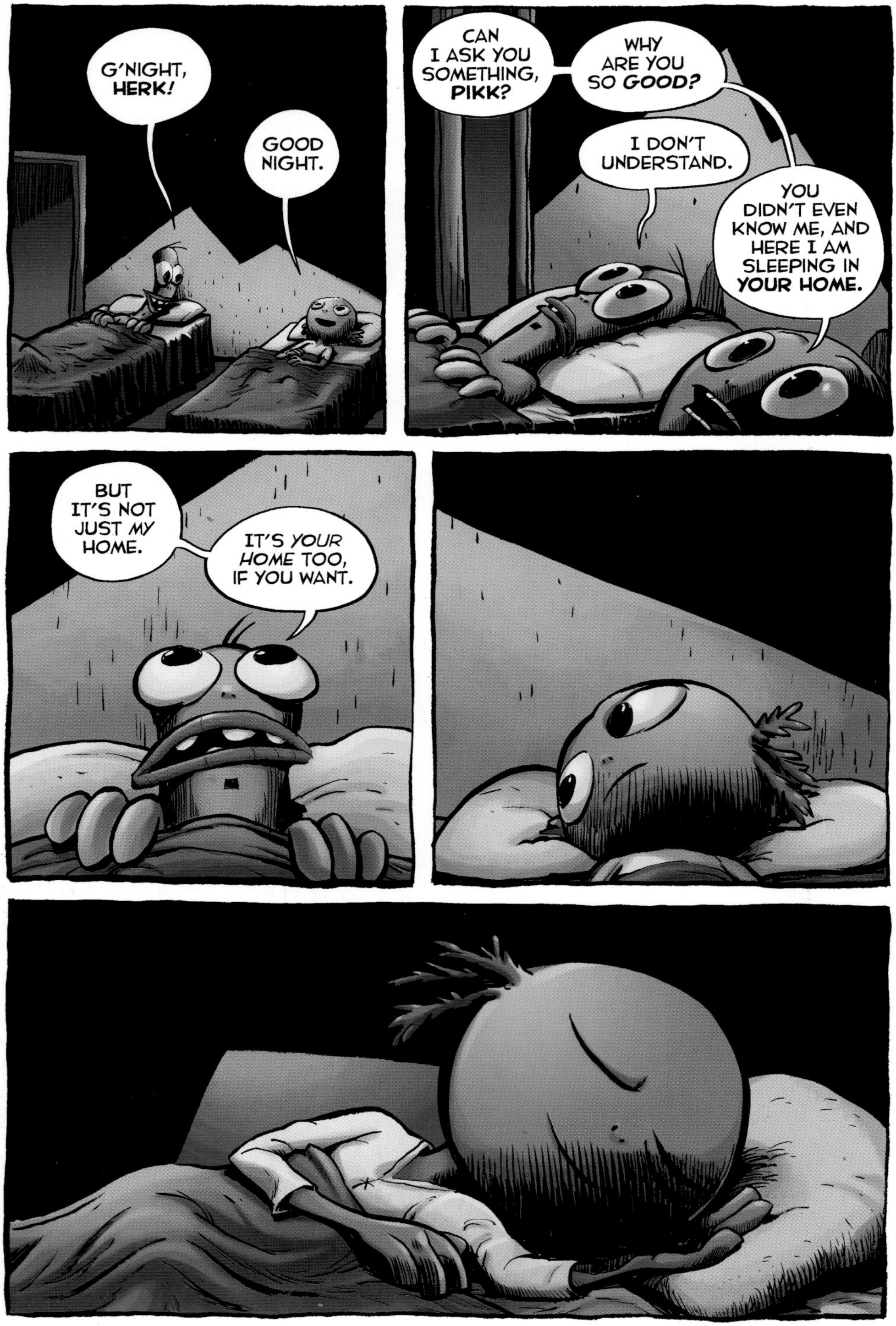
G'NIGHT, HERK!
GOOD NIGHT.
CAN I ASK YOU SOMETHING, PIKK?
WHY ARE YOU SO GOOD?
I DON'T UNDERSTAND.
YOU DIDN'T EVEN KNOW ME, AND HERE I AM SLEEPING IN YOUR HOME.
BUT IT'S NOT JUST MY HOME.
IT'S YOUR HOME TOO, IF YOU WANT.

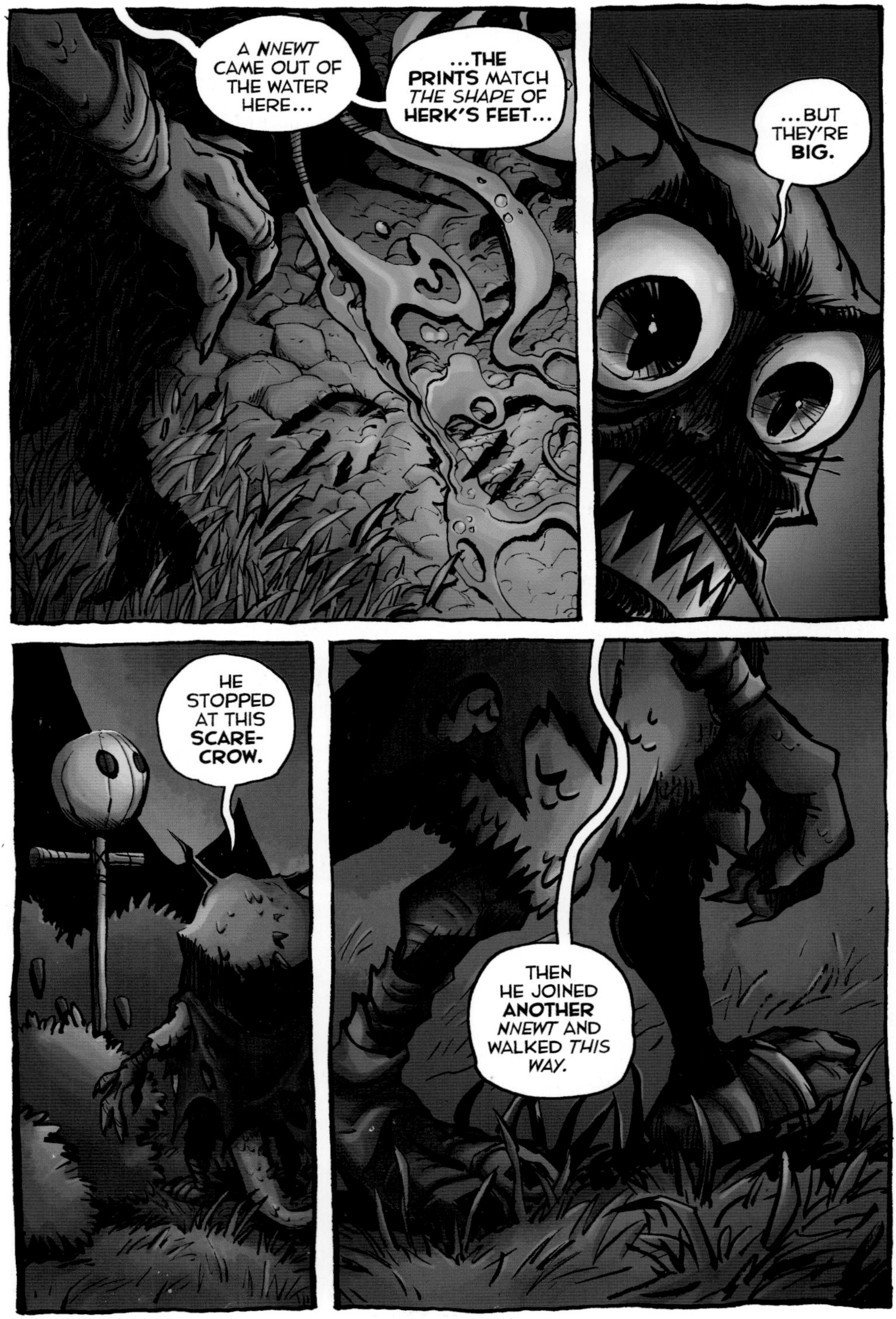
A NNEWT CAME OUT OF THE WATER HERE...
...THE PRINTS MATCH THE SHAPE OF HERK'S FEET...
...BUT THEY'RE BIG.
HE STOPPED AT THIS SCARE-CROW.
THEN HE JOINED ANOTHER NNEWT AND WALKED THIS WAY.

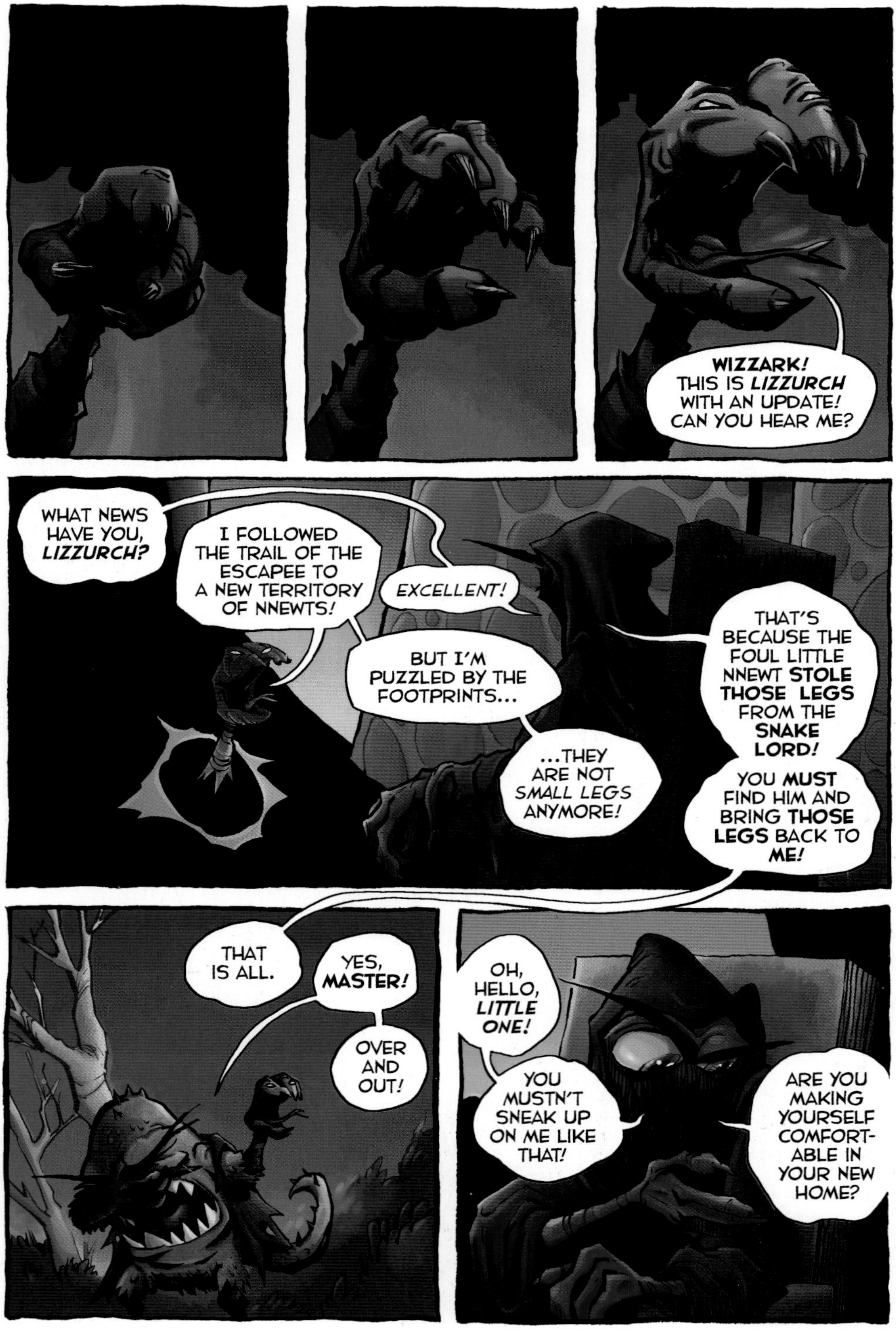
WIZZARK! THIS IS LIZZURCH WITH AN UPDATE! CAN YOU HEAR ME?
WHAT NEWS HAVE YOU, LIZZURCH?
I FOLLOWED THE TRAIL OF THE ESCAPEE TO A NEW TERRITORY OF NNEWTS!
EXCELLENT!
BUT I'M PUZZLED BY THE FOOTPRINTS...
...THEY ARE NOT SMALL LEGS ANYMORE!
THAT'S BECAUSE THE FOUL LITTLE NNEWT STOLE THOSE LEGS FROM THE SNAKE LORD!
YOU MUST FIND HIM AND BRING THOSE LEGS BACK TO ME!
THAT IS ALL.
YES, MASTER!
OVER AND OUT!
OH, HELLO, LITTLE ONE!
YOU MUSTN'T SNEAK UP ON ME LIKE THAT!
ARE YOU MAKING YOURSELF COMFORT-ABLE IN YOUR NEW HOME?

I WANT MY MOM AND DAD.
WE'VE ALREADY GONE OVER THIS...
...THEY'RE NO MORE.
YOUR ENTIRE VILLAGE WAS DESTROYED.
THEY WERE WEAK.
WE WERE STRONG.
I SAID I WANT MY MOM AND DAD!
I'M MAKING YOU AN OFFER GIVEN TO NO OTHER NNEWT...
...I WILL MAKE YOU STRONG.
I'M NOT AN UNREASONABLE WIZZARK. IF YOU BECOME MY PUPIL...
...I WILL LET YOU CHOOSE YOUR BROTHER'S FATE.

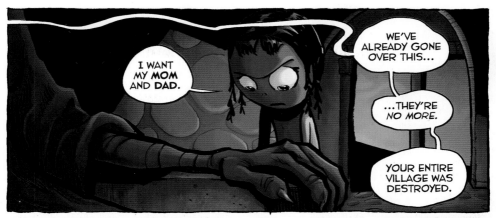

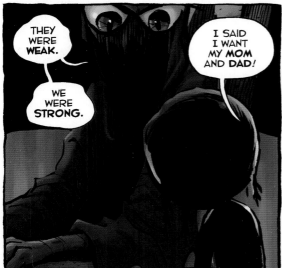

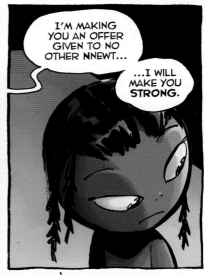

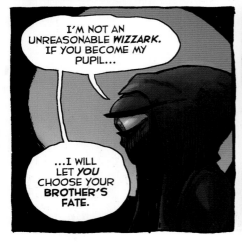

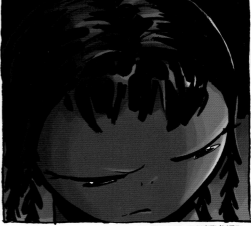

TO BE CONTINUED...

DOUG TENNAPEL is the acclaimed author and illustrator of GHOSTOPOLIS, BAD ISLAND, CARDBOARD, and TOMMYSAURUS REX, all published by Graphix. Among other honors, GHOSTOPOLIS was an ALA 2011 Top Ten Great Graphic Novel for Teens, a 2010 *Kirkus* Best Book of the Year, and a *School Library Journal* Best Comic for Kids published in 2010. BAD ISLAND was a *School Library Journal* Top Ten Graphic Novel for 2011 and a 2012 ALA Great Graphic Novels for Teens selection. CARDBOARD was named to the list of *School Library Journal* Top Ten Graphic Novels of 2012.

Doug is also the creator of the hugely popular character Earthworm Jim. He lives in Franklin, Tennessee, with his wife and their four children.